FOR CERTAIN
VALUES OF FAMILY

Manna Francis

CASPERIAN
BOOKS

www.casperianbooks.com

Cover illustration by Orit "Shin" Heifets

ISBN-10: 1-934081-14-0
ISBN-13: 978-1-934081-14-3

Thank you once again to Donna and Kimberley, for putting so much hard work into getting the Administration stories in print. And extra thanks go to my ever-patient husband, who should've received a mention in the last book for help with the technical plotting, but didn't. Sorry!

Table of Contents

Family Values

Chapter One

❖

Warrick's "serious conversation" voice normally gave Toreth a reflexive urge to leave the building as quickly as possible. The urge was dampened, in this case, by the fact that he was naked, and that Warrick had spent the last half hour massaging him into a boneless heap of pure relaxation. Maybe that had been the point.

"There's something I'd like to ask you, if I may?" Warrick said.

"What?" Toreth asked.

"I was just wondering..." Nothing, apparently, because the sentence trailed off—a rare occurrence with Warrick.

"Mm," Toreth said, and closed his eyes. Silence was fine by him. It had worked very well so far that morning.

After a minute, Warrick said, "It seems a long time since the revolt, don't you think?"

Where the fuck was this going, Toreth wondered? Then Warrick ran his palms down on either side of Toreth's spine, and talking didn't seem too high a price to pay to keep him doing it. Massage was fairly boring, after all, for the masseur. Now what the hell had Warrick asked? Something about the revolt, about—

"Well, yeah, it is a long time," Toreth said, his voice muffled by his arm. "Couple of months, anyway."

"Yes. Nine weeks since it started. Five since Carnac left I&I. And you've been here for almost a fortnight."

So that was it. He'd been expecting this, because he'd known that there was only so long Warrick would be able to bear the invasion of his previously spotless flat. "You want me to go back to my place?"

"That's not quite what I—"

"It's not a problem. I still haven't got round to sorting things out there, that's all, because..." No reason, really, except that he had pushed it so far down his priority list that it had dropped off the bottom. "I'll get Sara onto it."

"No, you misunderstand." Warrick paused to trickle more oil over Toreth's lower back. "I'm not complaining. Far from it. If I wanted you to leave, I would say so."

True enough. However, now that the topic had come up, the ignore-it-and-hope-no-one-notices strategy was fucked. "I'll sort it out."

"Of course." Warrick sounded oddly tense, although his hands didn't give up the pressure as he rubbed his thumbs in circles at the top of Toreth's thighs. "If that's what you want to do."

What else would he...? And then Toreth realized. "Are you—" No, it was a ridiculous idea. Obviously another misunderstanding.

"Mm? Am I what?"

"Are you asking if I want to stay?"

"I didn't wish to make any assumptions." Warrick worked his hands slowly higher, driving out the incipient tension. "I'm not expecting an instant decision one way or another. Some indication of your long-term plans would be helpful, that's all."

Toreth thought it over. Or tried to think it over. He considered telling Warrick that if he was hoping for serious mental exertion on his part, he should stop, or at least move his hands somewhere else. At this moment, or probably any other, he could think about domestic arrangements or he could have his buttocks massaged, but he couldn't combine both. Of the two, he knew which he preferred. He squirmed slightly, which was as much movement as he could summon the energy for, hoping to direct Warrick's fingers somewhere that would distract them both from the question.

Warrick seemed serious enough about not expecting an immediate response, because he obediently stroked down, pausing briefly for more oil. A finger teased him for a while, until he was wriggling again, involuntarily this time, then pushed gently into him.

"Ah...mmh. Yes. Nice."

"Charmingly monosyllabic," Warrick said.

If he could manage to open his eyes and look around (both of which seemed unlikely), he'd be able to see Warrick's face. But he didn't need to—he could hear the smile in his voice.

What he wanted to say was, Please, God, yes, keep doing that. More and more, for as long as I can stand it, and then fuck me. Come inside me, with me, then let's fall asleep here and I'll answer your stupid bloody questions later. A lot later. Instead he dragged himself up onto his elbows and went straight for the difficult part. "Do you want me to stay?"

"That's an interesting question." The slow, easy rhythm of Warrick's finger inside him didn't falter. "Or a complex one, at any rate. I have given it some thought."

It was probably extensive practice in the sim that meant Warrick could discuss and fuck at the same time. Toreth had always thought it was a very unfair advantage, but he wasn't about to start complaining now. That raised the awful prospect of Warrick stopping.

The continuing silence suggested Warrick expected a contribution to the conversation. Monosyllabic seemed to be working so far. "Yeah? And?"

"Occasional disagreements notwithstanding, I enjoy your company. I certainly enjoy the convenience of having you here, whenever I *want* you."

Toreth moaned as a second finger joined the first, stretching him until he deliberately relaxed to accommodate it. Much tenser than he ought to be.

"It's also, ah, significantly less disruptive than I expected," Warrick said.

"Disruptive?"

"In terms of clothes and towels on the floor, mess in the kitchen, and so on. And, incidentally, I do appreciate the effort."

Toreth might have taken offense, if Warrick hadn't finished the sentence by leaning forward and trailing feather-light kisses down his neck and upper back.

"No problem," he managed once his spine had uncurled.

"Good. I realize that I'm not the easiest person to share accommodation with, even on a temporary basis."

Toreth grinned into the crisp pillowcase, fresh on the bed last night. "You're fine. For an obsessive-compulsive control freak with a clean towel fetish."

"Mm. Indeed. However, to return to the discussion, I wouldn't be opposed in principle to extending the experiment. On the other hand—" which Warrick slid down between his legs, slick with oil, stroking his balls gently, "—there are downsides to the idea. The flat is fundamentally too small for both of us, if you were... intending to spend a lot more of your time here."

Move in, Toreth nearly said. Just say move in. We both know what we're talking about. But, somehow, he couldn't say it. The urge to leave, or at least to end the conversation, tugged at him again. The difficulty of concentrating with Warrick doing *that* made it a challenge, though, rather than an ordeal. "So...mmh, yeah, again...so what?"

Warrick changed position, lying down beside him, propped on one elbow. "It would seem logical to move somewhere larger," he continued. "One reason I raise the question now is that, in view of the recent upsets, SimTech has reappraised my security assessment. They've asked me to consider moving somewhere with fundamentally greater protection. Actually, the head of security is being rather insistent about it. I need to know what kind of place I should look for."

"I suppose so." Toreth shifted on the bed. "Can you—a bit. Deeper...ah, yes. Fuck, that's good."

Warrick laughed softly. "Nice to be appreciated. Anyway, that brings up a second point. I own this flat—or to be accurate, SimTech owns it. The same would be true of a new flat. Would you have a problem with that?"

"Why the fuck would I care?"

11

"Honestly? Because I've made mistakes in the past and bought things for you, or arranged things to do, which were too expensive, and you disliked it. I'm sure I'd feel exactly the same if our financial positions were reversed."

True enough. He considered it carefully, or as carefully as he could manage. "It'd be different."

"Are you sure? Why?"

"I could always apply for another flat if I didn't like it. I wouldn't have to stay there. But . . . "

"But?"

"I'd have to register the change of address. And my status in the new accommodation."

"Ah. I'd forgotten all about that. Is *that* a problem?"

Ridiculously, yes. "No. Does it matter what the hell it says in some file at the Department of Population?"

"Not at all, as far as I'm concerned. I'm sure we can find a suitable box to select."

There was silence for a few minutes, except for murmurs of appreciation and encouragement. Toreth began to hope that the conversation had run its course and they could get down to—

"There are other things. Such as—" Warrick stopped and, more annoyingly, his hand stopped as well.

Toreth nudged up with his hips, to no effect. "What?"

"Do you ever take people back to your flat?"

"Do I—? Oh, you mean fucks."

"Yes. Fucks." He started stroking again. "Because that is something I couldn't tolerate. What you do away from here is your own business and I accept that, but—"

"I wouldn't do it. I wouldn't want to. I never take anyone home now. Only you." He paused. "That's something else."

"What?"

"We keep most of the gear at my place. If we," lived together, "didn't have somewhere else, it would all have to be here. Or wherever. For people to see if they started nosing around. Dillian, for example."

He bit back a moan of disappointment as Warrick took his hand away and knelt up again, sitting back on his heels. "She wouldn't."

Tempting to agree, just to make him come back. "Jesus, you're joking. Of course she would. What would she think about the drawerful of stuff that was looted from my place?"

Warrick hesitated, then said, "She'd be upset."

"Upset? She'd throw a fucking fit, and then she'd have me arrested and you committed. I know how she feels about it. She thinks I beat you up, to start with. And that's before she gets on to what I *do* do to you. Remember what she was like about the cabinet?"

"*I* remember—how the hell do you know?" Curiosity, with irritation keeping it company.

Oh, fuck. There was such a thing as being too relaxed. Warrick hated the idea of their sex life being a topic of outside discussion. Putting the blame on Dillian was a risky strategy, but in this case it was true. "She had 'a little word' with me about it. She said you'd shown it to her." It wasn't necessary to add "which you never told me."

"Well...yes, I did. She noticed the bruises, so I had to say something. And what did she say?"

He shrugged. "I don't remember. It was a long time ago."

"Toreth, what did she say?" A nonnegotiable tone of voice.

"The usual. I don't like you, I'm keeping my eye on you. Be careful with him. If you hurt him, I'll et cetera."

"Et cetera?"

"Call Justice, I expect—I've usually stopped listening by that point." Dillian would be happy with this, anyway, spoiling a so-far lovely morning without even being there.

"It's none of her business, as I have made abundantly clear in the past. I'll remind her the next time I see her."

Better and better. "Don't bother. There's no point—it won't do anybody any good. You won't change her mind, and she doesn't need extra reasons to be fucked off with me."

"I...very well." A further hesitation and then—finally—the combined massage and fingerfuck resumed.

It took five minutes for Toreth to get back to the same state of happy relaxation, during which there were no further comments from Warrick. However, his next words made clear what he had been thinking about.

"I have tried to explain it to her."

Toreth sighed and hunted for a suitable discourager. "It doesn't matter. Listen—what Dillian thinks about me is so far down the list of things I give a shit about that you'd pass housework before you got to it."

That drew a small laugh. "So little? But I didn't want you to imagine that I let her think things like that and didn't say anything. I could try—"

"Warrick, leave it. Don't give her ammunition. She's going to be bad enough as it is about me sharing a flat with you."

It took him a few seconds to realize that he'd said it, quite accidentally. "She's going to be." That sounded dangerously like a decision.

Silence. Then Warrick said, "Turn over."

Too much effort. "Why?"

"Because I want to fuck you. And I want to see your face while I do it." Warrick leaned down and gently bit the nape of his neck. "And, assuming the timing

13

works out, I want to watch your eyes as you come. Then I plan to come also, and very probably fall asleep soon afterward. After that I'm going to wing it. There may be a shower, and then coffee and some lunch and—"

"For God's sake. All *right*." Finally, he managed to roll over. "The fuck will do fine; I don't need your bloody schedule for the day."

He shifted across the bed, allowing Warrick to move above him, and brought his legs up smoothly, resting his calves on Warrick's shoulders. As usual, Warrick paused and looked down.

"God. That is so . . . I can't explain how much of a turn-on that is."

"Enjoy it while you can."

"Oh?"

Toreth turned his feet inward, running his toes through Warrick's hair. "Yeah. Because I'm not going to be able to manage it forever. It's not as easy as it used to be."

"Mm." Warrick kissed his ankle, then bit it gently. "Better make sure we get to the gym today, then. Shall we stop?"

"If you stop now, I'll probably kill you."

"In that case—" Warrick leaned down, stretching his legs, and Toreth curled up to meet him for a kiss.

Finally, Toreth thought, conversation over.

14

Chapter Two

❖

In a way, he hoped Warrick would think better of the idea and quietly forget it. For the rest of the week, it seemed as if he had. Nothing was said, nothing arranged. Toreth continued to stay at the flat, but it felt different—suddenly claustrophobic at odd moments. Unconsciously, Toreth had been aware of his residence there as a temporary thing. The possibility that it could become permanent, even though it would be elsewhere, had changed things.

At the end of the week, on Friday morning, a message arrived at work from Warrick. He read it over, several times, then went out to speak to Sara.

"I'm leaving at four today, or I'd like to. Is there anything urgent that I don't know about?" he asked, hoping for a yes.

Sara shook her head. "Nothing at all. You know how quiet it's been since, well..."

Since the revolt. Part of the problem was that the Administration's systems were still in confusion. The lack of work could largely be put down to uncertainty, though. It wasn't easy for a division devoted to investigating politically significant crimes to find cases when no one knew for sure anymore what made a crime of political significance.

"Where are you going?" Sara asked.

For a moment, he had a ridiculous urge to lie. Then he said, "Flat hunting."

"Oh, right." She looked back at the screen and he thought he'd got away with it, then invisible antennae twitched and she turned around. "On your own?"

The innocent inquiry didn't fool him for a second. "With Warrick. He's looking for a new place."

"A new place for him?"

"Who else?" Yes, lying was easier. It wasn't as though they'd actually *agreed* anything yet. "He just thought I might be interested to see what the places looked like."

Her eyes went wide. "You're moving in with him!"

Heads came up around the room. Toreth tried to ignore them. "Put it out over the fucking system, why don't you?"

15

She paled. "Sorry," she said, in almost a whisper.

He hadn't meant it that seriously. What the hell was wrong with her? Whatever it was, it—and then it hit him. Carnac. She was still feeling guilty about what she'd said to Carnac about his parents. He ought to have guessed at once, because this wasn't the first time; the weirdest things set her off about it. Toreth added another few euros to the debt to be extracted from Carnac if they ever met again. The bastard was going to have to put on some weight to come up with enough pounds of flesh to cover it.

For the moment, all he could think of to say was: "Fancy coming along?"

To his surprise, her face lit up. "Can I really?"

"Sure, if you like. Although I don't think it's going to be that exciting."

"What? The kind of places Warrick's going to be looking at? Who *wouldn't* want to?"

Well, himself, for one, but neither could he bear the idea of Warrick making the decision on his own. He felt unexpectedly better about the idea, though. Sara would be moral support—or, no, not quite that. Someone who came from his world, not Warrick's. Toreth paused and considered that last thought. Christ, but he was making a production out of this. They were only looking at a bloody flat.

Warrick picked them up in the SimTech car. He didn't seem in the least surprised to see Sara, although her inclusion apparently came as a shock to the other man in the car—Rob McLean. His expression of surprise was short-lived, though, and after a round of greetings the security consultant made a stoically silent fourth to the party.

Now that Sara's interest in McLean seemed to have waned, Toreth was willing to concede McLean wasn't too irritating. Hard to forget, though, that he'd been a witness to Carnac's little performance. When Warrick began to speak, Toreth was grateful for the distraction.

"I have two places to try this evening," Warrick said as they drove off. "One's a new complex—I have a recommendation for it from one of the sponsors. The other one's somewhere older. Even if you don't like them, it'll give you an idea of the size and layout I have in mind. Then I thought we could go back to the flat and look at specs for other places."

"Sounds fine." Toreth winced inwardly at his own voice—he sounded like Warrick was offering a trip to the morgue.

The drive felt like an eternity, although it was actually only fifteen minutes. The car turned left, a barrier lifted, and they drove down into an underpass—brightly lit and obviously newly constructed. Toreth glanced at Sara, who was craning her neck around, trying to get a glimpse through the darkened front of the car. Then the incline changed and they headed up again.

16

The complex opened up in front of them like a puzzle box, surrounding them on all sides—a mesmerizing construction of multilevel buildings in glass and white stone. An open area of grass and flowing water in the center softened the effect. The newness of the place—everything clean and sharp-edged—was overwhelming. It looked like a brochure, or a CGI presentation. Hearing a low whistle, he tore his gaze away from the window to find McLean looking faintly embarrassed. Sara, sitting opposite him with her mouth wide open, said nothing. That was how he'd describe it later to Chevril—classy enough to shut Sara up.

Toreth looked at Warrick. "Jesus fucking Christ. You have got to be fucking *joking*."

Warrick smiled, looking as delighted as if he'd built the incredible place himself in the sim. "Not at all. However, I should say don't get your expectations up too far. We'll be looking at one of the smaller flats."

They left the car outside the front entrance. Passing through the doors, which had no suspicion of a smudge on the glittering glass, Toreth felt a very strong sense that he ought to be on duty. He'd never been anywhere like this when he wasn't.

Warrick gave SimTech's name at the vast reception desk and then they waited there. Toreth looked around at décor and people. The whole place stank of money, of corporate privilege and Senior Administration weekday residences. The kind of place people like Tillotson dreamed of living one day, when they'd backstabbed and slimed their way to the upper grades. Toreth had never even thought about it.

When their guide arrived after a minute or two, Toreth was almost too distracted to notice that it was a very attractive young woman, with the same shiny, expensive perfection as the building. Not quite that distracted, though. He put "fuckable staff" down in his mental "pros" column.

McLean seemed to like the security, nodding approval to himself from time to time as they walked through the corridors. Toreth spotted plenty of obvious cameras, as well as a number of more discreet versions. There were equally discreet uniformed guards in evidence, some clearly armed. No doubt the security had been tightened up after the revolt.

The ground floor held expensive shops and a variety of restaurants, currently almost empty. There was also a vast and comprehensively equipped gym that Toreth tried to imagine having the freedom to wander into any time he chose. Another big plus, and it made the concept of living in a place like this marginally more real, but at the same time somehow more uncomfortable. Toreth felt like a... a something he couldn't remember.

As they walked through the endless corridors, he distracted himself with a search for the nagging word. Something he'd heard a long time ago and stashed away. By the time they reached the door of the flat, he had settled on either "concubine" or "catamite." Not that he could remember what the latter meant, but he didn't much like it.

17

Despite Warrick's warning, Toreth had prepared himself for something ridiculously vast; as it turned out, the flat was merely large. His own place would've just about squeezed into the combined living and dining area. There must be far bigger units in the complex, but Warrick wouldn't waste SimTech's money gratuitously. Still, it was comfortable for two, and definitely excessive for one, at least by normal New London housing standards. Toreth wondered if McLean knew Toreth would be moving in, and whether SimTech security assessed the suitability of cohabitees as well as habitations.

As they inspected the flat, Toreth derived a certain amount of amusement from the confusion the composition of their party caused their guide. Since Warrick—or at least SimTech—had made the appointment, she addressed the majority of her remarks to him. McLean had such an obviously professional air that he couldn't be anything other than paid security. However, she kept looking between Toreth and Sara, trying to work out the relationships, clearly wondering whether either of them ought to be included in the sales pitch. Judging by Warrick's occasional smile when the woman's attention was elsewhere, he'd also noticed her confusion and wasn't about to enlighten her.

The air smelled strongly of new carpet and fresh paint. "I'm afraid you can't go in," the woman said as she opened the bathroom door. Tiles shone, spotless. "They finished decorating this morning and the adhesive isn't cured yet. This section of the complex has only just been opened for sale and we're expecting them to go quickly. We brought the opening date forwards, despite the recent troubles."

"Or because of them?" Warrick asked.

"Yes." She stepped back to make room, addressing her next remarks to McLean. "We've had inquiries from a number of corporate security departments. We provide a full protection service, with a twenty-four-hour armed security presence."

McLean nodded. "I've seen the brochure. It's very impressive."

Sara had taken the invitation to look around at face value. As Toreth peered over Warrick's shoulder through the bathroom door, she reappeared beside him and grabbed his hand. "Come and look at this," she said, in a whisper that would have carried the length of the building.

She led him through an open plate-glass door and onto a large balcony. "Isn't it fabulous?"

The flat was high up and tucked away in an angle of the architecture, and he wondered how much difference that made to the price. Perhaps not as much as before if many corporates were retreating into havens like this. From up here, the activity in the complex was more obvious: a handful of expensive cars entering or leaving, people strolling between entrances or along glassed-in walkways. Toreth leaned on the railing and looked over the edge into the center of the complex, judging distances to cover and lines of sight.

"McLean won't like it," he said after a while. "Alarmed or not, this is a large exterior access."

"The whole complex is secure, though, isn't it?"

"Yeah, I suppose so." The comment crystallized the feeling he'd had since they drove in. The elegant, beautiful buildings made him think of the detention level at I&I. Closed off from the outside world—a prison. "Come on," he said.

Not surprisingly, they found Warrick in the kitchen, discussing fittings and fixtures options with the agent. Toreth waited patiently for about ten seconds, then said, "Are you done?"

It came out as more of a demand than a question, and Warrick looked around, surprised. "I...yes, I suppose so."

"Good. Let's go."

As they walked back to the entrance, Warrick asked, "What do you think of the gym?"

"Nice."

"Situation?"

"Well, it's within walking distance of I&I, if I use one of the other gates. Further than my flat, but not too much further."

"So, overall, do you like it?"

"It's fantastic. But—" He shrugged, unable to find the right words. "I mean, it's a bit..."

Warrick shook his head. "No, actually, it's a lot. I don't think I could live here."

Toreth blinked at him. "I thought you liked it," he said after a moment.

"I do. The flat was excellent. However, there is a fine line between security and imprisonment. This is much too far across that line for my tastes."

McLean, a little way ahead of them, must have heard, but he didn't comment. Toreth assumed that the security consultant had learned by now the futility of trying to change Warrick's mind once it was made up.

Sara sighed and tilted her head to gaze with exaggerated wistfulness at the entrance to the shopping area as they passed it. "And I was so looking forward to visiting you here."

Warrick patted her shoulder in mock commiseration. "You'll get over it. See what you think of the next place."

At the second prospect, they parked the car a little way away rather than use the secure underground entrance. The late afternoon sun colored the three white buildings a golden orange as they walked towards them. According to Warrick, they had been rescued, at an expense Toreth couldn't imagine, from the clearing of the ruins of the old city. The decontamination alone must have cost more than the construction of a new building. Something Toreth had never understood—what did it matter if they were the real thing rather than a modern copy?

At first inspection, the trio of buildings were nowhere near as extravagant as the complex they had recently left. Nor were they in one of the prized corporate residential centers. However, Toreth knew the area from cases he'd investigated. Set on the edge of the corporate heartland of New London, roughly halfway between the university and the Int-Sec complex, the flats had a respectable location.

"What do you think of it?" Warrick asked.

He liked the style of the exterior—clean curves, distinctive and idiosyncratic but not outrageously ostentatious, and he said so.

Warrick nodded. "Art Deco." He smiled suddenly, brilliantly. "I've always wanted to live here, or somewhere like here. But flats rarely come up for sale, because there are so few. They're not to modern tastes."

As they walked, Toreth examined the outer perimeter fence. Decorative metal, high and with regular notices warning of anti-intruder measures, nature unspecified. He liked the look more than the last place. At least the outside world was visible.

Across the road from the residential buildings stood a small commerce and entertainment complex of modern construction but in the same style. Same security, too, serving corporate residents from the surrounding buildings. According to the flat spec it was connected to the flats they were visiting by underground access. They bypassed the complex, to Sara's obvious disappointment, and carried on to the main residential entrance.

The unmanned gates opened to Warrick's ID, allowing them into a fenced courtyard area. A man emerged from a low, white building largely hidden by glossy-leaved evergreen shrubs. "Doctor Warrick?"

The first few minutes of the tour consisted of a potted history of the place, which Toreth ignored. He looked around the courtyard, noticing McLean doing the same thing. Both of them assessing the security, Toreth thought, if for different reasons.

It took Warrick a little time to pry out of the agent the detail that the previous owner had died here, of a sudden heart attack. The man obviously expected them to be put off by the revelation, and was plainly relieved when they weren't. "That might lower the price," Sara whispered to Toreth as they set off towards the building entrance, and he nodded. Not that it was anything to do with him, but the idea of a slight bargain appealed somehow.

As they climbed the stairs up to the third floor, Toreth heard Sara say to McLean, "It doesn't look as safe as the last place."

"It's not," he replied, sounding disapproving. "It's in the bottom quarter of the acceptable scoring."

"Scoring?" she asked.

"There's a system for assessing security provision in a building. And another

20

one for assigning a value to personnel. It's not *quite* as bad as it looks. This place does meet Doctor Warrick's required level. The security systems are top class, and there are a lot of concealed modifications to the structure. Sympathetic to the architecture."

Toreth looked over his shoulder. "You don't like architectural sympathy?"

McLean smiled slightly. "Not when I'm on duty, no."

At the top of the stairs, Warrick stopped and turned. "You're exaggerating the risk, McLean."

"Possibly." He didn't look at all discomforted. "But that's my job, too. I'd rather have completely modern construction with better-assessed materials."

"It's in the corporate high-security zone. If there's any sign of trouble, the whole district is saturated with corporate security forces. Not to mention Service troopers."

"*If* the troopers show up, yes."

Warrick shrugged. "A fair point." He turned to the hovering agent. "Please, carry on."

The flat was significantly larger than Warrick's current residence, but it was still a sane size for two people. It spread over two floors, which would be a novelty for Toreth. He'd never lived anywhere with internal stairs. It opened a whole new range of possibilities for fucking.

Downstairs there was a kitchen, living room, dining room, office, and a completely empty room with startlingly green walls that the agent called a library. Toreth boggled slightly at the idea of living somewhere with a *library*; Warrick seemed quite unfazed by the idea. Upstairs, the main bathroom contained an interestingly large bath, and Toreth spotted a strangely reassuring cracked tile or two. There was a second, smaller bathroom off the main bedroom with a spacious shower. Added to the one squeezed into an oddly-shaped room downstairs, Toreth realized they'd have more toilets than residents, which seemed wrong. Still, the place wasn't vast. Not so obviously corporate, either. Not so easy to imagine hordes of guests here, and corporate events full of tedious corporate tossers Toreth didn't know or didn't want to know.

There were two smaller bedrooms as well as the main one, and a room described in the particulars as a dressing room, which Warrick suggested would do as somewhere to keep Toreth's exercise equipment.

The master bedroom certainly appealed—even with furniture, there would be plenty of floor space for games. The large curved windows, filled with colored glass, flooded the room with tinted evening light. Best of all, the room was shaped to provide a large alcove opposite the central window. Probably meant for the bed, but there was room elsewhere for that. Toreth imagined the dark red velvet curtains looped back on either side, framing the alcove, the cabinet within it, and Warrick, his body dappled with sunlight through the colored panes. Panes and pain—Toreth smiled, surprising himself with the idea that he liked the place. So surprised, in fact, that he felt compelled to tell someone, to test the feeling out. "It's not bad, is it?" he asked Sara.

"No, I suppose not. No balcony like the last one, though."

"And has fewer shops?"

She grinned. "There is that. But it's further from I&I."

"The extra walk won't kill me. Or I can get a taxi and walk the last part."

"Not so convenient for nighttime calls."

Toreth shrugged. "If I'm further away, maybe I'll get fewer of them."

"No gym in the building," she said.

"There's a swimming pool in the basement. Probably something across the road, too."

Talking himself out of the problems with it. That had to be a good sign, didn't it? When Warrick asked him what he thought, he didn't have to feign enthusiasm. "It's great."

"If you want to think about it . . ."

That was the last thing he wanted to do. "No. I'm fine with it if you are."

"Excellent." Warrick turned to the agent. "I'll—we'll take it. I'll have someone get in touch with you to discuss details."

As they left the building, Toreth said, "Christ, can you just do that?"

"What?"

"Say you'll take it."

"Well, no. But I can tell Asher tomorrow, and she can clear it with the appropriate people. This flat is somewhat cheaper than the first one we looked at, which should please her."

Warrick's slightly sour tone caught his attention. "Is SimTech in trouble?" he asked.

"Good Lord, no!" Warrick stopped in the middle of the courtyard. "Or . . . not yet, at least. But the market for luxury items like the sim has taken a rather brutal hammering, so any savings are welcome."

"So why move at all?" Sara asked.

"I did offer to pick somewhere less expensive, or even stay at the current place, but—"

"Neither of those options are possible," McLean said with finality. "The security is what costs. All the corporate insurance schemes are increasing their required security levels for providing coverage. You'd be an uninsurable risk."

"So I've been told," Warrick said. "But security already did a first approximation check of this place, so I don't imagine there will be any problem. Will there?"

The security officer shrugged. "Not from what I've seen."

Warrick looked at his watch. "Shall we get something to eat?"

In a spirit of exploration, they tried one of the restaurants in the complex op-

22

posite. In view of Toreth and Sara's uniforms they avoided the more expensive-looking establishments, although the Eastern Mediterranean place they eventually selected would still have rated a stiff memo from Accounts if Toreth had tried to slide it past on expenses without a good cover story.

Conversation during the meal revolved entirely around flats and other domestic things, and was carried out primarily by Warrick and Sara. Toreth felt glad she'd come along, since he couldn't think of much to contribute. The easy spirit in which he'd agreed to living at the flat had slipped away, leaving him feeling oddly exposed. McLean sat in an apparently more contented silence, expressing professional opinions when required to do so. Someone else spectating on a world he didn't belong to, Toreth thought. But so was Sara, and she seemed quite at home and not in the least overawed by the evidence of Warrick's corporate credentials.

Toreth had liked the flat. As the meal wore on, he found himself having to deliberately recall that, silently repeating it. For a while, thinking of the master bedroom and the prospect of installing the cabinet there worked to ward off the growing unease. However, by the time the other three were discussing dessert, even that image had lost its power. The discomfort, vague and so impossible to drive away, grew until it was hard even to sit still.

Then he wondered why the hell he was bothering. There was no obligation to stay, no reason to put himself through this domestic tedium. Warrick wouldn't care, and keeping up a front for Sara was even more stupid, considering what she'd seen in the past. McLean could go fuck himself. Toreth stood up abruptly, dropping his napkin on the floor and not bothering to pick it up. "I've got to go."

No need to apologize or explain. Warrick simply nodded while Sara said, "See you on Monday."

Once the restaurant door closed behind Toreth, Warrick looked at Sara, who shrugged and held her glass out for a refill. A moment later, McLean discovered a tactful need to visit the toilet.

"What did you expect?" Sara said, when they were alone.

"More or less that, at some point."

"He'll be back. And he'll say yes to the flat."

"Do you think so?" he asked, surprised by her confidence.

"I know so." She had a mouthful of the wine. "Are you going to get new furniture?"

"Mm...yes. I'll have to pay for it personally, rather than taking money from SimTech, but I'll buy something new for the living room and dining room at least. Something in keeping with the building." Not the bedroom furniture—or at least he'd have to get new furniture that also matched the cabinet. The bedroom at the

23

new flat had conjured some irresistible images. He glanced down at his hands, automatically rubbing his wrists, then looked up in time to see Sara hiding a smile.

"Sorry," she said.

He shook his head, annoyed with himself rather than her. "I don't want to embarrass you."

She waved her hand dismissively. "Doesn't bother me in the least. Why on earth would it? Actually, I think it's all kind of sweet. You two." Before he could think of an answer to *that,* she glanced over towards the toilets, then lowered her voice. "Can I ask something that's probably none of my business? Nothing to do with chains."

"Go ahead."

"It's just . . . are you sure you want to do this?" she asked.

"I would hardly have asked him to move in if I didn't."

"Okay. But . . . well, you know what he's like about his flat. I mean, that he doesn't invite people there much. Ordinary people."

People other than the two of them. "Yes, I know."

"And I've lived with you. Not for very long or anything, but, well . . ."

"You couldn't help but notice that I'm an obsessive-compulsive control freak with a clean towel fetish."

"Um . . . yes. And I'm still really, really sorry about your carpet. And so is Bastard." She was blushing, but she pressed on determinedly. "What I wanted to say was, well, do you think there'll be enough room?"

That didn't simply mean in the flat across from the restaurant. "You mean, won't putting Toreth and me in the same flat, however large, be something like tying two tomcats in a sack and poking them with a stick?"

Sara snorted. "Except louder."

He picked up his beer and had a mouthful, savoring the hops. The chances of the cohabitation lasting was something he'd tried not to dwell on excessively. Second-guessing Toreth's reactions was an exercise in frustration that provided only an illusion of control in return. Despite the careful planning he'd put into his circumspect approach to asking Toreth to stay, Warrick hadn't really expected him to agree. The whole project had a disconcertingly uncontrollable feeling. Comparisons with his marriage to Lissa were no help. She'd shared none of Toreth's mess of issues regarding commitment and dependency. If they tried this and failed, what effect would that failure have on Toreth?

Out of the corner of his eye he saw McLean, hovering, obviously trying to work out if it was a conversation he could interrupt. Warrick set his glass down, consciously not aligning it with the other items on the table. "I don't know, Sara. Maybe, yes. We'll have to see."

Chapter Three

❖

Sunday brunch in the park had seemed like a good idea when Warrick sent the invitation. The park café was the setting for so many happy memories that he'd been sure it would be the perfect place. Even though in many ways they had little in common now, the café made a starting point. Hopefully they could go back to something they'd had a long time ago, before life in its infinite complexity and frequent unpleasantness had driven so many wedges between them. There they would know who they were, or at least who they had been.

Then he had arrived, and it wasn't the same place at all. Literally, since the building had been demolished. A large and grander new café had replaced it, built in unexceptional and rather soulless modern style, and the spotless white walls had none of the familiar, friendly shabbiness he'd hoped for. According to the polished steel letters set above the entrance, the building was only a year old—surprising that Jen hadn't mentioned it.

In the café, a floor-to-ceiling glass wall gave a view out over the main park, directly overlooking the complex paths and elaborate topiary of the formal garden in the center. At least that looked to be substantially the same. On the grassy bank closer to the restaurant, the hands of the floral clock stood still. Two uniformed park employees worked at planting out the dial, filling in the bare earth between the white hands and numerals. He was still absorbed in the view when Tarin said, "Keir?"

There was an awkward moment as Warrick stood up from the table and neither of them knew what to do. He half offered his hand, then Tarin took it and pulled him forwards into an embrace. No hesitation showed in his firm thump against Warrick's back. "Good to see you, Keir."

"And you. Glad you could make it."

When he stepped back, Tarin looked over the table, noting the other place setting, and he frowned. "That's not—"

"It's for Dilly," Warrick said quickly.

Tarin raised one eyebrow. "Quite a family get-together."

"Yes. I thought it would be nice for us all to see more of each other. Not just the three of us—Val, too, and Jen and Philly, but we can start small."

"Nothing too ambitious, I see." Tarin smiled slightly. "Reduces the chance of anyone getting knocked out."

Warrick grinned. "Sit down."

"This is a nice place," Tarin said as they sat. "Good choice."

Relief warmed him. "I had no idea it had changed so much."

"No? I bring Val here a lot, with and without Philly. I must admit I didn't like it when they knocked the old café down. Like someone had taken a bulldozer to my childhood." He shook his head. "Val and I took a piece of the wall home and put it in the garden, for a keepsake. Ridiculous how you can get attached to something like a building, isn't it?"

"Not at all. If it wouldn't bore you to tears, I'd tell you about the sim and the emotional recall linking of place memories."

"No, you should." Tarin picked the menu screen up, then set it down again. "Tell me rather than bore me, which I'm sure you wouldn't. I'd like to hear about it. And I'd like to try the sim, too, sometime—if you don't mind."

"Mind? Not in the least. When you come to stay—" He hesitated, thinking of the fraught circumstances of the original offer made after Kate's arrest. "If you still want to, that is."

Tarin nodded. "Yes. I haven't mentioned it to Val yet, but that's only because she'd pester me every time I see her until we do go."

"Then when you come down—"

"My God!" Dillian's voice echoed across the sparsely populated restaurant. "Tarin!"

Tarin looked over and waved, then smiled wryly at Warrick. "Do you think that means she's pleased to see me?"

Dillian hurried over, heels tapping on the mosaicked floor, and they both stood up again to exchange welcoming kisses with her. "What on earth are you doing here, Tar?" she said. Then her gaze swept over the table and she said, "Keir invited you?" She turned to him. "Why didn't you tell me?"

"I thought it would make a nice surprise. And besides—" He hadn't been quite confident she wouldn't come up with some excuse not to attend.

The two of them were being perfectly friendly, though, or at least more than simply civil. His own abrupt silence had gone unremarked. Dillian had taken her seat and was chatting happily to Tarin about how the park outside hadn't changed a bit. She too had noticed the clock, and before long they were deep in recollections of designs that had been planted in the face in past years.

The menu had been revamped completely. Without any meals from the past available to relive, Warrick picked beef and barley broth, with allegedly fresh-baked bread in which he would believe when he tasted it.

26

Dilly and Tar were still staring out of the window, pointing out parts of the formal garden that hadn't changed. Warrick examined the pair, trying to map their appearances back onto the childish faces he remembered. Dilly seemed easy, but perhaps that was only because of Valeria, who was so much like her as to suggest cloning. He wondered if it ever bothered Tar—probably not, since it would have to remind him primarily of Kate. Philly, who had never liked Kate, might find it a less pleasant effect.

Tarin himself Warrick remembered only dimly as a child. He should have taken the time to look at photographs before he came. His earliest memories were of Tarin in his midteens, and he remembered him most clearly later still, already almost an adult: not so heavyset, but with the same sandy hair—although thinning now—firm jaw and gray-blue eyes. He'd always seemed like the kind of person who ought to have frown lines, but even sitting next to Dillian, Tar was aging well, with a minimum of lines around his eyes and mouth. All three of them so much older, still, and with so much time wasted.

An approaching waiter interrupted Warrick's comparisons. After they had ordered food, Dillian turned to him and said, "Was this what Ash meant about news?"

"I'm sorry?" Warrick said.

At the same moment, Tarin said, "Ash Linton?"

"Mm-hm—that Ash. I spoke to her yesterday evening. She said Keir had some news, then clammed up and went all mysterious and said I'd better ask him because it wasn't for her to tell me." She looked to Warrick. "Did you tell her the three of us were having lunch?"

"Ah, no. There's something else." These were, he realized, possibly the two people in the world who would take this news worse than anyone. "Nothing very exciting, I'm afraid."

It was a measure of how well Dillian knew him that her eyes narrowed at once. "Oh? So what is it?"

"I'm moving flats. For security reasons to do with the revolt. I've found a place already, so it's just a question of the contracts being signed. You'll love it. It's rather larger than the place I have now, because—"

Dillian's eyes went wide. "*No,*" she breathed.

"Because Toreth is moving into it with me."

"Oh!" She leaned back in the chair and gazed up, apparently seeking inspiration from the vaulted ceiling. After a few seconds, she sighed and looked back. "Well, all I can say is good luck, because you're going to need it."

"I won't bring Valeria there," Tarin said in a precise, brittle voice. "Not if he's living there with you."

Warrick had been so absorbed by Dillian's reaction that he'd barely registered Tarin's icy silence. "But—"

"No. I won't have Val in a house with him." His normally ruddy cheeks had flushed a darker red. "And I don't want to hear about reforms at I&I, or changes to procedure, or any damn thing. He's a torturer, and it doesn't matter a damn what the Administration says he can or can't *do*, because it's what he *is*. If you think I'll let that sick, twisted—"

His voice had started to rise. No wonder Tarin had been so useful to Kate. Warrick closed the thought away and held his hand up. "Fine. I understand. I told you before, though, I don't expect you to see him or speak to him. I'll make sure you don't. I thought that was all right?"

"That was when he lived somewhere else. But if that's his home, then no. I won't take Val there."

Dillian drew breath, but Warrick interrupted before she could show which side she was about to take. "Let's talk about it later," he said. "We can do it over the comm instead of here. Let's not..."

"Spoil this place," Dillian said.

Warrick nodded. "Just what I meant."

After a long moment, Tarin nodded. "Sounds like a good idea. Since we're supposed to be getting along."

"Right," Dillian said firmly. "Let's have lunch and then go for a walk and see how many of the names we gave the topiary animals we can still remember."

"Tar will win," Warrick said. "I remember hearing Val using the same names."

So they moved on to safe topics, and it wasn't long before the crisis had passed and Warrick thought that at least they might make it to the end of meal without anyone throwing a punch or walking out. With all that, though, while the shared memories might help, he wondered if there was too much bad history along with the good. Had things between them degenerated so far that the best they would ever be able to hope for, as Jen would say, was no blood on the floor?

28

Chapter Four

❖

For a month, to Toreth's surprise, everything went like a wet shave—perfectly smooth except for the occasional small nicks.

Work grew busier, which made for a distraction from other things. Section heads were, crablike, sidling into new positions, subtly redefining their sections' remits to emphasize the "politically important" nature of the crimes they claimed, and de-emphasize the purely political. Corporate Fraud and Information and Communications Crimes were busy, as the corporations took advantage of the confusion to start another round of sabotage. General Criminal, whose catchall description had previously been a handicap, was well placed to bid for incoming cases. Tillotson developed a disconcerting cheerfulness which suggested the section was doing well in the postrevolt prestige wars.

Annoyingly, news of Toreth's planned house move had leaked out into the section. Chevril produced an endless series of cracks about corporate sugar daddies. The rest of the seniors backed him up. It was fairly good-natured, for I&I, but it grated. After a couple of weeks, Toreth had come in to work to find a box containing a cheap but very sparkly paste engagement ring on his desk, along with a bridal bouquet of pink plastic flowers. He'd slammed out into the main office and announced that if he found out who'd left them there, he'd be returning the gift with interest and a rectal speculum. It had caused a lot of laughter, but he got no more presents.

Outside work, things could have been much worse. The topic of the new flat had stayed in the background. Warrick had said so little about it, in fact, that Toreth had occasionally asked him how things were going. Reassuringly, the answers were never very interesting, as everything was being arranged by SimTech's legal department.

A few times Warrick had asked his opinion about something. Décor, mostly: carpets, wallpaper, paint, furniture. Nothing Toreth cared much about, but fortunately Warrick had made it easy by presenting a limited range of choices for each

29

item. Presumably, Toreth had decided, Warrick had already winnowed out all the options he couldn't live with personally. No doubt he would be happy with anything Toreth picked, so Toreth didn't give himself ulcers worrying about the decisions.

After the first couple, though, he'd paid more attention, hesitating over the choices and trying to read from Warrick which was the one he wanted, which ones he was less keen on. Naturally, it hadn't taken Warrick long to notice what he was doing and, equally naturally, to try to avoid giving anything away. Usually, reading Warrick was so easy that Toreth had enjoyed the challenge provided by the novel subject. Making it part of the game almost made it fun.

Today, though, the game was over and things weren't fine, or fun.

The day had started well enough, with bright spring sunshine, warm enough that Toreth had set off early and walked most of the way to work. He'd had to catch a taxi for the last part, because the journey on foot took longer than he anticipated. Walking to work was a habit he'd let slide when the streets were still too dangerous for an I&I uniform. On the way, he'd even thought how much more convenient it would be once they'd moved to the new flat.

He'd been in his office for five minutes before he called Sara in. As she closed the door, she looked apprehensive, as well she might. "What the fuck is that?" he demanded, pointing at the screen.

She didn't even pretend to need to look. "Accommodation form for the Department of Population, just like it says at the top."

"You filled it in."

"I thought it would save you time, that's all."

He couldn't reasonably make a protest. She'd filled in hundreds of forms for him in the past, both work-related and personal, and he'd never been anything other than happy to be spared the effort. "Is there any rush?"

"The deadline to let them know is today. Counting from the last time you were at the old flat."

Of course she would know that. Sometimes she was too efficient. "With all the chaos from the revolt, does it really matter? The whole citizen registration system is a bloody shambles. I doubt the DoP'll be handing out fines for late address changes. Have they even decided whether change-of-residence went out with movement notification?"

"Yes, they did, and no, it didn't. It's still in force."

He cast around for another argument, finding nothing. "Yeah . . . okay. Thanks for checking."

"My pleasure," she said as she closed the door, sounding as if she really meant it. No doubt looking forward to the housewarming, so she could try to pick up a rich corporate guest. If she got off so much on domestic arrangements, *she* should move in with Warrick.

He frowned at the screen. This was the real step. This meant abandoning all rights to his own flat, which had belonged to the Administration anyway, and having nowhere to go except Warrick's flat, which belonged to SimTech. Looked at like that, it wasn't much of a change. Except that it was. He'd said it to Chevril a hundred times: there was all the difference in the world between working for I&I and belonging to the Administration, and working for some corporate on a personal contract. Even though having the DoP know he was fucking Warrick on a regular basis wasn't anything like putting his name to a body-and-soul corporate contract, it provoked an oddly similar gut reaction.

The form sat on his screen, luring him back to read it again.

Relationships to other residents.

And Sara had selected *previously unregistered sexual partner.* Perfectly true, but the idea of having it recorded felt dangerous. Like a hostage to fortune, in some utterly illogical way.

Previously unregistered, meaning *now registered.*

Toreth closed the form without authorizing it. Maybe a professional corporate contract with Warrick would've been better, at that. At least then he'd be able to read the fine print.

He delayed all day, increasingly irritated because he knew why he was hesitating. An hour in the gym at lunchtime—usually a surefire pick-me-up—barely improved his mood. Sara didn't help, because she didn't nag him. If it had been any other deadline, she would have been in his office every half hour until he did what was necessary. She didn't even mention it when she brought afternoon coffee, unprompted and with biscuits.

When he opened his office door at the end of the day, wearing his coat, he stopped in the doorway, wanting her to say something. She didn't. She simply looked at him, also obviously waiting for him to have the first word. After ten seconds, he stalked back into his office, read slowly through the form one last time, and sent it off. When he emerged again, Sara had already escaped. Never mind. Another hour or so in the gym before he went home would work off some off the stress. Without really thinking about it, he sent a message to Warrick to tell him that he would be late.

Toreth opened the door of the flat and the rich smell of roasting meat poured out to meet him. A treat, obviously, because Warrick didn't do serious cookery midweek. On his way to the kitchen, Toreth wondered whether it was good news or bad—either could provoke unexpected cuisine. A rack of lamb sat steaming on the counter, and Warrick was doing whatever-it-was to the roasting tin to make gravy. Deglazing, that was it—a random technical cookery term Toreth had picked up. "That smells fabulous. What's the occasion?" Toreth asked.

"The purchase of the new flat completed today. Could you open that bottle, please?"

Toreth opened a drawer and took out the corkscrew—the one thing in the kitchen that he could guarantee to find in the dark. Holding the neck of the bottle steady with one hand, he turned the screw slowly, watching the spiral dig its inexorable way into the plastic and wondering if it made any kind of metaphor.

"That's most of the legal requirements fulfilled," Warrick said after a moment. "So all that's left is for the decorators to finish work, which should be the end of this week."

"That's great," Toreth said, while his stomach tried to claw its way out through his spine and run. There went all the relaxation benefits of an hour's worth of lifting weights.

"The new furniture isn't all ready yet," Warrick continued. "But we can use what's here until it is. I suggest we move on the thirtieth of April, if that's acceptable."

"Don't see why not." A week. One fucking week.

"I'm afraid it's a Tuesday, but the corporate-level security-rated removal services are fully booked right now. It was that or wait another six weeks, which would complicate the sale of this place—SimTech could use the money."

Six weeks would be fine by him. Another year would be better. "All my stuff's here anyway. They can just sling it in the transporter without me if I can't get away."

"Asher happened to be in the office while I was organizing it, and she asked if we were having a housewarming. I said it sounded like an excellent idea." He paused. "If you do, too, of course. But I didn't think you'd object to a party."

"Me? God, no." Or to a drink right now. He swigged a mouthful from the wine bottle, hoping Warrick wouldn't notice.

"Any suggestions for a date?"

"How about—" He picked a day at random. "The Saturday afterwards?"

"I'll organize things, then. Let me know how many people you want to invite."

"Uh-huh. Sure. Sara. Chev and Ellie. B-C, Mistry. Nagra, I guess. Maybe a few more."

"Call it a dozen or so, then?" Warrick said. "Bottle, please."

Toreth watched while Warrick splashed wine into the tin and stirred the gravy. Now was the logical moment to mention his own news—get all the stressful crap out of the way in one go. He organized the words in his mind, getting the right casual tone. His chest felt strangely tight. When Warrick had set the bottle down again, Toreth said, "Speaking of legal requirements, I sent the change of address off to the DoP today."

Warrick seemed to appreciate that meant something, because he tapped the spatula on the side of the pan, laid it down on the chopping board, and turned around. "Really? Excellent timing."

"Yeah." Breathe, he told himself. "Couldn't be better."

Warrick's brow furrowed very slightly. "Are you—"

"Why don't I get the plates out? And a couple of glasses, if you want to drink the rest of the wine."

"Thanks." Warrick turned back to the bubbling gravy without further comment.

Toreth laid the table, thinking about the mismatched assortment of cutlery and plates at his old flat. Had the looters left any of it in a usable condition? Probably not, and in any case most of it had been there when he moved into the flat. All that had really been his was the assortment of glasses stolen from bars around New London.

Warrick seemed happy to leave the topic of the flat alone, and for the duration of the meal, they talked about other things. When they'd finished eating, Warrick made coffee. As the water boiled, he said, "The last of the flat forms arrived this afternoon, too—utility provision, complex fees, and so on. I don't think you need to sign anything, though. Just let me know what information you need to have in order to arrange accommodation allowance payments from I&I."

"I want to pay half the bills." Even though it hadn't crossed his mind before, Toreth suddenly did want to. "Even if it's more than the allowance."

"It's not necessary," Warrick said carefully.

For what definition of necessary? Toreth folded his arms, knowing he must look childishly stubborn.

Warrick turned off the heat under the coffee brewer. "It's not even as if half would be an equal division. Everything I pay for this place goes through SimTech, and there are all sorts of tax considerations and allowances. It would be insanely complex to calculate what it's really costing me. Far simpler if you just pay whatever's the maximum accommodation allowance Int-Sec will give you for private arrangements."

"I'll work it out," Toreth said. "Or send everything to Sara, and she can do it."

"A large proportion of the money goes towards the corporate grade security. That's my expense, not yours. And—" He sighed. "To be brutally honest, you can't afford it."

It didn't help that this was exactly the kind of thing he'd assured Warrick wouldn't bother him. "My salary will cover it. Just show me the fucking paperwork."

"Very well." Warrick took out his hand screen and expanded it. He passed the screen over and sat down opposite Toreth, his face impassive.

The vacuum brewer gurgled and splashed its way through its usual routine while Toreth read the numbers half a dozen times and still didn't believe them. Fuck it, Warrick was right. He couldn't pay half. He couldn't even pay a quarter. He was going to be a kept man, at least in terms of who paid for the security fences and the guards. Sara had long cherished an ambition to be a kept woman, but he wondered if she'd really like the feeling any more than he did. He put the screen

33

down, resisting the urge to throw it. "Okay. I'll get Sara to find out what the accommodation section needs to know."

"Toreth, I'm sorry. I had no intention of making you uncomfortable. But I'm afraid there is no other way around that particular point."

Toreth stood. "I'm going out. For a walk." The lie sounded unusually awkward.

He half hoped Warrick would protest. No such luck. Warrick merely looked up, then nodded slowly. "I shan't wait up for you," he said, his tone only faintly ironic.

Outside the spring evening still felt pleasantly warm, so he did actually set off walking, away from the campus. He could find a taxi once he'd decided where to go. For the first half kilometer he considered simply crashing at Sara's for the night. However, to his irritation, despite the fact that he was alone, he couldn't stop thinking about Warrick, or about the new flat. In the end he decided that he needed a real distraction. Not running away—not like it had been after Carnac. An orderly retreat and regrouping. He had to get his life back to normal, and he knew just how and where.

If there had ever been a Gegi involved with the management of Gegi's Bar, Toreth had never met him or her. Since he'd first been there over ten years ago, that put any hypothetical Gegi a long way in the past. The bar stood on the edge of an entertainment district not far from the Int-Sec perimeter, on the far side of the complex from I&I. While the area itself was respectable enough, Gegi's was far from it. Sara refused even to cross the threshold. The place had escaped the revolt largely undamaged, though, and tonight it looked reassuringly busy; since the lifting of the curfew, business had been brisk.

Gegi's Bar had three kinds of patrons. The first and by far the smallest group went there almost every night. They all knew each other, by sight if not by name. They sat in regular groups having, Toreth presumed, regular conversations. Why the hell they'd chosen this vast, dark, noisy place, out of all the bars in New London, he couldn't imagine and hadn't asked. In fact, he'd never spoken to any of them, even though some of them had been there when he'd first visited the place. But then Toreth didn't go to Gegi's to talk. At the other end of the spectrum, there were the irregular clientele—the vast majority of the crowd. They made single visits, or came for a few days, then disappeared. Sometimes they would return, after a space of time, and sometimes they would transmute into the third type, the semiregulars. Semiregulars were the people like Toreth, for whom Gegi's was only one stop amongst many. A frequent enough one, however, that the bar staff remembered names and drinks, and occasionally even details of jobs and lives.

Semiregulars and irregulars shared something—they came to this place to look for someone, because Gegi's primary reputation was as a pickup bar, and one where it was possible for almost anyone to find someone to their specifications. In fact, it was a little more than that. The upper floor contained private rooms—small, scrupulously clean and chargeable by the half hour. Not that Gegi's encouraged the presence of professionals on the premises. In fact, being unlicensed for that kind of business, and in addition situated between the Int-Sec and Justice complexes, the management discouraged it strongly and on occasion painfully. The rooms were simply for the pleasure and added convenience of the customers. They prevented those who were in search of very short-term liaisons from having to leave the building once they had acquired a partner. The rooms were both a profitable sideline and kept up the bar sales.

Not surprisingly, Toreth had never taken Warrick there. It wasn't the sort of place to take a regular thing, but more than that he hated the idea of the kind of attention Warrick would attract. The default assumption was that, outside the hermetic enclaves of the regulars, everyone at Gegi's was available. Warrick would stand out as especially available, being a clear social cut above the usual—Gegi's did not attract a large corporate clientele.

He bought a drink and abandoned the bar to prowl. The noise soothed him— music and voices, loud and tangled into an incomprehensible web of sound, but familiar and comfortingly detached from him. He let it wash over him, run through him, easing the tension. After half an hour, he felt normal enough to start hunting in earnest.

He'd considered the ideal pickup as the taxi drove him across the city. Physique wasn't important, or even gender, but married would be good. Someone who didn't do this regularly—someone looking for something new and dangerous, maybe needing a little persuasion to take the final step. Someone he'd have to concentrate on. A couple of targets suggested themselves immediately, matching the pattern he'd built on the way over. He'd almost picked one for an approach before he processed why they'd attracted him. One man, one woman, both dark-haired, both medium height, both with high cheekbones and pale skin.

This was supposed to be a distraction, not one of those annoying evenings when he found himself fucking someone while mentally cataloging all the ways in which they weren't Warrick. He tried again, surveying the bar slowly. There—that was better. A man, taller than Toreth, with wavy light brown hair framing a long, mobile face. He was watching the women openly and the men surreptitiously. Check another box. And then, final clincher, the man turned a little and revealed the ring on his finger. Third finger, left hand—check.

In business for the night.

35

Chapter Five

❖

Toreth told Sara about the housewarming party as soon as he arrived at I&I the next morning. Predictably, she thought it was wonderful.

"Who's coming?" She grinned. "Other than me, of course. I have to be there, just in case he's got any rich single friends I haven't met yet. Do you want me to tell people?"

"Yeah. Tell anyone on the regular team who's free—don't bother with the new pool lot. Mention it to Chevril, tell him to bring Ellie so I can show her the bedrooms. And..."

Who else should he invite? Mike Belkin, maybe? And his wife, he supposed, except that Toreth had no idea of her name. He'd met her maybe twice, and all he remembered was that she was mousey and bruised. Then there was Bevan, who might be married at the moment—he often was. Bev was a politically sensible invitee, anyway. Daedra, Christofi, Liz Carey and her boy toy...I&I acquaintances, not friends.

Toreth had a sudden vision of Warrick's flat filled with I&I faces—all his regular drinking crowd, which was what Sara meant by "people." Few of them were people Warrick would want there. Nor were any of them witnesses Toreth wanted to his official inauguration as corporate pet. Which was now less than a week away. Shit. His heart was beating far too fast, and he wondered vaguely if the idea of actually moving in was going to give him his first ever nonphobic panic attack. Or maybe this counted as a phobia, too. What was the medical name for a fear of new flats?

"Toreth?"

He blinked at her. Not surprisingly, she was looking at him curiously. He was about to tell her to keep it within the team, maybe including Chevril, when he paused. Why the hell shouldn't he invite people? Warrick kept saying it was *their* flat. Fine. Then he'd treat it like his, and fuck Warrick if he didn't like it. And fuck anyone at I&I who wanted to make cracks about his rich corporate.

36

The resolution seemed to dilute the panic to manageable proportions. "Keep it down to a dozen or so and try to avoid the ones who throw up and start fights. Send the names along to Warrick when you've got an idea of who's coming—we don't want security shooting anyone not on the list." He paused, then smiled at the image. "Well, you could leave a couple of people off."

Sara smirked back. "I can think of a few I wouldn't miss. So—" She paused. "What?"

"So...you're really moving in there?"

"Yes, of course. Why wouldn't I be?" he asked with determined cheerfulness. In a few months he'd look back at all this and think what a fucking idiot he'd been to worry about it. "Right, since the Administration was still paying us last time I checked the account, what have we got on today?"

Sara gave him an odd look, then turned to her screen. "The Isinpharm corporate burglary is looking very good. Justice got the main suspect last night."

"Justice?"

"Yep. He was at a squat where they picked up a dozen indigs in a random illegal pharmaceuticals raid. His description came up on the ident system—which is the first miracle, the problems the system's had—and they held him in situ, *and* they didn't mess up the crime scene. Nagra was on call, so she went out with—" Sara frowned and paged down a few screens before she gave up. "A couple of pool investigators. None of them stay around long enough for me to remember their names."

Short-staffing was still crippling the section; pool staff were assigned for the exact time they were required and not a minute longer. That made it extra nice of Justice to be helpful for once. "Well?" Toreth asked. "Did she find anything?"

"Yes. All the stolen pharmaceuticals, plus the matching formulation data. But this is the really good part—while Nagra was there, the corporate sab contact turned up to collect the stuff and pay. Somehow he managed not to notice two Justice cars parked in plain view down the street, and he walked right into the middle of it with a case full of negotiables."

"Stoned, probably."

"That's what Nagra reckons. Because Nagra was there, there weren't any arguments about who gets the arrests. Our two prisoners are downstairs. The corporate sab has three previous arrests, no convictions, so there should be no problem with a decent damage waiver."

This, Toreth reflected, was why he liked his team. Juniors who solved his cases for him before he even got to work were just what he tried to recruit. "Insofar as any of the waivers are decent, anyway."

"Well, the best we can get, then. Nagra went home to bed about six thirty," Sara continued. "But she left a lovely IIP. In my obviously totally unqualified opinion, it's pretty much wrapped up. Except..." She raised her eyebrows and shrugged.

Except that there were no interrogation staff free to have a nice, friendly, new P&P-style chat with the prisoners. "Okay, I'll do it."

"Before you do, the news about Isinpharm got back to Tillotson already, and there's a new IIP filed for a corporate kidnapping. No ransom demand so far, but there are some forensics that look quite promising. All the files are here, and there are even a few witnesses to talk to."

He considered. "Tell B-C to take charge of the kidnapping for now and he and Mistry can carve up the interviews however they think is best. I'll do the interrogations this morning and then join in."

As he went through into his office, he caught himself whistling.

"I'll be moving on the thirtieth," Warrick told Asher as he closed her office door behind him. "And Toreth suggested Saturday the fourth for the housewarming, if you're free."

"I think so—I'll check with Greg."

In the corner of her office, the last few drops of a fresh brew were splashing quietly into the pot. The rich smell reminded him that his caffeine levels were far too low for a weekday morning. "Do you want a coffee?" Warrick asked.

Asher smiled. "Aren't I supposed to ask you that?"

"Yes, but I can't wait for you to remember your manners."

"Pot, kettle," she said as she stood.

"I didn't manage to find time for a cup this morning." And with only one of them there, the idea of making coffee had seemed oddly pointless. Ridiculous, when he'd drunk morning coffee in solitude for years.

"What's that?" Asher asked, nodding towards his hand.

He held up a large airtight box. "I brought biscuits. Ginger, shortbread, madeleines, cantucci, and those forever unnamed coconut-chopped walnut-syrup-crisp things—Jen's recipe. All homemade."

"Good Lord. In that case, definitely coffee. I'll pour it."

He took one of the low upholstered chairs. Asher set the cups on the table and sat opposite him. Sipping his coffee, Warrick watched her pick out a couple of biscuits. They hadn't been a deliberate attempt to bribe his fellow director into a good mood, but they couldn't hurt. He was anticipating a difficult conversation.

"Why the bounty?" Asher asked indistinctly through a mouthful.

"I had an unexpectedly spare evening, and I realized I hadn't baked anything at all for weeks. It's wonderfully therapeutic. Once I started, I ended up getting rather carried away. I had to send out one of the security guards for extra flour."

"I should make some myself, but somehow I never find the time." Asher sighed. "I remember baking biscuits with you and Dilly and Jen. I'd like my kids to have memories like those, but I can't see myself finding the time. I feel guilty already."

"You and Greg will make wonderful parents. Have you heard anything about the reproduction license application?"

"No. We should still get on the corporate fast track, I hope, but apparently the Department of Population is deluged." She tilted her head slightly, quizzical. "I've just realized —you're the only person who hasn't asked if we're doing it because of the revolt."

The idea had crossed his mind. "Well, I knew you were thinking about it before. And you're both far too sensible to rush into anything." With the opening presented, he couldn't help asking. "So, is that the reason for trying for a license now?"

"I don't—I mean, my parents asked that, so did Greg's, even Jen dropped a few subtle questions last time I saw her." Her mouth quirked. "It's starting to annoy the hell out of me, truth be told. And I've been telling everyone so firmly that it's nothing at *all* to do with the revolt that I'm beginning to wonder if I'm protesting too much. It's so hard to think about it objectively."

"You have plenty of time. The application, and then—" He waved vaguely, suddenly realizing he had no idea of the details of the process. Lissa and he hadn't made it that far through the DoP maze. "Implant removal—that must take time, too?"

"Three to six months for full fertility to return for both partners, for the majority of couples," she said promptly, then smiled. "I have a horrible feeling that I'm going to turn into an awful baby bore."

He laughed. "You couldn't possibly. But I'm afraid it's really not my field. I can give you a good estimate for code delivery, but..."

"I don't think it's quite the same, somehow." Asher shook her head, smiling slightly. "So, talking about family rearrangements, Toreth's really moving in with you?"

"We're moving in together, but yes, basically." With other people he might pretend, but he'd known Asher for too long. "He didn't back out when I mentioned a date, so I think there's every chance he'll go through with it."

"Well, I have to say I never expected it."

"Nor I." He picked up a squishy, sticky walnut square. "The revolt changed a lot of things."

"Yes." Asher looked down at the table for a moment, and Warrick wondered if this was the start of the conversation. However, when she looked up, Asher said, "I had dinner with Dillian last week. She seemed...slightly unenthusiastic about the idea of the two of you in the same flat."

"Ah. If she had any expectation of it lasting, I'm sure she would have been more than 'slightly.'"

"And you?"

"I'm trying to keep my expectations realistic."

Asher smiled, looking satisfied. "I'm glad to hear it. At least now we can finalize the sale of the old flat, too. That will please the bank."

Warrick frowned. "Are they making trouble?"

"Not really. They were sniffing around to see whether we might like to borrow money at a *very* reasonable rate. I told them we have other places to raise it if we need it."

"And do we?"

"It's possible." She sighed. "We'll have to make a decision soon, Keir. We can't keep delaying."

"There are still units shipping from the production plant. We have work for months, even building and programming flat out."

She laid the half a ginger biscuit in her hand back down in her saucer. "I grant you we have a long backlog of orders, and the cancellation penalties are keeping most people on the list. That doesn't change the fact that new orders are below even the lower boundary of the original projections."

"Not far below," he countered.

"Perhaps not. But I don't want to hit the end of the current list with no money in reserve and no prospect of an income."

"What about the negotiations with the Administration Leisure Centers people? Did they follow up their first inquiry?"

Asher grimaced. "I got a new set of requirements from them first thing this morning. They want the stripped-down basic units, no custom programming, and a price to match."

"But if we had spare capacity at the factory, presumably it would be worthwhile?"

"Perhaps. But take a look at the requirements from this morning when you have a chance—I'm almost certain they only approached us because they think that they can use the prospect of a deal here as leverage when they negotiate with P-Leisure over the same contract." She sighed. "From that point of view, it's a waste of our time. Still, the longer it goes on, the more contacts we'll make in the Leisure Center administration."

"As long as we're careful not to offend P-Leisure by looking as though we're actively trying to poach their customers. They've been very generous over the years, and it's to everyone's benefit if they get it all back several times over. Did you talk to Tavi Lennox-Phull?"

"Yes—she knows what the Leisure Center people are up to as well as we do. Handy to have an old friend of yours working for P-Leisure. She isn't worried—she knows we can't yet match P-Leisure on that kind of deal." She smiled, a neat but combative show of teeth. "Just give me a few years, when we have the new production facilities. Then I'll show you an income stream."

40

He grinned back. "And I look forward to swimming in it. But for now all we've got is our technical expertise and experience of innovation. We can't stop research."

Asher gave an exasperated sigh. "And I've never suggested that we should. Just that we refocus on the immediately useful applications."

"How will that save money?"

"If we have fewer experimental programs, that means we can move the developers from there—who are all the best developers—and put them into the core projects."

"And that will let us cut staff? No—out of the question."

She held up her finger. "We won't have to sack anybody. We've been expanding the staff year-on-year since we started. If we simply stop recruitment for new places and to replace people who leave, then we'll save a lot of money over the projected budget. That was one of the ideas behind short-contract flexibility, if you remember."

This was really a discussion that ought to happen with Lew present, but he couldn't help his reply. "We have to keep developing."

"We have to be sensible."

"Do you think P-Leisure and the other corporations with development licenses will 'be sensible'? No. They'll have their eye on the long term."

"They're larger," Asher said. "They can afford to."

"And we're smaller so we can't afford not to."

"I acknowledge the dangers, but it's better to make decisions now than to let the situation fester. People will be happier with a decision made and a plan in place."

"Not that decision," Warrick said with finality. "Have you spoken to Lew?" Asher nodded. "What does he say?"

She quirked an eyebrow. "Guess."

It wasn't hard. "That we should cut back the software budgets and concentrate on the next generation of sim hardware?"

"Right. And *you* insist that the software is the most important part of the business."

"No, I think software and hardware research are equally important. We should keep both as they are."

She smiled, somewhere between exasperation and affection. "What am I going to do with you?"

"Nothing, not yet. Leave it until the end of the month. Or a little longer than that." As she started to protest, he said lightly, "You wouldn't want to spoil my birthday by wrecking SimTech, would you?"

She set her cup down firmly on the table. "Keir, I'm not trying to do anything of the kind." To his surprise, she sounded genuinely annoyed. "Do you think that

41

I don't appreciate the importance of research and development? This is my corporation, too. Don't you dare behave as though you're the only one who gives a damn about SimTech."

"I'm sorry, Asher. I know quite well that I'm not."

"Good. You said it, Keir—we have to keep our expectations realistic. We can't hide our heads in the sand and hope the economic turmoil from the revolt will simply vanish. But—" Her voice softened. "We can wait for a while still, I suppose. And I have no choice, if we three can't agree on what to cut. I'll cobble something together to tell the staff."

"Thanks."

She shook her head. "Two weeks, Keir. That's as long as I'm prepared to wait."

That evening, Toreth felt unexpectedly uncomfortable as he opened the flat door. It was the first time he'd stayed away all night in the last few weeks, which was weird in itself. Warrick wouldn't make a fuss about it, since he obviously hadn't expected Toreth to come back to the flat. However, it meant that Warrick knew for sure where he'd been. Not like before, when Toreth had his own flat and there was always the possibility that he'd been tucked up in bed with a warm glass of milk and a good selection of porn. This, he realized suddenly, was what it would be like all the time at the new place.

Where were you?

Stoned out of my mind on probably illegal drugs in a flat owned by a guy who had no clue he was fucking an I&I para.

Maybe he'd just take the easy route and lie. Say he'd been at Sara's. He didn't like that thought either, though. It wasn't that he minded lying—far from it. Lies were what kept life smooth and easy. However, the idea of lying because he felt obliged to, rather than because he wanted to, that was something different.

Toreth found Warrick in the kitchen, cooking again, something that smelled unusually unappetizing. Warrick didn't comment about anything from the previous night—not the argument over the bills, not Toreth's abrupt departure, or the fact that he hadn't returned. Sticking very much to the rules, which was a relief.

"What are you making?" Toreth asked. "Smells awful."

Warrick looked around. "Deviled kidneys. Treating myself. I called in at the fresh produce market on the way home."

"The place stinks."

"The flat management system will take care of it." Warrick began methodically turning the sliced kidneys. "I'll tell it to turn up the filtering. I'm sure it will be gone by the time you get back."

"Back from where?"

"I'm sorry. I thought you were going out?"

Why would...oh, yes. Section birthday party for someone he'd never liked that much anyway. Annoying that Warrick remembered events like that when he didn't. It felt too much like Warrick keeping an eye on him. The irritation crystallized the earlier unease into an urge to test the rules, and to hurt. "Yeah, I am. In fact, I should change and go, or I'll be late."

"Well, have fun."

"I will. I did last night, at least."

Warrick's shoulders stiffened slightly, but he said nothing.

These days Toreth didn't do this, and he'd forgotten how much fun it could be. "I went somewhere I don't think you've been. Pickup place not far from I&I."

"Really," Warrick said.

"It's not a bad place, if you just want a quick fuck. Lots of potential."

"I'm sure there was." And then, the words forced out unwillingly, Warrick added, "Man or woman?"

"Man. Luckily he didn't live too far away, so it saved me the price of a hotel. Amazingly enough, his wife was at her sister's."

"How very fortunate. What was he—" Warrick shook his head and slid the contents of the pan onto a plate. "No. That would be a bad habit to get back into, wouldn't it?"

So determined to be reasonable, not to argue. "Didn't feel at all bad to me. Blowjobs never do."

"I meant myself, since obviously 'getting back' would be redundant in your case." Warrick turned suddenly and his voice sharpened. "You are nothing if not relentlessly predictable."

"Yeah, well, I needed to unwind. Not all of us get to spend all day in the sim fucking teenage graduates who'll do anything for a job at SimTech."

"Even if that were anywhere near accurate, it's hardly the same as bar-crawling all night in a desperate attempt to track down the tiny remaining handful of New London citizens you haven't already fucked."

Adrenaline was starting to kick in, bringing with it the first stirrings of anticipation of the makeup fuck. "So? I thought what I do away from here is my business."

Warrick paused, then said calmly, "Indeed it is. I'll consider the topic closed."

"You fucking started it."

"No, I did not." He pointed at Toreth with the stinking spatula and a drop of sauce spattered onto Toreth's shoe. "*You* brought it up, quite deliberately, for reasons we both thoroughly understand. But if you want an argument I'm afraid you'll have to find someone else for that as well. Have a good evening."

The sudden exposure of the subtext infuriated him. Treating him like a fucking child, and it only made the anger hotter to acknowledge that there was a certain amount of justice in that. "Fine, I will have. And a nice fucking night, as well. I'll see you tomorrow. Maybe." Without waiting for a reaction to the announcement, he went off to shower and change.

Dressing to go out didn't improve Toreth's mood. Sara had mentioned the birthday party as he left, and he'd managed to forget on the journey home. He had no real desire to go; if he wanted to do anything tonight, it was take himself back off to Gegi's or somewhere equivalent. Before the revolt he wouldn't have gone to the party—wouldn't even have bothered with an excuse. Now the pressure to attend was politically unignorable. Everyone in the section seemed to feel a ghostly urge for solidarity from the still-empty desks and offices. Enforced socializing irritated Toreth as much as enforced anything else.

Two or three more minutes and he would've left the flat. He'd been delayed anyway—when Warrick answered the comm, Toreth was still in the process of looking for his coat, which he thought he'd thrown down somewhere in the living room.

"Yes?" Warrick said. Something about his stillness, a sudden change in attitude after the casual greeting, penetrated Toreth's bad temper and made him stop his search and watch.

There was a long pause, during which Warrick drew breath to speak half a dozen times. Finally Warrick said, "I can't . . . Jen. Jen, listen to me. Stop . . . is Dilly there with you now? Let . . . let . . . Jen, let me talk to Dilly. Please. Let—Dilly? Tell me what happened."

Half a conversation—after that Warrick was mostly listening, nodding, the blood draining from his face. Warrick pale and distracted was usually something that Toreth found very appealing indeed. Not this time. He looked sick, shocked. Family bad news, Toreth guessed. When the call finished, Warrick's first words confirmed it. "It's Tar."

"Is he dead?"

"Not . . . not yet. Jen's at the hospital, with Dilly. They're giving him a ten percent chance. One of them said less."

"What the hell happened?"

"I don't know—no one seems to. Dilly hasn't been there long and Jen's not . . . Dilly said there was a collision. Tar was in a private car—or a taxi, they're not sure yet—that went out of control. He's been unconscious since they brought him in."

Sounded like a mess. "They'll have done a DNA check. Next of kin would be in his medical file."

"Valeria's all right," Warrick said, as if he'd asked. "She wasn't in the car with him."

"Yeah? Good."

Warrick sat down abruptly on the arm of the sofa. "Did I tell you he was coming to stay at the flat?"

"Tarin? Here?"

"Yes. Or no—the new flat now. With Val. They were coming for the weekend. I arranged it, oh, weeks back. When you were..." The sentence trailed off.

"I thought you didn't like him?"

"Yes. So did I. For years and years." He sounded lost. "Strange, isn't it?"

Toreth kept silent, feeling uncomfortably and surprisingly out of his depth. Over the years he'd spoken to a lot of people who'd just had bad news: kidnaps, murders, violent assaults, rapes, financial ruin—more or less everything in which I&I might conceivably have an interest. On many occasions, he'd *been* the bad news, arresting suspects or explaining damage waivers to prisoners. It was just that he'd never actually been involved before. Invested in the outcome of cases, yes, but the people never. Not that he cared if Tarin was dead, alive, or somewhere in between. He felt something, though—an odd echo of Warrick's obvious distress. Sharpened, perhaps, by the memory of the stupid argument in the kitchen.

Not so fucking impervious now, was he? Toreth enjoyed the thought for a moment, then he shrugged the feeling aside. He considered the range of options, settling for doing what Warrick would have done. "I'll make some tea."

Warrick looked up, focusing on him for the first time, and smiled slightly. "Thanks. But I don't have time—Dilly wants me to go there right away."

"You've got time for tea. I'll make it. You call a car and tell SimTech security where you're going. They'll throw a fucking fit if you just disappear. Pack some things, too—you'll probably need to stay tonight." Slightly to his surprise, he found himself adding, "I'll come with you, if you like."

Toreth waited until Warrick nodded, then he went back into the kitchen. He could call Sara from there; at least this would make an acceptable excuse to skip the damn party.

Chapter Six

❖

Outside Tarin's room in the ICU, Toreth leaned against the spotlessly white wall, listening to the medic explaining the situation to Warrick. Toreth had heard it all before, dozens of times, and this woman seemed competent enough at it. Telling the distressed relative what had happened, what they had done for the victim—patient—so far, and what more they could do, had to be the pain-in-the-arse part of the job. Not that Warrick appeared particularly distressed, unless you knew what to look for. Probably she did.

The SimTech security guard stood a little way down the corridor. Toreth had recognized her at once when they met her by the car at Warrick's building. He knew the recognition was more than his general familiarity with SimTech staff, but it wasn't until she introduced herself as Alicia Dean that he remembered speaking to her during the old investigation at SimTech. Right now she looked slightly uncomfortable but completely professional and very alert. Not surprising, since there'd been an unexplained accident involving a corporate family member.

Single phrases from the medic caught his attention, creating a picture. More details than Dillian had given over the comm: the accident had happened at around four fifteen. Tarin had been on the way to collect Valeria from school, and only a hundred meters away from the building his taxi had inexplicably been hit by a delivery tanker carrying something flammable. The fire had started at once, with suggestions of an explosion. Injuries from the impact. Burns over Tarin's whole body—his clothes burned off him.

At least, Toreth thought vaguely, they wouldn't have had to peel them off, and the flesh with them. But he was distracted by the knowledge of what would come next...soon. Any moment now.

"We have him in a flotation tank while—"

Hearing the dreaded words at last, Toreth gagged, hands clenching as he fought for breath, his senses hijacked by fear.

Warm, medicated, oxygenated fluid buoyed him up, keeping him hydrated.

Flowing in, circulating around him, flowing out to be purified and eventually returned. Pumping through the mask into his scorched lungs. In his nose, in his mouth, in his throat—it didn't matter that it was keeping him alive because it felt like drowning, except that it went on and on.

Sickness swept over him, making him glad of the support of the wall. Toreth had never in his life experienced a flotation tank. He didn't need to. He'd seen them working, and that was enough to build the false memory from other terrors. Just one more thing in the world to avoid. If he'd known that it was *this*, he never would've come with Warrick. If he could've made it the length of the corridor he might have left, and damn what the medic or the security guard thought. Unfortunately, it was taking all his strength to stay upright.

Eventually, it registered that the medic was finishing her spiel. Toreth struggled for composure, succeeding to the extent that when Warrick turned towards him, he didn't seem to notice anything amiss. "Dilly took Jen home before we arrived," Warrick said. "Once I've seen Tar I'm going on to Kate's . . . to the house. I'd be, ah, very pleased if you'd come, too."

"I said I would, didn't I?"

"Yes, of course you did."

He watched Warrick turn, start for the door to the room, reach for the handle—

"Don't go in," Toreth said suddenly.

Warrick stopped. "Why?"

"Because you don't want to see him." Out of the corner of his eye he saw the medic watching them, her face expressionless. Dean had her attention fixed on the far end of the corridor.

"It might be the last chance," Warrick said.

"It makes no fucking difference. He'll be completely out—" Toreth's throat tightened. "And you can't touch him or talk to him, so there's no way he'll know whether you're there or not. Have you ever seen anyone with those kinds of injuries? No? I have. If he does die, you'll be glad not to remember what he looked like. Trust me on this."

Warrick seemed to be weighing up the idea. Finally he said, "Dilly saw him."

"Jesus Christ, it's not a bloody competition. You—" Why the hell was he bothering? His own pathetic fears? He had no obligation to follow Warrick through the door. "Fine, go in if you want to. I'm waiting out here."

Warrick hesitated a moment longer, fingers resting lightly on the door, then nodded. "Very well." Toreth wasn't sure what he meant until Warrick dropped his hand and turned back towards him. "Let's get back to the car."

All the way there, Toreth had to fight back the smile, annoyed with himself over the ridiculous feeling of triumph.

Trust me on this.

47

At Kate's house, Dillian greeted them at the door, for once too distracted to disapprove of him. Dean's presence didn't seem to register. Of course, Dillian was corporate, too, and used to ignoring minions. He'd bet any money that she wouldn't be able to describe Dean in an interview tomorrow.

"Did you see Philly at the hospital?" Dillian asked after she'd closed the door. Warrick shook his head.

"You must have just missed her. She brought Val here, then went back to the hospital when we got home. She said she'd stay there tonight."

"Good—that there's one of us there, I mean. How's Jen?"

"Keir, I'm so sorry. She called me before she went to the hospital, and by the time I got there she'd already gone in to see him, and she just...went to pieces. She told me she'd call you, and then when I got there she hadn't done it." She bit her lip. "I should have done it myself. I—oh, God. I'm sorry."

Warrick put his arms around her, dark head bowing down to hers, rocking her gently. "Shh. It's not your fault. I'm here now."

Dillian had obviously been crying, and as they went through towards the kitchen, Toreth reflected on how much more popular people became when they died. Or, in this case, didn't quite die. The atmosphere was palpably that of a bereavement, though—neither Warrick nor Dillian was the sort of person who would take a ten percent chance and pin serious hopes on it. Ten percent was a backstop figure medics used because they hated it when patients they'd pronounced hopeless surprised them and lived.

Outside the kitchen door, Warrick paused, then turned to Dean. "I assume you want to check over the security?"

"If I could, please. If it's not acceptable, I'm afraid I might need to call some more personnel from SimTech."

"Do whatever you think is necessary. I sent your ID to the security system from the car, so you have full access for now. When you're done, wait in the living room. I'll be through to talk to you later."

Dean nodded and faded tactfully into the background. Toreth wondered if functional invisibility was something they taught at security training school. It would be a handy trick to learn.

Jen was waiting for them in the kitchen. Warrick went over at once, before anything was said, and embraced her with the ease and warmth that always left Toreth feeling uncomfortable, somewhere between jealousy and distaste. Over Jen's shoulder, Warrick mouthed, "Tea." Toreth went to start it, but Dillian intercepted him.

"I'll do it," she said.

Busy with the tea things, and slicing one of the cakes that seemed to be a permanent fixture of the house, she nevertheless managed to spare time to direct the occasional unwelcoming glance at Toreth. Hadn't taken her long to get back to normal, Toreth thought. Fuck her. He hadn't come here for her. He was supposed to be here providing...well, moral support for Warrick, he supposed. Whatever "moral support" was. With Sara it usually amounted to alcohol and light flirting, which unfortunately wasn't likely to do the trick here.

His uncertainty didn't seem to matter, though. It quickly became apparent that his contribution, moral or otherwise, would be limited. The conversation now underway in the kitchen didn't concern him. Practical arrangements, who needed to be contacted and told what, discussions about Valeria and Tarin's wife Philly—family matters, and he wasn't family. He didn't need Dillian to tell him that. Hanging around on the edge of things, unregarded and unwanted, he wondered whether he shouldn't just go and leave Warrick in Alicia Dean's capable hands. Warrick didn't need him, Dillian didn't want him, Jen seemed scarcely to register his presence. Why the hell had he come here at all?

He stopped picking currants off the cake on the work surface beside him and thought about that. Shorn of the disgusting self-pity, it wasn't a bad question. Why had he come? He didn't usually feel a need to trail around after Warrick like a puppy on a leash, and although it was tempting to wrap it up in some stupid association with the new flat, it wasn't that, either. Partly it was the same feeling he'd had in the flat: the attraction of seeing Warrick helpless, faced with something he couldn't push aside with a mask of indifference and a cold smile. Something that couldn't be smoothed away with the magic touch of money and status, or solved by cleverness or corporate contacts. Something leveling.

So Toreth had seen it, and now he should go, before the shine of the experience tarnished in the face of Warrick's composure and competence.

There was also a professional angle here, though—someone who, if he wasn't technically a corpse, was a close approximation of one. An accident, or an attempted murder, with nothing to choose between them at this point. There were, at most, suggestive circumstances: Warrick was corporate, Tarin had some interesting political views. He wouldn't submit an Investigation in Progress based on that vague a suspicion unless the victim was important enough to merit it.

Justice would doubtless think the same thing, assuming they even heard about it. The Transport Safety Division would have first call on the investigation. Only if they found signs of illegality would Justice take an interest. At that point, Tarin's unwitting link to Int-Sec should flag up a blazing stop sign as soon as Justice pulled his file. Toreth would probably be able to tell that by how quickly and enthusiastically Justice dropped the case.

Or maybe there was no flag, now that Kate was gone. An investigation might end up digging too deep and revealing Tarin's resister connections. That led into such a world of shit he didn't want to think about it. All hypothetical anyway,

Toreth reassured himself, until the accident was proved to be something more. Leaving it alone would be the sensible thing for him to do, too, but a nagging compulsion wouldn't let him. Toreth didn't believe in intuition—feelings like this were usually triggered by sound reasons that he hadn't consciously put together yet. Almost reflexively, he began assessing the group in the kitchen, looking for guilt, for aberrant reactions, for knowledge out of place.

Jen interested him. From Warrick's partial comm conversation and Dillian's words when they'd arrived, he'd expected their aunt to be hysterical. Certainly the obviously shaken woman in the kitchen made a contrast to the sharp, sardonic Jen he'd met before. She seemed controlled enough, though. Possibly she'd pulled herself together for her nephew's benefit. At the moment she was stubbornly resisting Warrick's gentle suggestions that she might want to lie down for a while.

Dillian looked at least as upset as Jen. Toreth would have expected her to deal reasonably well with a shock like this—certainly better than she seemed to be. Her job as an extreme environments structural engineer must involve at least a level of familiarity with unpleasant accidents. On the other hand, it was only a few weeks since Kate's disappearance, which complicated the situation, so perhaps her distress was partly due to that.

Warrick was—Toreth caught himself before he extended his assessment farther. No one in the kitchen was a realistic suspect—he needed to be more methodical. Talking to witnesses was the first step. What did children drink? Sweet things, probably. He poured a glass of tonic, then made himself a gin and tonic. As he picked up the drinks, he glanced at the group around the table—still engrossed in their conversation, and paying no attention to him. He murmured a vague, "Won't be long," and slipped out of the kitchen.

To his relief, Dean was nowhere in sight. Finding Valeria's room proved no challenge to his investigative powers—her name was painted on the door. He balanced the glasses in one hand in order to knock. When there was no reply, he knocked again, then opened the door and went in. Valeria sat on the bed, with a screen balanced on her knees. She didn't look up.

It had been a long time since he'd taken the introductory pediatric interrogation course. As far as he could recall, though, the basic principles were no different from adult interrogation—certainly not at level one. He managed to close the door without spilling anything and tried a neutral opening. "Hello, Valeria."

Now she looked up, her expression brightening briefly. "Uncle Val!"

Nice to be wanted by someone. "We'll make a para-investigator out of you yet. How are you?"

Her expression closed down, making her look disconcertingly like Warrick. "I'm fine." She had the family talent for packing a lot of feeling into not many words. These two clearly said, "go away and leave me alone."

"Is there anything you want?" he asked. "Anything I can get for you?"

"No. And I don't want to."

He considered the statement for a moment. "You don't want to do what?"

"I don't want to cry."

"Fine by me." Sniveling kids were even worse than the standard kind.

"Auntie Dillian said I ought to," she said, concentrating fiercely on the screen again.

Memories surfaced, unpleasant and unwanted, of what it was like to be a child, trapped in a world of adults with incomprehensible rules and demands that could never be satisfied. Anger he couldn't control welled up, directed at Dillian. Christ, but he hated pediatrics—he always had. "Well, Auntie Dillian," should mind her own fucking business, the stupid bitch, "probably meant you could if you wanted to."

She shrugged. "Maybe."

But they both knew that Dillian hadn't said that. He took a deep breath and reminded himself of one of the basic level one approaches: make yourself a friend to the prisoner, someone who isn't as frightening as the guards and the cells and all the distant noises. Be someone who can help them. He walked over to the bed, trying not to loom over her. "How about a drink instead?"

That produced a spark of interest. "What is it?"

"One of them's tonic, and one of them's gin and tonic. Guess which is yours."

"Gin," she said promptly.

"If you like."

As he expected, she took a single sip and wrinkled her nose up in disgust.

"It's an acquired taste." He swapped the glasses. "Means you have to drink a lot of it before you get used to it."

"I know what acquired means."

"Well, good for you." Precocious as well as obnoxious. Useful in the current situation, however. He sat on the bed and glanced around the room, which seemed to have all the mod cons a nine-year-old might want, and all surprisingly tidy. Jen's work, or did Valeria share Warrick's neatness?

"Nice room," he said.

She nodded. "It's big. I like it more than my other room, but I don't say that to Mum. Her flat is really teeny."

He didn't actually know anything about the domestic arrangements. "You don't live here all the time, then?"

"No. I live with Mum, but I come here to stay with Dad a lot. And Auntie Jen and Granny, before Granny went away." She frowned at him. "Do you know where Granny is?"

He ignored the question. "Can I ask you something?"

She set the glass down carefully on the table by the bed and pulled her knees up against her chest. "Okay."

51

"Do you always get a taxi home from school?"

The question didn't seem to surprise her. "Only on Tuesday."

"Why Tuesday?"

"Because I have band practice. I play the violin. Usually I go home with Sarah's mum, 'cause Sarah lives near Mum and me. But Sarah isn't in the band, so Dad picks me up and I come here with him. Mum comes for me later, or sometimes I stay all night."

Routines, which were always the first point of danger. It would be interesting to know how many people had access to that information. Toreth wondered if he dared look to see if it was noted in Tarin's security file. "Did you see the accident?"

She shook her head. "Some people at school did. Katty did."

"Who's Katty?"

"She plays the flute in the band. She's really good, lots better than me. She's my best friend." She looked down at the screen again. "We wait outside together after band, because there are some other girls who don't like her and I look after her. But yesterday I stayed inside."

"That's very nice of you—to do that for your friend." Praise wherever you can, he remembered, as long as you don't praise answers to direct questions. "Why didn't you wait with her today?"

"There was a man outside the school fence. When we went outside first he was watching us. And—" She shrugged. "It was creepy, so we went and waited inside. We took turns to go out and look to see if Dad was there."

"Was the man there every time you went out?"

She nodded. "I told Ms. Plaice and she said it was okay. But *we* thought he was creepy. We thought if only one of us went outside, then whoever was inside could tell a teacher if he did anything bad."

"Very clever," he said absently. Someone watching the school on the one day Tarin would be there? A slim, tenuous link, but it might be worth chasing up. "Did you see the man's face?"

She nodded. "I went up quite close to him, once. He was on the other side of the fence, so it was okay. He smiled at me."

"Yeah?" Toreth considered options. If he'd been at I&I, he could have started putting together a profile for the ident system and called in a pediatric interrogation specialist to keep the evidence as untainted as possible. However, there was no way in hell Warrick or Dillian would let him take Valeria to I&I. "Did Katty see him, too?"

"Maybe. I didn't talk to her. She went home with her mum, like I did—she was crying. I didn't cry."

"Good for you. Your friend—does she ever come round here to, um, to play?"

"Yes, sometimes. Uncle Val..." She looked up at him, the expression in her

52

dark eyes reminding him of Warrick again: curiosity and calm intelligence. "Are you investigating?"

Shit. "Yes, I am. But unofficially. Do you know what unofficially means?"

She squinted thoughtfully. "Kind of."

"It means...not because of my job. On my own." It had to be worth a try. "Secretly."

"Secretly?" As he'd hoped, the idea seemed to appeal. "Does Uncle Keir know?"

"Ah...no, he doesn't. Nor does anyone else."

"Auntie Dillian?"

"No." Christ, he hoped he wasn't going to have to go through the entire list of their mutual acquaintances.

She pondered the answer for a while, then said, "Auntie Dilly won't like that."

"Maybe not."

"So I won't tell her. You shouldn't tell her, either," she added seriously. "Granny says don't tell people things if they'll get upset about them."

Words to live by. "Kate...your granny's a very smart woman."

Valeria nodded slowly. "I want Granny," she said, and he saw the tears beginning to well. And then, "I want Daddy," and the flood started as she reached out for him.

Oh, fucking hell. He held her close against him, wishing that he had one of his investigation team here to do this part for him. Mistry, for preference. She'd hold Valeria's hand and blow her nose and somehow get half a dozen useful bits of information in the process. Comforting witnesses was something Toreth had written out of his job description, along with various of the other tedious but necessary chores. What was the point of being a senior if you had to do crap like this?

A soft, startled exclamation caught his attention, and he looked up to find Dillian in the doorway. The expression on her face almost made up for the damp patch growing on his chest—absolute, unbelieving shock. He nodded to her. "Dillian."

She came into the room, hesitating halfway between the door and the bed, obviously wanting to take Valeria away from him but seeing no way to do it. He decided to make it easy for her. "Valeria?" He eased back a little, lifted her chin. "I have to go."

She nodded, accepting another incomprehensible adult necessity. Still, it took her a while to let go of him. As he went to pass her, Dillian halted him, her hand on his arm. "Keir said you stopped him from going in to see Tar," she said in a low voice.

"Yes."

"Thanks." Her hand tightened. "I mean that."

He couldn't help his reply, or the harsh tone. "I didn't do it for you."

The hurt showed in her dark eyes, which were usually so calm, so arrogant—

53

so like Warrick's, and he took a vicarious pleasure in it before she covered the expression and walked past him to the bed.

Toreth killed some more time by offering to fetch a takeaway for a rather late dinner. He'd half expected Warrick to insist he'd cook, but constant tea-making seemed to be satisfying his usual crisis-induced domestic urges.

It was a relief to be out of the house, and he took his time, changing his mind more often than was strictly necessary before he finally selected Italian. As he sat in the restaurant, nibbling bread sticks, he considered the information he'd got from Valeria and the worries her outburst had begun to stir.

Valeria could want her granny as much as she liked, but she wasn't going to get her. If someone had tried to murder Tarin—and he reminded himself that so far that was only a suspicion—then there was a chance Kate could also be dead. He'd never asked Warrick the details of how he'd arranged his mother's release. Now might be a good time to find out exactly what had happened. How could he do that without arousing any suspicions on Warrick's part?

There were several possible reasons why Tarin was in hospital. The first was that he'd had a genuine accident. Even with traffic control, such things could happen. But even if the Transport Safety Division investigation concluded the collision had been accidental, that could simply mean that any saboteurs had been talented.

Sabotage was certainly a possibility to consider. Family tragedies could be used to distract corporate heads at critical times; extortionists who couldn't get to a primary target might go for less well-protected family members. A target assessment should have revealed that Dillian would make a better victim, but on the other hand, Warrick had apparently invited Tarin to his flat, so they'd obviously been talking recently. Toreth wondered if anyone else had known about that invitation. Come to that, he wondered why Warrick hadn't said anything about it to him. Probably because Toreth wouldn't have been happy about it. Given Tarin's resister connections, it was sensible to avoid contact with him as far as possible. "Resister" and "political criminal" might be in the process of being redefined, but that didn't mean it was safe to fraternize with one. Even—or especially—when fraternizing had a more literal meaning.

The attack on Tarin could be the first shot in a larger corporate sab campaign—a threat made against other family members would now be that much more effective. If this were the case, Warrick should be receiving a demand soon. That wouldn't be Toreth's problem. SimTech security could deal with it. He pitied the poor fucking sabs who tried to tangle with Warrick.

On the other hand, it might have nothing to do with Warrick. Tarin might have had enemies of his own, either personal or connected with his idiotic ideals.

Toreth's experiences of resisters suggested that they were fractious and definitely not above eliminating someone they saw as a threat. Resister infighting would be even less of Toreth's problem. Except that . . . Toreth was connected to all of it. He was a para-investigator, and so a target for resisters, too. He knew far too damn much about Kate's Citizen Surveillance history. And he made a legitimate target for corporate sabs wanting to reach Warrick—his unease at being a registered partner suddenly felt far less illogical.

"Sir?"

Toreth looked up, startled. The waiter stood at the counter, holding the heated boxes. Toreth paid and left, still half absorbed in working through the possibilities. The more he thought about them, the less he liked them.

Dinner was unsurprisingly quiet. The dining room reminded him of his meal there at New Year a few years ago, although the subdued voices now made a striking contrast to the cheerful noise then. The takeaway was excellent, and to Toreth's slight surprise everyone, including Dillian and Jen, ate well. Valeria, dressed in pajamas but looking determinedly awake, stuffed herself.

At least her presence reduced the amount of discussion about Tarin, which was beginning to grate. Neither Warrick nor Dillian had liked the man, as far as Toreth had ever noticed. Toreth couldn't put the abrupt reversal down to hypocrisy, because he'd seen it too many times before with sudden deaths and serious injuries. The tendency of death to wipe clear the flaws of the deceased played hell with investigations.

He found himself looking around the table at the others. Alicia Dean had declined an honest invitation from Jen to join them and taken her meal into the kitchen, so the table was family only. Now that Tarin wasn't there to spoil the effect, the transgenerational resemblance was frighteningly strong, and it made him think of the family portrait in the living room. Kate was missing, of course, but Valeria made up the numbers. Presumably she had been too young to be included when Cele painted the picture, or maybe she hadn't even been born.

He stopped and rewound the thought. When Cele had painted it. That opened up a possibility he hadn't thought of before. After the meal, he left the others to clear up and went to find a quiet corner to make the call. "Cele? It's Toreth. Have you heard?"

He listened impatiently through the usual litany of "how awful."

"Yeah, it's terrible," he said eventually.

Her next question surprised him. "Where are you?"

"Kate's . . . I mean, Jen's house. With Warrick and Dillian and a very stoney SimTech guard."

"Good. I'm glad you're there." And the genuine-sounding relief at his answer surprised him even more. "Poor Tarin. And poor old Keir. I bet it's hit him harder than you'd expect, hasn't it?"

"Yeah. Listen, I need to see you about something. It's urgent."

"What is it?"

"I'll tell you when I see you. Is tomorrow morning okay?"

"I have to be somewhere at eleven."

"Great. I'll be there before then."

"What—"

"See you soon. Bye." He canceled the call before she had the chance to ask any more questions. Better not to display too much curiosity over the comm.

Jen and Dillian were still tidying up the remains of the meal. Toreth found Valeria sitting in the living room with Warrick, who was listening to her read. Warrick looked by far the more exhausted of the two. When he saw Toreth, Warrick smiled, then yawned. "Time for bed, Val. I'll take you up."

She shook her head. "I want Uncle Val to."

"I don't think he—"

"It's okay, I'll do it." Toreth grinned at Warrick's startled expression.

"Well, if you're sure," Warrick said doubtfully.

"What, you think I've got an ulterior motive? Give me another seven or eight years for that. Who do you think I am, Lew Marcus?"

Warrick's eyes narrowed. "Toreth, that isn't at all funny. On any level."

Ignoring him, Toreth turned for the door. "Come on."

They climbed the stairs in silence. Inside the room, she looked up at him. "You're supposed to tuck me in," she said.

"Forget it. You can manage."

She stared at him for a few seconds, then suddenly laughed. Once in bed, she looked up at him solemnly. "Read me a story?"

"You can read your own. I saw you just now, remember?" He sat down at the end of the bed. Valeria sat up expectantly, eyes bright. "You were telling me earlier about the man you saw at school."

She nodded.

"If I asked Cele—Auntie Cele—to draw him, could you tell her what he looked like?"

She thought about it, scratching the elbow of her pajamas with her thumb. "I s'pose so," she said finally. "I could try."

"All you have to do is try. It doesn't matter if you can't remember in the end, just that you do the best you can, and you don't make anything up." He considered options for a moment. "Are you going to school tomorrow?"

"I don't know. I don't think so. Mum didn't say if I was or not."

"How about your friend Katty, the one who saw the accident?"

"Don't know."

"Okay." How the hell was he going to arrange this without Warrick or Dillian finding out? Maybe Jen would help. The problem was that he didn't know her well enough to be sure he could rely on her to keep quiet about it.

"Uncle Val?" Valeria said quietly. "I didn't tell anyone about the investigating."

"Yeah? You're a good girl." He stood up and turned to go.

As he put his hand on the light switch, she said, "Leave it on, Uncle Val, please."

He paused. "Do they usually let you have it on?"

She hesitated. "Yes. Always."

The lie was utterly transparent. He let go of the switch. "Fine. See you in the morning."

With any luck, it would annoy Dillian.

Warrick wasn't in the room they'd shared the last time Toreth had visited the house. For a moment, Toreth wondered if he'd got the right room, then he saw the bags folded and stacked in the corner. When he checked, he found their clothes neatly placed in the chest of drawers. Jesus, sometimes the man's tidiness really did verge on the compulsive.

It felt odd to be spending the night at Kate's house again, Toreth thought as he undressed. Odd that her shadow still lay on it so heavily. He'd spent only one New Year there before Warrick had thought better of the idea and not invited him again, but he remembered her quiet domination of the family. She had been gone for two months, and her presence seemed to have faded little if at all.

Eventually, tired of waiting alone in the bedroom, Toreth grabbed a dressing gown and went in search of Warrick. Toreth only found him because the door to the room he was in was ajar. A bedroom he didn't recognize—Tarin's, presumably. Inside it was dark, the only light coming from the street outside. Warrick stood by the window, arms folded tight across his chest, looking out.

"Are you coming to bed?" Toreth asked.

"Yes. Go on, I'll catch up." His voice was thick with tears. "I won't be long."

Oh, Christ. Wanting desperately to leave and pretend he hadn't seen this, Toreth went over and stood behind Warrick. Pause, deep breath, then he placed his hands gently on Warrick's shoulders.

As far as he expected anything, he thought Warrick might turn around, and the idea of that, of having to hold him as he'd held Valeria, made him feel queasy. The pleasure at seeing Warrick brought low had transmuted entirely into unease. However, Warrick didn't turn, although he did lean back against him, and one hand crept up to tighten over Toreth's. Otherwise he stayed as he was, crying almost silently, the tears glistening in the light through the window. Shaking a little.

It felt very strange. Not unbearable, not even particularly unpleasant, but strange. Staring out of the window, through their dim reflections, Toreth thought about all the witnesses and prisoners he'd watched cry. About Sara in the hospital, years ago now, or at I&I with that bastard Carnac, or over her latest broken heart. It was easy. Piece of cake—nothing to it.

Eventually, Warrick sniffed once or twice and pulled away. "Go on," he said again. "I won't be long."

"Okay."

Back in the room, he spent a minute or so considering what would work best, then switched off all the lights, got into bed, and pretended to be asleep.

By the time Warrick appeared, the pretense had almost turned into reality. The soft closing of the door woke him enough to listen to Warrick moving in the dark, undressing, then standing by the bed. "Toreth?" Warrick asked softly.

He kept still, breathing slightly irregularly, until finally Warrick climbed into bed beside him. Then it was simply a question of timing the movement right so that they met in the middle, accidentally, and Warrick's arm slipped accidentally around him. Why, he wondered sleepily, did he still bother pretending?

Chapter Seven

The other side of the bed was empty when Toreth woke in the morning. He checked his watch hastily, hoping he wouldn't be late for Cele, but it was still ridiculously early.

He found Warrick downstairs in the kitchen, talking to Jen. "Warrick, Sara called," Toreth said. "I've got to go in to work—I'm sorry."

Warrick looked around. "That's fine. Thanks for coming out here in the first place. Do you want the car?"

"I'll get a taxi. I'll call later, see how things are. If you're still out here, I'll come back this evening."

Warrick nodded, then stood. "If you can wait just a moment, I'll add you to the security system." He hesitated, as if expecting a protest, then added, "In case we're out when you arrive."

❖ ❖ ❖

Cele's flat-cum-studio was filled with clear spring light. She made coffee, then took it over to the giant cushions on the floor by the floor-to-ceiling windows in her work area. As they settled down, the expensive view caught his attention and he realized what an easy shot they would both make for a sniper in any one of dozens of places. Paranoia levels high and rising.

Cele looked at him expectantly. "What's so urgent?"

On the way over he had considered how to approach the problem—the best idea seemed to be to say as little as possible. "What do you know about what happened?" he asked.

Despite the question sounding more professional than he meant it to, she answered without hesitation. From the phrases she used, she'd obviously got the story from Dillian, and possibly spoken to Warrick as well. But she gave him no reason to think she knew anything more than the publicly available facts.

When she'd run through the events, he said, "And what do you know about Tarin?"

She glanced at him sharply, then turned away to refill her coffee cup. When she settled back into her cushions, her wariness was unmistakable. "What do you mean?" she asked.

"Come on, we both know he has some dangerous friends." Which sounded better than "traitorous." "And a lot of risky opinions."

"Do we?" she asked.

"Cele, I'm not planning to arrest him out of intensive care. Christ, how long have you known me?"

At that she did look a little embarrassed. "It's just not something any of us would ever talk about. At least..."

"Not in front of me. And believe me, I'm grateful. But right now we can't afford to ignore it. Politically, things are volatile. Opinions like his might not be treason anymore, or even a reason for an arrest, but on the other hand they might be. And whatever the official position turns out to be, they're still potentially bad for your health."

She looked at him, still uncomprehending, then her eyes went wide. "Christ on a crutch—you think someone tried to kill him."

"No, I don't. I think it's possible."

"Who?"

"I have no idea, and there's no safe way of asking anyone else to look into it." Play it down. "*If* there's anything to find out in the first place. It could be nothing more than an accident. The reason I'm here, though, is that Valeria saw a man hanging around her school yesterday morning. And I thought you could—"

"Whip out a pencil and draw him for you?"

"Got it in one."

She cocked her head, one polished silver earring flickering sunlight. "Do Keir and Dilly know?"

"No. It'll probably turn out to be nothing, and they've got enough to worry about."

She nodded, a little reluctantly. "What about Tarin? Will he be safe in the hospital?"

"Yeah. Those places have too much security for anyone to get to him easily. Besides, odds are he's going to die anyway."

Cele stared at him, then said, "So that would make it a pointless risk to go after him again unless they say he might pull through?"

"Right. Don't worry about him."

"That's one way of looking at it." She studied him for a moment longer, then added, "I'm glad I don't live in your world."

That gave him pause for thought. Cele was a close family friend. Not as close as him, in the sense that she wasn't currently fucking any of the family (unless there was something still going on with Dillian), but there was an outside chance that she could be in danger. Then there was Asher Linton, the other New Year regular at Kate's house, and a SimTech director to boot. He'd also carelessly forgotten Philly, who as the putative target's wife was potentially in more danger than any of them.

Well, more targets meant more chance of a corpse showing up that wasn't his own, which improved the odds of finding whoever was behind it. On the other hand, too many accidents in a row would make Warrick suspicious, and if that happened, Warrick would want to do something. He was a talented amateur, but an amateur he still was and he could stir up a lot of danger. Too many complications, and he began to wish his suspicions had never arisen in the first place. He felt hemmed in by the uncertainty of the dangers, and having to worry about Warrick as well as himself was an unwelcome novelty.

"What are you thinking about?" Cele asked.

"Warrick." He looked up and smiled, with his best show of natural charm. "If I'm looking blank, I'm usually thinking about Warrick."

"Sweetheart, you *never* look blank. Not even when you're sleeping and/or passed out." Before he could ask for an elaboration, Cele stood up. "That reminds me. I've got something for you. Although I'm not sure if now's really an appropriate time to show you, but..."

She hunted through a rack, then returned with a portfolio.

"Keir called me about the move and the housewarming, so I was looking for a present for him. This is from the good old days, when he had time to pose and I had time to draw purely for fun."

He shifted around on the cushions to sit side-on to the window, to improve the light, and opened the file. Studies of Warrick sleeping. In most of them, the bed was a shadowy presence, sketched in with a few lines to give a context for the figure. Faces, hands, torsos, full length. Frowning, he wondered when the hell Cele had had a chance to draw these. She always said—and Warrick had always said—that they'd never fucked.

Cele cleared her throat quietly. "He slept at the studio for a while, way back when. A different place—I couldn't afford anywhere this swish. I never laid a finger on him, although God knows I was plenty tempted. But he was engaged to Mel; they'd had a fight, which was why he was there at all."

Without looking up, Toreth nodded. Pretty much what he'd thought, he told himself. Repeating that a few times made it feel almost true. Reassured, and with Tarin completely forgotten, he took his time. He'd never watched Warrick sleeping—until this moment he'd never even considered it. What would be the point? He wanted to do it now. To study him, to map out the differences in his body between now and these images from years ago. To see if he looked the same: vulnerable, guarded, irresistible. He touched sleeping lips with his finger, wondering.

What are you dreaming? About fucking your precious Lissa? Or about something else—something she couldn't give you? A cock inside you, chains on your wrists...

So many subtle nuances of expression, so many varieties of sleep. He had no idea how long he browsed, or even how long he spent looking at a single drawing of Warrick on his side, perhaps nearing waking, his cock hard, his hand lying curled carelessly beside it. His slight, inviting smile made Toreth want to reach into the paper, shake him awake, and fuck him into the mattress until they both came screaming. Except that Warrick hated fucking before breakfast. What a criminal bloody waste, if this was what—

A soft scratching made him look up. Cele now sat on the floor a little way away, leaning against the window, a large sketchbook on her knee.

Cele smiled. "Carry on, Seven Inches—don't mind me."

But he couldn't, not once he'd realized he was being watched. He set the portfolio aside. "What are you drawing?"

"You and your gorgeous cheekbones. Come see."

Feeling oddly reluctant, he went to crouch beside her.

She had indeed drawn his gorgeous cheekbones. His face was, so far, the one clear part of the drawing—everything else was sketchy but expressive lines. As he watched, Cele was filling in the details of his arms and shoulders, the open portfolio on his knees, his hands lifting a sketch to get just the right angle for the light—what was on the paper wasn't visible. Everything faded gently away from the focus of his face, with mere hints of the cushion and the rest of the background.

His face, looking at Warrick's face. Nicely recursive. Like all Cele's work, it was very good. Very true to life, or he assumed it was. Sketch-Toreth was intent on the drawing in his hand, absorbed, oblivious to surroundings and observer. And his expression was... Oh, Christ in heaven. Burn it. Burn the damn thing right now.

The pencil stopped moving. "Well?" Cele asked. "Any good?"

Toreth stayed where he was for a long moment, appalled and yet unable to look away, then he stood up and looked at his watch. "Not bad. Finish it, if you like. I have to go—I'll get in touch about Valeria. We need to do it soon, though."

"Okay. Do you want to take one of those old ones? In exchange for giving me this." She lifted the sketchpad.

"Yeah, sure. Thanks."

He skimmed through the sketches again, for form's sake, but he knew which one he wanted. She signed it with a flourish, gave him a sleeve to protect it, and let him out of the studio.

At I&I, Sara was waiting for him, agog to hear the news. He told her the public version: unlucky accident, with SimTech considering the possibility of something corporate. There was no need to worry her with his speculations. Back in I&I, away from the gloomy atmosphere of Kate's house, the idea of a deliberate murder attempt seemed less plausible. All he really had was Tarin's resister background and the word of one child witness that a man might have been outside the school. He almost wished he hadn't spoken to Cele about it, even though he felt confident she wouldn't tell Warrick or Dillian.

He was surprised to get a call from Cele only half an hour after he reached the office. "Toreth? I'm going to Kate's place this afternoon. Dillian and Warrick have to go back to the hospital with Philly, and they don't want to leave Jen on her own with Val. I didn't tell them I was calling you."

What a star. "Great. When you get there, see if you can have them invite her friend over—the one who saw the accident. 'Katty' is all I know."

After a few minutes' thought, he copied the appropriate section on eliciting descriptions from child witnesses from the P&P and sent it to her. That shouldn't be too risky. He thought about going straight back to Kate's but decided against it. The later he got back, the less time he'd have to spend with Dillian glowering at him. Besides, the more work he could get done today, he more time he'd have free to devote to unofficial investigations later.

Toreth sat in Jen's kitchen, which was becoming familiar, and watched Cele sketching. She had Valeria's rapt attention, or at least all the attention she could spare from a plate of biscuits. The girl seemed to be enjoying the process of producing the likeness, which was good from the point of view of keeping her cooperation, but bad in that it made her more likely to drag the sketching out and distort her recollections. He kept quiet but listened carefully, making sure that Cele stuck to the protocols he'd sent her.

The house was silent except for the soft scuff of the pencil and Cele's occasional questions. Jen was asleep upstairs, and the SimTech security guard had gone with Warrick. "How about that, sweetheart?" Cele said, turning the sketchbook towards Valeria.

Valeria studied the drawing with a thoughtful frown. "His nose is wrong."

Cele rolled her eyes, but all she said was, "Wrong how?"

"It was pointier." Valeria dipped her last chocolate chip cookie into the glass of milk and nibbled.

"Okay." Cele began to erase lines. "I'm not sure you should give her any more of those," she added without looking up. "And if you do, you're responsible for cleaning up the consequences. I traded my maternal instincts in years ago for a pair of genuine leather trousers so tight you could count my pubes."

Toreth paused, hand on the biscuit tin. Valeria eyed him hopefully. On reflection, he decided Cele was probably right. The brat was certainly smart enough to spot a bribe pattern. She'd already provided a description and a second recounting of the events that was clearer than many he'd heard from adults.

"How about that?" Cele asked at length. "Give it a good look, sweetheart."

After a lingering glance at the tin, Valeria obeyed. "It's okay," she said eventually.

Cele laid the sketchbook down on the table and all three of them examined the drawing.

"I know him," Cele said at length.

"What?"

"I have no idea where from, but I've seen him. I'm sure I have. Or someone who looked damn like him. Or maybe a picture of someone." She shook her head. "I can't put my finger on it."

"Well, that narrows it down. Val?"

Valeria shook her head. "He doesn't look like anyone except him."

It was almost three by the time Valeria's friend arrived. Toreth lurked in the hall while Jen and Cele spoke to someone he assumed at first was her mother, but who turned out to be a child minder, summoned at short notice.

"Ms. Waller said that Katherine could stay for as long as Valeria wanted her to, but you were to make sure she wasn't upset."

"Of course," Cele said soothingly. "Don't worry—Val doesn't seem to want to talk about it."

"I think she just needs one of her friends," Jen added. "Someone familiar, someone her own age."

"Sure. Makes sense." The minder didn't sound interested. "Would it be okay if I didn't stay? Only I have things to do. I'll leave my comm number."

A score, Toreth thought. No need to pry the child away from a clingy parent.

It took another half hour before Katherine and Valeria were alone in Valeria's room. Leaving Cele with instructions to keep an eye out for Dillian and Warrick, Toreth went upstairs with the sketch. He paused outside the room, running through the questions he wanted to ask. This would be so much easier if he could involve Mistry. She'd sit and chat to the kid and then an hour later she'd somehow have all the important facts run through three times and a summary distilled from them ready for him. He didn't appreciate her enough.

When he went into the room, they were sitting at opposite ends of the bed, legs stretched out and feet touching. They both seemed to be absorbed in reading separate screens, which made him wonder if they were really so friendly after all.

They both looked around as he entered, then put down their screens in almost mirror gestures. "Val, would it be okay if I had a word with Katty?" he asked.

Valeria nodded but stayed put, looking grimly determined. Toreth decided it would be easier to let her stay. He set a camera on the dressing table, making the gesture as casual as he could, then sat down on the floor beside the bed. "Do you know who I am?" he asked Katherine.

She nodded, sitting very still, her hands under her thighs. "I told her," Valeria said. "And that you were investigating."

He put his finger to his lips and she nodded. "I'd like to ask you some things about yesterday morning," he said to Katherine. "Can you tell me what happened?"

She looked down at her feet. "I went outside, and I was standing by the fence when there was a bang. A really loud bang." She shifted on her hands. "I looked up the road and there was a big fire."

"What happened then?"

"I went up to the gate to see it better. There was the big fire on a transporter and all around on the road, and there was a car in it, all twisted up. But I only saw it for a minute before Ms. Plaice came out and we had to go in. She said it was goulash."

He considered for a moment before he got the word. "Was there anyone else watching? In the street?"

She nodded. "Lots of mummies and daddies. Of people who're in the band. They were shouting all different things."

"Anyone else?"

"Don't know."

He laid the drawing on the bed beside her. Before he could say anything, she nodded. "He was right by the gate, but he wasn't looking at the fire. And he wasn't shouting, like all the others. He looked at me. And he looked at the school and then Ms. Plaice came out and I didn't see him again."

"Ms. Plaice teaches music," Valeria added.

He nodded, without looking away from Katherine. "Have you seen him before?"

"I don't know."

He was prompting too much, but he couldn't see another way forwards. "Have you seen him at the school before? Someone's father, maybe?"

She was starting to look anxious. "Maybe. I might've done."

"Do you——"

Valeria said brightly, "Hi, Auntie Dilly."

Toreth turned around, only then realizing that he hadn't properly closed the door. How long had Dillian been standing outside? Long enough, judging by her expression—she looked ready to add a murder to the recent mayhem. He cleared his throat. "I didn't hear you come in."

"I can tell that." Before he could stop her, she crossed to the bed and picked up the sketch. "Who's this?"

Valeria kept quiet, but Katherine piped up immediately. "He was at our school on the day that Mr. Marriot—" Valeria kicked her and she stopped, glancing worriedly between Valeria and the adults.

"Downstairs," Dillian said, looking directly at Toreth, cold and furious.

He nodded. There was no need to have his only witnesses contaminated by witnessing this, too. Toreth followed Dillian out, pocketing the camera on the way.

"How could you get him involved? How the hell could you let him talk to Val? How could you *encourage him*?"

Dillian waved the sketch towards Toreth without looking at him. Toreth crossed his arms. To his surprise—and relief—so far most of her venom had been directed at Cele. He'd gathered only third-person scorn. He wasn't about to push his luck by saying anything. Warrick had also said nothing so far. Perhaps he was waiting for Dillian's fury to blow itself out, although Toreth caught the odd appealing glance thrown in Warrick's direction by Cele.

"If you thought it wasn't an accident, why the hell didn't you call Justice?" Dillian demanded of Cele—rhetorically, because since she'd slammed the kitchen door she hadn't paused for longer than it took to gather a fresh lungful of outrage.

"Dilly—" Cele said for the fifth time.

"If there needs to be an investigation, that's Justice's job, it's not anything to do with *him*."

"I said that Toreth could speak to Val," Warrick said.

Dillian stopped dead, her mouth open. After a moment she tried to speak, but nothing came out except a protesting squeak. Luckily she was too surprised to check Toreth's reaction, because he knew he must have looked as stunned as she did.

"I thought it was for the best," Warrick continued.

"The *best*?!" Dillian was starting to wind herself up for another assault when Warrick stood. He crossed the kitchen and stood beside Toreth, hip touching his, hand behind Toreth on the counter. Presenting a united front. For his part, Toreth managed some kind of a neutral expression, although it was a struggle.

"I'll spell it out if I have to," Warrick said. "Tarin did and said some dangerous things in the past. Do you really want Justice to start taking a close interest in him? What else might they find? What about Philly and Val?" He gestured around the kitchen. "What about us?"

Dillian closed her mouth, then sat down, the sketch crumpling in her hand.

"Toreth offered to look into it, I accepted. Blame me, if you have to blame anyone. Certainly not Cele."

"Oh." Dillian looked down and rubbed her nose. When she looked up, she was flushed. "I'm sorry."

"Don't worry about it," Warrick said. His voice had softened, and he crossed over to crouch beside Dillian, putting his arm around her. Toreth couldn't help smiling. Classic Warrick—attack and retreat, punch hard and then offer a soothing hand. God, he must be a demon in corporate negotiations.

"Everyone is upset," Warrick said. "And I'm sure no one will take anything to heart." He looked up. "Right?"

Cele nodded and turned to Dillian. "Already forgiven and forgotten, sweetheart."

The door opened and Jen looked in. "What on earth is going on? The noise woke me up." She sounded more like the Jen Toreth remembered—sharp and collected. "It gave me flashbacks to twenty years ago. What's wrong?"

"Nothing," Warrick said as he stood. "Frayed tempers, that's all. Why don't I—"

Toreth mouthed "make some tea" along with him, and caught a faint smile from Cele.

"I'm going to see Val," Dillian announced. "I'll take something up to her."

"I'd lay off the chocolate biscuits," Cele said.

Toreth detached himself from the discussion going on around him and thought about what Katherine had said. "Maybe a parent at the school" was the best identification he had. Odds were the girl was only trying to be helpful. Valeria hadn't recognized him, and she seemed like the sharper observer. On the other hand, he did have a possible adult witness—the music teacher.

"Toreth?" Warrick's voice. Toreth looked around. He'd just poured water into the teapot—through the wisps of steam, his eyes were cold. "Could I have a word?" Warrick said. "In the living room."

"Nice move in the kitchen," Toreth said.

"You had no right." Warrick's voice was low but furious. "No right at all."

Toreth blinked. "I thought—"

"I meant what I said—I'm quite sure that Dillian had no need to blame Cele for what happened. Now what exactly do you think you're playing at?"

"I'm not playing at anything. Far from it. I'm talking to witnesses, which is my job."

"Not here. Not without my permission, unless you have a warrant you didn't show me. Why the hell didn't you tell me?"

"Because you'd have thrown a fit like Dillian—just a different fit. You were dead right in there, you know. What if Justice takes an interest? There should be a big hands-off flag in Tarin's security file. But Kate's gone now, so what if there's no flag anymore? What if they press an investigation? Besides, don't tell me it never crossed your mind there might be more to it than an accident."

"I've hardly had time to think about it, have I?"

"Bullshit. Professional tip—if you're going to lie, just lie. Don't make it into a question, because it's a real telltale. I knew you'd think of it. So I wanted to look into it quietly and find out if there was anything to worry about. If there had been, I'd have told you right away. Until then, the fewer people who knew about it, the better."

"I see." After a moment, Warrick's shoulders relaxed. "And I admit it's logical, although I still wish you'd told me. I'm sorry I was a little sharp."

And I'm sorry your sister is such a fucking bitch. "No big deal."

"What was the sketch Dillian was going on about?" Warrick asked.

"Oh. Valeria saw someone at the school, just before the accident. She thought he might be watching her. I asked Cele to sketch him. Probably nothing to do with anything, but I'll look into it. I can do it a lot easier from I&I—ask around a bit, get a photocomposite made up, maybe run a systems search with a borrowed code. It'll only take me a few days to do it perfectly safely. You've got enough to do without running an investigation."

Warrick smiled wryly. "True. Well, then, thank you—and be careful."

"Fuck, yes. Sit down, I'll get the tea."

"Bring the sketch in," Warrick called after him.

In the kitchen, Jen and Cele glanced up when he came in—from the sudden silence he surmised they were talking about either himself or Dillian, or possibly both. As he crossed the room, Cele turned her head to follow him, then winked at him out of sight of Jen. At least she was still talking to him, which might be useful later.

Jen had the sketch in front of her, smoothing out the creases. "Who's this?" she asked.

Toreth looked over her shoulder. "Someone Valeria saw outside her school before the accident."

Jen nodded. "The source of the argument," she said drily. "But what I mean is *who*? His name."

"No idea." With two mugs of tea ready, he paused by the table and turned the sketch towards him.

"Do you think the accident wasn't one?" Jen asked.

Toreth glanced at Cele, who shrugged slightly. Jen was too sharp to lie to, and there was little point now that so many other people knew. "Maybe. I've got no real evidence one way or the other. Mostly it's that I deal with far too much crap like this at work, and it kicked off my paranoia."

"I see. And Dilly was upset because you talked to Val?" Jen frowned thoughtfully. "It doesn't seem like her to go off the deep end like that, if that was all it was."

"Everyone's upset." He shrugged. "And she doesn't like me."

"I've noticed." She paused, then added, "Kate was very fond of you."

Noting the past tense, he looked at her curiously. She smiled wanly. "I was there when she was arrested. Keir told me that Kate was in some kind of trouble, that she'd had to leave the Administration. He also said that it's unlikely she'll be back, so I try not to let myself hope. One more thing we shouldn't talk about, I suppose."

You have no idea. "Yeah."

"I wish she were here now—she was always stronger than me, although most people would tell you it was the other way round. I'm all front, I'm afraid."

Cele snorted quietly and, remembering Jen's performance in defense of Tarin, Toreth tended to agree with Cele. "I wouldn't say that." Fuck, for all he knew Jen could work for Cit Surveillance, too. He looked down at the drawing. "Don't suppose you recognize him, do you?"

"No . . . not really. There's something a little familiar."

"Dillian said so, too," Cele added.

"What?"

"She said she thought she recognized the man." Cele smiled wryly. "Once she'd calmed down and actually looked at the sketch. But then she changed her mind."

He nodded. He'd looked at the damn picture so often he was beginning to think the same thing himself. Probably the guy just had one of those generic faces that every witness you spoke to thought they knew. Still, he'd see what Warrick could do.

When he went back to the living room, he found Warrick in a chair, his head back and his eyes closed. However, he looked up when Toreth closed the door, and he took the tea with a heartfelt, "Thanks."

"Here you go," Toreth said as he sat beside him. He laid the sketch on his knee and blew on his tea to cool it. "Bonus points if you *don't* think you recognize him."

"But I do," Warrick said quietly. "I think I met him recently."

Startled, Toreth looked up. Warrick had gone very still. "You—where? Who is he?"

"He probably isn't a colonel in the Service."

"Huh?"

Warrick smiled fleetingly. "After you told me that Kate had been arrested, I came here. I found a number on her computer and sent a message to Citizen Surveillance to say she was in trouble. Someone who looked not unlike this man arrived at SimTech later that evening. He was the one who arranged her release."

Damn it, he *knew* he should have asked Warrick more about Kate. "Why the hell was he at the school?" Then he regretted the question. He could think of a dozen reasons, all very unhealthy, but what he really needed was a way to kill the whole conversation before—

"We have to find out who he is."

Fuck. Too fucking late. "Whoa. Hang on a minute." He grabbed for the first distraction that came to mind—something from the list of leading questions for witnesses. "How sure are you it's the same man?"

"Well..." Warrick hesitated, studying the sketch. Toreth smiled to himself. Ask a witness that and they always started looking at the differences, not the similarities they were fixed on earlier.

"Moderately sure," Warrick said at length. "But not one hundred percent, I admit. Or even...it is only a sketch."

"Right. So you want to go looking for trouble because you *think* this guy looks like someone you met for, what, twenty minutes? Did he tell you his name?"

"No, he didn't. But..." Warrick trailed off, frowning thoughtfully.

"What?"

"Someone else might know," Warrick said slowly.

"Who?"

"Didn't you say that Carnac had a copy of Kate's security file? If the man I met was involved in handling her, wouldn't that be recorded? Then we could compare the handlers to—" He pointed to the sketch.

"I don't remember seeing handlers' names. But then I wasn't close reading for detail." Being too worried at the time about looming humiliation and death. "So, yeah, they could be. But I don't have the file."

"Carnac may well have, though."

"Oh, no. No fucking way."

"The idea doesn't appeal to me, either." Anger flattened Warrick's voice. "If I never spoke to the man again it would be no loss."

"Fuck. Shit." Toreth gave it twenty seconds' thought and still couldn't convince himself. It wasn't possible, even if his life and Warrick's life and the future of the Administration had depended on it. "I can't. If I lay eyes on the bastard again, I won't be responsible for my fucking actions."

"I wasn't suggesting that you go." Warrick sounded horrified. "I'll speak to him."

"Go? Hang on. To fucking Strasbourg?"

"Of course. I can hardly ask him for a file like that over the comm, can I?"

"There has to be a way of getting a secure message—" Toreth shook his head sharply. How the hell had they ended up discussing this as if finding a starting point for raiding Cit Surveillance files was a desirable thing? "Not Carnac." He gritted his teeth and forced the word out, hoping it would be enough. "Please."

Warrick's eyes widened briefly in surprise, and Toreth didn't know whether to be glad or not that the plea had had the desired impact.

"Very well," Warrick said. "So what do you suggest? There has to be another way."

"There's no need to rush into things. We don't even know whether we need to do anything at all."

Warrick raised his eyebrows. "Whether?"

"Even if he *is* the same man you saw at SimTech, we've no proof he was behind it. Maybe he was hoping to stop it and didn't get there in time. If he rescued Kate, there's no reason to assume right off that he'd try to kill Tarin. Or it could be a complete coincidence. Aren't you the one who always says the world's full of coincidences? We haven't even heard from the Transport investigation yet—it could easily have been a genuine accident. Let's not start kicking wasps' nests until we've got a reason to, huh?"

Warrick stared at the drawing for a long moment, as if hoping it would speak. Then his head lifted and he nodded slowly. "That's sensible, I suppose."

"Good. A few days, that's all I need." Toreth folded the sketch and slipped it into his jacket pocket. Wanting to distract Warrick, he asked, "How did things go at the hospital?"

"You were right yesterday—I wish I hadn't gone in to see him." He leaned his head back against the chair and sighed, then added quietly, "And I wish you'd been there today."

Meaning, maybe, come with me next time. Tarin would probably be better company than usual at the moment, but the idea of the flotation tank was too much. "No, you don't," Toreth said. Warrick turned his head and started to say something, but Toreth carried on over him, wanting to get the conversation over with. "Not unless you wanted the distraction of me throwing up all over the room, which is what I'd have done. It's the tank."

Warrick's face cleared. "Of course. I'm sorry. I ought to have remembered."

"You've got other stuff to think about." In a way, it was a relief that his stupid loss of control in the Jacuzzi hadn't made a bigger impression.

Warrick didn't say anything more, so after a while, Toreth said, "We had to interrogate a witness in a tank once, after a resister bombing. She had chemical burns, vapor damage to her lungs."

"Really?" Curiosity surfaced. "How did you manage it?"

"They woke her up in the tank and we asked the questions through a nerve-induction earpiece. She did have one good hand, so she typed the answers for us. She kept choking on the—" He swallowed. "Before we started the interview, I went to the toilet and stuck my fingers down my throat. Then I took an antinausea shot. I still spent the whole three hours one breath away from puking on the floor. She died a couple of days later. Systemic poisoning. So what did the doctors conclude about Tarin?"

"Nothing, so far." Warrick looked up at the ceiling again. "The choice is simple enough. They can carry on the treatment, or they can let him die. It wouldn't take long. The doctor we spoke to said they're struggling to keep him going as it

71

is. Even if he makes it through the next few days, there's a strong possibility he could die later if they can't suppress the infections. He'll require constant medical support for . . . well, a long time. In the unlikely event that he pulls through, it will take months of treatment before he can leave the hospital. Not just skin replacement—muscle groups, some organs." Warrick swallowed. "His hands. They couldn't make any firm long-term predictions; they haven't been able to assess him conclusively for brain damage yet. Although that was the one thing they were optimistic about."

Sounded like a hell of a lot of hassle and expense to go through for someone you didn't like. Warrick had stopped talking, so Toreth asked, "What did you tell them?"

"Nothing. Philly is his registered next of kin—they're technically still married and they never changed it after the legal separation. But she wants Dilly and me to decide. I think she wants us to let him go, but she can't make herself say it because of Val. And I just don't know what to do. I don't—" He stopped dead, then looked around. "I don't know why I'm telling you all this. I'm sure you're not interested."

"No, carry on. I don't mind." This was just what he needed to know to predict if the potential killer might feel the need to follow up his first attack.

"I didn't know Tar well enough to even begin to guess how he'd feel about it. It would be much easier if Tar had left any indications of what he'd want—" Warrick shook his head. "I have no room to talk. I've done nothing like that either, even though the SimTech legal department asked me to."

"I have," Toreth said. "Not much, but enough for that. About all it is good for. I've got a whatsit—patient directive—in my medical file, saying that they can't put me in a flotation tank. Under any circumstances. Full body burns, whatever. *I'm* never going in one of those fucking things."

"But—"

"They knock you out. I know. But knowing it's possible . . . no. It's the idea of them fucking up the sedation. Of waking up in there. It happens. The odds are one in a thousand, maybe, but I'd rather die. Isn't that stupid?"

"Actually, yes."

Toreth ignored him. "Your lungs are full of the stuff they put in the tank, and you're breathing it. The water—the supportive fluid for burns to the lungs. Can't speak, can't move—odds are the sedation would wear off before the muscle relaxant. They might not even notice you'd come round. You'd be—"

With difficulty, he forced himself to shut up before he talked himself into a full-blown panic attack. Not looking at Warrick, he drank the cooling tea, trying to clear his mouth of imagined saltiness. What would flotation tank fluid taste like? Beyond the basics, flavor was mostly scent. Could you taste at all if your nose was full of liquid?

72

"I wouldn't let it happen," Warrick said suddenly.

Toreth blinked at him, lost.

"If the alternative was that you'd be dead or crippled, you'd go in the tank. I have very good lawyers—they'd force the hospital to treat you while they found a way to tear the directive to shreds." He stood up and shrugged. "I'm sorry, but that's what would happen. If it's any consolation, in the very unlikely event of it ever being an issue I promise I'd have the sedation constantly monitored. Now, if you'll excuse me, I need to talk to Dillian about what we're going to tell the doctors tomorrow."

Toreth stared after him, too surprised even to protest. What the hell did Warrick think it had to do with him? He had no right to make any announcements like that. Sara had been Toreth's registered next of kin for years. In a crunch, she'd probably give in to Warrick, though, which was a thought he didn't like. Of course, once they were cohabitees, registered sexual partners, boxes ticked and forms filed at the DoP, that would give Warrick some say in things. Toreth didn't recall offhand if it included next-of-kin rights, but it might. He didn't like that either, any more than he liked the idea of things being the other way around, of being responsible for Warrick. Corporates made targets, too, so it wasn't impossible that—

Toreth shook his head. What a morbid bloody train of thought. What he needed was a drink.

Chapter Eight

❖

The next morning Valeria proved unexpectedly useful by announcing that she wanted to go back to school. Toreth offered to drop her off on his way back into the city. It had the double advantage of reducing the chance of his visit to the school ringing warning bells and of pissing Dillian off beautifully. In fact, Dillian was still trying to think up reasons why he couldn't do it when he loaded Valeria into the taxi. Toreth climbed in behind her and closed the door firmly. "Wave to your aunt Dillian," he prompted as the car set off.

Valeria knelt up on the seat and waved out of the back window; Toreth added a wave of his own from behind her. Dillian waved back, looking ready to punch something, and Toreth hoped Warrick was out of the line of fire. Valeria sat down, and Toreth opened his hand screen and started reading. With luck the kid could take a hint.

"Why doesn't Auntie Dilly like you?" Valeria asked after a minute.

Because she's a bitch. Or just possibly because she's got a huge fucking hard-on for her brother and she hates that I'm the one who's fucking him. "What makes you think she doesn't like me?"

She didn't manage to hide the snort of laughter. "She's not very nice to you?"

"It's not that she doesn't like *me*. She just doesn't like my job."

"Why?"

Toreth thought it over. "Okay. At school, do you like the strict teachers, or the teachers who let you piss about and misbehave in class?"

She giggled. "I like the nice teachers."

"Right. Well, part of my job is like being a teacher for grownups. We make sure that citizens don't misbehave, and try to catch them if they do. So a lot of people don't like us."

That seemed to make sense to her. After a moment, Toreth returned his attention to the screen. However, the silence didn't last very long.

"Does Auntie Dilly think you should let people misbehave?"

74

"Not quite." Toreth sighed and closed the hand screen. Suddenly, this cover story for getting into the school didn't seem like such a great plan. "Look, you know it's a bad idea to say some things?"

"Like what?"

"Like, you don't think the Administration is a good thing. Don't you have citizenship classes?"

"Oh, yes. On Mondays, Thursdays, and Fridays."

"So they tell you the Administration's a good thing, right? That you should do what the Administration says. 'The government is best that—'" He frowned. Pity he'd skipped so many of his own citizenship lessons at her age. "Right. 'The government is best that ensures the greatest security for the greatest number.'" Or something like that.

She nodded. "But Mr. McVade said last week that sometimes we have to think about things for ourselves and decide if they're good or bad."

Toreth raised an eyebrow. Teachers spreading sedition? There was a snippet of info that might come in handy. "Fine. But I bet he didn't say that before there was all the trouble in the city, did he? Before that, he said you should trust that the Administration knows what's best and don't ask questions, didn't he?" She nodded again. "Well, you should stick to what he said the first time, because if you don't, you could get into deep sh...big trouble. And my job is making sure that people *do* do what the Administration says."

"Why?"

"Because if people don't obey the law, then the Administration won't work."

"Why not?"

"Because..." Jesus, how did *anyone* work in Pediatric Interrogation and keep their sanity? He took a deep breath. "Look, remember what I said about not asking questions? Well, that's a good example of a question you really, really shouldn't ask."

"Oh. Okay. Only Dad always says you should ask 'why' if you don't understand something."

And that is exactly why the fucking idiot is doing a deep-fried crispy chicken wing impersonation in an ICU. "For some things. Not everything. Not the things they tell you about in citizenship classes, to start with." How the hell had they ended up here? "I thought you wanted to know why Dillian doesn't like me."

"You said. Because of your job."

"Right. Because my job is to stop people from misbehaving, which includes asking 'why' too much. Sometimes your father used to ask questions he shouldn't have done. She thinks I'd tell people about that and he'd get into trouble."

That seemed to give her pause for thought. "And did you?" she asked very quietly.

"Nope. Can you guess why?"

75

He watched her thinking it over. Then her expression cleared and she smiled. "Because you're one of the nice teachers!"

God, in a few years she'd probably be a real heartbreaker. He hoped he'd still be around to find out. "Got it in one. That's me. One of the nice teachers. And now I've got some work to do."

She craned her neck, trying to see the screen. "Are you marking homework?"

He looked at the file, which was B-C's IIP for the day before. "Yeah, in a way."

The school looked like the brand of minor corporate/middling Administration outfit that could afford to provide a decent level of security. Also the kind of place where the management would be nervous about losing its reputation for the same. A large new extension suggested a recent Administration grant or corporate tax-deduction gift, but the other buildings were old. In places they could do with some work.

He took Valeria's hand and walked into the school. He'd thought he might have to flash his ID, but in the end he was welcomed in the entrance way by a slender, gray-haired woman in her fifties, with slightly rabbity teeth. Katherine stood next to her. "How are you, Val?" the woman asked.

Toreth blinked, but Valeria was already answering, "I'm fine, Ms. Plaice."

"I'm very glad to hear it. Now, Katty, I want you to take good care of Valeria today. Go along to registration with her now."

Katty took Valeria's hand and led her off, looking delighted with the responsibility.

"I don't think we've met before?" Ms. Plaice asked.

"No." He considered lying, then weighed up the chances of Valeria and Katherine keeping his name quiet if asked. "My name's Val Toreth." She raised her eyebrows at the name. "Yes, it is a coincidence, isn't it? I live with Valeria's uncle, Keir Warrick. Can I have a word with you somewhere private?"

She showed him to a small, obviously communal office—not as spruce as the public parts of the building, which suggested either a stretched budget or a low priority on staff comfort. Once he'd refused a coffee and they'd sat down, she said, "I couldn't help but notice your uniform, Mr. Toreth."

He smiled. "People do. Senior Para-investigator Toreth."

"Are you here about the accident?"

He didn't feel like exposing his interest to that extent. On the way over, he'd considered a variety of stories, none of which would stand up to close scrutiny. "Actually, no; I'm doing a favor for someone. I'm investigating a complaint by a parent." He waited until she stiffened, then said, "Nothing to do with the school as such. Someone said their kid had been approached outside the gate by a man who wanted to talk to them."

He waited for her to ask why the parents hadn't come to the school directly. Instead, she sighed. "I bet that what they didn't tell you was that they were breaking school policy."

"I'm sorry?"

"We ask people to come through the gate and drop off or collect their children in the designated areas. But there are always queues and consequently people who are too busy to worry about child safety."

"I, ah—" He rubbed the back of his neck, trying to look a little uncomfortable. "No. I'm afraid they didn't mention that."

"No doubt they said they thought a complaint would have more weight with the I&I name behind it."

As that had indeed been his cover, he didn't have to fake surprise at the statement.

She smiled, apologetic, obviously trying to reassure him that she wasn't blaming him. "It's happened before, Para-investigator. Do you have any details you can let me know without compromising the parent's identity?"

"I have a picture of the man."

Ms. Plaice studied the sketch carefully for a few seconds, then nodded confidently. "He's been there four or five times. I've seen him twice, personally, on band practice afternoons. I know all the regulars who collect the band members, at least by sight. He wasn't one of them, though there are always relatives or new responsible adults picking up the children for the first time. I saw him this week, in fact . . ." She hesitated. "On the morning of Mr. Marriot's accident."

He ignored her questioningly raised eyebrows. "Did he ever do anything suspicious?"

"Not as such. I noticed him because he was watching the children leave, but *I* never saw him approach a child."

"Why didn't the school call the Justice Department about him?"

"We did, a couple of weeks ago. We sent pictures from the security system. They investigated and told us that since the man had no record of unlawful behavior they couldn't do anything. Lack of manpower."

"Always the way. Did they give you a case number? I can pass it on to the concerned parties, and they can make their own inquiries if they're not satisfied."

"Just let me find it for you."

As he waited, Toreth studied the picture again. Cele had given the man a neutral expression, helpful in a witness picture. On prolonged inspection, however, it gave him a secretive, slightly sinister look.

The case number was handed over on a torn strip of paper, saving Toreth the bother of faking a problem with his hand screen. The fewer electronic trails he left, the better. "One last thing," he said. "Can you tell me where I might find a Mr. McVade?"

Through the window in the classroom door, Toreth could see but not hear the lesson in progress. McVade leaned on his desk, hands braced behind him. Toreth had expected him to be young, mostly because of his suicidally open expression of anti-Administration sentiments. In fact, McVade had a slightly crumpled, hang-dog face, and Toreth guessed him to be forty, although his untidy sandy hair and slightly scruffy clothes might be deceiving and he could be older. It would be easy enough to check in the security files when he reached I&I.

Finally, McVade stood up and turned to pick something up off the desk. He caught sight of Toreth and paused, eyebrows raising in a silent question. Toreth raised his own eyebrows and pointed into the room. McVade nodded, beckoning him in.

Closed, the door had hidden everything except Toreth's face. When Toreth opened it, McVade performed one of the most beautiful double takes Toreth had even seen, then sat down abruptly on the edge of the desk. The class, seated behind their screens, watched in undisguised fascination.

"Do you recognize my uniform?" Toreth asked as he strolled over to the desk.

McVade nodded, looking as though he were about to be sick.

"Well?" Toreth prompted after a few seconds.

"You're a—" He cleared his throat. "You're from I&I. The Interrogation and Investigation Division."

"Investigation and Interrogation—just think of the order we do them in. You really ought to be able to get that right, given your subject."

"Of course. Investigation and Interrogation." He turned to the class and gathered himself with an obvious effort. "Can anyone tell me what department the Investigation and Interrogation Division belongs to?"

After a long pause, a few hands rose.

"Alan?" McVade said, his voice rather high.

"The Department of Internal Security?" the boy said.

McVade sagged slightly with relief, and Toreth smiled. "I'd like you to step outside with me, just for a few minutes," Toreth said evenly.

McVade didn't respond—he looked as though he were trying to summon an excuse and the courage to use it. Finally he nodded. "Now, class, while I'm away I want you to start test number, uh, seven-six-six. Anyone who finishes that may play the next government history file."

Once in the corridor, Toreth looked both ways. Quiet enough. He returned his attention to McVade, who had his hands clenched in his pockets and his back braced against the wall. Toreth examined him with mild interest, wondering if the man was about to faint. When the teacher had started to shuffle his feet, Toreth said, "Mr. McVade, I have a question. Would you say that the Administration tries to do what's right for its citizens?"

"Of course," he said quickly.

"Of course. Would you say that children should be taught that the Administration has their best interests at heart? And that the people who run the Administration know what's right and what's wrong?"

"Well, yes. Para-investigator, all teaching staff are required to have extensive background checks and interviews about their—"

"Shut up," Toreth said evenly. "I'm not a citizenship specialist, but would I be right in saying that nowhere in the current curriculum does it say that children should be taught that it's important to learn to think for themselves about questions of right and wrong?"

Now his skin had the curd-pale coloring of one of Warrick's more exotic cheeses. "Oh, Christ," McVade breathed.

"Or maybe *I'm* wrong. Have they changed the curriculum and not told us?"

To his surprise, McVade straightened, taking his hands from his pockets and putting them behind his back. "I'm not saying anything else until I have access to an independent legal representative."

Even under the new P&P, McVade must know that was pushing his luck. "For a political crime like spreading sedition—and to minors at that? I think you know better than to expect a rep for that."

Some of the color had returned to McVade's face. "Then I demand to have the head teacher present before we continue this, this ... "

"Interrogation?" Toreth broke out one of his nastier intimidating smiles. "Mr. McVade, this isn't an interrogation. It's a friendly informal interview. Besides, the school wouldn't thank you for making the whole incident official. Even if it went no further, I'd have to put a note in your security file and the establishment's file. You know what that would mean?"

"My complete and irreversible unemployability?" McVade said bitterly.

"Right." Toreth relaxed his stance. "But I don't think it needs to go that far, do you? Not when it's all based on a misunderstanding."

McVade stared, obviously wondering if he'd misheard. Finally, he licked his lips. "Misunderstanding?"

"Do you know why I'm here? Someone I know has a child in one of your classes. We had an interesting little chat recently about your idiosyncratic interpretation of the citizenship lessons. I told her that she'd probably made a mistake and you just weren't very clear when you explained things. Kids that age can easily get the wrong end of the stick."

"Yes, they, er ... they can." McVade looked like a man trying to work out where the trap lay. "I'll make sure I'm clearer in the future."

"You do that. Nice talking to you, and I hope I don't have any reason to do it again." Toreth clapped him on the shoulder, and the man nodded fervently.

"You won't, I promise."

"You'd better get back in there, eh? Before the little bastards set the place on fire."

When Toreth arrived in the office, he found that Sara had left a physical note on his desk, in bright red ink on yellow paper, to remind him that it was Warrick's birthday a week from today. That, he realized, was after the move, assuming it all went ahead in light of the recent excitement. Warrick hadn't said otherwise.

The corporate kidnapping interviews had provided no immediate leads for Nagra and B-C. Everything they had so far pointed to amateurs trying their luck in the volatile political situation. That meant a higher chance of finding them eventually, but also that they probably didn't understand the corporate antiextortion rules. Very soon, it would dawn on the kidnappers that they had a high-profile victim on their hands, no chance of getting the ransom they wanted, and no backup plan. That was often bad for the victim.

As the case had ground to a halt, Tillotson was already sending memos suggesting that if Toreth didn't get somewhere soon, the four pool investigators he'd been assigned would find new work elsewhere. A two-day investigation was hardly old enough to write off as hopeless, Toreth thought, but he knew there was no point arguing. He applied himself to the case, trying—not always successfully—to avoid wondering what Warrick was doing.

By lunchtime, Toreth found his concentration wandering more and more often. Finally, he abandoned official work for a while. Nagra's attention would suffice for the kidnap victim, Toreth decided, while he concentrated on a genuine political criminal.

Oblique avenues of investigation into Tarin were limited, but at least Toreth could firm up the cover for his visit to the school this morning. McVade must have been telling the truth about his vetting for the teaching position, but Toreth pulled the man's file anyway. The "no action" flag caught his eye at once. Panic gave him a stirring adrenaline kick until he checked the details and relaxed. It was only a low-level warning, meaning no arrest and no interrogation, but also no absolute prohibition on contact. An informal interview at the subject's place of employment wasn't likely to arouse the wrath of...whoever.

The notes didn't specify the agency behind the watch on the teacher. That left a variety of clandestine divisions inside and outside Int-Sec as candidates. Without a higher-level access code there was no way of finding out which one, and Toreth didn't feel like attracting attention by digging for the information.

To hide his interest, he pulled Plaice's file, then those of five more teachers at random. Thankfully, they were all unexceptionally loyal Administration citizens. He logged the visit to the school as following up an anonymous tip-off about anti-Administration sentiment: no IIP to be filed and no specific mention of McVade.

After he closed the report, he sat and stared at the blank screen, biting his thumbnail. This was exactly what he'd worried about: that digging at any part of the case would turn up unpleasantness that was better left buried.

The I&I canteen had been one of the last parts of the building to reopen after the revolt. While it was closed, Toreth had got into the habit of making sandwiches, or at least of throwing an assortment of junk from the fridge into a box with a couple of pieces of bread. Mornings weren't his best time for culinary inspiration, or anything else, but on most days he'd surprised himself by opening the box at lunchtime and discovering a largely edible meal. It was easy enough when he had Warrick's miraculously well-stocked fridge at his disposal. However, faced with Jen's unfamiliar kitchen, Toreth had given up, so he'd been forced back to the canteen. As he queued, he noticed that they had taken the opportunity of prolonged closure to hike prices yet again. Probably they hoped no one would spot the difference.

"Toreth!" Chevril cut into the queue beside him, ignoring the muttered comments from the gaggle of admins behind.

"Elena not packed your lunch?" Toreth asked.

"Yes. Full of low-fat stuff." Chevril patted his stomach. "I ate it, and now I've come over for a bacon sandwich, if there's any left. How're you? Keeping busy?"

"Weren't you here yesterday?" Toreth asked.

Chevril shook his head. "Up north, doing work that should be done by a bloody junior if I had one. I got back late last night—after eleven, because the train timetables are still haywire. Elena was livid. So what happened here?"

"Didn't Kel tell you?"

"I've got better things to do with my time than track your every move." Chevril grinned, unabashed. "But now that you mention it, he said you'd been out of the office and no one knew why. I thought if Sara hadn't told even him, then it must be something good."

Sara was clearly getting paranoid about letting *any* information about him out. Of course, telling Chevril's admin was tantamount to sending out a division-wide message, high priority.

"Sorry to disappoint you, but it's nothing exciting," Toreth said. "Warrick's brother got himself badly smashed up in a car accident. Warrick wanted me to go over to the hospital with him."

It was, he realized, a perfect opening for a corporate toyboy joke, probably involving handholding. Instead, Chevril shrugged. "Good for you. No point having family crisis leave days in the contract if you don't use them when you get a chance."

He isn't my fucking family, Toreth thought irritably, then wondered how Sara *had* booked the leave. Surely she wouldn't do that to him?

"Getting anywhere with your missing bloke?" Chevril asked.

"Nowhere at all. And Tillotson's demanding results on one hand, and threatening to take my pool investigators away with the other. Usual brilliant management logic—if the investigation's taking too long, you can speed it up by cutting the team."

He made the mistake of pausing for breath, which left a conversational crack into which Chevril slammed his new favorite crowbar. "If you've *got* a team to cut, unlike some people..."

Toreth sighed silently and resigned himself to another round of Chevril's current top complaint: the hopelessness of trying to replace a team with no decent investigators to choose from. Chevril seemed to be surprised by how much work Sedanioni and the rest had done for him, and by how much he had to do now. Chev had been unlucky, as usual—Kel was the only survivor of his regular team who hadn't resigned from I&I.

Toreth tuned him out, waiting for his turn to bitch while no one listened. If he could be bothered. In an odd way, he realized, he almost enjoyed the pressure from Tillotson for results. Cases had been so few in the weeks after the revolt that it felt good to have a reason to moan about the head of section's impossible demands. It was about the only thing in his life that felt normal.

That evening, Toreth found himself missing his own flat more than he had for a long time. Although Kate's house wasn't small, it was surprisingly hard to find somewhere private in it. There was always someone around—one of the adults or, more irritatingly, Valeria. Tomorrow night, he decided, he'd sleep back at Warrick's flat, whether Warrick was there or not. Needing to be closer to work would be a perfectly acceptable reason.

Not long after Toreth arrived at the house, Dillian went to the hospital, which was something of a relief. In her place arrived Philadelphia Wintergreen.

Toreth had never met Valeria's mother before. After the years of wondering vaguely what she looked like—although admittedly never enough to pull her security file—she proved to be a mild disappointment. Certainly the woman was not as impressive as her name. Ten years older than Toreth, she wasn't ugly, but she was extremely serious. Granted, part of that might be due to a day spent at her husband's bedside (or was that tankside?), but Toreth suspected it was a permanent condition. Her straight mouth and dark brown eyes had no evidence of laughter lines around them. She even had serious hair, a uniform brown in a sharp-edged bob. On reflection, she was exactly the kind of earnest, solid type that Toreth could imagine Tarin marrying. It came as no surprise at all to find out that she was an official at the Department of Education, and an ex-teacher.

One thing that did interest him was how much she knew about Tarin's resister connections. When Warrick introduced her to Toreth she seemed wary, but as he had no reference for her usual reaction to strangers it wasn't conclusive. Curiosity piqued, Toreth made two coffees and took them through to her in the living room. She didn't look welcoming, but as he'd expected she didn't object as he sat down beside her.

"I'm sorry about Marriot," he said when he'd handed her a mug.

"Are you?" Her voice didn't waver, and she was examining him with curiosity. "I didn't think you knew him."

"Not well at all," he admitted readily. "We were both here for New Year, about three years ago. If you haven't heard the story from someone else already, he called me a psychopathic Administration torturer—behind my back, but within earshot." She stared at him and he smiled, trying to look a little self-deprecating. "I thought one out of three wasn't bad, for someone who'd barely spoken to me. He'd already given his opinions about Administration reform at lunch. Warrick was a hell of a lot more surprised than I was when Dilly called him about the crash. From what I heard that New Year I'd say Marriot's been damn lucky so far."

Her surprise had vanished behind a wary mask. "I didn't think the roads were so dangerous."

"You know what I mean." He set the mug down. "There's a reason I'm telling you all this. There will be an investigation into the accident, even if it's only by the transport safety people. They'll be working on the records and the vehicles already. If anything suspicious turns up, Justice will get involved. Maybe I&I. And in a case like this, the first place either of them will start looking for a culprit is at the victim's family and friends."

"Friends?" she asked drily. "That seems like an inappropriate word."

"Friendship's overrated. Most murder victims are killed by someone they know. And if Tarin had any friends who thought the way he did, it's not a healthy circle to be moving in. Advocating comprehensive reform of the Administration isn't something I'd put down on an application for life insurance."

Now she looked bewildered. "But the revolt, the change of Administration...?"

"Might make less difference than you think. Who knows what the hell counts as a political crime these days? Anyway, what I need to know is if Justice turns this accident into an investigation and starts looking hard at Marriot's associates, will they find anything?"

She shook her head, but it wasn't disagreement. Rather, she was fighting the instinct not to tell him. He wished he'd taken the time to change out of his uniform before he talked to her. At the school it had been an asset—here it was an enormous liability. Not that Philly looked to be the kind of woman who'd forget who she was talking to, even if he was stark naked.

"Ms. Wintergreen, I don't go looking for extra cases. Even if sometimes I have to try very hard not to see them." A little exaggeration wouldn't hurt. "In the past I've heard more than enough from your husband to have him taken in for interrogation."

She didn't even blink. "So why didn't you?"

"Because he's Warrick's brother. Half brother. Mud sticks, and you don't get mud any thicker than an arrest for anti-Administration resistance."

"From the sound of it, you already think you know enough to make up your mind about him."

"Yes. But is it *just* him?"

"We had some mutual friends he's still in contact with who weren't unsympathetic. And...I don't disagree with him." She gave him a challenging look. "I doubt any moderately intelligent, right-thinking person *could* disagree that there are fundamental problems with the Administration. If there weren't, we wouldn't have had mobs on the street."

Once she decided to go, he had to admire her for going all out. Toreth shrugged. "I don't care, as long as agreeing was all you did."

Her defiance damped down a little. "In my younger days, perhaps, I had a few more radical ideas. But it became too dangerous. There were too many arrests—whenever any plans were made, the Administration always seemed to be ahead of us. I felt sure, in the end, that someone was betraying us."

"There are a few intelligent, right-thinking people who admire the Administration and aren't so keen on anarchy."

She didn't react to the dig. "After Valeria was born, I decided it was too risky to stay involved. Tarin agreed with me at first, but...he changed his mind. The others talked him round. It...it doesn't surprise me that Kate has gone. For a long time I thought that she encouraged him in his views."

And then some. "I don't know anything about that. But what you're saying is that he's tied in and tied in deep, with people who've planned active sedition."

"Yes."

"That's what I thought."

"And now what?"

"I don't know." He was tempted to suggest she and anyone else involved should consider joining Kate on a one-way holiday out of the Administration. But Kate had escaped with the connivance of Citizen Surveillance. Without that kind of help, fleeing the Administration was an admission of guilt that was tantamount to a confession. "If you happen to know anyone who might have any evidence they'd like to get rid of, now is a good time to suggest it to them. Apart from that, I promise I'll do what I can for him."

That caught her by surprise. "Why?"

Jesus, obviously Valeria had inherited that question from both sides of the family. "For Warrick. And for me." Forestalling her question, he added, "Because mud sticks."

All the talk of mud at least gave Toreth an idea for finding some peace and quiet. Upstairs, the bathroom was empty and Toreth ran himself a deep, hot bath, which he felt he deserved. He even found a bottle of masculine-scented bath salts and tipped in a generous dose. If they were Tarin's he wouldn't be needing them for a while.

Although the bath was deep enough to get at least an illusion of buoyancy, hot water never tripped his phobias in the same way as cold, and the heat soaking into his muscles felt wonderful. He settled back to think over what he'd found so far. The conversation with Ms. Plaice had confirmed that the stranger outside the school had been there more than once. Four or five sightings, at least two coinciding with Tarin collecting his daughter from the school. Not conclusive, but suggestive.

Warrick's identification of the man as the Citizen Surveillance agent had upped the stakes. Was he tidying up loose ends from Kate's undercover operation? According to Warrick's account of their meeting, the man had been helpful enough, but that could have been a first-stage response and this the rather more final cover-up.

The unofficial killing of resisters by agencies like Cit was much like the unofficial annex deaths at I&I, only without the complication of a postmortem trial. If citizens were too well connected or difficult to arrest for other reasons, then a quiet accident helped the Administration run smoothly. It was a shame, Toreth thought uneasily, that Warrick wouldn't look at it in the same light. If he became convinced there was foul play involved, then he'd be out for blood.

A Citizen Surveillance connection gave him another focus—Kate. If Kate wasn't dead, then she might be behind the attempted murder. Still working for Int-Sec, or even on the run, she could see it as a necessary step towards tidying up the remains of her old life. Since she'd raised Tarin as a tool for Int-Sec to use in monitoring resistance groups, she'd probably not lose much sleep over eliminating him. He wondered how she felt about Warrick, who knew more than anyone about the circumstances of her escape. She'd always seemed fond of her younger son, for what little that meant.

There was the picture in the living room downstairs to consider: Kate, Jen, Warrick, and Dillian. If it was Kate behind the killing, then she might be thinking as much of her family as of herself, assuming she gave a fuck about any of them. Could Kate know that Tarin and Warrick were reconciling? That would give her an incentive to act before they grew too close. Killing Tarin now would go a long way towards shielding Warrick and the others from taint by association. There could be no subsequent arrest and interrogation, no trial, no messily public execution or re-education, no chance that he could say something to suggest Warrick or Dillian had ever expressed anti-Administration sentiments. If Kate's goal was to protect her other children, then if Tarin died the danger would be over.

Almost over.

Tarin had been cut out of the family in the letters Kate had written to her absent husband and excluded from the portrait. That left Toreth with the uncomfortable awareness that *he* wasn't in the picture, either. That omission was purely a function of time—the picture had been painted before he'd met Warrick. But had Toreth's name been in the recent letters?

Other considerations affected how much danger he was in. Did Kate know that he knew about her secret? Did whoever Warrick had contacted to arrange her release know that Toreth had been the source of the information? Could they have found out about his old mistake of pulling Leo Warrick's file? Warrick had said that he'd had messages from Kate, sent from outside the Administration. If she was free and clear, was it really likely that she would be behind Tarin's accident?

Toreth pushed his hair back, realizing as he did that he was sweating. He nudged the tap with his toes, letting a little cool water into the bath. While it ran, he debated the merits of telling Warrick about his teacher eyewitness. The longer he left it, the worse Warrick would be about the omission. However, he didn't want to give Warrick any ideas about leads to chase down. With any luck, Toreth had bought himself a few days' breathing space to decide what to do.

When Toreth went downstairs, he found that Dillian had returned, and she, Warrick, and Philly were locked in a deadly serious-sounding conversation in the living room. Toreth left them to it and spent a moderately entertaining evening talking to Jen. He managed to steer her away from amusing anecdotes about Warrick's childhood and towards stories about teenaged Dillian. A little ammunition was always welcome.

He didn't have a chance to talk to Warrick until they both went upstairs to bed. "How's Tarin?" Toreth asked as he roughly folded his clothes—which was getting to be a habit—and stacked them on a chair.

"He's still hanging on, barely, although even the doctors don't seem to know how he's managing it. He—" Warrick shook his head. "No. I'm sorry, but I've been talking about it all day, with doctors and family. I'll tell you in the morning."

"Hey, don't bother. I don't give a fuck anyway." At least while it still looked like the idiot would die without further help.

Warrick stopped stripping, his shirt half unbuttoned, and stared at him.

What now? Toreth wondered. It wasn't as if it was a surprise: Warrick had said yesterday that he knew Tarin's health was of zero interest to Toreth.

Warrick laughed suddenly, brief and humorless. "Lucky you. Sometimes I wish..."

"What?"

Warrick shook his head. "I wish we were back at the flat."

Obviously not what he'd been about to say, but it made a successful distraction. "What, right now? Why?"

"Because then there wouldn't be anyone sleeping in the next room. Or at least no one I'm related to."

"If you want to play, I can keep you quiet."

"'Want' doesn't really cover it." Warrick sounded strained and he glanced around a little helplessly. "But we don't have anything here. Not even the belt. And Dilly's sleeping on this floor."

Warrick stopped speaking as Toreth took his hand. He held it for just a couple of seconds, his thumb stroking gently over the palm, before he shifted his grip to Warrick's wrist and twisted it up behind his back, following the movement smoothly around to end up standing half behind him. Warrick hissed at the sudden pain, his hand flexing.

"Is this it?" Toreth asked.

"We can't..."

He twined his fingers in Warrick's hair and pulled his head back, leaning in to breathe the words into his ear. "Is this what you need?"

Warrick's eyelids closed, lashes dark against his skin, and he moaned softly.

"I asked you a question." He twisted Warrick's arm further up, forcing the pace. "Is it?"

"Ah! Yes. Yes, I need it..."

"That's right. I've told you before—if I want to take you, I'll do it anywhere I like. Any way I like." Toreth let go of his hair and stroked possessively down Warrick's neck, around his collar and inside his open shirt, cataloging the textures under his palm: smooth skin, rougher hair, hard points of nipples. He ducked down to bite Warrick's neck, wanting to hear his breath catch.

"Toreth, please—don't let me make any noise."

"And I can do it with or without toys. I don't need props. I don't need anything to make it work. Do you?"

"No." Warrick let out a long breath. "God, no. Only you."

"That's right. Only me."

Only me. Only me. The words stayed in his head in a constant background counterpoint.

In the end they had props, even if only the basics. He pulled Warrick's shirt forwards over his head and down his arms, leaving the wrists still buttoned, then pushed him face down on the bed. Toreth followed quickly, not giving Warrick time to find out that he could wriggle out of the sleeves if he tried.

With his arms trapped and Toreth's weight holding him down, Warrick was already lost in the game, his eyes glazing, dark and pleading. Toreth had made vague plans, ideas drawn from the stock he kept ready for impromptu sessions, but he dropped them all in favor of "just fuck him." Right now, that was enough. Nothing more elaborate needed for either of them.

Only me.

Only me, he thought, as Warrick struggled under him, cloth tearing in staccato bursts because even strong, expensive corporate-shirt cotton can only take so much abuse. The ripping cloth sounded louder than it was, but much quieter than Warrick. Toreth pinned him to the bed, fucking him hard while he kept his hand clamped tight over Warrick's mouth, smothering the noise.

And, God, it felt good. Unexpectedly, shockingly good, in a way it hadn't felt for a long time. Not just each deep thrust or Warrick's body hot against him, but the game itself: power and control, the rules building a wall around them, a solid barrier against the chaotic world outside the room.

Only me. Only us.

Chapter Nine

When the comm chimed, Toreth was surprised to see the clock say eleven. They'd been in bed for only half an hour. The comm hadn't woken Warrick, though—he slept deeply beside Toreth, and in the dim light he reminded Toreth of the pictures at Cele's. He looked younger and very peaceful, oblivious to the strain of the last few days. Toreth grabbed his dressing gown and slipped out into the corridor.

He had assumed it was work or Sara. No one else he knew called him in the middle of the night. However, it was Cele, looking exhausted. "Toreth, can you come over? I've got something to show you."

"Can it wait until tomorrow? Tomorrow evening would be better." There was a limit to how much time he could take off work before someone noticed.

"I think you should come." Her agitation finally registered, and some of the haze of sleep lifted. "I might have a name for the man in the picture."

Fuck. This could be difficult, especially if she wanted to tell Warrick. "I'll be there."

While he dressed, keeping as quiet as he could, he noticed the pain in his left hand—a deep ache that meant a bruise. When he was back out in the light of the corridor, he found a rough oval marked in the fleshy part of his palm, below his little finger. At some point Warrick must have bitten him, and damned hard, but he was fucked if he could remember it happening.

❖ ❖ ❖

When Cele opened the door to her studio flat, she was wearing an eye-watering screened-silk dressing gown which seemed designed to prove that the human eye really could distinguish sixteen million colors. "Come in," she said. "I just made some more coffee."

Inside the flat was more paper than Toreth had seen since the systems failures at I&I after the revolt. Single sheets covered every flat surface and made piles of varying heights on the floor. Portfolios took up the remaining space.

The windows were clear and the blinds raised. At night the flat seemed higher than in the daytime, and Toreth was acutely aware of how exposed he and Cele were, standing in plain view and backlit. "You look like shit," Toreth said as he dropped his coat on a chair.

"And that's the flattering version." She waved around the room. "I was up almost all last night, too, like a good little detective. I knew I'd seen the face somewhere, and I decided in the end I'd drawn it."

"Had you?"

"No. Or at least I don't think so—I can't have done. I don't know who he is, but I know who he looks like."

He tried to hide his irritation at the wild goose chase. "Really? Who?"

She led him over to the window, to the only clear space in the room, and picked up a closed portfolio from a crowded sketching table and handed it to him. It was labeled in Cele's writing, 'LW for K. Prelims. Pnc/Pho.' It looked old, edges scuffed and a line faded down one side by exposure to light. Inside he found a copy of the drawing she'd done for him at Kate's house, and three older sketches in pencil. In the old sketches, a smiling young man sat in a chair, with a baby in his arms and another slightly older infant on his knee. Toreth recognized him at once, with a rock-solid certainty that refused to supply a name or a context.

"Who is he?" Toreth asked.

"Keir's father, Leo, with Keir and Dilly. I did it for Kate from a photograph, a long time after he died. She'll have the finished picture at her house somewhere—she loves it."

He stared at the sketches, old and new. God, she was right. He'd only ever seen Leo Warrick once, in an old picture from a long-closed security file, but she was *right*. Add thirty-five years and this would be pretty damn close. And if that was true, it opened up all kinds of nasty possibilities.

For one thing, he'd left the sketch of the suspect at Kate's house. Warrick, Dillian, Jen—any one of them might suddenly see the resemblance. So might any old family friends who turned up at the house to lend support in a crisis. The first thing any of them would do was exactly what Cele had done—show the picture to someone else and ask if they saw the resemblance, too. If Warrick found out he would never let it go. And, although Toreth didn't recollect ever seeing it, the finished picture was at Kate's place, somewhere. In the house with Warrick, who could notice it any moment. With luck, everyone would still be tucked up safely in bed, and he could get back to the house and find the damn thing before it precipitated a disaster.

Coming back to the present, he realized his heart was beating double time and Cele was watching him intently. "It can't be him, of course," she said, "and

90

he didn't have any close family that I know about. So it's just one of those strange-but-true freaky coincidences, isn't it?"

He tilted the pictures towards the light and frowned. "Do you really think they look alike?"

Now she looked surprised. "Don't you?"

"Do you do a lot of age enhancement?"

"Well . . . no."

Thank fuck. "I do. Or a reasonable amount. Aged-up files for wanted suspects and missing corporates, that sort of thing. This doesn't grab me right away."

"Oh?" She didn't sound as if she entirely believed him.

"Don't get me wrong—I really appreciate the effort." He gestured around the chaos in the studio with the portfolio. "Look, I'll take the old pictures into I&I and get them properly aged up, and we can compare them with the sketch, how about that?"

He tried to put as much "I'm just humoring you" into his voice as he could, and from her disappointed expression she seemed to buy it.

"Sorry to drag you out of your nice warm bed and haul you all the way out here for nothing," she said.

"No problem. It's not your fault. Look at enough pictures, you see what you want to see." He grinned at her, trying to hide his desperation to get out of there. "It was worth it just for the dressing gown."

Back at Kate's house, all was quiet and still. The living room light was on, and as Toreth closed the main door, the SimTech guard stepped out into the hall, hand on his gun. Toreth greeted him in his best faux-corporate dismissive manner. He must have been getting good at it, because the man nodded and disappeared back into the room at once.

A quick, quiet tour of the darkened downstairs rooms revealed no picture of Leo Warrick. Toreth had expected that—he was fairly sure he'd remember the picture if he'd seen it previously, and he'd been in all the ground floor rooms except Kate's study. That was still kept locked, so he'd have to hope the picture wasn't in there. On the top floor, where Warrick was hopefully still fast asleep, there was a junk room and three guest rooms: one with Dillian, one with Warrick, one empty. None of them were likely to contain a prized picture. That left Kate's bedroom as the best target.

On the first floor landing, he set the lights low and considered options. One room was where he'd found Warrick looking out of the window. Toreth had assumed that was Tarin's room, and he didn't remember any pictures in there. He knew that one door was the bathroom. Valeria's name was on the door to the right of that, which left two other rooms, of which one would be Jen's. But unlike Valeria, the older members of the household didn't helpfully label their doors.

He opened a door, waited for a minute, then stepped inside, only to hear low breathing. He eased the door open wide enough to illuminate the room and found Jen asleep in the center of a double bed. Cozy, and he was struck once more by the thought that for her age she was still a looker. A resemblance to Warrick always helped, he thought as he closed the door.

The last room looked promising. It was feminine without being fluffy, and it had the cool, slightly dusty smell of somewhere unoccupied for weeks. He closed the door, switched on the light, and looked around. Plenty of pictures hung on the walls, including at least two of Cele's, but not the one he was looking for. Where the hell was it? He was about to leave and try Tarin's room when he spotted a picture on the wall opposite the door. That was the one—a man, two small children and unmistakably in Cele's style. It was half obscured by the wardrobe; an odd choice of location, he thought, until he realized it was perfectly placed to be visible from the bed.

He took the picture down and placed it on the neatly made bed, then pulled out the sketch of the Cit Surveillance agent and laid it beside the frame. Seeing the finished picture, he couldn't imagine how Cele had ever bought his doubts that they could be the same man. Warrick must be the older of the two children. Despite his distaste for the idea of Warrick as a child, Toreth couldn't help looking for a resemblance, and finding it. Dark eyes and hair, of course, but also a serious intelligence in his face as he looked up at his father.

If he simply took the picture and destroyed it, would that raise too many questions? It might be less risky to replace it with another one. He knew from experience that witnesses could remark on the absence of a picture even when they had no clue as to its subject. The human visual memory relied on shape and color, with details often lost. Perhaps he could find something upstairs that wouldn't be missed.

In any case, he could start by taking the damn thing away and putting it somewhere safe, like in a fire. The frame was only clipped together, and he had just pried the backing sheet away from the glass when he heard Warrick's voice.

"Toreth, what the hell are you doing in here?" Warrick stood in the doorway, wearing his dressing gown.

Toreth turned the dismantled frame quickly away from Warrick. "Nothing. Go back to bed. I'll be there in a minute."

Even to himself, he sounded like he was hiding something. Warrick's gaze swept the room and Toreth cursed silently. Of all the people in the house, it would have to be the one person who would be bound to spot that—

Warrick crossed to the bed. "You've got my father's picture there. Cele's picture." He looked down to the sketch on the bed, and Toreth saw the suspicion dawning. "Toreth, give it to me."

92

"Listen, trust me, you don't want to look. Just let me—"

"*Give it to me.*" It wasn't quite a shout, but the next one would be.

Toreth laid the picture flat on the bed beside the sketch, then turned both of them around to face Warrick. Warrick looked between them for a long time, and Toreth listened, wondering if they had woken anyone. The rest of the house was silent. Kate's room was silent. No cars passed in the street outside. Somewhere, distantly, an alarm was ringing, the noise so faint he could be imagining it.

Toreth set the frame on the floor, then studied the upside-down pictures, wondering if there was a chance in hell that Warrick wouldn't see it. When he looked up, Warrick was watching him. "When did you find out?" Warrick asked. He didn't *sound* angry. He didn't sound anything other than mildly curious, which was not a good sign.

"Tonight. Cele called me—she spotted it. I think I managed to persuade her she was seeing things. I wanted to have a look at the finished picture, see what I thought. And then—" He shrugged. "I didn't really have a plan."

Warrick shook his head slightly. "You intended to destroy it, didn't you?"

"Yes," Toreth said, and waited for the explosion.

Instead, Warrick nodded slowly. "I wish that you'd told me, but I do appreciate the very sound reasons why you wouldn't want to."

Toreth blinked at the unexpected reprieve.

Warrick leaned down and pulled the pictures across the bed, lining the edges up carefully. "It's funny, but seeing him in person it's not half so obvious as it is with these. I've looked at this picture all my life. There are others, of course, and Kate had some photographs, but this is special. Cele really highlights the important features, doesn't she? Goes to the heart of the subject." He touched the sketch gently. "Remarkable, if you think that this was from a description."

"Yeah, she's very good." Warrick's thoughtful tone was starting to disturb him. "Warrick, if it's him, then there's no reason anymore to suspect Tarin's accident wasn't an accident, is there? I know he isn't Tarin's father, but Jen told me he was fond of Tarin, right? Treated him like a son?"

Warrick was still looking at the pictures, stroking his palms over each other.

"There could be half a dozen innocent reasons he was there," Toreth said with all the conviction he could muster. "So there's no need to take this any further, is there?"

Warrick looked up. "And if he was responsible?"

"Even if he was, he got Kate out. If he arranged the accident, he must be trying to cut the family off from any association with resisters. Tarin's the only one who's a risk. You, Dilly, Jen—none of the rest of you have ever had any direct dangerous connections except for Tarin. Philly says she's been out of touch with the resisters for years. It's over now. Let it go."

Finally, the calm broke. "Let it *go*? Do you—you have no idea how Tar felt about him. He loved him—he *worshiped* him."

Toreth couldn't help comparing Warrick's pale fury now with his desperate need earlier that night and his absolute surrender to the game. If only Warrick would occasionally bring his submission outside the bedroom.

"That was thirty-odd years ago," Toreth said. "Right now, Tarin's a liability to everyone." Toreth tried to keep his focus, to remember what was important to Warrick. "What about everyone else? What good will it do them if you keep going at this until you blow the whole fucking thing wide open? That's the only way it ends. That, or Leo looks at you and the rest of the family and decides he can't keep all of you alive."

Warrick's expression hardened. "So you *do* think he was behind the accident."

Shit. "It doesn't matter what I think. We don't have any evidence, and it's too dangerous to look for more."

From Warrick's expression, Toreth might as well have been speaking Japanese. "I have to find him."

"And do what? Kill him?"

"No, of course not. I—" Warrick frowned, as if he hadn't actually got that far with the plan. "I don't expect you to understand."

No, of course not. No doubt Toreth's psych file said he wouldn't. "Warrick, however pissed off you are about Tarin, is that any reason to commit suicide?"

"There's nothing suicidal about it." Warrick was using the "I'm being perfectly reasonable" voice that made Toreth's fists clench. "All I have to do is find his name. It should be easy enough. The history of the operation will be in the Citizen Surveillance files—I'll get it from there."

He really wished Warrick wouldn't tell him things like that. "It's far too bloody dangerous. Warrick, ordinary citizens aren't even officially supposed to know that Cit Surveillance exists. It's a closed Int-Sec division. No contact numbers, no public records. What if you get caught?"

"I won't be," he said with absolute confidence.

"Do you have *any* idea how to get into the Cit Surveillance systems?"

"Not yet. But I'm sure I can find a way in."

"Yeah. And I'm sure you can get yourself arrested and land me in the shit with you up to both our fucking necks."

There was another silence, during which Toreth began to hope that Warrick was finally seeing sense. Then Warrick shook his head decisively. "I'm sorry, Toreth, but I have to try the files."

"*No.* Warrick, if you do anything, I'll—"

He stopped. He had to stop. What could he threaten to do? Leave? Maybe Warrick wouldn't even care, and it was pointless anyway, when they both knew what an empty threat it was. He'd tried that already and he hadn't even managed to stay away for a month before he'd crawled back the moment Warrick snapped his fingers. And what good would it do, anyway, after all this time? He'd still be

94

arrested if Warrick was caught. For a moment, Toreth felt tempted to tell Warrick about his own lead from the school. But that would only encourage Warrick to look harder, and the last thing Toreth wanted was the stubborn bastard pursuing the trail into a school where the staff's files were being flagged by unknown agencies.

Toreth took a deep breath. "If you do this, you do it on your own."

"I didn't expect you to help."

"Too fucking right. But not just that—if you get yourself into shit over this, don't expect me to try to pull you out. I'll be walking away from the whole fucking mess just as fast as I can. Forget flats and registered fucking partners. You can try your corporate connections and expensive lawyers and see how far it gets you with Cit Surveillance."

Faced with fire, Warrick had performed his usual retreat into ice. "I know what I'm doing."

"Bollocks. You have no clue what those people are like. Do you think *they* use the revised P&P?"

Warrick's eyebrows rose. "I lived with Kate for my whole childhood. I think I know exactly what they're like, and exactly what they're capable of."

Don't do it, please. Jesus, please *Christ* don't do it. Toreth wondered if begging would help. He suspected this time it wouldn't, and he wasn't humiliating himself on the off chance that it might. "Fine. Search the files, do whatever the hell you like." As usual. "But don't expect me to risk my neck pulling you out of *your* messes."

"Keir?"

They both looked around. Dillian stood in the doorway, wrapped in a dressing gown that Toreth couldn't help noticing flattered her figure very nicely. While Warrick crossed to her, Toreth swept the pictures from the bed and rolled them up, with the portrait inside Cele's sketch. He pushed the dismantled frame under the bed with his foot.

"What's going on?" Dillian asked. She stepped sideways, trying to see past Warrick, who moved to block her view.

"Nothing," Warrick said. "An overly loud discussion, which is now closed."

Chapter Ten

❖

Warrick returned from the kitchen to his office, carrying a tray of bacon sandwiches and tea. The aftermath of the revolt was still disrupting deliveries, and there had been no bananas available on the residential ordering system this morning. He hadn't wanted to take the time out to try one of the Saturday markets.

He settled down at his desk again, where the screens still reported no progress. It looked like being another late night. Weekends weren't the best time for exploring illicit entrances into new systems. During the week, the higher flow of traffic concealed attempts at breaking in. On the other hand, out of working hours breaches of security might not be chased up quite so quickly, giving him a chance to recover from otherwise fatal mistakes.

If he'd simply been lifting records from the normal citizens' security files database, it would have taken minutes at the most. That was something he'd done dozens of times—maybe hundreds. Even the I&I files, courtesy of Toreth, were accessible. Operational files at Citizen Surveillance were an entirely different question. After a solid day of work, he wasn't even certain that he was working on the right division. Semisecret government organizations didn't helpfully label their systems.

Between waiting for the results of his attempts to get into the database and thinking of new strategies as each one failed, he had plenty of time think about other things.

He poured a cup and leaned over it, breathing in the steam and letting it soothe his aching eyes. The caffeine was probably a bad idea, but he needed it, so he'd compromised on tea rather than coffee. He had a headache that had refused to yield to painkillers, and he could feel the tension knotting muscles in his neck and shoulders. Nothing to do with the computer work—he could spend far longer than this in front of a screen with no ill effects.

Anger at Citizen Surveillance and at Toreth caused a fair portion of the stress. He didn't blame Toreth for being afraid of the consequences of attracting Citizen

Surveillance's attention. It was something he understood very well, and it made its own contribution to the tight band of pain around his temples: fear of what might happen to Tar if he didn't succeed, and of what might happen to himself and others if he got caught.

He hadn't seen Toreth since the night of the argument. Toreth had taken a taxi back into the city first thing in the morning. When Warrick arrived at his own flat on Friday evening, Toreth wasn't there. Neither were about a suitcase's worth of his clothes. No doubt he was staying at Sara's, or at a hotel. That was Toreth's traditional second-choice solution to any argument between them: if sex wasn't an option, walk out. Hardly a surprise after all this time, but infuriating given the seriousness of the situation. Of course, from Toreth's point of view, the solution was easy—let Tarin die and the rest of them would be safer. No surprise there, either.

A message on the screen distracted him. Another failure, hopefully unnoticed. Even if his attempt was spotted, he'd covered the tracks as thoroughly as he could. He ate a sandwich while he considered the next most viable approach. Then he wiped his hands scrupulously and worked for a concentrated twenty minutes. Then it was back to waiting.

How long should he keep this up? Despite his front of confidence to Toreth, Warrick knew damn well that the longer he kept at it, the lower the probability that he would succeed in any given hour and the greater the chance of being caught. Eventually, detection would become inevitable. He needed to set himself a limit and then have the discipline to stick to it. On Monday morning, the removal firm would arrive. That made a good end point. The remainder of Saturday evening and the whole of Sunday was long enough to either find what he needed or be sure that he couldn't.

This morning, the hospital had reported Tarin as stabilizing. Even so, he'd discussed with Dillian whether to cancel next weekend's housewarming party in case Tarin's condition worsened. In case, really, that he died. In the end, Warrick had decided not to; it simply wasn't practical to arrange the next few weeks around the possibility that Tarin might die at any time.

And if that death wasn't natural . . .

He'd stick to his time limit, but if the systems search failed, he'd have to think of something else.

Shopping had been Sara's idea of something to do on a Saturday, but Toreth had put up only the token resistance required to preserve his reputation. He needed more clothes—all he had were what Warrick had bought for him during the revolt, plus the handful of survivors from his flat, and the new I&I uniforms. Yesterday at Warrick's flat, still angry and on edge, he'd packed the uniforms but not enough of the other things.

His suspicions should have been aroused when Sara had been so vague about where they were going. She'd kept him occupied in conversation during the whole taxi trip, so Toreth hadn't paid too much attention to their route. When the car pulled up, he realized why she'd been so keen to distract him. The shopping complex, in a residential zone where the flats were astronomically far out of the price range of mere Administration employees, was filled with shops that didn't display prices. If you shopped there, whether it was for clothes, food, furniture, or private cars, you shouldn't need to know "how much."

"I thought I said I needed clothes?" he asked.

She nodded earnestly. "Right. And in there are clothes shops. I thought your compensation finally came through? From the flat?"

"Half of what I put in for, and no explanation why they cut it."

"Are you going to appeal?" Sara pushed the door open and stepped out.

"Maybe. Probably not." He followed her out. "It'll be just as tedious as fucking with accounts at I&I, except with I&I accounts they know that I work in the same building and I can find out where they live."

She laughed. "It wouldn't matter, anyway. You can't scare Central Housing Division staff—they aren't even human." She hesitated briefly, then said, "Do you want me to do it for you?"

"Yeah, okay. If you like."

The taxi system requested additional confirmation of payment, and he leaned back in through the door. Satisfied with his I&I ID, the taxi finally pulled away. At least that perk hadn't yet been canceled by the new Administration.

The shopping complex guard—armed, Toreth noted—also accepted their IDs, although with less grace than the taxi. Toreth didn't bother to say anything, simply resting his arm over Sara's shoulders as he watched the guard silently weigh up the conflict between their no-doubt inadequate credit ratings and Toreth's senior para status.

Inside the complex, the floor was so spotless, even Warrick would have eaten his dinner off it. Cunning as ever, Sara broke him in gently with a detour into a toiletries shop called, originally enough, "Skin Deep." The assistants looked icily perfect and aloof, but they thawed out after a few minutes of Sara's determined enthusiasm. While she searched for the perfect shades of this lipstick, that foundation and the other eyeliner, Toreth taste-tested hand creams. His skin was getting rough from too much time wearing gloves down in interrogation. As they left the shop, he eyed her improbably large carrier bag. "How much of that are you ever going to wear?"

"Most of it. I got a lot of free bits and bobs. They always throw things in if you're nice to them." She peered into the bag and smiled with satisfaction. "Anyway, it's all still coming out of my comp money."

98

"Still?"

"Down to the dregs, but I did save on the furniture." She stopped outside a menswear shop. "Here we are."

This place didn't actually *have* a name, as far as he'd ever discovered, just a screen above the shop front where swirls of tasteful shades slowly chased each other around. Not a single artfully displayed item in the window carried a hint of a price label.

"I can't—"

"Just for underwear," Sara said innocently. "You know you have to."

He sighed and opened the door. She was right about the underwear. The nameless shop sold the only make that were absolutely, perfectly comfortable. That he knew that in the first place was entirely Sara's fault, because she'd bought him the original pack for a New Year present. Since then he'd tried buying underwear from elsewhere and they had just annoyed him by not being quite right. His bank account survived on his coming here alone and making a quick dash in and out. On that basis, he made a brief, futile attempt to head straight for the underwear section, then gave up. Sara sidetracked him onto a trail of other items, ending up, twenty minutes later, in the middle of a display of sweaters that Toreth was fairly confident the customers weren't encouraged to handle.

"It's blue," Toreth said doubtfully.

"Yes, it is." Sara unfolded the sweater and held it up, turning it around for a thorough critical inspection. "Duck-egg. It's a good color this year."

"But what about next year?"

"You'll still be able to wear it," she said with absolute confidence, "because it goes perfectly with your eyes. Which makes people think you get your cashmere sweaters dyed to order and you must be incredibly rich."

"I certainly won't be if we don't get out of here soon."

"No, really. You know people notice that kind of thing. I do. You could pick me up if you were wearing it." She offered the sweater and grinned. "If I didn't know you already, that is. Go on."

In theory, he reminded himself, clothes were one thing over which he didn't mind making an effort or spending money. A good wardrobe was essential for good hunting.

Toreth stripped off his own sweater and pulled on the blue one. It felt silky against his recently moisturized fingertips, almost waxy. He stroked it smooth, then found a mirror nearby. His hair was mussed, so he straightened it, checking out the look of the soft wool sleeves as he did so.

The thick knit managed to hang and cling at the same time. He imagined putting it on Warrick—just the jumper, nothing else—then rubbing his face against it, against Warrick's hard, muscled shoulders while he fucked him slowly and Warrick swore and pushed back against him and begged for it harder and faster. Smelling sweat and sex over the warm new-wool scent of the . . .

Sara coughed. With a start, he focused back on the image in the mirror. He looked distracted and slightly flushed.

Sex. He definitely needed more sex, very soon.

A pinch-faced assistant in a tight black dress lurked nearby, looking disapproving. Toreth took the jumper off and handed it back to Sara. "Yeah. It fits okay. Add it to the pile." He was about to suggest moving on somewhere more sanely priced when he changed his mind. What the fuck. If he was going to pretend to be a corporate in Warrick's—their—new flat, he might as well look the part. "I need some shirts. Let's see what they've got."

"How's Warrick's brother?" Sara asked as they browsed, with a determinedly casual edge to her voice that make him pay closer attention.

"Still very, very fucked."

"Does anyone know what happened yet?"

"No."

"Are you . . . " She fingered a plastic-wrapped pink shirt that there was no way in hell she could seriously be suggesting he buy. "Toreth, is there something going on?"

"It's nothing," Toreth said. "Absolutely nothing that you need to worry about."

Sara looked at him closely, then nodded and turned away, dropping the shirt back onto the display. "Okay."

The quiet voice again, and something he couldn't immediately identify that set his teeth on edge. Resignation, he realized after a moment, or at least an unhappy acceptance that she had no right to expect him to tell her anything, not anymore.

If he ever met Carnac again, Toreth was going to add a whole new chapter to the P&P especially for him.

More immediately, he decided he had a goal with Sara, just as with I&I, to put things back to normal. That meant finding some way to reprogram the reaction. Telling her to knock it off wouldn't drive the message deep enough to matter. If he said he didn't care that she'd told Carnac things about him that no other living person knew, then he'd be lying and she'd know it. Still, he could find another way; the Administration hadn't wasted years of training in how to make people feel the way he wanted them to feel.

Until he hit on the right approach, though, he could do nothing except ignore the sting of anger and carry on as if he hadn't noticed anything. "Come on," he said. "Let's pay and get out of here before I bankrupt myself. There's a café on the next floor up. I'll buy you a mocha."

Chapter Eleven

❖

On Monday, Toreth worked hard all day and spent two hours in the gym, and he didn't think about Warrick at all. After work he went back to Sara's flat, ate curry, and watched a truly appalling romantic comedy that she claimed Kel had recommended. It involved a mistaken identity setup that could have been sorted out fifteen minutes into the plot by any moron with a DNA scanner. He pointed this out a few times, until Sara threatened to throw him out of the flat if he didn't shut up.

It was only as he went to bed that he realized the house move was tomorrow. After that, if he wanted to collect any more of his belongings he would have to go to the new flat. Not a big deal, but Toreth hoped his own clothes would manage the trip safely, especially since they were all new. At least he had the expensive stuff with him.

On Tuesday, he almost caused a permanent and irreparable rift with Sara by waking up at six and going in to work. She seemed to feel obliged to go with him, which was fine by him, except that she also felt obliged to whinge about it the whole way. At lunchtime, their corporate kidnapping victim turned up—partially—as four separate pieces scattered across marshland on the edge of the river estuary. By the end of the day, the rising tally of body parts left him short of several bits, but however he phrased it in the IIP the man was still dead. That knocked the priority of the investigation down and, as Toreth had expected, Tillotson promptly reassigned all their pool investigators.

When he and Sara left for the night, Toreth still hadn't heard anything from Warrick. He wondered whether he should check in, just to make sure Warrick had put him on the security system of the new flat. A couple of times Toreth started to call, then canceled the connection. He wouldn't be able to resist asking how other things were going, and it was probably better not to know.

On Wednesday morning, as they were eating breakfast in Sara's flat, she suddenly dropped her spoon and said, "Shit. You hadn't forgotten that it's Warrick's birthday tomorrow, had you?"

Of course he had.

At work, he fucked sixteen things up before lunch, yelled at Sara, B-C, and Mistry over the lack of progress in the corporate kidnapping, then went to the gym. He ended up swimming lengths fast enough to leave a significant wake. His shoulders ached, his legs ached—because he'd been slacking on his exercise lately—but now he couldn't *stop* thinking about Warrick and his bloody brother. Warrick wouldn't give up, that was the problem. And that left the possibility that either he'd find Leo Warrick—or whatever the Citizen Surveillance agent was really called—or he'd get caught, and neither of those options were good for Toreth's life expectancy.

Toreth turned at the shallow end of the pool, took a breath, and kicked off, diving down underwater. He kept swimming, lungs burning, feeling the water flowing over his face and the panic rising. His body screamed breathe and his brain screamed drowning, until finally he touched smooth tiles at the far end of the pool with his fingertips and broke up for air, gasping, his knuckles white as he gripped the edge of the pool. He hung on to the side, treading water as his heart slowed.

There was, realistically, only one way to prevent disaster, and that was to find the man who'd been at Valeria's school himself. Dangerous as it was, it was probably safer than letting Warrick run around unsupervised until he brought Cit Surveillance down on both of them.

In the afternoon he abandoned official work to call Officer Lee at the Justice Department. As he waited for the call to connect, he felt the now-familiar twinge of doubt. Did she still work there? Had she died in the revolt? Admittedly, at Justice the odds of her survival were better but, as always, the few seconds' wait brought back the disorienting uncertainty. Not to mention a desire to hunt down every resister in the Administration and nail them to a wall as punishment for fucking up Toreth's life like this.

"Para-investigator?" Lee smiled on the screen, looking rather more pleased to hear from him than she ever had in the past. "You're alive and well, then."

"Never better. I need a favor, Officer. Can I drop in and see you after I finish here?"

"Sure. Call me again before you arrive and I'll meet you at the main entrance."

Paranoia twinged. "Can we make it a side door?"

She didn't looked surprised, but she did shake her head. "Impossible, I'm afraid. You'll see why when you get here."

He did indeed. The Justice Department was turning into a fortress, with a new double perimeter fence being erected. At the locked main doors, the armed officers on guard checked his ID twice, even with Lee standing there beside him. Before the pair of them could move into the main building, his ID and Lee's were checked at a second reinforced door.

"Jesus," Toreth said as they walked down the corridor. "*We* don't have this much security now. I thought you didn't get hit so badly?"

Lee shrugged. "We all saw the pictures from I&I. And we're the ones who are actually out on the street. The revolt blew off some steam, but it also made people realize what was possible. There's a lot of anger out there, Para-investigator. If the new Administration doesn't meet the expectations raised, there'll be more trouble. Maybe worse trouble." She looked at him sidelong. "Unless it's still treason to say that the Administration might be fallible?"

Toreth shrugged. "No one's told me otherwise. But I'm afraid I'm too busy to arrest you. You're not the only ones who're short-staffed."

"I heard you lost a lot of people," she said, her voice suddenly sympathetic.

"Yeah. And they were a lot of the best people." He gave her an appraising glance. "Want a job? I can guarantee a good starting grade."

She smiled wryly. "I don't think so. I'd rather keep a few names above me in the lynching list."

In her office, the other desk was occupied by a harassed-looking young man who was staring at a comm screen. Judging by his tapping fingers and clenched jaw, the soothing hold picture of a flickering shoal of fish wasn't doing its job. Toreth tilted his head towards the man, and Lee nodded. "Palano, can you give me ten minutes?"

The man looked up, startled. The dark rings around his eyes complemented his heavy five-o'clock shadow, and Toreth wondered if he'd been there all the previous night. "What?" Palano asked.

"Can I have the office for ten minutes?"

For a moment Palano looked as though he'd protest. Then he slammed the comm connection closed and stood. "Sure, why the hell not?" He groaned softly as he bent to pick his coat up from the floor, and straightened slowly with his hand to the small of his back. "Have it all evening. All night, for all I care. See you sometime."

"Vin, your shift doesn't finish—"

"Why don't you tell the inspector? They can sodding well sack me." Palano banged the door shut hard enough to rattle a shelfful of commendation certificates, which had even tackier plastic frames than the I&I variety.

"Maybe I should offer *him* a job," Toreth said.

"If you catch him before he gets a good night's sleep, he might even say yes." Lee sat down at her desk and pointed to a chair. "Now, what can I do for you? I hope it won't take too long, because *my* shift finishes in half an hour."

"I'd like a copy of a final case report," Toreth said as he sat down. "And I'd like to make sure there's no official link to your passing it to me."

Her eyebrows rose. "That sounds interesting."

"You don't want to know how interesting. But I can promise that no one will care about you pulling the file."

"Just if you pull it?"

"I'd rather not have people know I was looking. It'd put some noses out of joint. Besides, it's one of your files—I'd have to put in an official departmental request. These days it might take weeks, or it might never turn up at all."

She looked at him narrowly. "Okay," she said eventually. "But remember—"

"I owe you a favor. A big favor. I'll remember."

She took the case number and turned to her screen. "And I'll try to make sure I collect on it before someone strings you up. Right...here you are."

Peering over her shoulder, he scanned down the file. "Twenty suspect names?" he said in dismay.

"That's right." She flicked through the file—unfamiliar with the Justice format, Toreth couldn't follow her. "Very bad picture, apparently. Whoever it was knew enough to keep his face away from the school surveillance systems, or maybe he was just lucky. The best they sent us was a ten percent profile. These names are the twenty best fits who came up as resident in New London." She glanced over her shoulder. "At least, they were resident here before the revolt. Now that movement notification is gone, your guess is as good as mine."

"They told the school they'd identified the man and he wasn't a threat."

"I'm sure they did. That isn't in the file, but—" She looked around again. "What would you have done with a case like that?"

"Called the school to get them off my back and then not put it in the file in case the guy turned out to be a psycho. Did whoever ran the case check them out?"

"I shouldn't think so. No one's going to devote much time to a vague report like that. Let me see...no, just automated basics: a check for family links to pupils, basic c&ps looking for suspicious movement patterns or signs of kidnap preps like travel tickets or drugs. A search of the pupil roll in case there were any high-target parents listed, which there weren't. That was pretty much it."

Twenty names to choose from, and only the twenty best-fit names at that. Annoyingly—but not surprisingly—the record summaries didn't contain the full biographies or the historical image files. That meant no current photographs to compare to Cele's sketch, or pictures to compare with the young Leo Warrick, unless Toreth risked pulling their security files himself. Or unless...

"Can you pull the security files for me?" Toreth asked.

Lee raised her eyebrows. "Got a Justice case code and security authorization?"

"Of course not. Can't you do it anyway?"

"Nu-uh. Definitely not unless you tell me what it's about, why you want them and why you can't do it at I&I. A favor is one thing, but that..." She paused. "Well?"

No plausible lies came to mind and the truth was out of the question. "'Fraid I can't."

"Well, then, there we are. Do you still want the case file?"

"Yeah, might as well. Thanks."

As she walked him out, past the tight security, he pondered the differences between Justice and I&I. For a senior at I&I, pulling a basic security file didn't need a case number, a special authorization or, in fact, anything more than a desire to see the file. He'd used and abused the privilege on many occasions. Toreth had always liked the feeling of being higher up the food chain than Justice. Now he had the feeling of shadows circling, bigger fish who had slipped into the I&I pond and who might take an unhealthy interest in him and his unofficial investigations. Lee had told him once that she preferred the anonymity of politically unimportant crime, and right now he understood the feeling thoroughly.

He checked the files out in the taxi on the way to Sara's. He didn't want to do it at her flat in case she asked what he was working on.

As far as occupation went, none of the twenty men in the file were helpfully listed as a Cit Surveillance undercover operatives. A third of the men worked for the Administration; one of them—sixty-five-year-old John Sable, unmarried, parents deceased—was a senior administrator at the internal audit section of the Data Division.

Sable's job rang faint alarm bells because the Data Division name masked a multitude of sins from public scrutiny. The Administration knew well that knowledge was power. The DD was the only major cross-departmental division, working under the direct control of the Bureau of Administrative Departments. In its respectable guises, the DD gathered and organized the vast quantities of data on every citizen and corporation that was necessary to keep the Administration running smoothly. All the other departments fed information into it and took information out. On the shady side, a collection of Administration organizations whose main function was to keep a clandestine watch on citizens and corporations claimed the Data Division as home, or at least used it as a postal address.

However, there were plenty of perfectly legitimate administrators at DD. The huge amounts of data collected and controlled by the division required an equally huge staff. If he'd pulled this file up himself in the course of an ordinary investigation, he wouldn't have assumed Citizen Surveillance—maybe wouldn't even have thought of it. Nothing in the file looked out of place or remarkable in any way. Given that the man at Valeria's school might well be an undercover operative, he could just as easily be one of the other nineteen and listed as an accountant. Still, it was something.

He closed the file and decided to call Warrick. Warrick would probably make a fuss about Toreth hiding the Justice lead from him, but with luck Toreth could find out what Warrick was doing and maybe use this new lead to stop him.

He called Warrick's personal comm, which was switched off. Better not to leave a message. Toreth called Warrick's flat with a similar result. Shit. The inability to contact him made Toreth edgy. What the hell was the man up to? Eventually, he called the flat again and left an utterly neutral "call me when you've got time" message.

It was only as he finished leaving the message that he realized it must be the system at the new flat. Weird to think that Warrick would be there when he heard the message. The movers had been booked for yesterday and Warrick would've left some kind of message if things had gone disastrously wrong. So everything would be there, Toreth's own belongings included. Toreth hadn't seen the place since the decorators had finished, and as he closed the school suspect files, he thought he really ought to go take a look. Maybe not today, if Warrick wasn't there. Tomorrow for sure, since, as Sara had reminded him again before she left, it was Warrick's birthday.

The taxi was still three streets from Sara's house when Toreth told it to stop. He didn't fancy the idea of another evening of romantic comedies, not even in pursuit of his plan to end Sara's irritating nerviness around him. She wouldn't be surprised if he came in late, and the kind of fucking he was in the mood for wouldn't take too long, anyway.

Abandoning all thoughts of Warrick and Sara for the next hour or so, he ordered the taxi to turn around, and directed it to the nearest bar.

Chapter Twelve

❖

On Monday the move began as smoothly as could be expected, which was to say that Warrick loathed every second of it. He'd planned to stay in the flat all day, watching the removal company staff packing. However, although they were quick and efficient, seeing strangers handling his possessions—all his possessions—proved to be impossible, so in the end he went in to SimTech, despite having officially taken the day off.

Once there, the temptation of taking another crack at the unyielding Citizen Surveillance computers nagged at him. Using SimTech's systems for something so dangerous would be utterly unforgivable. In an attempt to distract himself, he decided to take full advantage of a day free of planned meetings to impose himself on various sim trials and room tests. It didn't noticeably improve his mood. Everyone he spoke to probed him, more or less discreetly, about whether there would be budget cuts. The less optimistic were really fishing for news of staff cuts. In all honesty, he could say nothing to reassure them.

On Tuesday, the trauma of packing transmuted into the trauma of the cross-city transportation of his belongings and unpacking at the other end. At least he trusted the SimTech engineers who arrived to move the contents of his office, which had been deemed too sensitive even for corporate-screened removal agents.

Now that he was in the new building, the SimTech security guards had been withdrawn just when he could have used an extra few pairs of hands. However, when the movers had, thankfully, gone, Dillian and Cele arrived to help. He couldn't turn Dillian down without offending her—hurting her wouldn't be too strong a word for it—but neither was he in the mood for confrontations and peacekeeping. Consequently, he was both relieved and disappointed when Toreth failed to appear.

By midafternoon he'd unpacked enough of the kitchen contents to make tea. The kettle had just boiled when Cele stuck her head around the door. She looked fetchingly hot and mussed, with an artistic smudge of dust on one cheek. "Did you put that there deliberately?" he asked, pointing to his own cheek.

107

She grinned. "Of course. Basic rule of anything dirty—you only ever get one big smudge, so put it on yourself and you know it looks good." She scrubbed her face with the back of her hand, which rather made the situation worse. "I got it moving the boxes with 'Toreth' written on them, which must be why it's so smutty. Where are they going?"

"Ah...the smaller bedroom which isn't the one opposite the bathroom."

"Right. Knowing you, I'm surprised you haven't got a floor map and codes." Instead of leaving, she sat down on one of the new kitchen chairs. "Classy furniture in here. Not cheap, either. I thought you were on an economy drive."

"I am. Dillian bought it for me."

"Mmh, of course. Perfect for her, a bit—" she sketched unmistakable feminine curves in the air, "—for you. Fits the flat, though."

"Beautifully. I'm sure I'll learn to love them."

"And Seven Inches?"

Warrick smiled and turned back to the teapot. "Furniture isn't one of Toreth's major interests."

"As long as it's strong enough, right?" She bounced on the chair, which failed to creak under the assault.

He laughed. "That's about the size of it."

"So...should I unpack his things?" she asked. "I'm guessing not, but I thought I'd check. Don't want the poor boy feeling left out."

"I think leaving it all packed is a good guess." At the moment he frankly doubted Toreth would ever stay long enough to unpack. "How do you want the tea?"

"No milk for me, thanks," Cele said. "Squeeze of lemon, if you've got any fresh. I couldn't find any last week."

He opened the fridge. "You're in luck. I managed to hunt a couple down in the complex opposite."

While he sliced the lemon he listened. The sounds of unpacking—thumps and occasional swearing—came from the upstairs landing. He ought to call Dilly down for tea, too, but there was something he needed to do first. When he'd sat down and poured them both mugfuls, he said, "Cele, may I ask you something?"

She set her mug down without taking a sip. "Uh-oh. Sounds serious."

"Are you and Dillian...?"

She rocked her hand from side to side. "That depends on exactly which question you're asking. Sex, yes. Friends, yes. Swearing of eternal mutual devotion, not so much. Which—" she held her hand up, "—I do not have a problem with. All is hunky-dory in Cele-land."

"And at the moment? I mean, in the last week?"

Her expression cleared. "Right. Tarin. No, I haven't had a visit, but I'm expecting one. Don't worry. I'll make sure she's all right. Zinfandel and sympathy and girl stuff."

108

"Good. I've been—well, busy. I haven't spent as much time with her as I ought to. I don't really know how she's coping."

"I think she'll be okay. But since we're prying, how are you?"

If anyone would understand—and be able to handle the recent events—it was Cele. But he had no right to use her for sympathy, especially not with this. "I'm fine."

Of course, wanting to shield her and managing to lie to her successfully were different things. Cele looked at him for a long moment while he struggled to keep his expression neutral, then she shook her head firmly.

"B-u-l-l-s-h-i-t. There's all this—" She waved to indicate the flat. "There's Tarin. I know SimTech's having problems because Ash and Dilly both told me, even though it somehow slipped *your* mind. And there's something not right with Toreth. Dilly said you were fighting at Kate's."

"We fight everywhere."

"Okay. If you don't want to tell me, I'm not going to strap you down and stick needles under your—oh, shit." She shook her head. "My bad. I'm sorry."

He brushed the apology aside impatiently. "There's no need to tiptoe round it. I'm perfectly well aware of what Toreth does for a living." He tried to lighten his tone. "Sometimes I think I should get a badge made up." He drew a circle on his chest with his finger. " 'Yes, I know he does.' It would answer so many questions."

Cele rubbed vaguely at her smudged cheek again, then sighed. "This is so fucked up."

"I'm sorry?"

"Everything. There are too many secrets. Listen, there's something I have to tell you. Even though maybe I shouldn't." She leaned forwards and lowered her voice. "I found a picture, something I did for Kate years ago. And the other guy I drew—the picture of the man at Val's school? There's probably nothing to it, but it looked a bit like—"

"I know," he interrupted quickly. "That was what we were fighting about. Toreth found the picture in Kate's room."

"Shit. Keir…"

He waited, listening to Dilly dragging something across the uncarpeted landing, and he prayed Cele wouldn't ask.

"Is it him?" Cele finished finally.

"Yes."

She sat back, mouth open, for once genuinely speechless. With things gone this far, he might as well finish it. At least that way she would understand how important it was to keep quiet. "He and Kate both work for Citizen Surveillance—they have all their lives, as far as I know. That's why Kate had to leave the Administration, and it's why Leo left her when Dilly and I were children. His cover was compromised. Now you can see why it's very, very important that this doesn't get any further."

"Toreth said it wasn't him," she said faintly.

"He's trying to keep it quiet, and I agree with him about that much."

"Jesus." She picked up her mug and took a distracted gulp, wincing at the heat. "You hear about it happening. Stories about undercover agents and secret departments and agents provocateurs. I heard some from my parents, hints about how the Service got its information. But . . . Jesus. *Kate*? I mean, *our* Kate?"

"I know." Horrendously inappropriate as it was, he couldn't help smiling at her expression of disbelief. "It is hard to credit, I'll grant you that."

"All that time . . . why did they get married? Because Citizen Surveillance told them to?"

"Presumably. But she loved him a great deal, I know that much."

"Everything she did, though. She was always so kind to us. To me and Ash, I mean. And, fuck, my parents are Service. God, what if I'd ever said anything?" She frowned, rubbing at her cheek again. "Maybe I did say something. I'd never remember if I had."

"Was there ever anything to say?"

"I suppose not. Not really. If you cut 'em in half they'd both have Administration stamped right through them. But everybody says things sometimes, don't they? They used to complain about the system, about bad postings and mad budget cuts, and the idiotic things Service Command did. And . . . God. Do you remember when Dad was caught up in that inquiry? After the Unification Day protest shootings? He had plenty to say about *that*. When I was just a kid I could've repeated any of it."

Now she was getting too close to things he didn't want her to think about. "I'm sure she kept her work and her family separate."

Cele didn't seem to be listening. "Kate's house was—I mean, people *always* talked there. It was liberal. Not like idealist, criminal liberal, at least not if you don't count Tarin, I suppose, but everyone knew it was okay to—"

"*Cele,*" he said desperately.

Then he could do nothing but watch comprehension dawning. "All Tar's friends," she whispered. "She knew who they all were. They all came round, they all talked there. Tarin talked to her. He must've told her . . . he had no idea, did he?"

"None."

"You did, though." The confidence in her voice was absolute. "Before now, I mean. How long?"

"More than twenty years," he said harshly, and waited for the condemnation.

"You knew all that time and you never told him?" She sounded surprised more than anything.

"That's right." He didn't let himself look away from her. "I never told him, because I was too afraid of the consequences."

"Oh, shit. Oh, Keir, I'm sorry." She reached out and took his hand. He grasped

110

it, squeezing far too hard because he heard her gasp. Before he could apologize, she was crouching by his chair with her arms around him. He returned the embrace, grateful for the comforting contact. He pressed his face into her hair and, dimly, thought how good it was that Toreth wasn't around to walk in on the scene. "I'm sorry," Cele said again. "I didn't mean to say—I should just learn to do my thinking with my mouth closed."

"It's okay," he said, trying to breathe past the tightness in his throat.

"No, it's not. I'm a moron. I spend way too much time alone in my studio and I talk to myself which is an incredibly bad habit to get into because it means that I do this stupid shit all the time. Okay, not usually quite this serious but I did once think that this guy in a gallery was the most boring human being that I'd ever had the misfortune to meet and somehow I managed to say it out loud. Which was more than a bit embarrassing because he *owned* the damn gallery and . . . and there I go again."

He laughed and hugged her tight. "You're forgiven."

"Thanks." She lifted her head and kissed his cheek. "Poor Keir."

The sympathy made him acutely uncomfortable. "Tar's the one who's been hard done by."

"Yeah, but ignorance is bliss. It must've been hell all those years, knowing and not being able to tell anyone."

He hadn't realized until that moment how odd it was that the secret was a secret no longer. "In the end, I just didn't think about it. There was always a chance I was wrong about the whole thing. I used to hang on to the doubts."

"What about Dilly? How did she take it? I can't believe she's been so calm. All she said was that you and Toreth had a blazing row and you wouldn't say what it was about."

"She doesn't know what it was about, and it's going to stay that way."

She released him abruptly and sat back on her heels. "Keir, you can't—you can't not tell her. He's her father, too. She's got a right to know."

"It would be better for Dilly if she doesn't know. And I don't have the first idea of what or how to tell her. I still have no idea why he was at the school, Cele. Do you understand? What on earth could I say to her?"

"That . . . well, I guess, that her long-lost, allegedly dead father isn't dead at all, but possibly he did try to murder her half brother." Cele nodded slowly. "Right. I mean, I can see it's hard. But . . . there must be some way." Her tone changed to determination. "We can do it together. We can think of something."

"*No*," he said, and her eyebrows rose. "Please, Cele. I don't want to see Dilly get hurt any more than she already has been, and that's all it could do to her. Kate and Leo are out of her life for good—they can't do any more harm and all she has left is the memories of them. And there's Jen. Should I tell Dilly but not her? How the hell could I tell Jen that her sister lied to her for her whole adult life?"

111

First Tar, now Dilly, a voice whispered. Sound reasons or not, he'd never felt like such a coward in his life.

Cele was deep in thought, biting her lower lip. Finally she looked up at him. "Okay, maybe you're right, at least for now."

He didn't try to hide his relief. "I know I am. Look, if anything happens to me, then you can tell her, if you think it's necessary."

"If...?" Cele held her hands up. "Whoa right there. No. This shit cannot be real. If something *happens* to you?"

"It's possible. Unlikely, I hope, but possible. This is dangerous knowledge, Cele, and believe me, you have no idea how sorry I am that you were dragged into it. But I promise you that when Toreth asked you to draw the picture, he had no idea who the man was."

She snorted quietly. "And worrying about me would've stopped him, of course. No, I'm sorry." The shock had dissipated and she was beginning to fidget on the spot, her usual energy bouncing back. "I hate just...gah. Not being able to *do* something to fix it for you."

He had to smile. "I know. If you want to help, look after Dilly."

"Oh, I'll do that." She smiled. "Hardship city. Okay. I'll do what I'm told, this once—keep my mouth shut and my hands all over Dilly. Don't make me regret it."

"I'll do my very best."

"Just so I can keep this straight, no one else knows about Leo and Kate? I'm not going to get strangers coming up to me and making cryptic remarks?"

"I sincerely hope not. Outside of Citizen Surveillance, the only people who know are myself, Toreth, and now you."

And someone he'd somehow forgotten. Carnac. The one alternative source for Leo Warrick's real name now that he'd abandoned the files. Toreth had asked him to stay away from Carnac, but if Toreth was withholding his help, he wasn't leaving Warrick with many options.

"Keir?" Cele asked.

"Nothing. I think it would be better if we don't talk about this again, all right?" When she nodded, if reluctantly, he touched her cheek briefly. "Good. Shall we take some tea up to Dilly? She sounds like she could use some."

Chapter Thirteen

❖

Hotel owners were one group who would regret the abolition of movement notification. It was the first trip away Warrick had taken since the revolt. He'd booked a hotel out of habit. In the prerevolt days it had been automatic. Unless he had been a hundred percent sure the trip would only take a day, it had always been better to book a place in advance and waste the price than to go through the complications of reregistering the stay if he couldn't complete his business in one day.

It wasn't until he arrived in Strasbourg that he realized he needn't have bothered. Perhaps the change was largely illusory—a credit and purchase check would still reveal everywhere he had spent money, and the Data Division would doubtless still log every use of his ID. However, the open, obvious face of Administration surveillance no longer watched over the airport.

It felt odd to pass through without the usual questions: purpose of visit, planned length of stay, temporary residence address. The ID scanners stood silent; many of the people filing beneath them glanced around before they walked through, occasionally breaking stride or pausing for a moment. Warrick understood their hesitation. As he passed through, he half expected alarms to ring and guards to be summoned. It was harder still to believe that he could change his plans, move on from Strasbourg to anywhere within the Administration that his fancy took him, and no one would care or question him. The unaccustomed freedom felt peculiar, even unsettling, and he wondered how long it would last, or whether the frank unfamiliarity would drive the citizens of the Administration to demand a return to what they knew. A few resister attacks against the new regime might be enough.

Warrick's personal freedom was limited by the presence of Rob McLean. When Emma Queen, head of SimTech's security section, had found out about Warrick's plans for unescorted air travel, she'd arrived in his office unannounced and reminded him about the postrevolt travel policies. She'd been as polite as ever, but also clearly annoyed at being forced into the position of having to lecture her employer.

Warrick had argued against a bodyguard. As he'd told Queen, it wasn't as if Strasbourg was a foreign country—it was as much a part of the Administration as New London, and probably more secure, given that the Judicial departments had their headquarters there. He had surrendered when the head of security threatened to involve Asher and Lew. The less close scrutiny of his movements by friends and family there was, the better.

As the taxi drew up, McLean opened the door, signaling for Warrick to stay in his seat until he'd checked that the street outside was clear.

"You'll have to wait down here," Warrick said.

McLean shook his head firmly. "I've got my instructions from Queen."

Warrick sighed and waited for McLean to scrutinize the area before following him out.

Warrick had confirmed the address three times with the taxi system. The slightly tatty office block was on the edge of the corporate district, and seemed to have suffered some damage in the revolt. As they walked through the doors, Warrick noticed the likely impetus for the resisters' attack on the building: above brand-new and very heavy security shutters, a screen announced the presence of a Service recruitment center. The smell of smoke lingered faintly in the air; he remembered how long it had taken to eliminate it from the SimTech production facility after the fire there.

Carnac's office, on the tenth floor, had no sign outside, not even Carnac's name. The screen by the door was switched off and dark. The small room visible through the glass-paneled door wasn't at all what sprang to mind when thinking of a socio-analyst. The walls had an obviously fresh and hastily applied coat of plain white paint, with spots of it on the worn brown carpet and matching low, padded, plastic-covered chairs. He could see only one door out of the room besides the exit to the corridor.

A vaguely familiar blonde woman sat behind a desk, aged somewhere in her midthirties. Her lips were moving rapidly—dictating at speed onto the screen in front of her, he guessed. She looked up as McLean opened the door, and Warrick noticed her hand slide under the edge of the desk. "Can I help you?" she asked.

Warrick followed McLean into the room and crossed to her desk. "I've come to see Carnac."

Her expression changed from a wary welcome to dismay. "Oh, dear. Do you have an appointment?" She peered at the screen. "I don't think I have any appointments listed for this morning. Hang on a mo, cherie, and I'll look again."

"No need," he said quickly as she started to page down the screen. "I won't be there."

"Oh!" She transferred the accusatory frown from the screen to him. "The socioanalyst is *very* busy."

"I've come—"

As he started to explain, the second door to the room was flung open, and Carnac appeared like a tall, blond genie. "Keir! How positively charming and delightful, and absolutely the last person I expected to find on my doorstep."

On the plane over, he'd imagined various openings to the conversation. Plainly, Carnac had decided to eliminate their last meeting from their mutual history. Fine by Warrick, as long as he got the information he wanted.

Carnac had crossed to the desk, still smiling. "Keir, this is my youngest sister, Colette, who has most graciously offered to help me out during some professional difficulties. Colette, this is Dr. Keir Warrick, who—" Carnac paused delicately, and Warrick waited to see what relationship would be claimed. "Who is someone I met for the first time a number of years ago," Carnac finished.

She didn't even blink at the odd phrasing. "Pleased to meet you, Doctor. Shall I cancel your appointments, Jean?"

"Do I have any?"

"A few." She glanced at Warrick and McLean, and Carnac gestured for her to proceed. This time the screen surrendered the information after only a few seconds. "General Thacker is due at twelve, with four guests he didn't give me names for."

"Ah, of course. The dear general. Keir?"

"I don't plan to be here that long."

Carnac nodded. "Then please—come this way."

The room Carnac had emerged from was packed with the contents of an office that must have been at least five times larger. Tiny paths squeezed between furniture and high-security filing cabinets. Half a dozen conference chairs were crammed around a magnificent walnut table, leaving barely enough room to sit in them. Warrick hoped General Thacker and his unnamed guests weren't heavily built.

He heard one of the chairs in the reception area creak as McLean sat down to wait. Then Carnac closed the door. "Temporary accommodation, I'm afraid," Carnac said as he worked his way over to a coffee machine that perched precariously atop a stack of boxes. "Socioanalysis and I have had a difference of opinion."

"Oh?"

"Yes. They are under the impression that they have unceremoniously tossed me out of their little club. I believe I resigned free of any debts or obligations. We are still working through the legal ramifications of our mutually exclusive versions of events. As you can imagine, lawyers are positively slavering with glee. However, the practical consequence is that I no longer have access to their premises. This was the best I could do on short notice, and the landlords were amenable to the idea of a short lease. I may be leaving Strasbourg soon. Please, sit, if you can."

Warrick squeezed his way into a chair.

"The coffee at least should be good." Carnac placed the cups on the table and then sat. "My own machine which came with me from my old office. As did everything else in here—I begrudged the idea of leaving any of it for Socioanalysis. On reflection, it would have been more practical to have put some of it into storage, but I think it has a certain je ne sais quois. A touch of the renegade, perhaps."

"A renegade being visited by generals?"

Carnac shrugged. "There is no doubt *someone* out there who would describe me as such. At the very best, my position is somewhat anomalous." He took a sip of the coffee and nodded. "Excellent. And I'd be grateful if you kept news of the general's visit between ourselves."

"You're the one who went out of your way to make sure I knew he was coming."

Carnac's obviously manufactured expression of indignation was as familiar as it was annoying. "I—"

Warrick held his hand up, and Carnac subsided, looking surprised. "I doubt you've genuinely forgotten an appointment in your entire life, which means that you wanted me to know. I'm not interested in discussing it. I didn't come here to play games."

"I see." The room was silent for a moment, then Carnac said, "So, in a spirit of both polite social inquiry and reconciliation, how is Toreth?"

Warrick counted to five. "Toreth is fine. He's moving into a new flat with me."

Carnac choked on his coffee, to Warrick's immense satisfaction.

"So I'm afraid to say that your plan didn't work," Warrick added when Carnac had stopped coughing.

"Plan?" His eyebrows arched again. "I had no plan. I merely spoke the truth."

Warrick considered the options—pursue it, which was what Carnac plainly wanted, or drop it. Word fencing with a socioanalyst was, to borrow a phrase from Cele, like getting into an arse-kicking contest with a centipede.

"I came here to ask you a question," Warrick said.

"My time is at your disposal." He gestured expansively, poise restored. "No charge."

"Is this office secure?"

Carnac's face didn't flicker. Since Warrick had come all the way out here unannounced, it must be obvious the conversation was something that couldn't be carried out over a comm. "To the best of my knowledge, which is the result of some time and expense."

"Toreth told me that you had a copy of Kate's security file. Is that true?"

"Yes."

116

"Did it have the real name of the man who married her? Leo Warrick."

"Your father."

"I know who he is."

"Of course you do. Yes, it did."

"Do you remember the name?"

Carnac smiled. "I still have the file. The whole history of the operation, if you would like to see it. Her reports about Tarin, her comments on the rest of her friends...and family."

The temptation was so strong that he almost gave way. All that stopped him was the image of Tar in the flotation tank, so helpless, so hideously burned that it was impossible to believe that it could be the man he knew. Reading Kate's file would tell him far too much about her double life, and that was also knowledge that could never be erased.

Carnac was watching him intently, and Warrick knew that if he asked for the whole file Carnac would hand it over, even though he had to be aware of the consequences. For the first time, he wondered why someone so apparently cruel and conscienceless would risk his life to engineer a revolt for the sole benefit of the masses he despised. So that everyone would have the freedom to make bad choices and destroy their own lives?

"I want the name," Warrick said. "Nothing more."

"Why do you want to know?" Carnac asked.

Warrick hesitated. Did Carnac know about Tarin? There was no reason why he should, and equally none why he shouldn't. "I want to know who my father is."

Carnac smiled slightly. "Perhaps the question should have been 'why now?' You've known for some time that Leo Warrick was alive. This sudden interest concerns me. In this delicate time—and with my current precarious political position—you're asking for a dangerous piece of information, as you well know."

"The only reason I knew he was alive was because I snooped in the computer of a Citizen Surveillance agent. Do you think I'd ever have wanted to risk my neck or Kate's by letting them know that? Now it doesn't matter. They already know— I told them."

Carnac stared past him, lips pursed. "Acceptable." His gaze snapped back. "If doubtless not the whole truth. There is a price for the information, though. Dinner."

The anger he'd been keeping back rose. "I have an appointment at the Science and Technology Division of the Legislature, and then I'm returning to New London as soon as I can. I have a flight booked this afternoon."

Carnac shrugged elegantly. "If the information means that little to you, why should I put myself at risk to give it to you? Your hotel, seven o'clock?"

No doubt the standards at the hotel restaurant would occasion some sarcasm from Carnac, Warrick thought as he waited in the bar. It wasn't a slum, but it was as far below the socioanalyst's gourmet standards as his current office was below his professional ones. Warrick found the idea oddly satisfying. Carnac might be blackmailing him into a meal, but at least it wouldn't be an occasion. Serviceable food, a brief conversation, and that would be all.

At least that had better be all. Exactly how much was he willing to give Carnac for the name? Warrick liked to think that he'd draw a line at the bedroom door—if not for his self-respect, then out of consideration for Toreth. In honesty, he didn't know. He did know that Carnac sometimes coerced his partners into bed. Would he do the same to someone for whom he professed—or pretended—to have some feelings?

Seven o'clock passed with no sign of Carnac. It wasn't until almost eight that it occurred to Warrick that something unpleasant might have happened to Carnac. Even with his dangerous political dabbling—obviously still continuing—his renegade office and the possibility that Int-Sec was pursuing him, the socioanalyst had seemed as untouchable as ever. In reality, if Socioanalysis had disowned him he was probably more vulnerable than most corporates. If his enemies had coincidentally chosen today to move, it would be annoying, but it would also be risky. By visiting Carnac's office, Warrick might have made himself a target of those same enemies.

McLean, no doubt, had already thought of that, though. If he hadn't raised it as an issue, then he presumably thought the risk was acceptable. In fact, McLean had said nothing during the wait. He was never talkative when on duty, but even by his standards he was currently unusually silent.

As Warrick watched him, McLean glanced at his watch and shook his head very slightly. "You'd rather we weren't here?" Warrick asked.

"Much. I'd feel a hell of a lot safer back in New London. I can't give you an accurate assessment of how much, though, because I don't know how dangerous Carnac is or what the risk is from associating with him."

"I don't think anyone has come up with a metric to quantify it."

McLean winced. "I wish you'd told me who you were planning to see. Queen will have my hide for letting you walk in there."

"Lucky for you that you aren't going to tell her."

McLean stiffened in his seat. "That's against security procedures."

"I know, and I'm sorry to place you in this position. But nevertheless. This is nothing to do with SimTech—I would've come alone if I could, but SimTech's involvement stops with your presence here. Carnac was at my flat the day before he left New London. As you know." McLean nodded. "What I spoke to him about today was related to that. So you won't tell Queen, or any of the directors. You can tell them all about the Legislature, but no more." Another nod. "Well?" Warrick asked.

118

McLean looked up from his mineral water and smiled wryly. "Well?"

"Was there anything you wanted to ask?"

"Not really. There's something I *ought* to ask, however. Does Toreth know that you're here?"

He'd been expecting a question about Carnac—which in a way it was, but not one he had a ready answer for. "I'm not sure. He may well have guessed. It's none of your concern, in any case."

McLean shook his head. "Your safety is my concern, and as you've already reminded me, I was there at your flat. Believe me, I don't like asking the question any more than you like hearing it."

"I'm sorry," Warrick said, meaning it quite genuinely.

McLean shrugged. "All part of the job. SimTech pays me more than well enough." He topped up his glass of water, then smiled. "At least I'll be there tonight to keep an eye on you."

"I should apologize for that, too. I wasn't expecting to actually use the hotel when I told Gerry to book it, so I was thinking more about saving SimTech the cost of a second room. I could ask again if there's another one free."

"I don't think so. Queen would prefer me in there with you, just in case."

Warrick had a mouthful of his orange and soda, and wished he dared have something stronger. McLean returned to his slow scrutiny of the room, his gaze moving back and forth, omitting no one, staff or guests.

At half past eight, when Carnac had still not appeared, Warrick decided he and McLean might as well eat. If Carnac arrived later, he would have to hand over whatever information he had without garnish of any kind.

The knock on the hotel door came at half past eleven. Warrick's first disoriented thought was that it was Toreth, and that snapped him awake. Or could it be a visit from Citizen Surveillance, or some other part of Int-Sec? He was out of bed and halfway across the room before he even remembered McLean. The security man intercepted him and waved him back. Then McLean checked the screen by the door, standing well to the side of the door. Warrick picked up a dressing gown to add to his underwear; McLean must have been sleeping fully clothed.

"It's Carnac," McLean said after a moment. "Alone, as far as I can tell."

"Let me see."

The security screen revealed Carnac standing outside, his eyes glazed, swaying very slightly. He lifted his hand with careful precision and knocked again, three times.

Warrick opened the door and Carnac blinked at him, hand still raised. However, when he spoke his voice was crystal clear, with not a hint of slurring. "I need to speak to you."

119

Warrick debated with himself for a moment, then moved aside. "Come in."

Carnac stepped unsteadily into the room, then stopped. "Good evening, Mr. McLean."

McLean returned the greeting with a nod, his attention divided between their visitor and the still-open door. Warrick turned to McLean. "Wait outside, please."

This time McLean didn't protest. "How long?"

"Fifteen minutes at the most."

"I'll knock after ten," McLean said as he closed the door.

"I'm drunk," Carnac said, then stopped speaking as he navigated his way across the empty floor and dropped into a chair. "As I'm sure you have noticed, being a very perceptive man in most if not quite all areas."

"Carnac..."

"Believe me, it gives me no more pleasure to turn up in this condition than it does for you to find me on your doorstep." He paused, frowning. "Or the equivalent term for the area outside a hotel door. Step seems inappropriate, somehow." He shook his head sharply. "Anyway, I'm drunk because it was the only way I could get myself here. In all probability, we won't meet again—I won't impose myself on you in the future uninvited, and I can't imagine anything else I have that you might want. As this is my last chance, I came to apologize."

Warrick couldn't think of anything in his life which had been simultaneously so funny and so very not amusing.

"To apologize," Carnac said again as Warrick sat opposite him. "Although not for what I intended to do to Toreth. Not even for Kate. We both know what she is and what she did."

"That doesn't leave much scope," Warrick said.

"If you would let me finish. I apologize for the injury I tried to do to you. I had my justifications—it was necessary for the Administration, it was better for you in the long run—but that is what they were. Justifications for something ultimately indefensible. You had never been anything other than generous and open-hearted towards me, and as repayment...in repayment..." He stopped, frowning, then took a deep breath. "What I mean is, to say my behavior was inexcusable would be an understatement of epic proportions. So, I won't try to make any excuses. I'm sorry, and that's all I have to say."

Warrick couldn't help himself. "How long have you been rehearsing that?"

Carnac didn't flinch. "I worked out the substance a few days after I returned to Strasbourg. I polished it up in the last few hours, between glasses. I decided that I couldn't bear to do it over dinner and I apologize for not calling to cancel. I was— it occurred to me that you might well return to New London if I did so."

Warrick would have sworn that he heard a catch in Carnac's voice. Manufactured or not, for a moment he had to pity him. He allowed himself to really look at Carnac, as he hadn't at the office, seeing the deepened lines and the change in his eyes—an awareness and acceptance of the possibility of defeat. Or perhaps it was that intoxication had stripped away the shield Carnac usually kept up and blunted his energy and the force of his personality. Or perhaps Carnac was being his usual manipulative self, and this approach was as calculated as his flawless verbal attack on Toreth.

"And an apology is supposed to change what you did?" Warrick said.

"I didn't think that breaking a dinner appointment was so serious a breach of etiquette."

It was easy not to return his smile, and after a moment Carnac's mouth relaxed back into bitterness. "Please, give me a little credit for knowing that some things cannot be undone. But I deeply regret what happened, and I thought you had the right to know that. In a way, I'm glad that it failed. Not the destruction of I&I, which I think we both wanted, but the part concerning you. If I'd succeeded, we—" he gestured between them, "—would have been doomed. I would always have known what I'd done and been too afraid of the consequences to tell you. The pressure of dishonesty would have destroyed any fledgling relationship. Either that, or honesty would have compelled me to confess."

Warrick sighed. "Carnac, there is no possibility of a 'we.' There never was, there never can be. I wish you would accept that." For everyone's sake.

"I do, now. The only surprise is how long I managed to delude myself that the possibility was there. And that self-deception disgusts me more than it ever could you."

Warrick didn't entirely believe him, but neither did he want to pursue it. "Did you bring the name?"

Carnac nodded, then fumbled in a pocket. He produced a folded piece of paper. "The name from the security file. I assume it is his real name, but I can't promise that." He set it down on the table between them, misjudging the distance hopelessly, so that his fingertips rapped sharply on the table.

"Ow," Carnac said, sounding startled. He sucked his fingers, then flexed his hand. "Surprisingly painful," he murmured to himself. "Interesting. I thought alcohol inhibited pain. Perhaps it does."

He really did sound thoroughly intoxicated. Warrick picked up the paper, then hesitated briefly before politeness won out. "Are you sure you're in a fit condition to get home? Perhaps you should leave it for an hour or two."

"A very kind offer, under the circumstances." Carnac rubbed his fingertips thoughtfully. "But you do have a flight to catch in the morning and I wouldn't want to keep you awake."

"I meant that you could wait downstairs in the bar. I'm sure they're still open."

"Ah, I see. I should have guessed. But I think I'll be on my way, for both our sakes. What would Toreth say if I spent two or three hours in the same hotel as you? More to the point, what would he *do*?"

The sudden change of topic caught him off-guard. "Nothing."

"Nonsense, as you well know. He's capable of killing, in anger or in cold blood, and we would both be in danger. All it would take for him to find me here is a credit and purchase check, and I'm certain he has no qualms about abusing his discretionary powers to keep a watch over his property. You don't—"

Drunk or not, Carnac hadn't lost his power to pick targets. "What did I say that sounded as if I wanted your advice on my personal life?"

"Actually, some years ago, you asked for it. I declined to give it, if you recall, because you would have ignored it. Of course you'll ignore it now, too, but still. Warrick, he is dangerous. More dangerous than you allow yourself to see. You should leave him."

"And find someone safer?"

"No," Carnac said sharply. "Not that. Please believe this has nothing to do with . . . with my regard for you. And I concede that I'm impressed by the hold you have over him, but—"

"I have nothing of the kind," Warrick said icily.

Carnac inclined his head. "An unfortunate choice of words. I should say, rather, that the depth of his feelings for you is a source of perpetual astonishment to me. But that only makes him more lethal. He has no frame of reference for understanding emotional connection. He's terrified by what he feels, and the thought of losing you terrifies him even more."

The urge to argue was almost irresistible, but anything he could say would only supply Carnac with more ammunition for the future. This had to be the end. "I came here to ask you for a favor and you have my gratitude for the information," Warrick said. "Don't presume on it."

The socioanalyst's gaze didn't waver. "The advice is still free. The choice as to whether or not to take it is, as ever, yours." Carnac stood, making it upright on the third try. Once there, he stood in silence for a few seconds before he nodded. "Then it seems there is nothing more for us to say."

Warrick shadowed him to the door and opened it. McLean stood opposite, apparently relaxed, his hands by his sides.

Carnac lingered in the doorway, seemingly unwilling to take his own assessment at face value. "It is your birthday tomorrow, is it not?" he asked.

"I—yes." He wondered why on earth Carnac would remember that.

Carnac straightened, and suddenly looked nothing but sober. "If you pursue this matter," he said softly, "however sound you believe your reasons for doing so to be, then you stand a good chance of not living to see another one. If you will take my advice on nothing else, then at least let Leo Warrick stay dead. You have done quite magnificently well without him so far—take that as a sign that you do not need to find him now."

"I have no choice," Warrick said.

Carnac smiled slightly. "We all have choices. Ask yourself this—what will it take to salve your conscience? At least consider the damage you will do others by the time you have punished yourself sufficiently for your sins of omission."

The sudden leap in the conversation left Warrick unable to think of a reply. After a moment, Carnac shook his head. He started to offer his hand, then apparently thought better of it. "Be careful, please, Keir. The Administration would be a far poorer place without you."

"And you." The answer was almost reflexive and it wasn't until the door closed that Warrick realized the ambiguity in it. He'd meant to tell Carnac to be careful— even that impulse wasn't entirely explicable, given the trouble he had caused for all of them. Would the Administration be poorer without Carnac? It would certainly be safer.

Chapter Fourteen

❖

The early-morning rush in the corporate section of the New London airport terminal had begun to ease by the time Warrick's flight landed. As the walkways carried them through the high, cool corridors, Warrick tried to decide what the hell he was going to do with Carnac's gift. He'd worried at the problem last night until he'd finally fallen asleep to the sound of McLean's quiet snoring. No easy answers had presented themselves.

Carnac's warning had given him pause, but he no longer had any idea how far, if at all, he could trust the man. His motives were unquestionably complex and in the past his ideas of what was best for others had proved to be idiosyncratic, to say the least.

The immigration hall opened up before them, its sounds reflected and blunted by the marble. Warrick barely registered the group of black uniforms by the immigration point. I&I uniforms were nothing out of the ordinary here. As he passed by, one of them stepped forward. "Dr. Keir Warrick?"

The man was unfamiliar—short and stocky, with sour lines on his face suggesting perpetual indigestion. "Yes?" Warrick asked.

"My name is Senior Para-investigator Avis, of the Information and Communications Crimes Section of the Investigation and Interrogation Division." He pulled out a hand screen. "I have a warrant for your arrest."

Oddly, his first thought was that it had to be Toreth, calling in a favor to try to scare him into dropping the investigation. "I want to speak to Senior Para-investigator Valantin Toreth," Warrick said.

Avis's eyebrows rose, the incomprehension looking quite genuine. "Why?" When Warrick didn't answer his question, Avis repeated, "I have a warrant for your arrest."

Warrick took the screen, still half convinced that Toreth was behind it. On the other hand, Avis wasn't a name Toreth had ever mentioned, nor did Warrick recall meeting the man at Sara's party.

Avis was fiddling with the handcuffs on his belt. Out of the corner of his eye, Warrick saw McLean step forward and two of the I&I guards move to intercept him. Warrick held up his hand to stop McLean. Avis looked between them. "Who are you?" he asked McLean.

"His name is Robert McLean," Warrick said. "He works for me, in the SimTech security department." McLean lowered his hands and the I&I guards released him and backed away slightly.

"Then unless he wants to get arrested for obstruction, he should go back there," Avis said.

The demand to speak to Toreth had been an irresistible impulse, but Warrick knew his arrest training better than to follow it up. He turned to McLean. "Go," he said firmly. "Call Queen, Linton, and Marcus, then get back to the main office. You can't do any good here."

"I want to see validatable ID and warrants before I let you leave with *anyone*," McLean said.

Avis sighed and offered his ID. Warrick turned his attention to the screen in his hand. The details on the warrant were infuriatingly vague—"pursuit of an investigation into activities falling within the remit of the Information and Communications Crimes Section of I&I"—but that was enough to shock him badly. "Information and communications crimes" could mean practically anything. Most likely was his abortive investigations on Tarin's behalf, but there were many older incidents. He'd made forays into corporate systems on behalf of SimTech, and while those wouldn't automatically be I&I business, the recent political upheavals made anything possible. Exposure of any of it could mean financial disaster for SimTech.

Beside him, McLean was working his way steadily through the group's IDs, to Avis's obvious and mounting impatience. "McLean," Warrick said. "Leave it." He turned to Avis. "I'm ready."

Warrick had never been arrested before. He'd considered the possibility during the investigation into the murders at SimTech, especially toward the end, but it had stayed hypothetical. For most of his adult life, though, he'd suffered from the low-grade fear that permeated all levels of the European Administration. Even further up the social scale, everyone with a gram of common sense feared the knock on the door that might herald arrest. Since its foundation, I&I had become the core of that fear for most citizens. The years with Toreth had dulled the edge for Warrick until he had begun to think of the black uniform as normal, no longer a cause for comment or worry. Now, as the group formed around him and escorted him through the building, the fear was back manyfold.

McLean was shadowing them, which Avis seemed prepared to tolerate as long as the security man kept his distance. He had his comm out and he was talking urgently. Warrick tried to keep his breathing regular. Once SimTech knew what was going on, the legal wheels would be put in motion.

The main exit hall had even more marble—white, red, black, and green—and high windows that poured sunshine into the open expanse. The front doors of the airport were in Warrick's sight, but not as accessible as they looked. Two-thirds of the way down the room, a thick, clear barrier ran seven or eight meters up towards the distant ceiling; it was marked only by two reflective strips at hip and shoulder height. Guarded openings pierced the barrier at intervals, with clear doors ready to be slammed down in case of trouble. It provided bulletproof security without spoiling the look of the corporate exit.

As they approached the barrier, Avis pointed him left, towards a side exit. Halfway there, Warrick spotted a familiar dark-haired figure hurrying towards them on the far side of the plastic. Hell. He'd forgotten all about Dilly. "McLean," he called over his shoulder. "Ms. Avens is over there. Get her somewhere safe. Take her to SimTech if she'll go."

At the possibility of trouble, the I&I guards took hold of Warrick's arms and started walking him quickly towards the exit. Warrick wondered vaguely why they hadn't cuffed him yet. They were almost at the doorway—thankfully there were no more open gaps in the barrier.

"Keir?" Dillian was keeping pace, her voice muffled by the barrier. "What's happening?"

McLean had doubled back to find a way through to his new charge and Warrick felt suddenly isolated. "Don't worry, Dilly. Everything will be fine. Go with McLean."

"No!" She had her hand on the barrier as she jogged to keep pace. Her bag slipped from her shoulder, bumping down to her elbow. "I'm not leaving you. What's going on?"

Then they had reached the door, going into a darker corridor, no marble or high windows. Dillian's voice faded, although to his relief it sounded as if McLean had caught up with her.

As the guards escorted him out to the waiting car, he thought not about Toreth but about Marian, leaving her office flanked by investigators, head held high. She'd gone through the same gates he'd soon be driven through, and emerged only in a coffin.

An anonymous note would do the job quite adequately, and be safer. Making the call in person would be spite, Carnac acknowledged, pure and simple. Or possibly spite mixed with pique and the remains of the second-worst hangover of his life.

Or possibly he was lying to himself about all of it, and the real reason was more distasteful still. When had he become so mendacious?

Last night might not have been his most eloquent performance, but he thought it had deserved a better reception that it had received. He'd hoped—and it had been hope, not expectation—to find a crack in Keir's defenses. And yet... and yet, he couldn't blame Keir for his coldness. Not "didn't want to," but *couldn't*. What was it about the man that had brought a trained socioanalyst to this pass? As a purely intellectual observation, it was fascinating. As a state of being, it was becoming intolerable. However, given the devastation wrought on the Psychoprogramming Division during the revolt, he had no option but to tolerate it. Recently his life seemed to be attracting irony like a magnet.

Carnac checked his watch. Keir's plane had now landed, meaning that he would be safely on his way to SimTech, where he would be surrounded by well-trained security. That left the perfect opportunity to spread a little misery, as well as actually do some good. Much as it galled him, he had to admit that the one person best suited to saving Keir from his own determined efforts at symbolic self-immolation was also the last person in the world Carnac would dream of asking for a favor. That didn't matter—the information could be conveyed in less direct ways, and Toreth's unerring instinct for self-preservation would make sure he tried to stop Keir.

Toreth answered his office comm looking slightly distracted. He still had his gaze fixed on something to the left of the screen as he said, "Senior Para T—" Then he caught sight of his caller and the word stopped midsyllable, frozen on his parted lips.

"Wait, please," Carnac said before he could cut the connection. "This is important."

"It had better be the end of the fucking world, because if it's not, I'm going to—"

"Please. No need for threats. I called to discuss our mutual acquaintance. I shall be brief: he is doing something dangerous, which is not entirely unheard of for him, and foolish, which is far rarer."

"How the fuck do *you* know what he's doing?"

"Well, I will leave that up to you to work out, Para-investigator. Although since the abolition of movement notification, I suppose that aspect of your job has become far harder."

"Don't try that crap. I know he's here in New London. He's..."

Carnac relished the dawning uncertainly. Really, it was too trivial. Incidental fun mustn't distract him from his serious purpose, though. "Did you know that he has developed a potentially unhealthy interest in genealogy?"

Toreth said nothing, which was as good as a yes.

"I hope you are not encouraging it," Carnac continued.

The direct goad worked better. "*Encouraging?* Do I look suicidal? Or stupid?"

Sometimes it was such an effort to leave the easy ones alone. "If he pursues this, he will be in danger, or rather, in even more danger. And so will others whose identities I'm sure I have no need to spell out. He must stop it, and soon."

"No *shit*. I can see why people pay you so much."

"It's a serious warning, honestly meant."

"This is all your fault," Toreth said with a hard-edged certainty that was actually rather unnerving. "If you hadn't come up with that fucking file in the first place, none of this would be happening. Was this in the plan? Did you work out a probability for getting him killed?"

"I, ah." Annoying as it was to admit, he had to say—"No. There is a limit to the outcomes I can consider. I work best with organizations, not individuals."

"An excuse. Big fucking surprise. If anything happens to—if this all fucks up because of you, you know what? I'll find you and I will tear your throat out." He smiled nastily. "Or maybe I'll do that anyway."

Distance, that was most definitely key to baiting Toreth. "This is rather straying outside the scope of my call. I don't wish to spend all day on the comm."

"Fine. So did you give it to him?"

And that went beyond easy. This time he couldn't resist. He arched an eyebrow. "Did I what?"

It took a moment for the innuendo to sink in before Toreth went absolutely white with fury and Carnac had to suppress a chuckle. "Did you give him the fucking *file*?" Toreth gritted out.

He didn't feel like sharing his inability to refuse Keir's requests. "He didn't ask to see it."

Toreth relaxed slightly, and Carnac wondered why it was so significant. Worry about the price Keir might have paid for it? Well, he had delivered his warning, so he could wrap up with a little self-indulgence. "By the by, I hear that you're moving into a new flat." On-screen, all the tension returned to Toreth in a rush. "That must be a distressing thought. Placing yourself into a domestic situation with a dominant presence over whom you have no control. It must...resonate for you."

Toreth simply stared for a moment. It took an obvious effort for him to unclench his jaw enough to speak. "You know what? Fuck you."

Oddly less satisfactory than he had hoped, Carnac mused as he stared at the abruptly blank screen. Petty revenge almost always was. He closed his eyes and pinched the bridge of his nose, which had little effect on the dull pain behind his eyes. After a moment, he opened the comm again. "Coll? I don't suppose you have anything to mend a broken heart?"

"A...I'm sorry, Jean? A what?"

He smiled bleakly. "Do you have any painkillers? I have a perfectly appalling headache."

Toreth leaned back in his chair and gripped the edge of the desk, because his hands were shaking with rage. "*Bastard,*" he said out loud. Unbelievable, arrogant—"Lying fucking *bastard.*"

Even that much coherence was costing all his concentration. It took a full minute before he could calm himself enough to start wondering where Warrick was. Not in Strasbourg, that was obvious. Carnac had been baiting him. Somewhere in New London, then. Somewhere he would call Carnac from, which probably meant the flat and not SimTech. Somewhere Toreth could find him and—

The comm chimed—an internal call, not that prick back for the parting shot he'd no doubt had ready. "*What?*" Toreth snapped as the screen brightened.

He recognized the woman as one of the receptionists downstairs. "Para?" she said uncertainly.

Toreth frowned, reaching for her name. "Madeleine? Is there a problem?"

In the background, he could hear raised voices, and Madeleine glanced quickly sideways. "Yes, Para. There's a woman in reception demanding to speak to you. She says that her name is Dillian Avens. She's rather agitated."

Toreth's heart sank. "I'll come down for her right away."

In reception, Dillian was waiting by the reception desk, apparently still arguing with Madeleine. A security officer stood nearby, on alert, his eyes fixed on her. Toreth wondered if she'd actually hit anyone, and whether he'd be able to smooth things over if she had. "Dillian?"

She turned quickly. "Did you have anything to do with this? What were you two arguing about?"

Oh, Jesus. Whatever had happened, he needed to get her out of here. He crossed the space quickly, caught her by the elbow, and led her to the side of the room. The guard looked at Toreth questioningly as they walked away, but he seemed happy to let them go. Of course, if Dillian took a swing at anyone now it was likely to be Toreth. "What the hell's going on?" Toreth asked in an undertone.

At least Dillian had the presence of mind to lower her voice, too. "Keir's been arrested."

The words weren't the shock they ought to have been. He'd known, somehow, as soon as he'd seen her.

"I was at the airport when it happened," Dillian was saying. "There was a group of men in I&I uniforms. I followed here as quickly as I could, but they won't let me see him."

"Of course they won't," Toreth said absently while his mind raced. "There's at least twenty-four hours before there's any external contact at all except with Justice reps." Or was that under the old system? He thought it still applied.

"What are you going to do?" Dillian demanded.

He'd told Warrick not to expect Toreth to risk his neck if Warrick managed to drop himself in the shit. The temptation to stick to the resolution lasted only a few

129

seconds. "Whatever I can. I'll need to find out some details first." Something she'd said suddenly registered. "Why was he at the airport anyway?"

"He was on a flight back from Strasbourg, I think. He was supposed to be back yesterday, then he called to say he had to stay overnight. I went to collect him because we had to be at the hospital this morning to speak to the consultant..."

He lost the rest of the sentence in the resurgence of anger. Strasbourg. Carnac had been telling the truth for once in his miserable life. More than that, Warrick had spent the night in Strasbourg and although every rational fiber in Toreth's body told him nothing could have happened between them, it couldn't stop the twisting in his guts. He held up his hand, and Dillian halted in the middle of whatever the fuck she'd been saying. "You get out of here," Toreth said. "I'll find him."

Oh, yes, he thought as he turned back to the lifts. I'll find him.

He'd kill them, Toreth decided on the way down the corridor to General Criminal. Warrick first, then Carnac. Or maybe Carnac first, because if he was caught between murders, he'd prefer to be sure of Carnac.

Sara was absent from her desk when he arrived. He soon discovered why— she was in his office, using his comm. When she saw him, she said goodbye and closed the connection. "Warrick's been arrested!" she burst out as soon as he closed the door.

"I know." He did at least get the satisfaction of being able to say that and of seeing her surprise. "Dillian was here. How did you know?"

"I got a call from one of the admins in ICC. She recognized his name from my tenth anniversary party. She remembered talking to him about the sim."

The name of Information and Communications Crimes was both welcome and unwelcome news; Political Crimes would have been worse. "Did she have any clue why they pulled him in?"

"A security breach, that's all she knew. Something high level, because she said Avis was looking pleased—he hasn't had a big case for a long while, even before the—" She hesitated, as she still always did when mentioning the revolt. "The trouble. It was a quiet arrest, though, and they haven't applied for a waiver yet."

Probably because they'd be waiting for reports from the systems specialists. "Fuck."

Sara was watching him narrowly. "What are you going to do?"

"I have no fucking clue. Jesus. Fucking *idiot*!" He slammed his palms flat on the desk. Sara jumped up out of the chair at the explosion, but it released some tension. No waiver meant there were probably a few hours' grace to try and salvage something out of the mess. "Right. Get back onto the network, find out whatever you can."

After she'd gone, Toreth sat down and tried taking deep breaths, which didn't seem to help because every time he managed to tamp the anger down a little Carnac's smiling image appeared in his mind's eye. Toreth had turned Warrick down—once, once in all the fucking time they'd been together—and the first thing Warrick had done was run to Carnac. Well, okay, maybe the second thing, right after whatever fucking stupid stunt he'd pulled to get himself arrested by ICC.

Focus, he told himself. A few weeks ago, he'd had a socioanalyst bent—to coin a phrase—on killing him and everyone else in the division. So Toreth ought to be able to cope with Information and Communications Crimes, even with Warrick acting like someone had been slipping him stupidity tablets. It was still tempting to leave Warrick to stew in his own juice, at least for a while. Why the hell should he make the effort to rescue him after *that*?

On the other hand, superficially attractive as it was to make Warrick sweat, if ICC could prove Warrick had been in the Citizen Surveillance systems they wouldn't stop asking questions until they'd found out everything. And "everything" went a long way back for both of them, so Toreth might as well not fuck around. Quick action, starting with his best shot. On that basis, he called SimTech and bullied the receptionist into connecting him through to Asher Linton.

Warrick's fellow director didn't look surprised to see him. She did look pale, and as worried as he'd ever seen her. "Rob McLean called from the airport when it happened," Asher said. "What's going on? Why have they arrested him?"

"I'm not sure."

"Is it something to do with Tarin?"

Jesus, over an open comm into I&I. The stupidity tablets must be on special offer in the SimTech canteen. "Can you do me a favor?" he asked, hoping she'd drop the question.

"Of course. What?"

"Tell the SimTech legal department to hold off. I think the arrest is a mistake, and the fewer people who get invested in making it stick the better. I don't want Information and Communications Crimes involved in a pissing contest with your lawyers."

"They're already involved. We've submitted an application for an outside representative."

"Okay. Well, if they say yes, don't send anyone yet. And if ICC is calling this political, it'll get turned down, anyway. If that happens, don't try again."

Asher's eyes narrowed, and he was wondering if she was thinking about Marian Tanit's death in custody. "Why?"

"Because if they think they have enough evidence, they'll just strip his corporate status to get rid of you. That's not going to look good, is it?"

"I don't care about that."

"But Warrick will. You know he wouldn't want this affecting SimTech. And it doesn't have to, if he's out of here quickly enough. That would be best for everyone, wouldn't it?"

Asher nodded. "So what are you going to do?"

"I can't tell you. You'll just have to trust me."

The silence stretched out. "I'm not happy about this," she said finally.

"You're not alone." Toreth tried not to let the relief show. "Give me until the end of today, at least. You won't get anywhere before then, anyway."

"Very well. But no longer. I won't leave him in that place."

It wasn't until that moment that it really hit him. Warrick was *here*. Downstairs on the detention level, in a holding cell or maybe an interview room. The shock drove any thought of Carnac from his mind. Fuck. He only had Sara's word that there wasn't an interrogation in progress right this second, that Warrick wasn't in an interrogation chair, that there wasn't an overworked and bad-tempered interrogator being careless with an injector *right now*.

"Toreth?"

He blinked at the screen, where Asher Linton was frowning, concerned. "Everything's going to be fine, Asher. Hold off on that rep, and I'll let you know the second I have any news."

As soon as Asher had gone, he called through to Sara. It took her a minute to answer the comm. "Any news?" he asked

"Just give me a bit longer. I'll come in when I'm done."

He sat and fretted, unable to shake the images. Sara had said ICC didn't have a waiver, but for level one the prisoner need only to have been processed into custody. Even with the revised P&P there was no requirement to wait for independent legal representation. Avis could start interviewing whenever the hell he liked. Warrick wasn't stupid, at least not under normal circumstances, but even the most intelligent people could trip themselves up if they were arrogant enough to start playing word games with trained interrogators.

Toreth weighed up Warrick's intelligence and arrogance, and hoped like hell the former would keep a check on the latter. In the long run, though, it didn't matter. High-level waivers might be a thing of the past, but Toreth had taken care to ensure that the bowdlerized Procedures and Protocols still had bite. The urge to go downstairs and find Warrick grew with every second. Could he possibly get away with just walking Warrick out of custody? Maybe, but what then? Warrick would have to get out of the Administration, like Kate, and Toreth would have to go with him. And that meant leaving Sara behind to take the heat. Warrick wouldn't want to abandon Dillian and the rest of his family. Then there were Warrick's friends, SimTech partners . . . spreading ripples. It was an impossible idea, bordering on suicidal.

Fuck it. It might be the only way. Impulsively, he stood up, but at that moment the door opened. Sara paused, staring, and he wondered what his face must have looked like. Then she came in and closed the door. "I couldn't get much more," she said. "The security violation is inside Int-Sec somewhere. There's an upper-third-level waiver ready to send to Justice, so they must think they have something. But as he's a corporate director, ICC is sitting on it until they gather more evidence."

Pretty much as he'd thought. Unfortunate, because unauthorized access to Administration security records was one thing that corporate status couldn't buy off. Corporates who wanted secure files were far safer sticking to the traditional route of bribery.

"Shall I go down to systems?" Sara asked.

"Huh? Why?"

"I could ask the specialists not to find anything. They might do it, for you."

One option he hadn't considered, and it only took him a few seconds to discard it now. "No. Or not yet. I don't want to owe them that kind of favor—they'd own my soul for the rest of my life. We'll have to try something else."

Warrick had never been handcuffed in anger before. As he paced the cell, the difference it made surprised him. The sick fear caused by being there canceled any erotic charge from the cuffs. They were simply a reminder of where he was, and of the absolute power I&I had over those who fell into its grasp.

Leaning against the wall, he studied the cuffs. They were so familiar—Toreth had filched more than one pair. A freshly stolen set lay in Warrick's bedside cabinet, a replacement for those looted from Toreth's flat. Avis hadn't cuffed him at the airport or in the car, only in the lift on the way down to this cell. Did that mean they weren't confident of their evidence, or just that in the new climate they were trying not to offend corporates unnecessarily?

The holding cell had no chair or bed—the choices were to sit on the floor or to stand. He stood. Sitting would make it too awkward to stand again when Avis returned. Prisoner depersonalization theory. He'd heard Toreth mention it occasionally.

The cell's gray wall merged into the gray floor. The corridors outside had been the same. When the lift doors had opened, the unpleasant disinfectant tang had nauseated him. He didn't recall smelling it the last time he'd been here—perhaps it didn't permeate the upper levels. Now his awareness of it had faded, although if he took a deep breath he could still taste it in the air.

He was underground, he knew that, but how far down was a different question. The heavy door let no sound in, and the absence of any evidence of other people was disconcerting; the air cycling system sounded loud. Toreth must have been somewhere like this, during his few days' imprisonment during the coup. The idea of this same cell in pitch blackness chilled him.

Back then, Toreth had said he'd known that Warrick would try to get him out. Warrick appreciated for the first time how much of a comfort that hope must have been. At least he himself had a whole legal department who were at this moment gearing up to rescue him. They could have him out faster than he had managed to rescue Toreth. The main problem with that theory was that Warrick was, in all probability, guilty of the charges, whatever they were. No doubt he would find that out when he finally made it to an interrogation room. He hadn't been so much as interviewed yet, or even told in detail why he was here beyond the vague arrest warrant he'd read at the airport.

Warrick knew he'd been stupid at the arrest. Mentioning Toreth's name to Avis had been as good as implicating him. At the very least it would draw Avis's attention towards Toreth. He only hoped Toreth wouldn't do anything to make it worse.

If Toreth did anything at all. The thought shocked him. It wasn't that he'd casually dismissed Toreth's angry words in Kate's bedroom, but he somehow hadn't felt that they applied here. Except that this was exactly the kind of danger Toreth had been thinking about—arrest, interrogation, secrets spilled in a widening pool. Maybe Toreth *would* abandon him. Warrick was well aware that the main reason their relationship had lasted so long was that he didn't demand more than Toreth was capable of giving. Self-sacrifice was not part of Toreth's makeup, and he'd have the justification of the warning given well in advance. He was still debating the possibility that he really was alone here when the door opened. The momentary flash of hope vanished at the sight of another uniformed guard.

The endless, identical corridors were another feature of the place that had to be designed for intimidation value. Two impassive guards escorted him along, barely looking at him as they opened and closed security doors. They displayed no curiosity about him at all, and he wondered whether they didn't know he was the lover of a para-investigator, or if they knew and didn't care.

When the guards opened the door to an interview room, Warrick recognized Avis at once. There was a tall, blond man behind him, and for a moment Warrick thought it was Toreth. Then he realized his mistake and the disappointment almost choked him. The blond man seemed familiar, however. He wore an investigator's uniform rather than a para-investigator's, and Warrick wondered if he had met him at one of the rare I&I functions he'd attended.

"Sit," Avis snapped.

The room held a single table and two chairs. Warrick sat in one, and Avis threw himself into the chair opposite. He looked furious. Without explanation, he thrust a hand screen across the table. Behind Avis, the blond man coughed. When he had his hand cupping his mouth, Warrick thought he saw him mouth something over Avis's head. Had it been "from Toreth"?

Warrick read, keeping his expression as neutral as he could. The first thing his eye picked out was a number he recognized at once: his security clearance code from his long-ago days in the Data Division.

The heading of the document said it was an authorization to use an outside agency to gather information. He scanned the rest: Toreth's name, a financial approval for expenses only, no consultancy fees, with a maximum of one hundred euros, and an impossible starting date—the day after Tarin's accident. Reading too much more would make it look as if he wasn't expecting the miraculous rescue. He dropped the screen on the table and called up his best corporate arrogance, remembering to keep his hands still so as to minimize the effect of the cuffs. "Well? Isn't it in order?"

Avis's shoulders relaxed a fraction. "Why didn't you tell me about this before?"

"You didn't give me a chance. You arrested me, processed me, and put me in a cell."

Behind Avis, the blond man closed his eyes briefly. Relief, Warrick hoped.

"If you'd told me at the airport, you wouldn't be here at all!" Avis said.

"Our lawyers are very strict about it: if arrested, say nothing until you've spoken to them in person."

"Then why the hell didn't *they* say something? We've heard enough from them."

"This is a private consultancy contract between myself and Para-investigator Toreth. Nothing to do with SimTech, so naturally they knew nothing about it. Once I had a chance to speak to a representative, I would have explained everything." He hesitated, then added, "I did ask to speak to Para-investigator Toreth, if you recall."

Avis jerked the screen back across the table and stood. He turned to the blond man. "Okay, I'll believe you. Thousands wouldn't. You can tell the sainted bloody savior of I&I that I don't appreciate sloppy IIPs. I've wasted my best people for days on this."

"Yes, Para." The aggressive tone didn't seem to faze the investigator. "But, to be fair, it's not the Para's fault if the system failed to register the outside agency authorization. It was all properly processed, but they're still dealing with systems disruption from the revolt."

"If you wanted internal systems security testing, you should have gone to the systems section. Or come to us." Avis's voice now held more grumbling than anger.

"I can't speak for the Para, but everyone's under pressure to save time and resources. Given the staffing problems and so on..." The investigator gestured vaguely.

"Huh. And don't I know it. ICC is right down at the bottom of the pile for new kit, new people, you name it. I'm working with half a team, and most of those are junk from the pool."

"Yes, Para, I heard that. General Criminal is right down there with you. Political and Corporate Fraud are taking the cream, as usual." There was a moment of almost tangible shared resentment against the other sections, then the blond man coughed again. "If I could..."

"Oh, right. Of course." Avis removed Warrick's handcuffs and slipped them

135

onto a loop on his belt. When Warrick stood, the para-investigator faced him squarely. "I'm sorry about all this, Doctor. But I'm afraid that I couldn't do anything else, given that you refused—"

Warrick waved the apology aside. "I understand completely. I, of all people, ought to appreciate the importance of system security. I'm just glad that the Administration is so vigilant."

"Thanks for being understanding." Avis turned to the investigator and made a shooing gesture towards the door. "Well, go on, then. Take him, take him. Some of us have real work to get on with."

Outside the room, Warrick paused. "I'm sorry, I don't recall your name."

"Investigator Ainsley Barret-Connor, sir." He glanced up and down the corridor. "If you could, um, come this way."

"Is Toreth in his office?" Warrick asked as they headed, presumably, for the lift.

"Yes. He asked me to take you up there." After a moment, Barret-Connor added, "But if I were you, I'd consider going straight home. I can tell him you insisted, if you like."

"Oh?"

"He's not a happy man. I mean, *really* not a happy man."

"No doubt." The idea was tempting but, of course, impossible. "I'd be grateful if you could show me the way."

"Yes, of course. Although . . . when I heard him talking to Sara, he was saying something about the socioanalyst." Barret-Connor glanced at him. "Carnac."

"Ah."

It was fortunate that I&I's designers had fitted the offices with indestructible—if ugly—carpets. They had survived the revolt better than the building's occupants, and now the carpet in Toreth's office had no problem standing up to his frantic pacing as he worked through and rejected increasingly desperate plans for retrieving Warrick from detention. The rescue plans alternated with more detailed and more enjoyable plans for exactly what he was going to *do* to Warrick once he did have him back. Warrick, he vowed, was going to regret his trip to Strasbourg. The deceitful, treacherous fuck would never—

The door opened, and B-C appeared for exactly long enough to say, "He's here, Para," let Warrick go through the door, and rapidly close it again. A question from Sara was cut off midsentence.

Before Warrick could speak, Toreth grabbed his shirt front in both hands and slammed him against the office wall. "You stupid fucking bastard!" Screw what the office could hear. "I told you!"

Warrick didn't even have the grace to look surprised. "Toreth, I'm sorry. I—"

"I don't fucking care. Idiot fucking—" He struggled to keep his voice down. "I told you you'd get caught. For once in your life, couldn't you have fucking *listened*? You were *this* close to screwing both of us." He shook Warrick again, the sweet rush of violence feeding the underlying turmoil of fear and anger. "*This* fucking close. And you still might. We could both end up in re-education, if we're *lucky.*"

"Perhaps you could take your own advice," Warrick said breathlessly.

"*What* did you say?"

Toreth tightened his grip, twisting his fists and pressing Warrick back against the wall. Warrick's hands closed over his wrists, fingers digging in—painful, but nowhere near breaking his hold. Futile, and somehow infuriating.

"Why don't you do it like you fucking mean it?" Toreth said. "That's not what they taught you in corporate safety school."

Warrick released his hold. "No. Not at all. They taught me how to break some-one's arm. But I'd rather not have to."

His hands flexed again, almost involuntarily, and Warrick gasped. "Toreth, if you would *listen* for a moment and let me explain..."

Toreth considered the idea. If he was going to kill Warrick, right here in Toreth's own office wasn't the place to do it. Better to wait until they got home, where he could do it with proper care and attention to detail and the right amount of screaming. "All right," Toreth said. "Make it good."

Warrick took a deep breath, then glanced down at Toreth's hands. He took hold of Toreth's wrists again, lightly this time. "Do you think you could possibly let go? It really isn't helping my concentration."

Déjà vu. Almost the same position, in the same office, as after Marian's death. Back here, after all this time. He pressed closer to Warrick, hips against his, and, unbelievably, the bastard was hard. He was actually fucking getting off on the fact that Toreth was one breath away from breaking his ungrateful neck. Anger flared again, then suddenly evaporated, and he started to laugh. Warrick looked at him warily, hands still loosely clasping his.

After a few seconds, Toreth managed to regain enough control to gasp, "You are sick, do you know that? Completely fucking sick."

"Oh, yes." Warrick's mouth twitched. "Yes, I know. If it's any consolation, the cell was no fun at all."

"Jesus. Jesus fucking Christ." If Toreth didn't shut up, the rest of the office re-ally would wonder what the hell was going on. Releasing Warrick, he leaned on the wall beside him, swallowing down the noise. He looked sideways at Warrick, who also seemed to be fighting laughter, and the hysteria threatened to break through again. Thinking about the danger helped. "Fucking idiot," he said.

Warrick closed his eyes and leaned his head back against the wall. "I am sorry."

"Fantastic. So what's the excuse?"

"No excuse." Warrick stood away from the wall and faced him. "You were absolutely correct. I couldn't get into the systems and I had to give up. I thought I'd cleared up all traces, but obviously I was wrong. Avis didn't tell me what they'd found, but whatever it was, it is entirely my fault. I'm sorriest of all that you had to take the risk to help me and I'm more grateful than I can tell you."

And that was it. Apparently that was supposed to be enough. He should kill Warrick for that alone, for expecting Toreth to just accept that pathetic apology as recompense for scaring the living fuck out of him. But somehow, with Warrick in front of him—alive, touchable, safe, not down on level C, not in an interrogation room condemning them both to death or re-education—the anger stubbornly refused to reappear.

Maybe he could get it back, because if he let himself start to think about where Warrick had been before he was arrested, and who he'd seen there, he felt the muscles in his shoulders start to tighten. But he suddenly discovered that he didn't *want* to think about Carnac. Not now.

He pushed away from the wall and strode over to the door. When he jerked it open, Sara scooted her chair away from right outside. B-C was by her desk—she must have been relaying the news to him. Beyond him, at desks and in groups, admins, investigators, and paras stood frozen. There was a moment of silence, then the rest of the office busied themselves with screens and conversations.

Behind him, Warrick started forwards, but Toreth snapped around and pointed to a chair by his desk. "You. Sit." Turning back, Toreth leaned on the doorframe. "B-C?"

B-C cleared his throat. "Para?"

"Good job, well done. Thanks. Now the show's over, so fuck off."

"Yes, Para." B-C almost tripped over his feet in his haste to comply.

"Sara?" Toreth asked.

She turned around from her desk, just as innocent as if she hadn't been eavesdropping. "Yes?"

"I want a couple of—"

"Coffees?" She picked up two self-heating mugs and handed them to him, far too smug for someone caught with her ear against the door. "Anything else?" she asked.

"No. No need for a mop and bucket."

She grinned and turned away.

"For the blood?" Warrick asked after Toreth had closed the door.

"Yeah." Toreth sat down heavily. "For some reason, there seems to be a widespread conviction these days that I'm some kind of fucking homicidal maniac. Which is funny, because I *used* to have a pretty stress-free life. Wonder what changed?"

Warrick sensibly left that one alone. He pried the lid off his coffee and took a sip. "Ah. That is very welcome. Even—" He had another mouthful. "Even if the flavor leaves something to be desired. Now. Exactly how much trouble are we in?"

"I don't know." Toreth opened his coffee and breathed in the comforting smell. "Sara made out the most innocuous outside agency form she could under the circumstances, and I asked Jenny to sign it and backdate it."

"Who's Jenny?"

"Tillotson's admin. There's been a lot of backdating and form-fiddling going on since the revolt. Systems keep going down, and half the time people aren't quite sure who to report to anyway. Plus I'm running a bit of a reputation surplus right now, which I might as well use while it lasts. As long as ICC doesn't make a fuss, it'll all get buried in the rest of the paperwork."

Warrick smiled. "Thank you."

"It's my fucking neck as well as yours. Did you read the form?"

"I didn't want to make it look as if I didn't know what was in it. Fortunately, Para-investigator Avis was too annoyed to ask many questions."

He frowned. "B-C should've been backing you up. Wasn't he?"

Warrick nodded quickly. "Very efficiently. He spirited me up here before Avis knew what was happening."

Always worried about treating the bloody staff well, even when they weren't his. "Good. Right. Well, if anyone asks, you were testing systems security because I thought someone might be pulling corporate security assessments out of the Int-Sec database to use in corporate kidnappings. Exploiting the trouble caused by the revolt."

Warrick frowned. "Those files have nothing to do with Citizen Surveillance."

"Then if anyone asks, you'll have to tell them that you fucked it up, won't you?"

"I would've had to be spectacularly inept." He sounded mortally offended by the suggestion.

"Good." Toreth grinned. "Trust me, that's what you want ICC to think. Or do you want to be on their lists as a shit-hot systems cracker?"

"Mm. Perhaps a reputation for crass incompetence is more appealing than I thought." He looked at his watch, then drained half his coffee. "If there's nothing else, I should go. McLean must have told SimTech what was happening, and they'll need to be reassured. They'll need to see me in person to be quite satisfied."

They had a great deal more to talk about—starting with Carnac—but Toreth was always willing to put off an unpleasant conversation. "Okay. See you later."

Glancing down, Toreth caught sight of a note on the screen. A memo from Sara. "Warrick?"

Almost at the door, Warrick stopped and turned. "Yes?"

Toreth leaned back in his chair and smiled. "Happy birthday."

139

Building security had let him in downstairs without a murmur, but Toreth paused in the entrance to ring the comm up to the new flat, not really knowing why. When Warrick answered he looked briefly surprised before his expression changed to a smile. "Come on up."

The flat door stood slightly ajar when he reached it, but Warrick wasn't there. Toreth pushed it open and stood on the threshold, looking at the hallway. Much as he remembered it from the visit with the agent, except that the checkerboard black-and-white floor had been thoroughly cleaned and polished, the walls redecorated.

Once inside he paused, wondering where to hang his coat. Hadn't there been a cloakroom? Yes—he found it again, just inside the door. He might as well get off to a good start. No doubt he'd be throwing his coat down on a chair before long, and watching Warrick grit his teeth keeping quiet about it.

He'd stopped off at Sara's to pick up his things, and carrying his suitcase and shopping bags down the hall made him feel like a visitor. "Warrick?"

"In the living room," Warrick called.

Warrick was waiting near the doorway, holding a stack of small framed pictures. He set them down on a table Toreth didn't recognize.

Toreth dropped his belongings and looked around. There was plenty in the room that he did recognize, mostly ornaments and pictures, including Cele's nude portrait of himself seated on a windowsill. However, the rug from Warrick's old flat, the blue one that they'd fucked on plenty of times, hadn't made it here. In its place were three new, smaller rugs in shades of gray. The suite was new, too. Everything looked different, even the familiar things, and he wondered if it bothered Warrick. Toreth put his hands on the back of the sofa and leaned on it. Nice and strong. "The room looks smaller," he said, as Warrick was obviously expecting a comment.

"Yes. Places always do with the furniture in."

"The carpet's blue."

"Quite so."

"Reminds me of something."

Warrick laughed and moved up beside him, standing half behind him, not quite touching. "I'm sure it does, since you spend so much time in front of the mirror—it's rather close to your eye color."

He thought about Sara, and the blue jumper packed in his bag. My flat, Toreth said to himself. My home. The words sounded wrong, because nowhere he'd ever lived had looked like this, so clean and tidy. At least nowhere recent, and certainly not anywhere he wanted to remember now.

It must resonate for you.

140

He should've come here earlier, when it was still a mess. "It all looks good," Toreth said with an effort.

Warrick touched his elbow. "So—now that you've finally made it here, we should celebrate."

"*Celebrate?*" Toreth looked sharply over his shoulder. "After what happened at I&I?"

"Yes. Close your eyes."

Obediently, Toreth closed them, and the strangeness of the new flat went away, or at least part of it. The background noises were new, too, he noticed now. The flat management system hummed quietly at a subtly different pitch, and somewhere in the building water tapped through distant pipes for a few seconds before stopping.

Warrick put his hands on Toreth's hips and turned him so that his back was to the sofa, then moved even closer, right up against him. His hair brushed Toreth's cheek as he leaned in. "We should celebrate," Warrick murmured against the side of his neck. "Because I could still be there, but I'm not. I'm here and so are you. That seems like an excellent reason for celebration. And a practical demonstration of gratitude."

"What—" He stopped as Warrick dealt effortlessly with the fastenings on his trousers, sliding down the zip and spreading back the fabric. Unfair distraction.

"Mm." Now Warrick was touching bare skin, exploring. "Well, this is *very* interesting."

"I ran out of clean underwear at Sara's. I meant to come here tonight anyway to pick up some more—fuck." He tried desperately to ignore the hand slipping down between his legs. "Warrick, I talked to Dillian. You were arrested at the airport."

Warrick withdrew his hand. A joint popped as he lowered himself to his knees, steadying himself with his hands on Toreth's thighs. "Ouch. All that unpacking did me no good at all. You need to get me back in the gym regularly."

Toreth took a deep breath, but he couldn't seem to open his eyes. "Did you see him in Strasbourg?"

"Shh." Warrick licked his cock once, slow and wet. "Later."

He was hard already. Of course he was, because it was Warrick touching him—Warrick, who knew exactly what he wanted and how he liked it. But he had to know how much of the truth Carnac had told. "Did you talk to him?"

"Yes, I did. It doesn't matter. He's not important."

And just for the moment Toreth was willing to believe him. He gripped the soft upholstery of the sofa and let his head fall back, and gave up thinking about anything.

Toreth sprawled on the sofa, waiting for Warrick to bring him a drink. If anything, the new furniture was even more comfortable than the old. Amazing how much more homelike the place felt after a stellar blowjob.

A mug appeared above him and he reached up for it. "Whiskey and water," Warrick said. "Sorry about the service, but I haven't unwrapped any of the crystal yet. The dining room furniture won't be here until tomorrow, and it didn't make sense to put everything away only to move it again."

Toreth took a mouthful. "Tastes the same whatever you drink it out of."

"Technically untrue." Warrick sat beside him. "The shape of the vessel affects the concentrations of organic volatiles over the surface. That alters the smell, which in turn changes the flavor."

Toreth stretched his arm out along the back of the sofa behind Warrick. "The sim?"

"Indeed. Modeling scent is challenging, to put it mildly. And very important, since it's one of the most evocative senses." Warrick leaned in and pressed his nose into the hollow of Toreth's collarbone, inhaling deeply.

I wanted to kill him, Toreth reminded himself. His arm slipped down off the smooth new fabric and ended up over Warrick's shoulders.

"We'll have to eat in the kitchen, I'm afraid," Warrick said, his voice muffled but his breath hot through Toreth's shirt. "As the dining room is out of commission."

"Let's order a takeaway Chinese and eat it in bed."

Warrick looked up at him, smiling quizzically. "In bed?" Before Toreth could reply, his smile broadened. "Why not?"

There was something incredibly comforting about sitting naked on a bed, with a naked Warrick, and opening takeaway cartons. True, there was a double-folded tablecloth on the bed, and a tray to hold the bowls and chopsticks, and coasters on the bedside table for drinks they hadn't even brought up yet. Even so, eating in bed was something they had done far more in his old flat than in Warrick's.

"Do you still want to hear about Strasbourg?" Warrick asked as he carefully folded back the last flaps.

"I don't know. Do I?"

"Carnac's new office might provide you with a certain amount of schadenfreude."

"Small?" Toreth asked hopefully.

"Tiny and incredibly cramped. He looked like a corporate refugee, and his entire staff consists of his sister. Socioanalysis has thrown him out."

Toreth couldn't help grinning. "Serves the bastard right."

"I imagine they don't want to get a reputation for bringing up traitors."

"Yeah. You'd think brainwashing him from the age of five they'd do a better

142

job of it. Cunt." He picked out a sticky tangle of deep-fried meat, chewed it thoroughly, and swallowed. "Did you get anything from him?"

Warrick seemed to be concentrating on his chopsticks, holding them together as if checking that the lengths matched. "A lot of warnings, once he worked out what I wanted and what I was planning to do."

"Nothing else?" Thank God for that. "Not that you could trust anything the bastard did tell you."

"He's not unreliable, within his limits. Like all of us."

Some more limited than others. Was he imagining the suggestion of that in Warrick's voice? Hard as he tried, Toreth couldn't avoid the memory of Carnac's farewell speech.

I know the details of the diagnosis in your psych file.

Toreth honestly tried to keep his voice light. "So, did you two have fun?"

"I went there to ask him about Tarin," Warrick said carefully. "Nothing more. I'd far rather never see Carnac again."

"But you did go to see him, didn't you? You went. You talked to the bastard."

"*Talked,* yes. And that was all. After what he did, and tried to do, I would have to be drugged unconscious before he could lay a finger on me."

As if a bastard like Carnac would balk at that. "So you say."

"If you want to check with Rob McLean, he was there with us almost all the time."

Pathetic, stupid...then his control was gone. "And McLean'll say what? Whatever the fuck you tell him to say. Why don't you just show me the script?"

"Do I make a habit of lying to you? Or asking my employees to do so?" Somehow he had the nerve to sound shirty about that. "Perhaps McLean isn't quite as reliable as independent professional surveillance—"

Not that, not now. "I promised—"

"But I think he makes a more convincing witness than, say, Sara." Every syllable rang clear. "Remind me, how many times have you called on her services to provide a cover story? If you can remember."

"It's—" It's not the same, because Carnac *mattered.*

Not that I imagine that makes you feel any less insecure or afraid of the idea of my being alone with Keir.

At the remembered words, his stomach tightened with still-fresh humiliation. Fuck it, he could feel his cheeks getting hot. McLean had been with them "almost all the time." Which meant not all the time, and it was so easy to imagine them together. He could tell himself a thousand fucking times that Warrick would never willingly touch Carnac, but if Warrick had wanted the information badly enough...

Oh, Jesus, yes. The P&P at work might have been cut down, but this could turn into a level eight argument.

"Do you want a drink?" Toreth asked. Without waiting for an answer, he slid off the bed, almost upsetting a couple of cartons. "I'll get beer. Something."

The longer trip down the stairs and the unfamiliarity of the kitchen gave him an excuse to take his time. He kept his mind blank—as blank as he could manage—because there was no way of thinking about Carnac that didn't leave him homicidal. Opening the fridge door, he found the beer bottles lying in a meticulously stacked pyramid, and he took one bottle to roll over his neck and face. He stood in front of the open door, ignoring the warnings from the system, feeling the slide of cool air over his skin until the last of the flush had gone and he started to shiver.

He put the warmed beer back, picked up two cold ones and closed the door. Find the glasses, open the bottles, pour. Nothing to worry about. Nothing. He kept the mantra up all the way back upstairs.

Warrick was waiting on the bed. He didn't look to have moved at all, or eaten anything, although he was still holding the chopsticks loosely in one hand. He was staring at the stained glass window, expression distant and thoughtful. He looked around, though, and raised an eyebrow.

"Here you are." Toreth handed over the beers and climbed back onto the bed more carefully than he'd left.

"Thanks." Warrick didn't say any more. He simply sat and watched Toreth warily.

Nothing to worry about. Nothing at all. "How did things go at SimTech?"

Warrick looked relieved to drop the topic of Strasbourg. "Lew and Asher were somewhere between delighted to see me and furious. I couldn't explain quite why I'd been arrested, but when we're feeling the financial squeeze it's the last thing SimTech needs."

"And news will be spreading."

"Of course. The corporate gossip network is terrifyingly efficient. The speed of my release will help."

"You are going to leave it alone now, aren't you?"

Warrick hunted through a carton and produced a straw mushroom, delicately pincered in the chopsticks. "I certainly won't risk the Cit Surveillance systems again."

"Another arrest would really fuck up SimTech."

His eyes narrowed. "I know perfectly well what's at stake. Not just SimTech—there's the rest of the family. You."

Me. Too fucking right, me. But Warrick's reply hadn't been a no. "But?"

"Everything I said before is still true. I owe it to Tar. I cannot let anything else happen to him."

"*Why*, for God's sake?"

"I've thought about that a lot lately. And . . . there are a number of reasons." He looked at the mushroom for a moment, then ate it. Toreth waited, but that was apparently it.

144

"Well, do I get to hear any of them?"

"Of course. The main reason . . . I knew for years, Toreth." Warrick shook his head. "I knew what Kate was, I knew what she was doing to him, and I let it go on because I was *afraid*. Oh, not just for myself. I did it for Jen and Dillian, too. For Philly, later, and then for Valeria. There were always plenty of justifications and excuses."

What the hell was he talking about? "What could you have done?" Toreth asked. "How old were you when you found out? Seventeen? She'd been running him for years, even then."

"I never tried." His voice was harsh with self-recrimination. "I never let myself even start to wonder if there was something I *could* do. Sins of omission."

"Sorry?"

"Something someone said to me. I'm sorry, Toreth, but I can't let this go."

"Carnac called me this morning."

Warrick frowned sharply. "He did what?"

"Called me at the office. Mostly because he's a prick, and he wanted to let me know where you'd been. Which, yeah, I have to hand it to him, that was a surprise, since *you* didn't fucking tell me where you were."

"Toreth, nothing—"

"But also because he wanted to know if I knew you were fucking about with Cit." Toreth took a deep breath. "Warrick, I think it's a bad idea, Carnac thinks it's a bad idea—why are you the only one who won't see that you're being suicidally stupid?"

"I made a mistake. It won't happen again. You have my word that I'll be more circumspect."

His voice had an icy determination that left a corresponding chill of dread settling in Toreth's chest. It also left Toreth with only one option, unpleasant as it was. "I think I have a lead on him."

"Really?" Warrick sounded surprised. "How long have you had it?"

"Not long. That's what the message I left yesterday was about, except that I couldn't leave anything explicit. I've got some names. Still nothing certain, but a start."

"I don't expect any help," Warrick said. "This has nothing to do with you, I appreciate that. If you give me the names, I'll take it from there."

"No. You'll just go right back to fucking around with systems you don't understand and if you get into hot water, I'll end up boiling right in there with you. Give me a few days. And while I look, *you* won't touch any fucking systems. Not Cit Surveillance, not the Data Division. Nothing. Okay?"

Warrick set down the carton and leaned back on his hands, examining Toreth assessingly. "Where did you obtain this new information?"

Justice's computer security wouldn't be as good as Cit Surveillance's, bu

145

Toreth didn't feel like taking chances offering them as a target. Being caught once didn't seem to have dented Warrick's self-confidence. "There was a witness at the school, and out of that I got hold of a couple of dozen names to check out. Can't tell you any more."

There was a brief pause. "You didn't say anything about a witness before."

"Yeah, well." He didn't have a justification beyond the obvious, so he didn't bother. "Look, I promise it's real information, and I promise it's a real chance to find him. But I need more time."

Now Warrick looked outright skeptical. "And if it gets nowhere, you'll tell me, of course. Just as you told me about the picture."

Fuck. "Of course. This time I'll tell you as soon as I know anything." Maybe.

This time the silence was longer, leaving the room quiet enough for Toreth to hear his beer fizzing quietly when he swirled the glass. Finally, Warrick grimaced. "I can't." As Toreth started to protest, he held up his chopsticks. "I promise that I have no plans to make any more attempts on Cit Surveillance, but I won't make any promises I can't guarantee to keep. If an opportunity presents itself, then I'll take it. I'm sorry."

So that was it. Impasse. Walk out, that was the traditional next step, and Warrick seemed to be expecting it. His gaze flicked over to Toreth's bags, lying against the chest of drawers, and Toreth could almost read his mind.

You didn't even manage to stay long enough to unpack.

Well, fuck him if he thought Toreth was that predictable. Toreth shrugged and drained his glass. "Well, okay. It's your funeral, among others. I just hope I get a chance to say 'I told you so' while they're cuffing me." He held out his hand. "Pass me the noodles."

For once he had the satisfaction of seeing Warrick utterly nonplussed. Warrick stared at his outstretched hand, then up to Toreth's face, as though he were speaking a foreign language. After several seconds, he picked the carton up and handed it over carefully, obviously waiting for the argument to start up.

"Thanks. Now let's eat before the food gets cold and the beer gets warm. And then..."

Warrick raised an eyebrow. "Yes?"

Toreth smiled. Not having a blazing row turned out to be easier than it looked. "Then I still have to think of something to give you for your birthday."

146

Chapter Fifteen

❖

In the taxi on the way in to work the next morning, Toreth did consider doing exactly what Warrick had so obviously suspected he would—nothing. If Warrick was pressing on anyway, Toreth might as well pretend to investigate for a few days before announcing that he'd found nothing. In the meantime, he'd try his damnedest to stop Warrick from causing more trouble. Maybe Cele could talk sense into Warrick if Toreth couldn't.

However, the best chance of stopping Warrick's lethal plans was to find Leo before him. More than that, the existence of the list nagged at him. A genuine, unpursued lead in an unsolved case, and one that he could even look into in reasonable safety. He had twenty names to check. The most logical way was to start with the most suspicious one and work down. Done with reasonable caution, that would fill a few days. As he studied the file again, he wondered if he would ever learn to leave well enough alone. Very probably not, he decided. Somehow, over the years, the job had got inside him.

It didn't take Toreth long to find what he wanted in the credit and purchase check attached to the Justice file. A bar—a regular drinking place for John Sable. As the taxi drove into I&I, Toreth made a note of the address, put his screen away, and called Warrick.

"Toreth?" Given that he'd seen Toreth only an hour before, Warrick looked predictably surprised. "Is there, ah, any news?"

"No. I'm just checking that you'll be busy at work today."

Warrick half smiled. "Very busy. There's a directors' meeting this morning, during which we'll no doubt decide to delay making unpleasant decisions for another few days. That should keep me out of mischief."

"Good. I'll see you this evening. I—" He hesitated, but the last thing he wanted was Warrick getting interested in where he was. "I might be late back tonight. It's work," he added. "Nothing to get alarmed about."

Warrick nodded, no trace of undue curiosity in his eyes. "I'll probably be working late, too. I'll see you when I see you."

By the time Toreth reached his stakeout for that evening, the weather had closed in, and a light drizzle dampened everything, blowing under awnings and into doorways.

Santiago's Bar was on the opposite side of the Int-Sec complex to I&I, conveniently close to the extensive buildings of the Data Division's Int-Sec branch. It was also packed with a Friday crowd buoyed by the start of the weekend. It looked like a respectable place, serving what smelled like good food. No doubt the main business came from lunchtimes and early evenings. From his c&p records, Sable followed that pattern.

The bar ranged along one wall, so Toreth bought a drink and took a seat at the end, which gave a view of virtually the whole place. The crowd was welcome. If the man was here tonight, there was that much more chance that Toreth would be able to take a first look at him without being spotted in return.

And if Sable was Leo Warrick, what then? Toreth wasn't sure. He sure as hell had no intention of walking up to a Citizen Surveillance agent and announcing that he knew who and what the man was. That was suicidal, even without considering the part where he asked Sable if he'd tried to murder his stepson.

He'd been there for an hour before he caught sight of his target. He'd missed Sable's entrance—the gray-haired, soberly suited man was already seated, alone, in a booth across the far side of the bar. Cele's drawing had been astonishingly good, considering that she'd been working without ident system assistance from a description given by a child witness.

Then Toreth saw Warrick. He stood inside the doorway, the light sprinkling of water on his shoulders already evaporating in the heat from the unit above the door. Must have come here in a taxi, Toreth noted automatically, because his shoes and the rest of his coat were dry.

Weirdly, the next thought that went through Toreth's mind was that he was dreaming. His brain had taken Leo's sudden reappearance, combined it with the memory of the post-Carnac evening when Warrick had dragged Toreth home from a bar and fucked some sense back into him, and twisted it all together into this nightmare. The helpless paralysis certainly felt like a nightmare. Warrick looked around the bar, his gaze moving over Toreth without giving any sign that he'd seen him, but as soon as he caught sight of Sable he stiffened. Toreth watched Warrick cross the bar, his gaze fixed intently on Leo. It wasn't a dream. How the fucking hell had Warrick got here? Followed Toreth? Somehow found the address himself? Not, please God, been back in the fucking Cit files?

It didn't matter right now. Warrick was already sitting down opposite Sable, who half rose, surprise plain on his face. Warrick started speaking, and given his recent record he was no doubt saying something stupendously stupid that would get them both killed.

What should he do? What *could* he do? Toreth divided his attention between his watch and the faces of the two men. They both sat in profile. Warrick was unreadably neutral; after the initial reaction, Sable looked perfectly calm, too. Probably planning how to have Warrick killed. Good job—or not—that the mob had dealt with most of Psychoprogramming during the revolt.

It took another two minutes before Toreth could force himself to stand. As casually as he could, he worked his way across the bar, keeping his face away from the pair at the table, until he could slot into the fortunately empty booth behind Warrick. "You're saying that you have no idea what happened?" Warrick said.

"No, I know the case very well. I've been watching the progress of the Transport investigation. The conclusion at the moment seems to be that there was a malfunction of the taxi guidance system, due to outdated software partially incompatible with the current Central Transport Division's traffic control systems. The rest of the company's vehicles are being examined. They seem to share the same fault, making sabotage unlikely. There may be a prosecution, if the corporation is found to be negligent."

"And then I suppose there'll be compensation for Valeria?" Warrick asked bitterly.

"Perhaps. I don't make the rules. I don't run Transport investigations, either. I'm just telling you what I know." There was a brief silence. "I'm grateful for what you did for Kate, but there are limits to what I can do and what I can tell you about—"

"No." Emotion cracked through Warrick's voice. "I'm a corporate. I live with risk every day. I understand it, I accept it. But I need to know that the others are safe. I have an obligation towards all of them, including Tarin. Especially Tarin. If they're in danger—if he's in danger—then there has to be something, some compromise, some way to avoid—"

"Keir," Sable broke in. "Please, listen to me. I understand your concern for your family and friends, but in this case it's badly misplaced."

"Citizen Surveillance isn't involved?"

"Officially, Citizen Surveillance doesn't even exist. But if it did, then I have no knowledge of *any* such activity. And, believe me, I have been watching the files."

"And that's all you have to say?" Toreth could hear the frank disbelief in Warrick's voice.

There was a long silence. "Keir, if . . . *if* Citizen Surveillance were involved, then I very much doubt that anyone's life but Tarin's would be in danger. The Administration protects its loyal citizens."

"I see." There was a long pause. "Then I don't think we have anything more to say to each other."

The booth creaked, and Toreth looked hastily away, grabbing a menu to scrutinize. Much too late, he realized he should have sat behind Sable, who was fur-

149

thest from the main door of the bar. Sitting here, they would both have to pass him on the way out.

"Goodbye, Keir," Sable said.

Warrick didn't respond. A faint shadow crossed Toreth as Warrick passed him, and he prayed Warrick wouldn't glance down. The footsteps didn't falter, and after giving it five seconds, Toreth lifted his head cautiously, keeping the menu high. He spotted Warrick at once, walking away across the bar. He didn't look back.

Then Toreth caught movement beside him, and glanced up quickly. Sable had left the booth, too, and Toreth wondered if he was going to follow Warrick. What the hell should Toreth do if he did? Follow both of them? However, after a couple of steps, Sable halted, within an arm's reach of Toreth. He stood perfectly still, watching his son stroll calmly out of the bar. Toreth studied him, trying desperately to read his expression. He stared a fraction too long, because the man looked down and caught his eye. Before Toreth could think of what he ought to do, Sable had taken a seat opposite him. "I'm sorry. Is this place taken?"

"No."

"Good." He turned away, surveying the bar with leisurely thoroughness before he added, "Do you know who I am?"

Toreth nodded mutely and wondered if he had time to get another drink before he died.

"Good. That simplifies things immeasurably. Is there somewhere we could go to talk? I have colleagues who may be along shortly, and it would be better for both of us not to be seen together."

Every instinct screamed "stay here!," but the protection would be largely illusory. Perhaps if he cooperated there might be a safe way out of this.

They walked down the street in silence, and then down a quieter side alley until they reached another bar—Gegi's. Toreth stopped outside and nodded to the door. "That okay?"

"Not somewhere I frequent," Sable said. "However, I had in mind somewhere more private."

"This is perfect, trust me."

Inside, Toreth turned to the nearest staff member and waved an attention-getting credit card. "Half an hour, please."

The sale went through unremarked and Toreth took the room number. As they headed for the stairs, Toreth wondered how many times he had done this. He always, previously, expected to survive it. In the room, he sat on the bed while Sable locked the door, checking it twice, then looked at his watch. "Half an hour?"

Toreth pointed to the comm by the bed. "If that's not long enough, they'll usually extend it, unless they're busy. Should be okay this early, even on Friday."

"I think that half an hour should be adequate." His cool voice sounded suddenly, startlingly, familiar. "You said that you knew who I was. Tell me."

150

What was the least he could get away with revealing? "You were outside Valeria Wintergreen's school on the day her father had his accident."

"Ah."

At once, Toreth had a very strong sense that he'd given the wrong answer. He thought about the other things he knew or suspected, and wondered if any of them would have been better.

Disturbingly echoing his thoughts, Sable asked, "Anything else?"

"Why don't you just tell me?"

Brisk shake of the gray head. "That would be unwise, for both of us. You have some dangerous hobbies, Para-investigator. As you may have heard me say, I've been watching the files."

"I thought it would bear some looking into."

"You didn't feel the need to request the case be transferred officially?"

"I didn't want to attract Cit Surveillance's attention. And…I didn't want to draw too much attention towards Warrick."

"Good." The approval sounded perfectly genuine. "I would hate to think that my son was involved with someone who didn't give *some* thought to his safety."

Well, that cleared up what Sable was willing to admit, and the tone of voice was perhaps a little less intimidating than it had been. "Believe me, it's been on my mind a lot recently."

"I can imagine." Sable smiled briefly. "Yesterday was rather stressful, but I expect that I had the best morning of the three of us. By the time I found out about the arrest, Keir had been released. So is there anything you wish to say to me?"

"Tarin's accident wasn't badly done." Toreth noted the brief flicker of surprise at the forthright assessment. "But you shouldn't have been there. It was too much of a coincidence."

"I had to make absolutely sure Valeria wasn't in the car when the incident occurred." His blunt tone matched Toreth's. "Katy would never forgive me if anything happened to her."

"It was still a mistake. If there are any more accidents, or Tarin dies and it looks at all unnatural, then Warrick is going to do his damnedest to find out who did it and to make sure they don't get away with it. He's looking already, you know that."

"If he pressed the matter, it would be unfortunate."

With grim amusement, Toreth wondered if a talent for understatement could be genetic. "Too fucking right. I've got no plans to end up on level C because Warrick's developing a taste for vengeance."

"How would you act to stop him?" The polite inquiry chilled him.

Toreth didn't rush to reply, giving himself plenty of time to try to work out the right answer. There probably wasn't one. "I'd ask him nicely not to."

That drew a dry chuckle. "And do you think that would help? If he's as much like his mother as he seems…" After a brief pause, he added, "In truth, I'm afraid it might

151

not matter. I had hoped Tarin's death would be enough to cut the connection. On its own, given time, it might have been, but events are happening outside my control."

Toreth's heart sank, if possible, even further. "Don't tell me his friends are planning something?"

"Not as far as Cit knows—but that's the problem. A certain amount of resister activity makes citizens glad of Administration protection, but the group Tarin associated with is too large and too well organized to be left uncontrolled. There will be arrests. I'm afraid it's become inevitable now that Kailynna is no longer monitoring the group. I've done my best to prevent it, but I'm only one man."

"What about the new Administration? Couldn't the council stop it?"

"Tarin's friends have rather more radical ideas than the new Administration is comfortable with. Before they were a highly valuable source of information; now they are a nuisance."

"Fuck." Thank you, Carnac. Toreth wondered briefly if Carnac would care that by exposing Kate he'd doomed a whole coterie of his precious resister friends. "What if they name Tarin?"

"That is the difficulty."

Footsteps sounded outside, a man and woman laughed as they passed the door. Toreth looked down at the floor, at the worn carpet, distracted for a moment by wondering if he'd ever had anyone in this room. Then he forced his attention back to the current problem. If Tarin's friends were arrested and they named him, Warrick would be fucked. A pity that Valeria wasn't old enough to take over her grandmother's role. Had that been Kate's intention? Pity, too, that Kate hadn't managed to bring Tarin up to spy willingly instead of having to use him as an unwitting—Fuck.

"How many people know about Tarin?" he asked slowly.

"Everything about him is in his file, and her file also. There are records of the operation."

"Yeah, but files can be lost. I mean—they could've been lost already, couldn't they? During the revolt?"

"Possibly. However, that wouldn't prevent Tarin's associates from naming him."

"No, but they might not know everything about him. What if he had been an active agent, if he'd been working *with* Kate? Not as an Int-Sec employee—that'd take too much fixing—but an informer. If that were true, then the accident would be a logical reason to bring the rest of the group in, wouldn't it?"

Sable's eyes narrowed. "Files would have to be altered...it could be done. But the investigation would very likely raise enough questions that the truth would come to light. The other resisters would certainly name him."

"Give me the case. Half my training is how to avoid planting ideas in prisoners by accident. I can do it deliberately. By the time I'm done they'll be convinced they've doubted Tarin for years. No one will know it's not genuine."

Sable gazed at him levelly. "Except you."

He swallowed, trying to keep his voice level. "I won't tell anyone."

"We both know that you cannot give that guarantee." His clipped voice sounded again very like Warrick's. "If asked the right questions, under the right circumstances, promises, however sincerely meant, cannot hold."

Toreth had to nod. It was something he'd spent his entire professional life proving.

"Still..." Sable rubbed the side of his neck thoughtfully. "I do believe you would have a powerful incentive to keep quiet."

My career, my freedom, my life. "Too fucking right."

"And besides, I've read—"

"My psych file." Irritation and relief loosened his tongue. "Yeah, yeah. You and the rest of the fucking planet."

Sable stared, then laughed. "Yes, I imagine it must be annoying."

Toreth shrugged. "I'm sick, but it pays well. What do you think of the plan?"

The faint noise from the bar below did nothing to soften the silence in the room as Sable gazed past him, contemplating the wall with complete concentration. Then he nodded. "I'm willing to take a chance on it, *if* you think it would be sufficient to stop my son from digging any deeper."

"Yes, it will." He'd convince Warrick or die trying. "With the right arguments."

"How can you be so sure?"

"He's not suicidal. And even if he was, there's Valeria—there's all the family. He won't put them in danger if Tarin is safe."

"And how does he feel about your safety?"

Toreth shrugged, uncomfortable with the basic idea and with the faint hint of threat he hoped he was imagining. "I couldn't tell you that."

"The last time—the only previous time—I spoke to him, he seemed concerned for your welfare. Well, if further reassurance is required, I will do my best to provide it. But hopefully he will trust *your* word that the danger is past."

Toreth blinked. "Yeah. I hope so, too." On the evidence of tonight, that wasn't a bet he'd want to take.

"Very well, then. I shall make arrangements. I may have to move quickly, so be prepared to be called in to take the case at any time. I'll begin the arrests as soon as the files are secure."

"I'll be ready."

"My influence at I&I is limited. If the case is given to someone else, we will all fall together."

"I'll be ready," Toreth repeated.

Sable nodded. "Then, if there is nothing more, I think it would be a good idea for us to go our separate ways." Without waiting for an answer, Sable opened the door and held it for Toreth. Walking past Sable—turning his back on him—sent a crawling sensation between Toreth's shoulder blades. The noise from the crowded bar below grew as they walked down the corridor, a reassuring beacon of safety and normality. God, he hoped there weren't too many more half hours like that in his future.

As they descended to the bar, Toreth felt a sudden, suicidal regret that he hadn't tried propositioning the man. He shouldn't want to—besides being significantly older than Toreth's usual range, he had a staunchly heterosexual air and Toreth didn't honestly think that he would get anywhere. The thought had a hypnotic fascination, though. He glanced sideways at Sable, abruptly absorbed by the idea of how he would look in bed, how he would look coming. The idea of stripping away Sable's poise and control appealed viscerally. An old, familiar urge.

Fucking Warrick's father.

Probably a good thing he hadn't asked. For one thing, if the man agreed, Toreth would never be able to resist telling Sara about it.

Warrick had seen Toreth as soon as he had stood up from the seat opposite Sable. How he'd kept the shock off his face, he didn't know. Thank God for years of practicing control in the sim. He'd waited outside the bar, watching them through the window, and then followed twenty meters behind as they walked to a new bar. Gegi's, the sign read.

Somewhere he'd never been. After five minutes outside, he'd risked venturing into the place. The bar was large and noisy, but he'd convinced himself he couldn't find them in there. If they'd left by another door he had no way of finding them. With nothing else to do, he'd got back outside, where watching the door seemed more likely to produce a positive result. Now he'd been waiting for more than fifteen minutes, attracting more attention than was probably safe although most of it was of the easily refused variety.

No one had lingered, and for that he was grateful for the miserable night. A recycling point a few meters from the bar's main entrance provided a bare minimum of shelter, but his hair was beginning to feel wet rather than simply damp. The chill wasn't helping his concentration. His mind was . . . well, certainly not a blank. But he couldn't get a grip on his thoughts, couldn't even begin to start setting them in order and making a plan. All he was certain of was that he had no intention of abandoning Toreth in there with—

Leo Warrick. John Sable. His father.

He couldn't connect the ideas, the people, together in his mind yet, and he wondered if he ever would. Leo, whose name had featured so prominently in his childhood: Kate and Jen's stories, the pictures, the belongings he and Dilly were sometimes allowed to play with. An illusion, but one that felt far more real than this, waiting outside a bar in the rain for a Citizen Surveillance agent to emerge. How long should he give it? What should he do if Sable left alone?

154

In the end, to his relief, they came out of the bar together. Toreth held the door open for Sable, who smiled politely and gestured for him to go first. Toreth closed his eyes for a second as he stepped out of the door, and Warrick wondered if he was expecting a gun or a knife. But there was no drama, nothing to differentiate them from the other couples who had left while he watched.

Couples. From his brief foray into the bar, it had been clear what kind of place it was. He couldn't help wondering whether Toreth would contemplate that, then decided he didn't want to know. Much of the trick with Toreth was knowing when it was better not to ask.

Warrick moved a little further back behind the recycler as both men looked up and down the street. Sable lifted his hand for a taxi, but Toreth caught his arm.

"Can I ask you a question?" Toreth said.

Sable nodded.

"Did you tell him who you are?"

"No. He told me." Sable smiled, warmly this time. It made him look almost like Cele's old portrait. Almost human. "I think, unfortunately, that I'm rather proud of him."

"Unfortunately?"

"Yes. I'm a servant of the state, Para-investigator. Emotions are an indulgence I can't afford. They complicate situations impossibly." He grimaced, turning away so that Warrick couldn't read the expression. "They cost too much."

The noise from the crowded bar came suddenly loud again as a group of young men left, making their way around Sable and Toreth without paying them any attention.

"My life would have been so much simpler if I had never met Kate," Sable continued when they had gone. "And the traditional qualifier is 'simpler but poorer.' Maybe that's so, but..." He paused for a moment, then shrugged and waved at a taxi. It cut through the light traffic and halted by the curb. "In the end, what's the point of wishing things had been different? We make our choices and have our accidents, and all we can do is live with the consequences. And pay the price. Goodbye."

Toreth stood with his hands in his pockets, watching as the taxi drove away. When it turned the corner at the end of the street, he turned and strode off quickly in the opposite direction.

The sudden departure took Warrick by surprise. By the time he'd started following again, Toreth had turned a corner, cutting through a short delivery yard into the parallel street. When he reached the street, Toreth was nowhere in sight. The pavements were busier here, people hurrying through the rain. Warrick searched the crowd for a blond head. Nothing. Had he crossed the road? Gone into a bar? Caught a luckily passing taxi? He picked left, as being the direction most towards the flat, and started walking.

A few seconds later a voice behind him said, "You're a fantastic programmer, but you make a fucking awful tail."

Warrick spun around, then relaxed. Toreth stood with his hands in his pockets, so ostentatiously casual that Warrick almost laughed. "You frightened me to death."

"Well, it'll save me from killing you the old-fashioned way." Despite his stance, Warrick realized, Toreth sounded furious. "You should leave this kind of thing to the professionals. What the *fuck* do you think you were doing?"

"What did it look like?"

"It looked like when you said last night you'd 'take an opportunity if it showed up,' you were lying through your fucking teeth because you already knew exactly where the bastard was."

Warrick dropped his gaze to the wet pavement, then looked up at Toreth. "Something like that, yes. I'm sorry."

"Which makes all the fucking difference." Toreth ran his hand through his rain-damp hair, slicking it back. Then he shook his head sharply, undoing the effect. "I should have guessed—no wonder you didn't give a shit about my lead. How the fuck did you find him?"

He'd hoped Toreth wouldn't ask that. "I had a lead, too."

"You—shit." His face twisted with dismay. "You got a name from fucking *Carnac*?"

"Yes."

After a frightening moment of silence, Toreth put his hands behind his back. Warrick saw his shoulders tense as he clasped his hands together hard. Not a good sign. "So much for fucking trust," Toreth said coldly.

"You were the one who said that information from Carnac wasn't reliable. Like you, I wanted to check things out before I did anything rash." Toreth drew a quick breath, but Warrick pressed on. "I did a credit and purchase check on the name and went to see if it was the right man."

Toreth groaned. "Cit must be watching the files, you do realize that?"

"They won't know it was me, I promise. I know those systems. There's no way they can trace—"

"They don't need to fucking trace anything." His voice was hoarse with the effort not to shout. "Jesus wept. You were there, in the bloody bar! You *talked* to him. Warrick, you shouldn't even have been in the place. It's too fucking dangerous."

"Are you working for SimTech security these days? If not, you're certainly beginning to sound like them. When I saw him—" Warrick paused, also trying to keep his voice calm. "Perhaps it was stupid, yes. But I had to know."

"And?"

"He denied he had anything to do with it."

"Did you believe him?" Toreth asked.

"Not for a moment. Whatever differences Tar and I have had in the past..." He shrugged one shoulder. "He's my brother, even if that man isn't his father. I refuse to let Tarin be dealt with like vermin because of whose son he happens to be.

156

I've never felt the need to indulge in corporate sabotage before, but something has to be done to stop Sable."

"*Kill* him?"

The bald statement made Warrick take a breath before he replied. "Yes, if necessary. Or to find something to hold over him. Perhaps even Kate's escape, if it was unauthorized. It worked for us with Alan Howes. It can work again."

Toreth looked away, frowning, his eyes fixed on the lights of the bar across the road. Cars passed, their tires hissing over the wet road, but Warrick didn't press him. "He spotted me watching after you talked to him," Toreth said at last. He looked back. "We talked about Tarin. We sorted something out—a way Tarin can be safe, if he survives. Something to clean up his name, get rid of the association to the resisters. But...fuck. Sable's in a risky position, too, and you have to stop pushing him. This once, let me fix it for you, on my own."

He sounded sincere, but then he usually did. "And I'm supposed to trust his good intentions?"

Toreth took a deep breath. "No. You're supposed to trust me." There were so many qualifiers and justifications that he could have added to that, but he didn't. He just waited.

Could he trust Toreth? Or, more accurately, did he believe him in this situation? Warrick was surprised by how much he wanted to say yes, to make the gesture, and he distrusted the feeling. Wanting to trust Toreth was not the same as that trust actually being realistic or sensible. However, for all his many, many faults and unreliabilities, had Toreth ever failed him over something this serious?

"Tarin will be safe?" Warrick asked.

"Absolutely. Now, and for however long it is in the future before he manages to do something else stupid. I can do it."

That decided him. "I promise" he wouldn't have believed for a moment. Toreth could make a hundred promises in a day and forget every one of them without a qualm. But a statement of ability was another question. "I can do it" made Tarin's death a matter of personal success or failure for Toreth, and more than anything, he hated to lose. So it was logic, not emotion, to nod, accepting the offer—to nod and see the relief in Toreth's eyes.

"I can fix it," Toreth said. "I will fix it. Just stay the fuck away from Sable from now on."

"You have my word."

"Great. Now let's get out of this bloody drizzle. I'm soaked."

It was flattering, Warrick thought as Toreth waved down a taxi, that someone whose own promises meant so little was so willing to believe Warrick's.

Chapter Sixteen

❖

Two days ago, sitting on the bed with Warrick, sharing food out of cartons, Toreth had felt at home. In fact, after they'd done the difficult conversation, they'd spent fifteen minutes discussing decorating before he'd even noticed. True, they'd been talking—yet again—about the exact best way to arrange the cabinet and curtains, but it was still pretty fucking domesticated as far as Toreth was concerned.

Two days ago, that was all. And now, today, it might as well never have happened. Toreth felt like a guest at the delayed housewarming, and a rather uncomfortable guest at that. Part of the problem tonight was that the mixture of other guests was almost disorienting. Their two worlds in collision. SimTech and I&I. A tall, bearlike man whom he vaguely recognized as Asher Linton's husband stood talking to Elena. Sara was flirting not terribly seriously with a young man Toreth had a feeling had arrived with someone from SimTech. Phil Verstraeten had his hands full carrying refilled wine glasses over to where Liz Carey appeared to be making friends with Jen. Toreth wondered where Cele was, and whether she'd finished the drawing of him yet.

There had been no news from Sable, and that hadn't helped. He felt as though he was waiting to catch something fragile, knowing that if he looked away for a moment he could hear the crash as it landed.

He felt a hand on his arm, and turned to find Dillian. "Can I have a word with you?"

If he'd been in a better mood, he would've managed something civil. As it was, he said, "I can't stop you."

"Have you seen Keir?"

"Not recently, no. Don't worry—I haven't murdered him and stuffed him down the waste disposal."

For a moment, she stood quite still, then she nodded. "There's no particular reason I should expect you to be polite, is there?"

He kept his voice low and even. "Not really, considering that the last time you wanted a word it was to tell me that you'd rather see me in prison than fucking your brother."

"Can we go somewhere quieter?"

"No, I don't think so. If you've got something to say to me, say it here." Some things he couldn't handle today, and a row with Dillian was one of them. Too many unforgivable things waited to be said that would put Warrick in a filthy mood if he ever heard about them—which he would.

To his surprise, Dillian didn't walk away. Instead, she stood, hesitating, then shrugged. "Fine. Here will do."

Fuck. Trapped in the open, he waited for whatever shit she wanted to fling this time.

"I'm not going to pretend I...no." She shook her head. "Bad start. All right— I don't know if you remember, but you told me once that as long as Keir wanted you, you'd still be around. I hoped for a long time that you didn't really mean that."

He laughed, not bothering to hide it. "For five *years*?"

She didn't answer that. Instead she looked up at him, her gaze steady, and said, "I want to say sorry."

Toreth stared, trying to parse the sentence in some way that made sense, then said, "You've got a funny fucking way of going about it."

"Yes, well—" She shrugged. "It's become a habit, I'm afraid. I do regret the way I've behaved before—some of the things I've said. To be perfectly honest, I still can't understand why Keir wants what he wants from you. I didn't—still don't—understand how you can..."

She trailed off, so he supplied the options. "Chain him up? Hit him? Fuck around?"

She winced slightly. "Yes."

"It's easy, really. I just—"

"Don't...I can't understand it. I'm not sure I'll even ever be able to accept it. But at the hospital, when you stopped Keir from going in to see Tar—that was very kind of you. And everything afterwards, after the arrest. And even if I overreacted a little to what you did with Val, I do understand that you were trying to make sure Keir was safe. And..." Dillian frowned, looking briefly so much like Warrick that he almost lost track of what she was saying. However much he disliked her, he still wouldn't say no if she ever offered.

"And everything that's happened," she continued, "it's made me realize that life is too damn short to waste it worrying about things I can't change. I spent so many years not liking Tar, and it never occurred to me that he could die and nothing would be put right. Stupid, but true. I can't bear the idea of ending up that way with Keir. Not about anything. Not even—" She stopped, but the words didn't need to be spoken. Not even you.

"Yeah, well, don't get worked up about it." Wanting the conversation to be over, he reached for standard, professional reassurances. "You'd be surprised how many people feel exactly the same in circumstances like that. More often than not, in fact. Perfectly natural."

She nodded. "Thanks. But it's not just the business with Tar. It's—" She waved her hand, indicating the flat. "I wasn't happy when he told me. But in a way, it does make a difference, knowing that he means this much to you. You're making a commitment to him by moving in."

Then she stopped, clearly expecting a response. The one thing that sprang instantly to mind made his hands clench, and this would be a very bad place to hit her.

Dillian continued, oblivious. "I can't fool myself any longer that he isn't different as far as you're concerned. That you don't really care about him."

Her words, so casually spoken, felt like a slap in the face, like a cruder echo of Carnac's venom. What fucking right did she have to say these things to him? "How I . . . what the hell has it got to do with you?"

"I only wanted to tell you that I—"

He grabbed her arms, squeezing tight, desperate enough to try that. Her eyes widened, her mouth still open on the last word, but at least it *was* the last. The effort of holding the anger back, of keeping his voice neutral, started a throbbing pain in his temples. "Shut up." He shook her arms, digging his fingers in tighter. "Just shut the fuck up and mind your own fucking business. What he wants has got nothing to do with you. He's—"

He's mine, but fuck it if he'd give her that much ammunition.

Out of the corner of his eye he saw Sara, scrambling down the stairs into the living room as quickly as she could without pushing people bodily aside. He daren't let her get to them—he wasn't going to let his anger with Dillian spill out and hurt Sara. Finger by finger, he forced his hands open, then walked away without another word. Behind him, he heard Sara's voice. "Dillian!"

Picking up a bottle of vodka from the table on the way past, he went off and locked himself in the cloakroom. There he sat on a pile of guests' coats, his heart pounding, drinking out of the bottle until he stopped shaking.

Once it had been all right. Back when it was just fucking, and how long ago had that been now? Before it turned into flats and families and next of kin and things he simply couldn't cope with. He couldn't do it. He couldn't live here. He'd screw it up, somehow, in the end, like he so nearly had just now with Dillian, and he and Warrick would have a row that couldn't be fixed by fucking. Then Warrick would throw him out, at least if Toreth instead hadn't killed him for his endless fucking *patience*.

This was enough. This was absolutely enough. Time to put a stop to it before things got completely out of control.

Toreth found Warrick in the study, sitting at the desk. He didn't look around as Toreth came in. After a moment, Toreth closed the door. "What the hell are you doing in here? Your f—Dillian was looking for you."

"I won't be long."

"What is it?"

As Toreth went over to the desk, Warrick pulled a file across it, hiding whatever he'd been looking at.

"What is it?" Toreth repeated.

"Nothing."

"Bollocks is it." Toreth reached over his shoulder and hesitated, his hand on the file, suddenly reluctant to know. Warrick didn't react, neither to stop him nor to encourage him. Long seconds of silence passed, then he lifted the file.

He really should have guessed.

"It arrived earlier," Warrick said. "Hand courier. There's a note with it. She says to let you know she's sorry she didn't have time to get it framed. She might be able to get here later, but she has a gallery opening she has to attend."

"Do you...what do you think?" What had Cele said about it?

"I think it's very good. But then all her work is. And the choice of subject is impeccable."

Toreth finally laid the file aside and stood looking at the finished drawing, his hands resting on Warrick's shoulders. What would Dillian say about it? "Why are you sitting in here?" he asked eventually.

Warrick leaned back, resting his head against him, making him think of the night at Kate's house. "I was trying to work out what you're looking at."

"And?"

"And I think I did."

Toreth didn't ask, and Warrick didn't elaborate. After a while, Toreth moved around to sit on the edge of the desk.

"Warrick..." Now that it came down to it, the words wouldn't come. He shouldn't tell him tonight, because he could foresee the most God-awful row or, more probably and more unpleasantly, an evening of frigid politeness in front of the guests until Toreth lost his temper and stormed out.

"What is it?"

"I can't live here. It won't work. I know you wanted to try it, but I'll just end up...or rather we'll end up—" The sentence was getting out of hand. He took a deep breath and went for the essentials: excuse, apologize, and shut up. "I should have said before, but I thought it would be okay. I'm sorry for...for the inconvenience." Christ, *that* was lame.

Warrick shook his head. "No real inconvenience incurred. I was telling the truth when I said I intended to move anyway and this flat is perfect. Thanks for letting me know. And I'm sorry if you feel I pressured you into agreeing in the first place—I didn't intend to."

And that was it. Toreth watched Warrick slide the drawing back into the sleeve Cele had sent it in and put it carefully away in a drawer. When he stood and turned there was an awkward moment of silence. Then he stroked Toreth's upper arm gently and smiled. "You look very nice. In the flesh as well as on paper."

"Thanks."

As they left the study, Warrick hesitated in the doorway. "You aren't planning to go now, are you?"

"Fuck, no. I'll stay 'til tomorrow." Why hadn't he waited until tomorrow to tell him? Or the day after? Or the week after? Or—

"Good. Did you say Dillian wanted me?"

They returned to the living room and the party. Once there, Toreth helped himself to another drink and waited for the sense of relief that stubbornly failed to arrive. He felt somehow cheated. Not that he'd wanted a huge, standup row over the issue—of course he hadn't. Even so, some kind of reaction would have been nice. Warrick could at least have *asked* him to stay, even though he'd have had to say no. The problem was that Warrick would've known he'd say no, which was precisely why he hadn't asked. Infuriating—but then Warrick so often was.

At least Warrick had taken it okay, or pretended to do so. His bloody patience again, or maybe Warrick had been having doubts, too, and he was relieved not to have to be the one to say something. The idea that Warrick might *not* want it, want him...

He found himself clenching his jaw, anger souring the taste of the drink. What irked him most was the fear that he'd really backed out because of Dillian, and even if he hadn't that she would *think* he had. God, she'd be happy about that. That on its own was almost enough to make him tell Warrick he'd changed his mind. Except that if he then changed it back, he'd look even more like an idiot. And what if Warrick didn't want him to stay there anyway? What if—

Forget it. He finished the drink and looked around for Sara, finding her talking to B-C. Looked as if her earlier target had made his escape while Sara was distracted. He worked his way over, summoning up a smile.

Chapter Seventeen

❖

The next evening, Toreth stretched out on Sara's sofa bed, finding the edges with his fingers and heels. Cracks. There were lots of cracks in Sara's living room ceiling, Toreth noted. Cracks and spiderwebs. The cracks were pretty evenly distributed, but the spiderwebs were in the corners. It all looked a very long way away and very close at the same time. If he reached out... of course, he couldn't touch anything. Arm raised, he traced a crack along through the air with his index finger. If he moved his hand quickly enough, there was a very slight blurring effect. Fun, possibly, in a very low-key and mellow way. It had been a long time since he'd taken any drugs that didn't make him want to fuck.

"Sara, what the hell is this stuff?" Toreth asked aloud.

"I don't know." Sara's voice sounded muffled, either because she was in the kitchen or because his ears were as fucked up as his eyes. "Why don't you ask her?"

The duvet was piled in a heap on the floor by the bed, and Daedra lay curled on it. She looked rather spidery, come to think of it, with her thin arms wrapped around her knees. Her plaits had slipped forward, covering her face in a faintly disturbing tangle, like thin bleached snakes. The one black plait crawled through the others. Bastard lay stretched out beside her, displaying scruffy folds of belly fur and looking as stoned as Toreth felt. He was purring, his lids almost closed, although Toreth could *feel* him watching. Daedra snored quietly in counterpoint.

"Can't," Toreth said. "She's asleep. But I feel weird."

"Weird?" Sara's voice sharpened suddenly. "Good weird, bad weird, sick weird, or paramedic weird?"

He looked over toward where her voice seemed to linger smokily in the air. She was peering anxiously around the kitchen door. "Good, I think."

"Mmm. Me too." Apparently reassured that he wasn't about to go into fits or throw up on any of her new furniture, she vanished again. Toreth blinked, watching her faint ghost fading out.

"What are you doing in there?" he asked.

"Looking for a drink."

"Get me something, would you?"

While he waited, he turned his head the other way and studied the vaporizer on the table. The oil in the clear bowl shimmered, currents curling around in it, driven by the heater below. He took a deep breath, trying to catch the smell, but like working on the interrogation levels, exposure had blunted awareness. Nothing sickly, though—it was spicy, with a hint of citrus, and he wondered if Daedra had scented the oil.

He hadn't forgotten the deal with Sable. On the table beside the burner lay a bag with wrapped injectors holding an antidote that Daedra swore would cancel out the effects in a few minutes. Without that, he wouldn't have agreed to the session, which would have made Sara as suspicious as hell. He couldn't recall the last time he'd turned down one of Daedra's special offers. And it was a huge fucking relief to turn his brain off for a while and destress, even if the relaxation was purely chemical. Sable, Tarin—everything was still there, but he didn't give a shit anymore. He vaguely remembered when his whole life had felt like that, but even that idea didn't cause any pain. Good stuff.

"I could put another drop in, if you like."

Under normal circumstances, he would have been startled by the closeness of Sara's voice. On the other hand, under normal circumstances he would have heard her approach. By the time he'd registered her presence and looked around, she was sitting on the bed beside his head, resting her elbow on the arm of the sofa. On a sudden whim, he wriggled around until he could put his head in her lap. She grinned. "Role reversal. Can I have your salary, too?"

He took the offered glass and raised his head to sniff cautiously. "What is it?"

"Citrus cordial. Lots of vitamin C."

"Thanks." He downed half the tart drink. "Ahh. What did you say when you came in?"

"I could put another drop in. In the burner. Or a couple."

What had Daedra told them? He couldn't remember the details. "She said the dosage was important. Something per cubic whatever per hour. I wouldn't fuck with it if I were you."

"Okay." Sara sipped her drink, then took a deep breath. "Nice of her to come up with something relaxing."

"Yeah." He waved vaguely. "It's even sorted out that fucking cat. You should keep some in a spray can and dose the bastard every morning."

For some reason, that seemed terribly funny. He was still laughing when Sara punched him in the ribs. Unfortunately, she caught him right in the last tender spot from the revolt. He jerked and splashed his drink over his chest, startlingly cold. "Ow. Jesus, watch what you're doing."

"Sorry." She rubbed his ribs gently. "Hey, I forgot to say welcome back. I'm going to have to start charging you rent."

"Yeah." That seemed funny, too. He grinned up at her, enjoying the novel view of her breasts. "You didn't even fold the bed up."

"I didn't get round to it. You've only been gone a couple of days."

He grunted agreement.

"And, well, okay, I did wonder if you'd be back."

"Huh?"

"With the housewarming yesterday. That seemed like a good time. I mean, if you were going to... well, you know. Bottle it."

"Bottle..." Even through the cotton-wool haze, the suggestion smarted a bit. What the hell was she talking about? "I didn't bottle anything. Couldn't. I never bottle."

"Of course not. So, just out of curiosity, why're you here while Warrick's sleeping all on his lonesome?"

Sound point. He did have to wonder about that, because while the drug wasn't revving his libido, his body liked the idea of another blowjob. Blowjobs always feel good—hadn't he said that to someone recently? Maybe Warrick would be awake when Toreth got home.

Something touched his hair, and he thought of spiders. However, it was Sara, gazing down at him expectantly. "I don't have to spend every fucking minute of my life with him," Toreth said.

"Sure," she said. "'Course not. Never said you did. But your suitcase is in the corner because...?"

Shit. He really had walked out that morning, hadn't he? He'd almost forgotten. But when he checked, the suitcase was indisputably there—the same one he'd taken from Warrick's months ago. And as he looked at it, everything came back. Warrick had been his usual patient self, which had only made it worse because by the time Toreth had finished packing, he'd been back to feeling that if Warrick asked him to stay he would.

No. He was better off out of there. Much better. A few days away, then Warrick would be settled in the flat and everything would be back to normal. All the ridiculous "our flat" rubbish would be ancient history. "I didn't *bottle* it," he said firmly. "I just decided it was a lousy idea. We'd drive each other mad in a month. If that long. Why wait until he throws me out?"

Sara was running strands of his hair through her fingers. "He puts up with an unbelievable amount of shit from you already. What could you possibly do that would be *worse*?"

"Well..." He stared at the cracked ceiling. "I could wait until bloody Dillian comes round one day, drug her stupid, then fuck her in front of him."

She snorted. "Yeah, okay, that would do it. But, I mean, really. What's going to go wrong?"

He didn't know and he didn't want to think about it. "Anything and everything."

"I think you should give it more of a try. Living with someone isn't *that* difficult. I've done it. And, um, okay, none of them lasted, but it was never the living together that screwed things up. I even stayed friends with them after." She frowned thoughtfully. "'Cept for the one who was a total jerk and stole stuff, too. Rick. Do you remember him?"

"Uh-huh." He certainly remembered holding the creep by the throat and bending him backwards out of Sara's flat window prior to extracting financial compensation from him.

"Never should've given *him* the door code in the first place," Sara continued. "Everyone said that. *Everyone.* But he was just so incredibly gorgeous that he sort of made my brain go stupid while I was looking at him. And God, he was so good in bed." She sighed. "Screwed like an *angel.* Hey, do you think maybe that's Warrick's problem?"

"What? Screwing like an angel? That's not a problem, trust me."

She giggled. "*No.* I mean, his problem with *you.* You make him go stupid." The idea seemed to please her. "You know, that explains it *all,* 'cause if I were him—"

"Sara," he interrupted.

"Yeah?"

"I appreciate it, really. Whatever the fuck it is you're trying to do. But just shut the fuck up, huh?"

"Okay." She smiled and smoothed his hair into place. "You can stay as long as you like."

Chapter Eighteen

❖

Not seeing Warrick for a while turned out to be a good idea on more than one level.

On Monday lunchtime, Toreth took his team out for lunch. Andrew Morehen had returned, with only a slight limp to show that his right leg from below his knee had been grown in a lab and grafted on. Everyone had crowded around him that morning, eager to greet him. And not just Toreth's team either, but what seemed like half the General Criminal office. The revolt was still a sharp enough memory that people were grateful for any sign that its legacy was diminishing.

Toreth didn't like the idea of leaving the office, but he had no highly active cases and it would've been out of character not to take the excuse for a lunch off the Int-Sec site. He did make sure that his comm was on, and on his way out he asked Kel to call him if anyone came looking for him.

As they walked across to the new, more solid security fence surrounding the Int-Sec complex, Toreth couldn't stop himself from thinking about the plan. How long would it take Sable to act? More importantly, how long would Warrick be willing to keep his promise? Toreth didn't doubt that Warrick had meant it, but suppose he discovered some new piece of information, or came up with another insane plan to do with Sable?

In one way, he'd chosen a brilliant time to leave Warrick's flat. Once Tarin's friends started to be arrested, Toreth would be grateful not to be there when Warrick found out. On the other hand, without supervision, Warrick could be doing anything. Right that moment he could be inventing some bullshit corporate-lawyer justification for breaking his promise. If he were arrested again, Toreth might well not be able to help him. And that was still a more optimistic outcome than if Warrick messed with Cit directly.

Toreth forced his attention back to the conversations going on around him. Usually, on a celebratory trip, people would still be talking about the completed case. On this occasion, with no case and no one particularly wanting to talk about

167

limb grafts on the way to lunch, conversations had wandered. Behind him, Nagra was talking to B-C and Mistry. "People aren't *all* idiots. Recruitment for the interrogation courses won't be back up for years, if ever. Who on earth would even think about joining I&I right now?"

Nothing new in that debate. He already knew she was edgy because the juniors were being pushed to take on more interrogation work and she didn't want to end up on the lower levels full-time. Nothing he could do about it except what he was doing already, which was fight to keep his team together and functioning as an investigative unit. Not for the first time, he wondered how things would have gone if he'd hung on to the Assistant Directorship after Carnac had gone. Badly, he expected, although it was all relative. Things weren't exactly fabulous right now.

He shook his head, and switched his attention to Morehen and Sara, walking a few yards ahead. The snatches of conversation and the body language proved interesting enough that after thirty seconds he closed the gap between them.

"We're going for a drink now." Sara sounded amused and she glanced up at the investigator.

"I meant, not with the team. You and me, on our own."

"And why would I want to do that?"

"Why ever not?"

"Andy, I met your girlfriend at the hospital when I came to visit you. Very blonde, very pretty?"

"Kira and I broke up last December." Morehen ran his hand through his hair. He'd grown it out while he'd been off sick, and Toreth wondered if the close crop would make a reappearance soon. Did he know that Sara preferred longer hair? "In fact, if we hadn't, I would've been on holiday in Amsterdam with her the day it all happened."

"So she was only visiting every day because she felt guilty?"

"Probably," he said, then paused. "Anyway, who said anything about girlfriends? I asked you if you wanted to go out for a drink, that's all."

"I've been asked out for more drinks than...well, let's just say a lot of them. I know what a drink sounds like, and I know what a date sounds like. And *you* know that I've always said I don't date at work."

"Actually, you've only said that occasionally. What you've *always* said is that you don't screw your b—" As he hit that dangerous word he glanced back over his shoulder, too quickly for Toreth to drop back to a subtle distance. Morehen colored and snapped his gaze away.

Without looking around, Sara said, "Which bar shall we go to, Toreth?"

"Café Seville," Toreth said. "Seems appropriate for today."

Morehen's neck followed his face's example by flushing red. Behind him, he heard Nagra laugh. "That's B-C's favorite, too," she said.

Despite its southern name, the bar's trademark was its tall, extremely blonde and uniformly stunning waiting staff, male and female. Whether they were all natural blondes or whether bleached applicants had a chance, Toreth had never established, although the shortness of the uniform's skirt or shorts meant it was nearly possible to check.

Toreth grinned and dropped back. Even if Morehen wanted more than a drink with Sara, he was out of luck tonight. He wondered if she'd tell him that Toreth was staying in her flat. Really, it wasn't surprising that rumors about the two of them had made the rounds of the I&I gossip network for so long. Suddenly he thought of Harry Belqola, back in the SimTech investigation, provoking Sara's ire with his tactless assumptions. Had Belqola survived the attack on I&I? Toreth didn't remember seeing his name on any lists; maybe he'd resigned or been transferred elsewhere in Europe long before the revolt.

Behind every random jump in his thoughts, he could feel the tension drawn tight. When would the call come? Once the arrests started, Toreth knew he'd feel better. Then it would all depend on his own skills, and he didn't believe in false modesty. He could do what was required. But could Sable? And if Sable failed, what the hell could Toreth do next?

"Toreth? Hello? Anyone in?" Sara sounded amused.

They'd reached the bar, and he had ground to a halt, staring into space. With an effort, he pushed the worries aside. "Sorry. I was looking at the shutters again."

The others looked blank, but Sara nodded. He'd mentioned it to her the last time they'd been here.

Reasonably priced drinks and decent tapas, combined with its proximity to the I&I exit from the Int-Sec complex, made the Seville a popular drinking place for Int-Sec staff in general and I&I in particular, sufficiently so that it had been targeted in the revolt. The owners had stoically repaired and refurbished, adding heavy steel security shutters painted to look like sun-bleached wood. They were something which would have been unthinkable this close to Int-Sec before the revolt. Today the shutters were folded back to let in the spring sunshine. Still, they were a constant reminder that short-lived as the revolt had been, its scale and violence had shaken everyone in the Administration, not just the heads of department and the socioanalysts.

Inside the bar, the medley of music and voices seemed no different from the time before steel shutters had become a necessity for peace of mind. "I'll buy," Toreth said.

He asked for orders from the team, barely listening. He knew what everyone there drank. So did the man behind the bar, whom Toreth recognized although he had no idea of his name. There was already a lager under the tap for B-C, and he was making Mistry's invariant vodka and orange—her celebration drink, because she didn't like alcohol but she felt she had to fit into the group. We're all creatures of habit, Toreth thought as he watched. We all like a routine. God, he hoped that he'd be able to have one again, soon.

"Pernod and coke—" Nagra's disgusting selection, "—and a G&T." Toreth glanced around to where Sara was involved in a comm conversation. "Make it a double. Whiskey and soda for me, and a glass of mineral water—that's all." The last item threw the man very slightly. Toreth grinned. "He's still on the antibiotics."

Just as Toreth paid for the drinks, his comm chimed. He listened while Jenny relayed the message, and tried to keep the nervous flutter of anticipation out of his voice when he replied. After he pocketed his earpiece, he eyed the whiskey, thought about downing it, then left it on the bar. "I have to go," he said to Sara. "Tillotson wants to see me about a new case. You carry on without me. Don't be too late."

"Okay." With no idea of the significance of the summons, Sara's attention was already wandering back to Morehen. "I'll bring you something back for lunch."

The head of section looked annoyed, but he still seemed to feel obliged to offer Toreth a coffee. Toreth wondered how long the aura from his temporary assistant directorship would last.

"Have you been doing work for another division without my knowledge?" Tillotson asked.

For once Toreth didn't have to fake innocence entirely. "No, of course not."

Tillotson picked up a hand screen and waved it as though there were an especially annoying fly in the office. "Then why did Citizen Surveillance call me and *demand* that I assign this case to you?"

Toreth accepted the screen warily. He took his time looking through the file, but the information he needed had been helpfully placed near the front. Thank you, Sable. "Oh, right," Toreth said. "I followed up a tip-off, and I accidentally crossed paths with an ongoing Cit Surveillance investigation." He smiled at Tillotson's alarmed expression. "No need to panic. I called someone up and sorted it out quietly. Unofficially. I suppose this is their way of saying thank you." Letting the section head think that Toreth had friends in Cit Surveillance wouldn't hurt. It was possibly even true.

Tillotson took his time digesting the information. When he spoke again, the edge of irritation was gone. "Yes, well, from what I saw, it should be simple enough—there's a mass of evidence already, so all they want is for you to secure confessions, get as much additional information as possible, and pass a watertight case to the Justice system. I said that an interrogation team could handle it, but they asked particularly for you to take it."

"Like I said, it's a gift. Nice, easy case to wrap up—it'll be good for the section. And it'll annoy the hell out of Political Crimes."

"Mm." Tillotson examined him carefully, then nodded. "They were quite insistent about the watertight aspect."

"I'll do my absolute best, sir."

Tillotson had no idea how sincerely he meant that.

Warrick was fortunately alone in his office when the call came through. He was surprised to see Jen—he couldn't remember the last time she'd called him at work, and she looked more panicky than he'd seen her since right after the accident. Then the obvious explanation hit him. "Is it Tar?"

"Yes. I mean, no, there's been no change for the worse. But I had a call this morning—three calls. People have been arrested. Friends of his. It happened last night, everyone taken at the same time. And—they're saying it's I&I."

"Shit." And then, reflexively, he said, "Sorry."

"I think even Kate would agree that it rates an expletive. What should I do?"

"Hold on. I'll call Toreth."

While he waited for the connection, he wondered what the hell he could do if this wasn't part of the plan. Probably nothing. At least, in a way, Tar was safer at the hospital. He tried not to think about Toreth's story of interrogating his burned witness.

To his surprise, although he'd called Toreth's personal comm, Sara answered. "He's not available. Can I help?" she asked brightly, so much the admin that she almost looked like a stranger.

"I have to speak to Toreth in person. It's urgent."

Her expression didn't flicker. "Is this about your brother?"

He hesitated. "In a way, yes."

"I thought so. He said not to worry, everything's under control, just like he said before."

Warrick waited for a moment, but she seemed to have finished. "That's it?"

"That's the whole message." She sounded piqued that he'd suggest otherwise, but again the mask stayed in place. He thought of the open-plan office, of all the people who might be watching.

"Can I speak to him?"

"No. He's got a new case. He's down in interrogation right now. A big group of resisters were brought in this afternoon and he's running all the interrogations personally."

Oh, God. "Thank you," he said automatically. If she replied, he didn't hear it.

He stared at the blank screen. Everything was under control, just like Toreth had said. That could mean only one thing. Sorting something out, a way that Tarin could be safe, his name clean with no association to resisters—this had to be it.

When Toreth had said it, Warrick hadn't imagined anything like this. Lost files, maybe, or bribery or threats. He should have pressed harder, asked for more details. What could he do about it now? It took only a few seconds' thought to supply the answer.

He returned to Jen, swapping the connection to the strongest corporate grade security SimTech possessed.

"Well?" she asked.

"Yes, it's definitely I&I."

"Should I call anyone? Warn any—"

"*No.*" He interrupted without thinking. "For God's sake, no. Whatever you do, don't get involved. Just...let things take their course. Tar's perfectly safe, I promise. Toreth will make sure his name is kept out of it. There's nothing to worry about on that score."

She searched his face. "You're quite sure?"

"Yes. And if he isn't, there's nothing anyone can do about it now."

Toreth stood in the gray corridor outside the interrogation room, taking slow, calming breaths and ignoring the curious looks from the guards. Hundreds of prisoners over his career, thousands of hours of interrogations, and few of them had been as important as these ones. The first man he'd selected should be the easiest, but if he didn't get it right then he'd lost one of his best chances.

When Toreth opened the door, the prisoner at the table didn't look up. Seeing the name on the prisoner list had been a surprise in one way, and in another so logical Toreth wondered why he'd never considered the connection before. He crossed to the table and dropped his hand screen on it. "My name is Para-investigator Toreth. But you already know that."

Now his head snapped up, his eyes widening incredulously. "You?"

"Hello, Mr. McVade. We have a lot to talk about this time. An awful lot of information for you to go through and confirm for us. Or correct." He smiled coldly. "Think of it as marking homework."

McVade straightened in the chair. "Who was it? Who betrayed us?"

God, he could have kissed the man. "Do you remember my little visit? When I said I'd been talking to one of your pupils? Well, Valeria Wintergreen was the good citizen then, and she's the daughter of good citizens." He watched the implication sink in, then sat down. "Shall we get started?"

172

Chapter Nineteen

❖

Sara authorized the transcript of the previous interview, then switched on the screen to watch the progress of the latest one. It should be finished soon, which meant yet another transcript and yet another late night. She wouldn't complain about it.

Toreth stood in front of his prisoner, listening to her confession, turning an injector over in his hand. Given that he must have read the terms of the waiver out to the woman, it was amazing how he still managed to give the impression of having available near-limitless unpleasant options. Sara wondered how long it would take for the reputation of I&I to fade to the point that simple fear of the uniform would no longer work as an interrogation tactic.

Without consciously noticing, she nibbled the last patch of nail varnish from her thumbnail and moved on to her index finger, worrying at a chip on the edge. What was going on down on the interrogation levels? After three days, she had no more idea than when Tillotson had so suddenly assigned the case to Toreth. Kel had asked her about it again at coffee that morning and she'd had to say she couldn't tell him. She couldn't admit that she didn't really know. She knew that whatever it was had something to do with Warrick's brother. She knew Citizen Surveillance had asked for Toreth specially—Jenny had told her that but hadn't known why. And that was all she knew.

Toreth had given her the orders on the first day, once and once only; he'd put nothing in writing. "I want every part where Tarin Marriot is accused of being or implied to be an informer. That's the single most important thing. Even if it doesn't have high direct evidential value, it goes in. Got that?"

She'd nodded, expecting that he'd say something about *why*. To start with, why he was handling the case at all, given the rules about personal involvement with prisoners. However, that first conversation had also been the last one that hadn't dealt purely with the details of the case. She'd barely even seen him since, despite the fact that he was still sleeping on her sofa on the nights he came home at all.

Although she tried not to, although she told herself Toreth knew what he was doing, she worried about not understanding the case. If she wasn't up to speed, how would she spot if she messed up the transcripts? How would she know if something on the admin network was relevant, or if there was danger from somewhere inside the division? Most of all, she wished he'd tell her because she wanted to know that he still could.

What had he told her, really, since Carnac had left? He'd come to her flat too stoned to know where he was and she'd fucked that up by trying to give him something he couldn't accept. He'd told her about moving in with Warrick, except that he'd let that slip by accident, and she'd messed it up in two seconds flat. Outside the things which really mattered, he was as friendly with her as he'd ever been, but that meant nothing at all because he could socialize flawlessly with people he'd happily see dead. Carnac had been right about one thing: all that made her different was that he trusted her. Had trusted her.

He was just her boss, that was all. It seemed a very long time since that had been the mantra she'd lived with. Not a friend—just her boss, just a para. Not, supposedly, someone who could care at all, or be hurt. Well, the division psych assessors could take their para profiles and stick them where the sun didn't shine.

On the screen, the guards were helping the woman up from the chair, and Toreth glanced up at the camera. The corner of the screen indicated the feed was no longer an active interrogation, so Sara closed it and got back to work.

Before she began the next transcript, she checked the messages, first her own and then Toreth's. With him down in interrogation all day, she'd tried to keep his inbox as empty as possible. She scanned down them, sorting them rapidly into things she could deal with and things he would want to see, until she hit one which made her stop.

To Warrick's great relief, Cele had offered to come to the hospital with them. She stood close beside Dilly, her hand resting in the small of Dilly's back. She'd provided calm, silent support while Dr. Caillat went through the treatment options for the last time. Warrick had taken charge of Philly. She kept her eyes fixed on the tank, never looking away, rarely even blinking.

The last of the sickening mess of burned flesh had been concealed since Warrick's last visit. The synthetic skin matrix covered Tarin, smooth, hairless, wrinkled and folded in odd places. It—he—looked nothing at all like Tarin. Tarin had had a mole on his thigh, Warrick remembered. He remembered more than he would have guessed from their childhood together, about Tarin as he'd been as a teenager and a young man, when he'd seemed so much older, so grown up. All in the distant past, before Warrick had made the mistake of looking on Kate's computer.

174

If it was a mistake. Looking back on it, he couldn't decide whether or not he wished he'd had the sense to stay away. How would things be different? No one could say, and he certainly didn't know that they would be better. Would Kate still be here, or could things have gone worse for all of them?

Cele nudged him gently, having obviously noticed his abstraction. When he glanced at her, she raised her eyebrow and he smiled reassuringly.

The medic paused fractionally at the exchange, then carried on. "Right now the tank system is keeping Tarin breathing, or at least helping him to breathe. It's taken over the functions of his brainstem. It's been several days since the last of the edema subsided and we've finished the matrix layers, which means that now is a good time for us to consider disconnecting the substitute stem system."

"Then what happens?" Philly asked.

"Hopefully, Tarin will keep breathing on his own. All the scans we've taken indicate that he should. There was some damage to parts of his brain, but the regrowth stimulators seem to have worked very well. We've done everything we can to make sure that he's capable of breathing unsupported. The only thing left is to let him try."

Philly nodded. "I need to think about it."

"Take all the time you want."

Warrick had seen the brain scan results himself. Caillat had been predictably surprised that he knew how to interpret them, so he'd told her about the sim, which shared technology with the ICU tank. They'd talked about the sim for a while, about potential medical implications, while Tarin lay in the tank, unconscious and immobile. If the tank was as sophisticated as the sim, they'd be able to talk to Tarin and ask him what he wanted. If, that was, the damage to his brain had been limited enough to make that possible.

"If he can't breathe, what then?" Dillian asked.

"This isn't an absolutely irreversible decision," Caillat said. "The autonomic management can be restored, if it's done quickly. But there is a chance that the reactivation will fail at that point. If that happened, we would have to take more drastic measures to directly stimulate the necessary pulmonary nerves."

"No," Philly said.

"I beg you pardon?" Caillat asked.

Philly was looking at the tank again. She shook her head minutely, her gaze never leaving Tarin. When she spoke again, her voice was barely audible. "I don't want that."

Warrick took a step towards the medic. "She means that if Tarin stops breathing and the brainstem substitution doesn't function again, then it finishes there," he said quietly. "That you'll let him go."

"If you could speak up, Ms. Wintergreen," Caillat said. "For the recording system."

She nodded, then cleared her throat. "Yes. That is what I meant." She nodded again. "I'd like you to do it, please. To switch off the system."

"I'll do it now."

There was nothing to it—a few changes on the screen, with no visible response in the ICU tank, no reaction from Tarin. They waited in silence for long minutes until Caillat turned to them.

"It looks like he's handling the switch well, although you know that I can't make any guarantees." She glanced away for a moment to check the screen. "It will take a few hours until we're absolutely sure, but this was a big hurdle, so we can all be pleased he's cleared it."

"I'll wait," Philly said.

"You're welcome to stay here, of course. I'll have to leave soon, but I can send in someone to sit with you."

Warrick crossed the last distance to the tank and touched the warm plastic with the palm of his hand. He didn't, he realized, feel as relieved as he'd expected he would. Of course this wasn't any kind of resolution, just one more step on the long journey that could still be cut short. Infections, any one of dozens of other medical dangers, and the outside threats from Sable and Citizen Surveillance that were fortunately still unknown to most of those gathered in the ICU.

A single sob caught his attention, and he turned. Dilly was crying, hand to her mouth to stifle the noise. "I don't want him to die," she said brokenly. "I don't. He can't. It's not *fair* if he dies."

If only that made any difference.

"He won't die," Philly said firmly in what Tarin had always called "that damned teacher voice," and Warrick realized that he hadn't seen her cry once since the accident. Did she really believe Tarin would live?

"I want to tell him I'm sorry," Dillian said. "I've said things to him before and—I want to tell him I love him and it didn't matter, all the rest. I just—" She wiped her eyes with the heel of her hand. "I'm sorry, Philly."

She turned away towards Cele, who gathered her in her arms. "You cry, sweetheart. Nobody minds."

"I wanted to tell him I loved him," Dillian repeated, her voice muffled by Cele's shoulder.

"I'm sure he knows," Philly said, and Warrick wondered if he was imagining the deliberate stress on the present tense. "And he loves both of you. He always did, even when you disagreed." Philly looked at Cele. "I think she'd be better somewhere else, don't you?"

"Come on." Cele urged Dilly towards the door. "We can come back tomorrow. Tar's not going anywhere, is he?"

There was a moment of appalled silence, then Dilly started to laugh, still sniffing. "No, he isn't."

Dr. Caillat followed the pair of them out of the room. When the door closed, Philly shook her head, smiling slightly. "She's amazing."

176

"Cele? Yes, she's certainly that."

"I have to ask you something, Warrick." The smile vanished and she looked directly into his eyes, then stepped up close and lowered her voice to a bare whisper. "Now that it looks as though there might be a chance, is he safe? I heard about the arrests."

"He's safe." Or, at least, I hope to God he is. "Toreth is doing his best to protect him—and all of us. Tar won't be named."

"Because mud sticks," she murmured.

"I'm sorry?"

"Nothing." She stood up straighter. "I'll have to thank him, when I have a chance. Which will be strange, don't you think? When I&I will also be responsible for whatever happens to some people I've known for a very long time."

He didn't have an answer to that.

When Toreth finally came back upstairs, Sara was still working at her screen even though it was long past the time she should've gone home. A coffee waited for him on his office desk, and he sat down and grabbed it. Double-check the interrogation lists for tomorrow, and then they could go home.

Movement made him look up. Sara was hovering by the door. "You didn't need to wait for me," he said. "I know the way to your flat by now."

"A message arrived, earlier," she said.

Toreth sighed. "Fuck. I hope this is something good. You have no idea how badly I want a shower and something to eat right now."

"Well...it's from your mother."

The first time, after the revolt, only surprise had made him hesitate. "Tell her to piss off."

"She wants—"

"Do I look like I give a shit?"

To his surprise, she stood her ground. "She wants to see you."

For a second he almost asked to see the message, but Sara had no reason to lie. About to repeat his previous instruction, he stopped, hit by a sudden insistent feeling that he was missing an opportunity. Of course—the dangerous topic everyone knew better than to bring up. Could this be a chance to undo some more of Carnac's precious handiwork? "That'd be a first," he said. "Unless she's finally lost her last fucking marble. She isn't calling me Angel Baby, is she?"

"No." Despite the curiosity plain on her face, Sara didn't ask.

"My brother," Toreth said, and left the opening dangling as he watched her, waiting for the response.

She took the bait. "I didn't know you had a brother."

"Not many people do. You remember their flat, the pictures on the wall? That was him. He's dead."

"Oh. I'm—" She stopped. "I'm sorry," maybe? Whatever remained unuttered seemed to block any other response. "Oh, I see."

Toreth sipped his coffee. Pull gently, so they don't feel the hook, that was the way. "We went out to a park on my birthday," he said eventually. "My fifth birthday. He and I wandered off and—" he shrugged. "There'd been a lot of rain that summer, supposedly, so the river was high. Some woman saw us in the water, dived in, and grabbed me. By the time she'd hauled me out and gone back, he'd been swept away. They found him a couple of days later, caught in a backwash under a weir."

Unsure exactly how to pitch the story to get the reaction he wanted, he kept his voice neutral. Perhaps he'd overdone it; Sara seemed to struggle for a response again. He was about to add something more, to prompt her, when she said, "It must've been terrifying."

"Yeah, I suppose so. Although I don't remember it. Nothing at all. Not even us falling in—however that happened." He shrugged again. "Some people thought I pushed him in."

"And—" She bit off the question, but Toreth answered it anyway.

"I might have done. But . . . " He shook his head. "How the hell would I know? She thought I did."

"You mean, the woman who rescued you? Or your . . . ?"

His stomach tightened up unexpectedly, old anger and new. "Yeah. Her." He stood up suddenly, forced into movement. Sara flinched, and he thought for a moment she was about to flee. Annoyed with himself on a new level, now, for breaking the mood, he pressed on, driving the words out as he paced.

"I saw it every time she looked at me. She hated me for taking her fucking little angel away, but later on, as I grew up, I frightened the shit out of her. Her own fault, the stupid bitch. If she hadn't spent so much time convincing herself I'd killed him . . . " Toreth shook his head, trying to stay focused on now, on giving Sara something she'd have no choice but to believe in. "That's why when I stabbed that kid and Justice sent me to the retraining facility, they didn't even try to appeal. They were glad to see the back of me."

"They didn't do anything?" Sara put her hand up to her mouth as the appalled protest escaped.

"Well, Gee told me she'd made a private representation to the Justice system. She wanted me locked away. She said, when she looked in my eyes, she saw someone capable of killing." He laughed. "Which, yeah. When I was looking at her. You've seen the flat. Do you know, they never touched his room? Probably still haven't."

Sara nodded. "I remember the photos, and the flowers. I remember . . . " Her voice trailed off uncertainly again, like she was afraid of saying the wrong thing.

Wasn't that enough proof for her, yet? It was all she'd get today, in any case, and he was already regretting the impulse. Toreth breathed in deep, trying to force out the tension from his body. This had been a bad idea. He wanted to hit something, and the real target wasn't here. And the anger was making him unprofessional. Close the connection down, that was the rule. Tie it in, bring it back to where the session had started, so that they wouldn't suspect you were deliberately building confidence. "So whatever the fuck she wants now, I'm not interested."

"But what do I say to her?" Sara asked. "I already told her before you didn't want any more messages."

"Delete her messages and forget them. Tell her I'm dead." Toreth turned away, jerking his jacket off the hook so firmly that for a moment he thought he might have torn the collar. "Do whatever you have to do to get rid of her, just don't waste my time with it again. Now, come on. Let's go home. I'll buy dinner on the way."

Chapter Twenty

❖

Toreth still hadn't called, and Warrick honestly didn't know whether he wanted to hear from him or not. Good news would be reassuring, of course, but when good news probably meant "the interrogations are going well," it would still be hard to stomach. And bad news would deliver itself, one way or another. Warrick had thought about working at home until whatever happened happened, then had discarded the idea. If things went wrong, if he were arrested again, then where it happened would make no significant difference to SimTech.

After lunch, which he ate in his office, Warrick went down to the research suite again. He had a meeting scheduled later that afternoon with Asher and Lew, which meant decisions to take that he'd really rather avoid. He couldn't, of course. He couldn't let his personal problems, however currently impressive, damage SimTech. He could, however, avoid thinking about the meeting until he absolutely had to.

The gingerbread house room he'd taken Toreth into had been completed, and he'd accepted Silis Reddick's offer of a guided tour. She seemed flattered by his presence, and he tried to give her and her work his full attention. The room more than justified the lead programmer's obvious pride. For once, though, Warrick couldn't see the room in technical terms. What would the team from this project do next? The fairy tale series of rooms had paid for itself and coincidentally been a technical challenge, but whatever Asher said, it would upset the programmers to have to close down some of the more experimental research.

After he'd walked around the gingerbread house and nibbled furnishings and fabrics, he followed Silis out into the sugary garden.

Silis was one of the most average women Warrick had met. He'd once described her as such to Dillian, and then had to spend ten minutes unsuccessfully explaining that he hadn't meant it as an insult. Dillian had insisted it was a perfectly awful thing to say about a woman, so he'd never used the description again. However, she was absolutely and literally average—in height, in weight, in her midbrown hair and undistinguished blue eyes. Warrick wondered if it was one reason she had taken so readily to designing outlandish sim rooms. What would she think of cutting back to focus on commercial simulation and sex industry applications?

"Here," Silis said, and whistled. A multicolored bird flew down from the roof and perched on her hand. Silis stroked it for a moment, then jerked out two tail feathers, one purple, one yellow. The bird cocked its head and squawked. "Off you go," Silis said, and it flew away to perch in a toffee-apple tree.

She offered Warrick the feathers. He took the purple one and sucked it experimentally. It didn't dissolve, but it did taste strongly of plum brandy. "Different flavor for each feather?" he guessed.

Silis nodded, twirling her own feather. "This one is Advocaat." She looked around the garden. "There are marshmallow rabbits somewhere, too. Kind of shy at the moment, but once you get hold of one it's snuggly as hell and they taste great. Perfect for kids."

The idea of taking a bite of a still-moving rabbit, even a virtual one, seemed mildly disturbing. "I don't remember mammals and birds in the contract."

Silis's enthusiasm abated slightly. "Er, no. But we were ahead of schedule and under budget, so I thought a couple of extra touches might go down well. The artificial life suite people loved the idea."

"I'm sure they did. And I'm sure the customer will be delighted, assuming they wish to teach their children to eat live vertebrates."

"Ah." Silis looked at the yellow feather in her hand. "I didn't . . . well, we just thought it would be cool."

Programmers, he thought irritably. "Major object additions have to be cleared by the project manager, you know that."

"Okay. Yes, I do know. I'm sorry." She looked up sheepishly. "Um . . . does this mean you don't want to see the sugar mice?"

"Sugar . . . ?"

Silis reached into her pocket and produced a squirming handful, which untangled itself into three life-sized mice which were, indeed, made of pink sugar. Not the smooth, amorphous mice that could be found in patisseries, though. These were clad in spun-sugar fur and had bright pink eyes and twitching whiskers. They sat up on their hind legs in Silis's palm, curved their tails behind them, and began to warble a three-part harmony arrangement of "Three Blind Mice" in high treble voices.

"They are . . . " Warrick bent down and examined the creatures more closely. Tiny teeth and claws, little pink tongues—every detail flawless. A ridiculous waste of design and programming time . . . and exactly the sort of thing he would've wanted to create himself at one point, back when the sim was ninety percent inspiration and ten percent perspiration. He straightened up to find Silis watching

181

him anxiously. "They are absolutely perfect," he said, and grinned at her expression of relief.

"Try one," she suggested. "They're edible."

He gave it serious consideration for a couple of seconds until the mouse he was eying clapped its paws together and led the group into a change of key. "I couldn't possibly," he said.

"That's what everyone says."

"How do they taste?"

Silis smiled. "Like pink sugar mice. Or at least they're supposed to—I couldn't bring myself to eat one, either."

Warrick turned slowly, surveying the room, taking in every detail of the whole appalling, tacky, overly elaborate monstrosity. He stepped back, down the path, to look up at the house. Gilded gingerbread walls, lollipop windows, barley-sugar thatching, icing trimmings . . . it was one of the most hideous things he had seen in his entire life. And yet, it filled him with wonder. Silis moved up beside him and placed a mouse on his shoulder. It stopped singing and stuck its nose in his ear, whiskers tickling.

"It's incredible," Silis said. "Not this room, the whole sim. Isn't it?"

"Yes." Inexplicably, there was a lump in his throat that it took him a moment to think away. "Yes, it is."

"I do envy you—I can't imagine how cool it must be to know you're the person who thought of it in the first place. Who made it possible."

"Thank you. Although it's a team effort," Warrick added quickly. "It always has been."

In his heart, though, it was still his.

He left Silis there, the mice perched on a toffee-apple tree branch and singing a medley of rodent-themed songs. As he worked his way out of the straps, he tried to marshal his arguments to persuade Asher that the development programs had to stay.

He found Asher in her office, with Lew Marcus already there waiting for him. When he entered, without knocking, they looked up, then at each other.

Lew sighed. "Reddick showed you her bloody mice, didn't she?"

"I'm sorry?" Warrick said in surprise.

"You know there are rumors going around about budget cuts?" Asher asked. "I overheard a conversation in the canteen at lunchtime."

"Oh?" Warrick asked.

"A few of the senior programmers were hatching a plan to persuade you otherwise. Apparently they seemed to think they knew just how to appeal to you."

Lew nodded. "I knew we were in trouble when I heard you were in the sim."

Warrick started laughing. He simply couldn't help it. The idea that the primary way the programmers hoped to change his mind was by showing him again just how much fun—how cool—the sim was, made him unfeasibly happy. Singing pink sugar mice and alcoholic birds.

"Keir," Lew said irritably. "Be serious."

"I'm sorry." He managed to get the laughter under control because he couldn't afford to annoy them.

Lew didn't look appeased by the apology. "We've got to make a decision, and one way or another it has to be now. And not on the basis of singing sugar mice."

"Keir," Asher said sympathetically, "I don't want to give you any extra stress just now, but we have to be sensible."

Sensible. The word gave him the opening he needed. "Why start now?" Warrick asked. "Was it sensible when we founded SimTech? I turned down a perfectly good and very lucrative corporate contract to do it. Lew did the same with a solid Administration research post. You had an excellent future at the investment bank. We gave them up to work out of your house, Asher. We all took risks. So did the people who came to work here from the neural remodeling project. We didn't make them any promises, because the odds were against us making it through the first year, never mind ending up with a salable product. They trusted us to do our best to make SimTech work."

"And we are doing," Asher said. "I'm not suggesting sacking them, or anyone else."

"No, you're just taking away every reason that the staff we most need have to stay. The only edge we have is our people—the people who don't want to work somewhere like LiveCorp, somewhere with a culture that stifles creativity. People will start to leave, and it won't take them long."

She looked genuinely surprised. "I think our staff have more loyalty than you give them credit for. Besides, in the current climate, I think they'll prefer to keep the jobs they have."

With that she might have a point, or even two points. But that was a risk *he* wasn't willing to take. "And if you're wrong? What have we got left if they go?"

"Technology," Asher said firmly. "Patent revenue and proprietary tech licensing that can nurse us through until the unit sales pick up."

"And when the sales do pick up and all our best people have gone? Who'll do the work the new customers want?"

No one spoke. Warrick stood in the center of the room, and it suddenly occurred to him that he'd been lecturing, something that both Asher and Lew hated. Asher sat straight and immovable. Lew was still leaning on the edge of the desk, rubbing his thumb along the top edge of Asher's screen. Warrick couldn't read his expression—he looked to be absorbed in watching his hand move.

"We have to make the decision," Asher said. "We can't put it off forever."

"You both know what my position is," Warrick said.

Lew didn't look up.

"Then if we can't agree, we'll have to vote," Asher said. "I say we cut the research program back, as outlined in my proposals."

"I don't object to savings in principle," Warrick said. "Of course not. I'll spend as long as you want looking at other places to cut back, but we have to keep the long-range, speculative development. It's what keeps the programmers happy and they're SimTech's future. I can't support your whole plan. I say we hold out for as long as we can, even if we have to eat into the reserves, while you try to find someone to pick up more licensing. Lew?"

Lew looked up. "Were the mice really that good?"

"Yes."

He smiled thinly. "Maybe I should have a look at them. It's a while since I've been in the sim."

"Lew," Asher said. "Vote, please."

He straightened up. "I vote with Warrick. Nothing personal, Asher."

Asher nodded. "Well, Keir, I hope you're right. Because if we take this risk and it doesn't work out..."

"I know," he said.

After five days of interrogations filling all his waking hours, coffee breaks were beginning to feel like the only anchors of sanity in Toreth's world. Except that they were coffee breaks down on the interrogation levels, which were no one's idea of fun. The office levels felt like a ghost town, with locked, empty offices on every corridor. The surviving interrogators made for equally depressing company, since the prime topic of conversation was how fucking useless the new Procedures and Protocols was and how much harder it had made their lives. Predictably, everyone had forgotten that the P&P had saved all their ungrateful necks from Carnac.

When had resister vermin suddenly developed rights? was the most common question he heard. Toreth felt like asking the same thing as he slogged through interrogation after exhausting interrogation. These days a maximum-level waiver was still better than nothing, but not by very much. After he'd sat through one too many interrogator diatribes on how the only hope for I&I was a few good resister attacks to shake up the Administrative Council and give them some backbone, Toreth suggested that the interrogators ought to get together and organize one. He hadn't liked the thoughtful silence that followed. At least if he was arrested for sedition, the interrogation wouldn't hurt too much.

184

For his next break, he abandoned the underground levels and headed upstairs. Seeing daylight seemed strange, and so did the greetings from people he passed. He felt tense and strung out, and locked into a working mindset. Or maybe it was just a week of talking to prisoners and interrogators, neither exactly normal company.

Even the General Criminal coffee room seemed wrong. There were too many unfamiliar faces—pool staff, juniors, and investigators. However, Toreth spotted Chevril and Mike Belkin standing together by the coffee machine, which looked to be broken again. Kel was poking around inside the open side, keeping up a running commentary that the seniors ignored.

No fucking coffee. Wonderful.

"Hullo, stranger," Chevril said as he approached. "Getting anywhere with your jigsaw chap?"

Still occupied by the afternoon's interrogation, Toreth stared at him blankly. "With my what?"

Chevril rolled his eyes. "With your corporate kidnapping. Did you find all the pieces? Or are you too good to do any actual work like the rest of us these days?"

"I'm slaving my arse off for Cit Surveillance down in interrogation, as you bloody well know. Nagra's running the kidnapping, for what it's worth, and frankly I don't give a toss how it's going."

"All right, all right," Chevril said. "Good God. Ask a civil question…" Toreth saw Chevril's gaze flick down to Toreth's left hand, then back up again. "You'd think someone who was living in the lap of luxury would—"

So had Chevril been the source of the engagement ring? The flash of anger caught him by surprise, flaring up out of control almost before he felt it begin. He managed only a moment of resistance before the sounds in the room dimmed and he was moving forward, the surrender to fury feeling so sweet, so right. Then Mike Belkin caught his arm, fingers digging in hard, and the unexpected contact pulled him back from the edge.

Kel had stopped talking. Chevril was staring at Toreth, open-mouthed. Toreth blinked, wondering what the fuck had happened.

"Toreth?" Belkin asked, his voice low.

He nodded sharply. "I'm fine."

Belkin raised his eyebrows. "Yeah? Because much as I'd love to watch you kick the well-deserved shit out of Chev…" He nodded across the room.

To Toreth's astonishment, Tillotson was seated in the far corner, his admin Jenny beside him. How the hell had Toreth missed him when he came in? Too much on his mind. "Thanks," Toreth said to Belkin. "I owe you."

Belkin released him. "I'll remember."

Toreth turned to Chevril, knowing what was expected. "Sorry about that." He couldn't risk pissing off his oldest allies. "I've not had much sleep for a couple of days."

"Forget it." Chevril still looked a little pale.

"I've fixed the infernal machine," Kel announced slightly too loudly. "Coffee's here for anyone who thinks it's a good idea."

It sounded like a very, very good idea.

Chevril and Belkin left him to sit alone. Toreth drank his coffee and brooded for a few minutes until Sara arrived, trotting into the room and looking around anxiously. When Toreth checked, Kel was watching him. The admin gave an apologetic twitch of his shoulders and eyebrows. Interfering fucker.

Presumably because there was no mayhem currently in progress, Sara went to get a coffee. Toreth wondered what she would have done if she'd walked in to find him plastering Chevril across the wall.

"Don't ask," Toreth said as she came over. "And tell Kel to mind his own fucking business in future."

"I was just wondering how you were, that's all." She sat beside him and blew on her coffee. "Being as I didn't see you this morning. Or yesterday evening." She glanced at him sideways. "Were you at Warrick's?"

His first reflexive response was, what the fucking hell has it got to do with you? However, antagonizing Sara wouldn't make the best prelude to asking her for yet more unpaid overtime over the weekend. "No. I slept here." Funny how the chairs that had been so uncomfortable last night felt so good right now. Maybe if he just lay down for . . . he tried to keep in mind the interrogation room bookings he had for the rest of the afternoon and evening. "Probably will tonight, too."

"Are you sure?" She was looking at him with open concern. "How much longer is it going to take?"

"Three days. Maybe two. No, three sounds more like it." And might just kill him. "How's the Justice submission going?"

"I'm processing it as fast as you send the transcripts up."

"I want it ready to send the day I finish."

"It will be. I'm still filing individual submissions, so the whole lot will be ready when the last one's done." Not surprisingly she was frowning, as he'd given her the same unnecessary reminder every day since the interrogations started. "You know, it'd be a lot easier if you'd tell me what's going on."

"I just need you to slant the transcripts the way I said and not ask any questions."

She lowered her voice. "Look, I already know it's about Warrick's brother, and Citizen Surveillance is involved." She hesitated for a moment, then said, "Is it something to do with *him*? Carnac? You said Warrick had been to see him."

Which was just about the last name he needed to hear. "Which part of 'don't ask any questions' didn't you understand?"

"Okay. No questions."

And there was the tight tone in her voice that pissed him off more every time he noticed it. Had he completely wasted his fucking time telling her about Aaron? "It's a pointless risk for you to know, that's all," he said.

"I understand." Judging by her close scrutiny, there seemed to be something utterly fascinating in her coffee.

"Sara, it's not—Sara, look at me." She lifted her gaze from her mug, already looking guilty. And *frightened,* shoulders hunching to protect herself from . . . what? Him? And that prodded the rousing anger again, because after all this time, she of all people ought to know better.

"I'm sick of this shit," he said, keeping his own voice quiet. "What are you expecting me to do? Smack you into the middle of next week because you shot your mouth off to Carnac about my fucking parents?"

After so long downstairs, he couldn't stop himself from cataloging her responses—knuckles whitening as she gripped the mug, her eyes wide and horrified because the things she didn't want exposed were being laid out. It was so easy, and it felt just like it had with Chev: his control gone the fuck knew where, leaving him sliding towards something irresistible and dangerous.

"Did you think I wouldn't *notice* the way you've been creeping about? What else do you want me to say? That what happened at Warrick's flat was your fault, too? That Carnac couldn't have done it without you?" Choosing the words had an almost sexual charge, the hot pleasure of twisting the knife into someone who had been stupid enough to let him know exactly where to place it. "That you betrayed me and I'll never forgive you? That I'll never trust you with anything important again? Is that it?"

She swallowed, her eyes glistening.

"Well? Did I miss anything?"

"No," she whispered, so close to the edge of breaking he could taste it. He could finish it—her—off right now, if he wanted. Another few words would do it, or just leaving her alone to think of them herself. What would she do if he walked out now, he wondered. Go home sick? Spend the afternoon crying on Kel's shoulder?

Apply for a transfer?

The thought dug in like Mike Belkin's hand on his arm. She wouldn't do it— guilt would keep her here with him. But the possibility snapped him back, leaving him sick and scrambling for words. Fortunately, training kicked in: break and rebuild to order, even without drugs or neural induction probes. He softened his voice, reaching out to touch her shoulder. "Well, then listen to this, because you're hearing it just once. Nothing's changed."

She frowned at him, bewildered by the switch. "But—"

"Shut up." He smiled to take the sting out of the order. "Whatever you did, however badly you fucked up, I trust you exactly as much as I always did. Which means I trust you more than . . . fuck. Just—" Oh, yeah. That level of coherence

187

boded well for later interrogations. "Not one bit less that I did before, anyway. And if I don't tell you something it's not because I think you can't keep a secret. It's because I'm worried about what you could tell Internal Investigations if they've got you strapped into a chair, because those bastards didn't give up *their* P&P, yet."

The desperate relief in her eyes should have had a kick like fucking, but he was too tired to really enjoy it. "So you can stop this bollocks right now, you hear? No more moping around, and that's an order."

Sara sniffed quietly. "I'm really sorry."

He wished they'd done this somewhere he could do one of the natural follow-ups: hug her, take her out and get her pissed and flirt with her. All he could do here was squeeze her shoulder. "Nothing to be sorry about. Just stop fucking *doing* it."

It seemed to be enough, though, because she smiled slightly. "I'll try."

"Thank fuck for that." He downed a third of the coffee and sighed. "If you want to do something useful, you can go up to level six and tell Daedra I need something that'll wake me up and still leave me legally competent to interrogate."

"Of course." She leaned over and pecked him on the cheek. "I'll bring it down to you."

After Sara left the room, there was a low wolf whistle from across the room. Typical of the spineless bastards to wait until she was out of earshot. Came to something when paras were more worried about pissing off your admin than they were about annoying you. Without looking around, Toreth raised his middle finger in the general direction of Chev and Belkin, then finished his coffee. He rinsed his mug clean and left it draining by the sink, ignoring the notice which strictly forbade so doing.

Chapter Twenty-one

❖

Despite what he'd said in the coffee room the day before, Toreth hadn't put up too much protest when Sara had suggested he come home with her, and get some sleep on an actual bed, not coffee-room chairs. She hadn't bothered trying concern, just highlighted a handful of mistakes he'd made in the afternoon's interrogation transcripts and sent them down to him "for clarification." He'd glanced through the transcripts, his face expressionless, then shook his head. "I won't get this done any faster by fucking it up. Knock it on the head for today—I'll make it an early start in the morning, instead."

Sara had agreed that sounded like a good plan, and canceled the evening's later interrogation suite bookings. That would win her a few brownie points on level D, as well; no one wanted their Friday evening spoiled by extra workload.

Sara hadn't even asked if Toreth wanted her to work that weekend, too. She'd simply set her alarm so that she would have time to make breakfast for both of them and pack something for lunch. At least, being May, the sun rose early enough that it didn't feel too much like a punishment when they arrived at I&I with the dew still thick on the grass, gray as the clouds overhead.

One of the reasons she'd bothered to make sandwiches was that it made Toreth take a break and come upstairs at lunchtime, at least long enough to eat them. Despite him falling asleep about half an hour after they'd arrived home, he still looked exhausted, and deep in midinterrogation distraction. As they shared out the sandwiches at her desk, Sara said, "I'm really sorry, but I have something to do this afternoon. It won't take long, I promise."

"Something to do? Is it Morehen?" he asked, with an unexpected flash of humor.

Taken by surprise, Sara was annoyed to find herself blushing, although she realized a moment later it was probably a good thing. "No," she said. "Nothing like that. It's a family thing—Fee needs me to help with something at her place. I wouldn't go, but..."

"Right." She'd already lost his interest, as soon as the word "family" appeared. "Just make it quick."

"An hour or two at the very most."

"Good."

As soon as they'd finished eating, he stood up, brushing crumbs from his shirt. "Right, back to it. They aren't going to interrogate themselves down there. Catch up with the transcripts as fast as you can when you get back. Oh—and say hello to Morehen for me."

"I'm not seeing Andy!"

Toreth grinned. "Likes blindfolds, does he? I should've guessed, with him coming from Political Crimes."

She threw a pencil at him, and he caught it and tossed it neatly back before he headed off the lifts. The little exchange left her smiling. Sometimes, Sara found herself believing that things could be okay, after all.

Sara recognized the woman at once. Not so much from the single meeting nine years ago, but because sitting on the other side of the café window, even distorted by dribbles of rain on the glass, there was something of Toreth about her, in the angles of her face and the blonde hair. "Glynis," that was how she'd signed the messages. Not "mum," or even "mother."

Despite the filthy weather, Sara hesitated outside. Why had Toreth told her so much, so suddenly? Was it a loyalty test after Carnac? He'd said that he trusted her just as much as before. He'd told her "do whatever you have to do." How would he react, though, if he knew she'd arranged this meeting? After his outburst in the coffee room, the prospect of what he'd do if he found out about this almost made her turn and run. Instead, she took a deep breath, and put her hand on the cold metal door handle.

Inside, the warmth of the café stung Sara's wind-chapped cheeks.

"Hello," Sara said tentatively when she reached the table.

Glynis stared at her blankly, then a slow recognition bled into her face. "You—yes. I do know you. Valantin brought you to our flat, once, didn't he?"

"That's right. I'm Sara Lovelady. I work for him."

"Is he here, then?"

"No, I'm afraid not."

She'd expected disappointment or perhaps, after their last meeting, no reaction at all. The woman let out a sharp breath and closed her eyes for a moment. "Oh."

"You sound relieved," Sara said.

Glynis looked at her measuringly. "He isn't coming later?"

"No. I passed your message on, but he said no." Uninvited, Sara sat down at the table. Glynis didn't react. "Maybe if you tell me why you want to see him, I can talk to him, get him to change his mind."

After a long silence, Glynis said, "I don't know what he's said to you about us."

"Almost nothing," Sara said. "Well. He told me he had a little brother who died. Drowned, accidentally."

"Yes, I suppose he would say that. Oh, this is difficult to explain."

A young waitress cleared her throat beside them. Sara ordered a coffee, wondering how the meeting would look to an outsider. Toreth's mother looked almost as uncomfortable as Sara felt. When the waitress had gone, Sara shifted in her seat, filling time by taking off her damp coat and hanging it over the back of the chair. Now that she was here, she didn't know what to say. Every opening felt blocked by worry over what Toreth would want her to reveal.

"Do you have any children?" Glynis said suddenly.

Sara shook her head. "I've never met anyone I wanted to make an application with."

"Well, believe me, it's terrible when something goes wrong. How can you ever admit to people that motherhood isn't wonderful? It's impossible."

"You mean...when his brother died? Surely anyone would—"

"God, no. Long before that. And I tried with him," she said earnestly, as though Sara's belief in that was important. "I really did try. We'd wanted a baby so much, but after Valantin was born, there was always...I couldn't *connect* with him. When I finally talked to the medics about it, they sent me to a psychologist. At least she listened to me."

"Did it help?" Sara asked.

"No. She told me my expectations were far too high. She had a pet theory, blaming the reproduction licensing system for creating pressure, but she could hardly put *that* on an official Central Records medical file. But she agreed it wasn't entirely in my head. She recorded it in his medical file—she said I found him 'unresponsive to affection.'"

"But he was just a baby. How can a baby be unresponsive?"

Glynis stiffened defensively. "You see what I mean? No one ever understands. I thought, since you've worked with him for so long, you might, but..." She sighed, the moment of anger hidden. "I don't know what was wrong with him, but it wasn't my fault. We applied to the DoP again, and when his brother was born, things were so different. Aaron was an angel." Her face softened with a grief which seemed as fresh as though the years passed had been days. "So easy. So sweet and loving. Always smiling. He said 'love you' before he said anything else."

Maybe because he'd heard it more. Sara couldn't help seeing it from Toreth's side, an imperfect disappointment pushed aside by a fawned-over younger brother. And then she caught her breath, because what was that other than a motive for the very thing she didn't want to think he'd done? "What about Toreth?" she asked reluctantly.

Glynis pressed her lips together, then shook her head. "At first he didn't seem to care about Aaron at all. It was only when Aaron started toddling that Valantin would sometimes be cruel. He'd pinch Aaron to make him cry, leave bruises—we punished him, which just made him more secretive about it. Once, David caught him filling the bath with water. He said he wanted to give Aaron a bath. God, I was so blind."

"But maybe he really did want to—"

"I tried to watch them all the time, but . . ." Glynis looked away for a moment, her mouth twisted in bitter self-reproach, and then her expression set into the cold, contained lines Sara remembered. "I did my best with Valantin, even afterwards, even when I couldn't bear to look at him. But if I'd given him up when it first started, made someone take him away no matter what people would think about it, Aaron would be alive. I can't ever forget that, or forgive."

Herself, or Toreth? "You don't know for sure that Toreth pushed him in." Sara tried to sound firm. "You can't."

"Can't I?" All emotion had left her face.

The waitress returned with the coffee. Sara shook a packet of whitener, tipped it in, stirring slowly while she tried to think what to say next. "Toreth says he doesn't remember what happened," she said eventually.

"I know. But the thing you have to remember about Valantin, always, is that you can never be sure if he's telling the truth. Never. And anyway, even if he did remember, do you think it would bother him? Do you think he'd lose one minute's sleep over killing someone?"

Sara dropped her gaze from the direct challenge.

"I tried to tell Justice what I thought happened," Glynis said. "They weren't interested. I took Valantin back to the psychiatrists, and that's when they first diagnosed an impairment of affect and a statistically raised risk of adult personality disorder."

The professional words came easily, and Sara wondered how often she'd reread the report. "But didn't they do anything?"

"No. They retested him later, and they said the impairment had diminished to below the intervention threshold. We couldn't afford to pay for private treatment, and the Administration wouldn't."

"So they said he was okay." It seemed perverse to argue when she knew how paras were recruited, but Glynis's rigid insistence infuriated her.

"Or he learned to pass the tests." The coldness hadn't changed, but now Sara felt she could see the strain behind the words, guilt or anger or pain. "He always was clever."

"If that's how you feel, why did you send the messages? Why—" Sara waved her hand around the café.

"I'm not sure I can tell you." Glynis leaned back in her chair. "I don't even

192

understand it myself. With all the chaos and violence, I suddenly...I don't know. People, friends and family, they know where he works, and I knew they'd ask about him, and how could I say I didn't know anything? Perhaps that was part of it. But I sent the first message, and then somehow I couldn't stop. When you answered and said he was alive, I thought that would be the end of it."

"He really is all right," Sara said. "And I&I is much safer, now. Nothing's going to happen to him."

"I know. I can't...I've tried not to think about him for years, now. Since he didn't come back to the flat the year after he came with you. I was so happy, then, and David, too, that it was finally over."

"But I thought—" that they'd made him go. Which was ridiculous, really, because who could *make* Toreth do anything he didn't want to do?

Glynis was watching her expectantly. "What?"

"Nothing. Just a—I interrupted you, sorry."

"The thing is, somehow I haven't been able to push him out of my mind again. And in the end I decided if I could just see him, be sure he hasn't changed, then perhaps it would stop."

"Oh." For herself, then. Nothing to do with Toreth. No change of heart after so long. Sara decided she might as well feel the disappointment on Toreth's behalf. He wouldn't, even if he knew.

"Has he changed since we last saw him?" Glynis said.

In the coffee room, when she'd thought it was all over, Toreth had told her that he trusted her, that nothing was different. Sara still wasn't sure that she deserved the chance, but she'd take it. And after all her screwups, she could do one good thing for him now.

"No," Sara said. "Not at all."

When she got back to the office, Sara found three interrogation transcripts waiting. Three prisoners in less than two hours—either they'd all broken quickly, or Toreth had decided the new waiver was useless for them. She held her breath as she checked the file codes. All marked to be processed for evidential submission, which meant success.

Kel was working the Saturday, too, even though Chevril wasn't in the building. "What are you looking so pleased about?" he asked.

Probably wondering where she'd been all this time. "Work, would you believe. Sad, isn't it?"

"It certainly is—and on a Saturday, too. Not that I have any room to talk, but still. My dear, you need to tell young Andy to take you out somewhere nice for the evening."

That was one harmless piece of gossip she didn't mind encouraging. "When the case is finished, maybe," Sara said. Kel shook his head, and went back to his own screen.

Toreth worked until past nine, by which time Kel was long gone. Sara sat alone in the shared office, rattling through the transcripts as they appeared, and trying not to think about when the place had last been so empty, after the revolt. When the final prisoner of the day had been sent back to the cells, Toreth looked up at the camera and said, "Still there?"

"Yes. I'll pick up your coat and meet you at the door, if you like. Save you coming all the way back up here."

She tidied her desk up hurriedly, and then ended up waiting for five minutes at the exit until Toreth arrived. He looked exhausted, again, in a way that hadn't been so obvious on the interrogation feed. He seemed to be barely focusing on her, probably still thinking about the day's interrogations and what he needed to do tomorrow. Almost, she didn't tell him, but after they'd climbed into the taxi, she said, "I've sorted everything out, by the way. With—with your mother. She won't be sending any more messages."

"Yeah?" He looked at her properly this time, the distraction lifting. "Well, good. Thanks."

She smiled back. "Any time."

"Mm." For a moment, she thought he was going to say something more about it, then he said, "Are we getting a takeaway, again? We should stop somewhere."

"No. I filled up the slow cooker this morning, so hopefully it's all turned into something edible."

"Since when do you have a slow cooker?"

"Since a couple of days ago. It arrived the evening you slept here. Warrick told me all about them," she added, and then almost bit her tongue. The mention of Warrick's name didn't seem to have any unfortunate effect, though, because he just nodded. "It seemed really easy, and I thought, since I'm working late so often, why not?"

Toreth snorted skeptically. "I hope Warrick gave you a recipe, too."

"Hey!" she said, having to work to sound properly indignant. It felt so nice to be joked with, again.

194

Chapter Twenty-two

❖

Opening the door to the building, Warrick reflected that at least the new flat meant that SimTech no longer required he put up with the continual and continuously irritating presence of a guard. The one who'd accompanied him home had left in the car. He was getting used to the peace and quiet again. Although perhaps things were a little too peaceful.

It had been ten days so far, Warrick thought as he stepped into the lift up to the flat—a relatively long absence by Toreth's standards, even considering the reason he'd gone. The lingering memory of Carnac's last visit made it seem longer still, stirring the old fear that sometime, perhaps this time, Toreth wouldn't be back.

Ten days since the housewarming. The seven working days had passed pleasantly enough. At SimTech they were still hammering out the details of the corporation's future. Now that *a* decision had been made and announced, the atmosphere had begun to improve, as Asher had predicted. He'd been busy all day at SimTech, and with the relief of a quiet, empty flat to come home to. Most evenings he'd managed to persuade himself he preferred it to Toreth's occasionally overwhelming presence. That was balanced, of course, by the nights sleeping alone, and mornings waking up still alone.

I'll never leave you.

He had made a commitment to Toreth and in return he had . . . nothing concrete. A brief flirtation with flat-sharing and a few weeks when he'd suspected he might even have enjoyed Toreth's undivided sexual attention. What else had he expected? Something more than Toreth was capable of, that much was clear. Annoyingly, he'd suspected that Toreth had wanted to be asked to stay, but at the same time he'd known that if he *had* asked, Toreth would have felt bound to refuse. A relationship based on not pushing was sometimes tedious and frustrating in the extreme.

There must have been a point when the idea of cohabitation had become so compelling. Warrick wondered whether it was something else he could blame on

Carnac. Toreth probably did, if he thought about it that clearly. Carnac's fault or not, the desire was there now and he saw no practical way to eradicate it. So he would tolerate it until it waned of its own accord and things returned to the way they had been. He'd feel better once Toreth finished fucking his way back to stability and returned—which, in all probability, he would, sooner or later.

When he opened the door, everything was quiet. Warrick imagined he could feel the emptiness of the flat, a flatness in the way the air moved when there was no one else there to stir it.

Toreth had called, in any case, every other day. He claimed to be busy at work, and perhaps he was. Perhaps, given Jen's reports, it was better that they hadn't seen each other, because—

As Warrick reactivated the security system, the lights went out.

He froze in place, mind racing with stories of corporate sabotage and kidnappings, few of which ended well. Footsteps behind him, quick and confident, reached him before he could react. A hand clamped over his mouth, and a cold voice whispered in his ear, "Keep very still."

Toreth. Warrick didn't relax, but the flavor of the tension changed. Relief, anticipation, and a spicing of anger.

"I've been waiting," Toreth continued. "I have something for you." Metal traced a line down his cheek, then Toreth loosened the hand over his mouth. "Do you know what that is?"

Fear thrilled through him, whipping up the adrenaline left by the shock of the darkness. "A knife?"

"Yes—very good. That's why you're going to do exactly what you're told to do. Because I'd hate to cut you...by accident. Now, hold still."

Something touched his face—a blindfold, bound securely around his eyes. Then Toreth moved away a little, probably for the lights, and Warrick turned and went for the door, or at least for his best guess as to where it was. He made barely three steps before Toreth caught hold of him with expert ease, spinning him back against a wall and pinning him there.

"Now that was stupid. Luckily, I have a cure for that."

Musical ring of a chain being lifted, and then a collar fastened around his throat. Not *the* collar, of course—that had been looted from Toreth's flat. Only "a" collar, and he was surprised to find it made a difference. He wondered what it looked like and lifted his hands to touch it. Toreth allowed it, briefly, then a pull on the chain drew Warrick down the hall.

At his old flat, or Toreth's, he could navigate in the dark. Here everything was unfamiliar. Dangerous. The stairs left his mouth dry and his stomach fluttering at the feeling of space and danger, and something else. Exposure, uncertainty: a flavor of the Shop, perhaps, the only other place he'd navigated stairs in the dark with Toreth so close.

Reaching the landing was almost a disappointment. A door opened—the room Toreth had originally chosen as his own, or so Warrick thought. Toreth guided him across the room, then stopped him. The knife stroked his cheek once more and he held himself still against a flinch. Probably not sharp, a distant part of his mind told him. He didn't listen too closely to that.

"Strip."

He hesitated, until Toreth took him by the hair, pulling his head back.

"Do it."

Cold metal whispered against his throat and clinked gently against the collar, and he obeyed. Once naked, he stood waiting, shivering although the room was pleasantly warm. He heard Toreth's breathing, imagined him looking. Defenseless against him.

"Good. Now, there's a bed in front of you. Lie down on it. On your back."

He felt for the bed, did as he was instructed. A soft, steely click sounded as the chain from the collar locked into place.

"Spread out your legs."

Another cold touch against his ankles—unlined metal cuffs. They'd never had those before, not for the bed, and the idea of Toreth buying them, looking for them especially for him, made his stomach twist. Toreth in the Shop, sorting through heaps of chains. Perhaps trying them on and—

"Give me your hand."

Not the instruction he'd been expecting, so it took him a moment to obey. A hand touched his, pressed a small bottle into his fingers. The flat of the blade slid up his throat, then the knife angled and the edge pressed lightly across the skin.

"Now, listen to me. Are you listening?" Warrick nodded very slightly. "When I've finished doing everything I want to do to you, I'm going to have you. I'm going to fuck you." Dark, cold voice, spiraling down his spine. "So, before we get started, you're going to get ready for me. You're going to do it yourself."

Warrick managed to draw enough breath to make a whisper. "No."

"And if you don't—"

"*No.*"

The knife stroked across his throat, ending up with the point pressing beneath his chin. Christ, it *felt* sharp enough. He froze in the chains.

He'll be careful, the voice said. Even if it is sharp, he'll be careful. Warrick shut the reassurance away, imagining what the pain would be like, sharp as the knife itself. Something he'd never felt, and he shivered.

"Wrong answer," Toreth said calmly. "Try again."

He struggled not to let himself nod. "All right. Yes."

The knife lifted away. With his hands trembling, it took three tries to open the bottle. Oil spilled over his fingers, cold against his belly, and he gasped. Toreth laughed softly and took back the bottle. "Go on. Do it. Fuck yourself for me."

197

Even though there was some slack in the chains, it wasn't easy to reach. Warrick choked himself on the collar once or twice before he finally found the right angle.

Strained as the position was, the touch of his own fingers inside him lifted the arousal to a new level. More oil trickled over him, cooling his aching cock, and his hips lifted. Without conscious guidance, his free hand slid up his thigh, and he whimpered as he touched himself, fingers curling around—

The blow across his face caught him by surprise, sending a shock through him like a jolt of electricity and leaving his cheek stinging.

"No!" Toreth said. Fingers dug into both his wrists, pulling them to his sides and pinning them down onto the bed. He lay back, panting, wondering if Toreth had enjoyed watching. "I didn't tell you to do that."

Yes, judging by the roughness of his voice.

His wrists were released, and a moment later Toreth's fingers pushed into him, not gentle, making him arch his back, hands tightening on the sheets. God, yes, *please,* more of that. He groaned with disappointment when they withdrew.

"Good enough. Now—" A tap of steel against his shoulder for emphasis. "Put your hands above your head."

Metal closed around his wrists as Toreth stretched his arms into position and locked the chains in place. Then Toreth moved away, leaving him alone for a moment. A space for him to become used to this, to refocus, the world shrinking down around him to this isolated, separate place. Their game.

So long since the last time. And this time, novel and so more exciting, with the added danger of the knife. Even if Toreth couldn't do anything more than threaten, imagination could make it real enough to—

The bed shifted, and he felt Toreth kneel beside him. A brush of bare skin again his side told him that Toreth had stripped, too. Then he felt the light touch of the edge of the knife again, sliding across his stomach, and the fear tightened.

He won't do it. Not that.

Please.

Please yes, or please no?

"Comfortable?" Toreth asked.

The tip of the knife pricked against his sternum. The pressure increased, and then the knife moved and *cut.* Only a short distance, but the sudden pain shocked him out of stillness, made him jerk against the chains hard enough to bruise his wrists. A cut, not a blow. Probably not much more than a scratch, but it felt so different, made a different shape in his mind, brilliant and frightening. Over it came an image of the wound itself, blood welling.

Toreth laughed, twirling the point of the knife against him. "Struggle all you like. It won't help. Shall we try that again?" The knife drew a line of fire, a thin trail of pain from midchest to navel.

"No. Stop it." His unsteady voice sounded like a stranger's.

A third shallow cut, shorter, crossed the second below his ribs. His muscles, taut against the chains, held him absolutely still.

No. I want it to stop. Even as he thought that, the knife sliced down his thigh and made it into a lie.

"Please, no." He tugged at the chains, and the pain came again, diagonally across his chest, nerves flaring into glorious life.

Safe word—there was the safe word. Two words, and it would end. The ease of the escape route, his absolute confidence that Toreth *would* stop at once if the words were spoken, forced him to accept the inevitable. Another two long, deliberate cuts, and he stopped even pretending that he was going to say it. He relaxed in the chains, waiting for the next contact of steel on flesh. His quick, shallow breathing made the wounds on his chest hurt with a vividness that brought tears to his eyes, soaking into the blindfold.

Again. Do it again.

Instead of another sweep of the knife, Toreth paused. The bed shifted as he leaned down close. His skin felt hot against Warrick's and even where they didn't touch Toreth heated the air between then. "It hurts?" Toreth murmured into his ear. Calm voice, measured and controlled, but without the former coldness.

"Yes."

"Too much?"

"No."

"Shall I stop?"

"No!"

A soft laugh followed, then Toreth licked a slow path down his chest, following the line of the last cut. So intense, so arousing, that the pain beneath was barely there.

Toreth moved again, finally settling into place kneeling astride his left thigh. A hand slid lightly down his chest, waking pain. Over his stomach, warm and slippery—with blood. With his own blood. When it touched his cock he arched up, pulling on the chains. "Fuck me." Not meaning to say it yet, but unable to hold it back. He felt movement on the bed. "Fuck me, pl—"

A hard kiss silenced him. "I will. Eventually. But for now I think I prefer this." The knife touched him again, poised. "Next one..."

A rapidly diminishing part of him knew he shouldn't want this so badly. "No. Please, don't."

A pause, then he felt the sharp edge laid lightly against his mouth, and he held steady. "Quiet," Toreth said. "Quiet, or I'll gag you. Shall I do that?"

Trying not to move his lips, Warrick whispered, "If you want to." He noted, distantly, that he meant it, although in truth he was having enough trouble breathing as it was.

199

Yes. Yes, to whatever Toreth wanted. Trusting him to know what was right. Giving up control.

The knife lifted away without cutting him, but when Warrick licked his lips he tasted a hint of blood from the blade.

"Next one...here." Short cuts, only an inch or so, were spaced over his whole body. Every slice felt separate and distinct, Toreth waiting in between until the initial pain ebbed away.

"Do you know how good you look like that? Can you imagine it? I should have done this a long time before. I thought about putting you in the cabinet. Letting you watch it in the mirror. But this is better."

Gradually cutting deeper with each stroke, Toreth teased out the minutes. The pain grew slowly worse, never quite becoming unbearable, until eventually it became unbearable for a different reason. Toreth's hand on his cock was a balancing focus of sensation, rubbing him slowly, keeping him on the edge and never quite doing enough. Caution forgotten, he twisted in the chains, begging Toreth to finish it, and knowing that he wouldn't yet.

Nothing he could do to stop it.

He hurts you. He wants *to hurt you. He's dangerous.*

Dillian's words from years before echoed through him, blending with the exquisite pain as Toreth flayed a tiny patch of skin from his biceps.

Keir, listen to me. He could do whatever he wanted to you. When you're like that. He could kill *you and you couldn't stop him. You couldn't do* anything *to stop him.*

Sometimes—afterwards—he wondered what she'd think if she knew he used it like this.

He hurts you.

He could do whatever he wanted to you.

He *wants* to hurt me.

I couldn't do anything to stop him.

Whatever he wanted.

He's dangerous.

Anything he wanted.

Anything.

Submerging himself in the words, he sank deeper, drowning. Slipping away, the knife driving the real world further out of reach, until Dillian's voice was a blur, meaning lost along with even the memory of a safe word. Everything finally dissolving into an aching emptiness, bound about with pain that focused every sensation inwards.

The chains at his wrists and ankles unfastened, and he felt the blade against his throat, nestling under the collar. "Turn over. On you knees."

Warrick had no resistance left, although Toreth had to repeat the order twice before he finally managed to obey. Blood slicked his body, making his thighs slide against each other as he turned and knelt.

Open and vulnerable.

The chain still held his head down against the mattress and the knife moved away for a few seconds as Toreth locked his wrists to the collar. Warrick moaned helplessly, links biting unnoticed into his hands as he clenched them on the chain, pulling on it.

Needing it now, so much.

Now.

Panting the words out. "Please. Toreth. Please."

The knife traced a path down his spine, barely slicing through the skin. Or perhaps it was cutting deeply and he couldn't feel it because now Toreth was in him, filling him, taking him, possessing him, strong hands controlling and directing, and nothing else mattered.

Nothing else existed.

Will and desire surrendered absolutely.

Sense of time lost along with sense of self, the ecstatic submission stretched out forever. Never-ending, pure and perfect, he reveled in it until the shock of his orgasm, forgotten and utterly unexpected, tore even that much coherence away from him.

Later—minutes, hours, days—and on the dim edge of consciousness, he felt Toreth unfasten the manacles and collar. Warrick rolled onto his side, still panting. Mess. The sheets would be a hell of a mess. He didn't want to come back to reality, to have to face the aftermath.

Fingers stroked his face, and a gentle mouth kissed him back to full awareness. Surprisingly, there was almost no pain beyond the usual aches in his wrists and ankles. It didn't make sense, and he couldn't force himself to think clearly enough to work out how it might be possible. His skin tingled in places, tight and hot like sunburn, but nothing worse than that. Delayed-action analgesic on the blade?

Then Toreth kissed him again, and undid the blindfold.

He sat up and looked down at himself. No blood, no cuts—not a single mark on his skin. Surprise washed away the remaining stupor. But he'd felt it. He'd felt the knife. He ran his hand down his chest, still half expecting to find sticky blood. Instead, his hand slicked over oil and semen. It wasn't—

"I *felt* it," he said aloud.

Looking up again, he found Toreth sitting facing him, hugging his knees to his chest, grinning. He looked so happy, so incredibly pleased with himself, that Warrick nearly said something stupid. What he said in the end was, "How did you do it?"

The grin broadened. "Was it good?"

"It was incredible. How?"

"With this." Toreth offered him a long knife, with a bluish metal blade and a dark blue handle with silver inlay. Warrick wiped his hand on the sheets and took it.

It had a thick, blunt blade—so blunt that when Warrick pressed it hard against the pad of his thumb, it did nothing more than dent the flesh, not hurting at all. The handle, however, was bulky enough to conceal electronics and a power supply. He found a switch on the base, and a sliding control concealed within the pattern on the handle. He pressed the switch, moved the control to the lowest setting, and slid the blade across his palm. An awareness of sharpness, nothing more. He increased the setting and tried again. This time he sucked his breath in—the cut felt so real that he couldn't believe it when no blood welled along the line. Obvious, once he thought about it with a mind unclouded by desperate arousal. "Nerve induction."

"Yeah, spot on."

He didn't want to ask. "From work?"

To Warrick's intense relief, Toreth shook his head. "We don't have anything that pretty."

"From the Shop, then."

"Yeah. I asked Fran what she'd recommend for a late birthday present."

"Is it legal?"

"Technically, maybe not, although I can't imagine even Justice getting excited over something with that sort of output." He shrugged. "I suppose if they really wanted an excuse to hold someone they could stretch it to a charge of possessing specified equipment."

"So w—" He caught himself, not quite in time. "So I shouldn't put it on display in the living room?"

"Probably not."

Remembering something, he put his hand to his mouth. "I tasted the blood."

Toreth held out his left hand, the index finger extended. There was nothing to see, but the suggestion was obvious; when Warrick looked around he spotted a pin on the bedside table. The bottle of oil stood beside it. Yes. He'd poured the oil on himself, as Toreth must have known he would, and then he'd forgotten all about it. So much careful planning. A gift for him, more so than the knife. Also, in another way, a reminder. This is what I can do to you. This is what you need me for. Toreth's power over him. Frightening, sometimes. It had been so real . . .

Warrick turned the knife over in his hands and sighed.

"What?" Toreth asked.

"Nothing. Or, actually, I was thinking it's never going to be the same as it was just now."

"Why not?"

202

"Because I'll know what it is. I'll know it's nerve induction."

Toreth stared at him. After a moment he said, "You didn't think I'd really *do* that? With a real knife?"

"Well, no, I—" He shook his head. "Not now, no. But maybe I did when it was happening. To be perfectly honest, I'm not sure."

"Fucking hell." Toreth sounded shocked. "I thought you'd guessed it was faked somehow. Why didn't you tell me to stop it?"

"I didn't *want* you to stop." The realization of that shocked Warrick. "I thought . . . no, I didn't think anything. I just wanted more of it. It was beautiful."

Toreth laughed. "*Beautiful?*"

"Yes. No other word for it."

"Better than the suspension fucks?"

"Hm. I don't know." The act of analysis and comparison, so familiar from work, helped diffuse the unease. "No, probably not. But it's different. Not quite so overwhelming. I was aware of where I was for far longer."

Toreth nodded. "The pain isn't continuous. It gives you a chance to keep focused. Plus, there's no actual damage, so the pain isn't genuinely cumulative, either. A lot of it's psychosomatic—the nerve induction kicks it off, then your body thinks it's injured so you feel it even after any effect from the kit's worn off."

"That's probably it, yes." Toreth had an excellent mechanistic understanding of pain. Not to mention a better understanding of how Warrick's body would react to it than he had himself, which was deeply unsettling if he thought about it for too long.

Toreth shook his head. "You're fucking insane. I can't believe you let me do it if you thought it was real."

Nor, now, could Warrick. He examined the idea more carefully, then shrugged. "At the core, I must have known you wouldn't break the rules. I didn't think anything quite that coherent at the time, but that's the reason."

"I didn't know we had rules for that."

"Perhaps not as such, but I still trust you not to break them."

"Yeah, well, if you say so." The sound of Toreth becoming uncomfortable with a conversation. "I just thought you'd get off on it."

"And you were spectacularly correct." He set the knife on the table and then lay down, moving across the bed to make space. After a moment, Toreth followed suit, stretching out with a sigh and closing his eyes.

He looked tired, Warrick noticed suddenly, now that Toreth's face was still—deeply tired, the result of a long-term lack of sleep. Fit, though. He'd got back the last of the muscle definition that he'd lost during the revolt, so whatever he'd been up to over the last ten days involved exercise. Warrick reached out and traced over Toreth's stomach. Toreth smiled without opening his eyes and tensed the muscles.

On reflection, Warrick decided that now didn't seem like a good moment to start delving into Toreth's activities during his absence, and particularly not the fate of Tarin's friends. He could ask later. He reached out and switched off the light, fingers brushing over the cool steel of the knife blade. They dozed for a while, close but not touching. A comfortable distance, after the intensity of the sex.

In the end Warrick did rather more than doze, eventually awakening with a start to a crash and Toreth swearing vividly in the darkened bedroom.

"Are you all right?"

"Yeah, fine. Tripped over something. Shit. Mind your eyes, I'm putting the light on. Isn't the voice recognition for the flat system working yet?"

"No. But at least I found the problem—it won't play with the new security system SimTech insisted on. And since I can't switch off the security, we'll have to push our own buttons for now."

Warrick shaded his eyes, blinking at the light, then looked around. Most of Toreth's small collection of possessions were still stacked in boxes in one corner, beside Toreth's battered sofa. He made a mental note to ask Toreth whether he wanted to leave everything here for the time being.

Toreth leaned on the wall by the door, rubbing his foot, and glaring aggrievedly at a box placed with booby-trap precision on the route between bed and doorway. "My own bloody fault for leaving it there," Toreth said. "I only brought it to put the chains in. Didn't want to get myself arrested by overzealous guards if they spotted me wandering through the place with them over my shoulder. Are you hungry?"

"Yes, actually. Shall we go out? Or I could cook."

"No need. I arranged to have something delivered by the complex—it's due any minute." Toreth stood up and looked over. "Unless you'd prefer to go out?"

"Here is perfect."

While Toreth waited for the food, Warrick went to the en suite bathroom. The extra space and new fittings were still an enjoyable novelty. He stood under the hot water, lathering himself thoroughly, and thought about the session, and about Toreth. Thinking something he'd thought so often before: he'd never find anyone else who could do that to him, someone whose needs meshed so perfectly with his own, who would know him that well. Who could always find another boundary and draw him across it so skilfully that he didn't feel it pass until it was too late. It would be insane to jeopardize what he had for some ridiculous urge for cohabitation. The topic had to be forgotten. The alternative was to let it drive Toreth away for good.

Leaning against the cool tiles, he closed his eyes and traced the lines of the imaginary cuts through the soap on his chest. Unmarked, his skin remembered every slice, and he could almost feel the nerves responding to the electronic deception. Pain without consequences, dangerously seductive. Thinking about the knife, about hands on his body.

Surrender and ecstasy.

Toreth.

He heard a laugh, and opened his eyes to find Toreth watching him. "The food's here. But if you keep doing that you're not going to get a chance to eat any of it hot."

Warrick shook his head, dismissing the images, and raised an eyebrow. "That looks like a rather ambitious threat from where I'm standing."

"Yeah, probably." Toreth grinned. "But I wouldn't put money on it. Can I join you?"

"Please do."

Toreth shed his shirt and trousers—presumably donned to answer the door—and stepped into the generously sized shower. Warrick passed him the soap and thought how very homelike it felt. He wished...

On a sudden, dangerous impulse, he asked, "Where have you been since the housewarming?"

That was a rule broken, and the surprise in Toreth's eyes reflected that. However, he answered after only a slight hesitation. "Sara's, mostly. And a couple of nights at work, when it didn't seem worth leaving. Although I'm not so keen on sleeping in the holding cells these days."

"I can imagine. Have you looked for anywhere permanent?"

"No. No time. I suppose I'll put in an application for accommodation. Might even get the old place back. But...well, because I registered here they'll classify me as voluntarily homeless. They're still working through a huge fucking backlog from the revolt. Could all take months—I might end up looking for somewhere private to rent, but that's always a nightmare to sort out with Housing." Toreth put his head under the spray and Warrick waited until he emerged, shaking water from his hair, and continued. "Sara's fighting Accounts for me over putting a hotel on expenses. But even if they say no, I can always find somewhere cheap enough when Sara finally throws me out." He hesitated, and Warrick wondered if he was going to suggest another alternative. In the end, Toreth said, "It's no problem, really."

"Mm." His recent resolution seemed to have failed already. There was no harm, Warrick told himself, in taking a chance. If a compromise could be made, it was up to him to find a way to do it. Toreth certainly wouldn't, or couldn't. "You're more than welcome to stay here. On a purely temporary basis, naturally. Just until you find somewhere else."

No sound but splashing water as Toreth apparently thought it over. Warrick didn't, honestly, hold out much hope—even by their standards, it was a thin fiction. But might it still be enough?

Eventually, Toreth shook his head. "No."

Well, it had been worth a try. "Up to you, of course. If you—"

"No, Warrick. Shut up for a minute." Warrick did as instructed and waited. "Right. If you're still okay with it, I'd—" He sighed, sounded exasperated. "Do you know what I've been doing since I saw you last?"

"I have a rough idea."

"Then I'll fill in the detail. I've been interrogating prisoners, fifteen, sixteen hours a day, plus paperwork. Luckily Cit Surveillance put a priority on the case, and most of the interrogation staff are dead or still on the sick, so no one thought it was odd. That's what ... eight days ..." His eyes narrowed. "Fuck, call it a hundred and twenty hours of interrogation. Which was really a hundred and twenty hours of making sure a decent number of them ended up with something on record to say they secretly suspected your brother was an informer."

"An—" Warrick hesitated, somewhere between relieved and horrified that his guess had been correct. It made a strange twist on Carnac's plan of using Kate's file to frame Toreth. "Did it work?"

Toreth grinned suddenly. "That's a pretty fucking insulting question."

Warrick couldn't help smiling in response—easier now that interrogation no longer meant everything it once had. "Very well. How well did it work?"

"About as well as I expected—good enough to convince anyone who wasn't completely paranoid, which I suppose might not be good enough with Cit." He shook his head. "No, it should be okay. If Sable fixes the files right, Tarin might even end up with a pension. Or at least a medal."

Warrick's throat tightened. "No. Tar can't ever know about this."

"Jesus. Relax. I was joking. By the time he's up to hearing about anything, it'll be long over and done with."

Warrick reined himself in. The arguments could wait until later. With Tarin still in intensive care, there was little point starting a fight over something that unfortunately might well remain hypothetical. "What—" Warrick hesitated, then forced himself to ask. "What happens to them all?"

"Not a lot, for all the hours I put in. They had the right kind of stupid ideas, but they seemed to do a lot of talking and not much actual resisting—you can probably thank Kate for that. Looks like mostly she used them to soak up information about resisters from all over the place, and made sure they never did anything so dramatic themselves that they had to be taken down. So Cit requested low-level re-education for most of them, and the rest just got the fright of their fucking lives. All part of the kinder, gentler new Administration." Toreth's grin emphasized the tired lines around his eyes. "Lucky bastards. It's a good job for them—and you—that they didn't get arrested before the revolt."

"Thank you," Warrick said. "For trying to help Tar and for taking the risks. I'm grateful." He stroked Toreth's arm, wanting to make sure he believed it. "Very grateful."

Toreth shrugged. "No big deal. It was my arse on the line, too."

The silence was becoming uncomfortable by the time Warrick added, "What I don't understand is what any of this has to do with your living arrangements."

For a moment, Toreth looked genuinely blank. Then he sighed again. "Just that I've had a foul week asking trick questions and then making the answers work out, and I can't be bothered fucking around doing the same thing off-duty."

"Ah. And?"

"The last primary interrogations wrapped up at lunchtime. So I left Sara to do her stuff, went to the Shop, and bought the knife and the chains. Then I came around and spent the afternoon asleep on your sofa."

"It's very comfortable."

"Yeah, it is. And all my crap is still here anyway, and like I said, it will be a nightmare trying to find another place. So, what the hell, I might as well just—" Toreth's gaze flicked away, searching around the shower as though he were looking for a way out. Finally he looked back. "Can I still move in?"

"Yes."

"Great. Thanks. I, well, I decided..." The sentence trailed off.

"That you miss the cooking, the cleaning, and my drinks cabinet?" Warrick asked lightly.

Toreth didn't smile. "No. I miss being able to fuck you without having to get in a taxi and drive all the way over here first. Because I've been too poleaxed to go out and find anyone closer." He hesitated. "No. Shit. I didn't mean..." Warrick could feel the tension growing. "I mean, it seems stupid, finding somewhere else when you have this huge place. And—"

"You don't need to explain."

"Thanks." Toreth put his arms over Warrick's shoulders, then leaned his forehead on his right arm, his cheek warm against Warrick's. "I went to the gym, too, after work, every bloody day. And before, most days. I absolutely fucking hate the gym first thing in the morning. But if you let it go too far, it takes forever to get fit again...I am so fucking knackered, you have no idea." He sighed again.

Warrick said nothing. He linked his hands at the base of Toreth's spine, almost an embrace, and held him, savoring the rare surrender.

"You know what?" Toreth said. "I'm sick of living out of that fucking suitcase. I just want to have somewhere to call home."

207

Boys' Toys

❖

"Oh, I'm afraid I won't be able to make it to the gym tomorrow," Warrick said as the waiter set the after-dinner coffees on the table.

As Warrick reached for the milk, Toreth took his wrist and slowly pressed his arm down onto the table. Warrick resisted, to not very much effect. Toreth had the advantage of leverage and of their being in a very respectable restaurant where even this much of a display of intimacy was drawing covert looks from nearby diners. Finally, Toreth held Warrick's hand flat against the table. "See? You want to get anywhere, you need to put more effort in. And more regular effort."

Warrick smiled, although his gaze was fixed on their hands. He flexed his wrist and Toreth tightened his grip. "I have no intention of turning myself into a narcissistic, hair-waxing bodybuilder," Warrick said. "I'm trying to improve my cardiovascular fitness, that's all. It keeps down the directors' health insurance costs."

"Whatever you're doing it for, it's still no good if you don't keep it up." Toreth ignored the waxing jibe, because saying "I use growth-retardant cream" didn't improve the situation. Plus, they both knew how much Warrick liked the consequences of his so-called narcissism. "What's so important?"

Warrick looked up. "I'm supervising a sensory sampling session at a security training center, of all places. It's a last-minute rush because we have a customer considering buying a sim-based training system. They've asked us to bring the demonstration forward. And, frankly, right now we'll do anything we can to chase customers."

"Who's buying?"

"Ah … an Administration department, is all I can say. They're looking for a way to model and test new nonlethal riot suppression equipment. It's all part of the kinder, gentler Administration."

Sounded like the Service. "They can't draft in some lucky recruits?"

Warrick raised a sardonic eyebrow, which looked odd when his hand was still pinned to the table. "If they were in a position to do so, which obviously I can't comment on, I suspect the problem would be that 'nonlethal' doesn't actually imply 'nondamaging.'"

"So they're letting you look at the experimental kit? Sounds interesting."

"I'm sure it would be. However, most of the equipment doesn't exist yet, even in prototype, and the proposed designs are all tied up in confidentiality clauses. It's the usual problem—until we get the contract they won't give us the information we need to prove we can fulfill it. So, in lieu of that, we'll have to demonstrate that we can provide an accurate simulation of a riot environment, including current control technology."

"You're going to have *riots* in the sim?" Considered alongside the meadows and the sex programs it sounded utterly bizarre.

"We are indeed." Warrick worked his hand out from under Toreth's. "It'll be a good project, if it happens. For one thing, we're planning to use it as leverage to significantly expand the scope of the Yes development program. With the backing of the department in question, that application should go much more smoothly."

Toreth wondered whether KA-41 was still around, and whether it would wake up next to find itself in the middle of a simulated mob, having the shit beaten out of it by baton-happy security troopers. "So what are you doing at a security training center?"

"Firearms data acquisition. Most of the rooms required we can build from what we have, but firearms is one area in which we have no material at all. We need environmental recordings and subjective sensory information, all the usual things. We can't gather it while there are other people using the place, because of the background input levels. Of course, we can tune and filter, but —"

"I get the idea," Toreth said before the conversation degenerated too far into technicalities. "Bottom line is, you're far too busy to make it to the gym."

"Yes, I'm afraid so. The center's been very accommodating but, unfortunately for my muscle tone, Saturday is the only day we can set up our equipment in suitable conditions. Of course," he added, "you're welcome to come along. I don't imagine it will be very interesting, but you could always provide some data."

Toreth had made the mistake before of volunteering for sim trials which had bored him more thoroughly than an hour of Tillotson at the monthly section meetings. "What does that involve?"

"Firing a gun while we monitor your brain and peripheral nervous system." Warrick's lips twitched in a mostly hidden smile. "No deep scans, so it won't require you to stand still for too long."

"Well..."

"It would be a help. More subjects are always better, and there are a limited number of trained SimTech guards I can call in at such short notice. Certainly not ones who already have firearms experience."

"So I'm cheap fucking labor now?"

"Oh, no." Warrick smiled wickedly, adding a slow blink that sent straight to Toreth's cock a good proportion of the blood supply that had been about to start work on digesting his dinner. "I wouldn't say *cheap*."

Well, that settled the after-dinner entertainment.

While he watched Warrick stirring his coffee in careful clockwise-counterclockwise patterns, Toreth considered the proposal for tomorrow. He didn't have anything better planned, and although it had been a few months since he'd been on an intensive refresher course, he was pretty sure he'd be a hell of a lot better with a gun than Warrick. It was always nice to beat Warrick at something. Not forgetting the infamous evening of pool, of course.

"Will you be doing any shooting?" Toreth asked.

"No. I'll be needed constantly for the technical parts. It has to go quickly and smoothly. Besides, I've never even fired a gun." Warrick shrugged. "Perhaps I should learn, but I try not to dwell too much on the unsavory side of corporate life. I pay other people to do that for me."

"Okay, then. I'm on." Then, just because of the earlier conversation, he added, "I'll be going to the gym first."

"I'm sure you will. There's no need for you to be there first thing in any case. It'll take several hours to set up and calibrate." Warrick smiled again. "Come for lunch. I'm treating everyone to reasonable caterers to compensate for hijacking their weekends. And then afterward you can show me how well you handle a gun."

The air in the large underground firing range felt cool and made Toreth glad he'd brought his jacket. Considering that people fired guns in there daily, the place was remarkably clean and well decorated. No doubt the company ran training courses for corporate higher-ups who didn't share Warrick's aversion to guns. The setup was familiar from the Int-Sec training section: targets and the stopping wall behind them, a row of cubicles across the end of the room. However, he could have guessed its purpose blindfolded; the smell of propellant, oil, and hot metal was unmistakable. For the moment, there were no weapons in sight, because the SimTech staff were everywhere in the room, placing sensors and running leads for the equipment that would take neural readings from the volunteers.

When Toreth had arrived, Warrick had nodded to him, then returned to a conversation with a woman Toreth recognized from his visits to SimTech. He remembered her because she made him think of all the witnesses over the years who had described someone as "average." These so-called "average" people usually turned out to have at least half a dozen features that ought, in Toreth's opinion, to have been obvious to a blind drunk. Whereas this woman really *was* average, to a degree that was itself noteworthy. Average and not at all Warrick's type, which meant he could spend a few minutes contemplating her spectacular dullness with little more than detached curiosity. Finally, the conversation broke up and he let his gaze move on.

Relaxed by the morning at the gym, Toreth didn't mind waiting. He lounged against the wall, watching the technicians scurrying around setting up equipment. It made a nice change to have the leisure to watch other people working. He kept one eye on Warrick as he moved calmly through the chaos, handing out orders and curt praise.

Building the place underground had been a clever—if expensive—idea, by-passing all sorts of regulations to allow the setting up of a full-size range in the heart of the corporate district. As he waited, Toreth wondered idly what they charged for training, and what they'd be gouging SimTech for the hire of the whole place for a day.

As the clock on the wall crawled slowly towards noon, he detected a change in the room. The activity wound down slowly, with people forming into small groups, chatting. After another ten minutes or so, Warrick moved to the center of the room and called for silence. "As some of you have so astutely spotted—" he glanced at the first group of technicians to have stopped work, who tried to melt behind each other, "—it is lunchtime. We'll break for one hour, to allow the equipment to bed in and calibrate background. Please don't come back before then; I don't want any sensors disturbed."

When the last of the technicians had cleared from the room, Warrick was still engrossed in a screen linked to a square, matte black box that Toreth thought was the central neural scanner control. "I thought we were going for lunch," Toreth said.

"In a moment. I have one or two things I'd like to check first."

Having had previous experience of Warrick's "moments," Toreth adjusted his expectation of lunch down to a hasty sandwich in about fifty minutes' time, and left Warrick alone in the vague hope that it would speed things up. A cabinet on the side wall held an assortment of weapons-related junk. Toreth poked through it idly, pausing when he found a small plastic bottle. The label read "gun oil" and the small print below classified it as nontoxic. He knew that without checking, because he recognized the brand from years back.

"You can fuck with this stuff," Toreth said, tilting the bottle to watch the thin oil coat the inside. "I&I sent a bunch of the juniors on a training exercise run by the Service. God only knows why—I've been at I&I for fifteen years and I've never needed to know how to light a fire and build a shelter under a sodding bush. Probably we'd all pissed off our division heads, somehow. It was the middle of winter, too. Everything was ankle-deep in mud, and it was fucking *freezing*, so we had to keep warm somehow. You know what the funny thing was? Every single one of us independently smuggled in drugs and booze but no one thought to bring lube. Fun days."

"Buggers can't be choosers," someone had said, which had seemed a lot funnier at midnight when he was out of his skull.

"Sounds absolutely delightful," Warrick said with heavy sarcasm. "Doesn't it sting?"

"Not really. It's synthetic oil, plus something to stop you from going rusty." He was about to drop the bottle back into the box when he changed his mind and put it in his pocket. "Where are the guns?"

"Over there." Without looking up, Warrick waved to a metal door set flush in the wall. "It should open to your iris scan."

The recess held an extensive and impressive collection, including a couple of semiautomatic rifles that Toreth hoped he wouldn't be expected to fire. His lessons for those had been a long way in the past. The handguns he was more familiar with. He wondered where the ammunition was—not in the same place as the weapons, which was sensible. In any case, if Warrick didn't want the sensors disturbed, that probably meant shooting was out until after lunch.

"Up to standard?" Warrick asked from right behind him.

Toreth managed to control his surprise well enough not to embarrass himself by jumping a foot into the air. "Rule one," he said testily. "Don't sneak up behind armed people."

"You aren't armed." Warrick moved him aside and surveyed the cabinet. "Mm. They're beautiful, aren't they?"

"That's not the word I'd use. I've seen what the bastards can do."

"Well designed, then. Objects designed to perform a function, and to do it well, are always appealing." Warrick glanced at him. "To an engineer, that is. Technology has its own aesthetic."

"Try having some fucker pointing one at you in anger and see how aesthetic that feels, that's all I'm saying. They're not toys." Toreth unlocked a catch and picked up an automatic pistol, feeling the weight. It fitted his hand well. He tilted it, watching the dull shine of the light on the black metal. Spotless condition, and top of the range—just the sort of thing to appeal to corporates. He tested the action of the slide, then thumbed the button to pop up the small sight screen at the back of the gun.

Warrick hadn't said anything more, but Toreth could feel him watching. "I'll show you how it works later, if you like," Toreth said. "Piece of piss. The gun does all the aiming and puts the result up on the screen. The fancy ones will even do facial recognition for target exclusion—stops overenthusiastic corporates from shooting their own security in the excitement. I've tried firing something with old-fashioned physical sights and it's bloody hard work."

Turning, he scanned slowly around the room, pleased by the steadiness of his aim. On the screen, the virtual sight dot brightened and dimmed to indicate range, shrinking and expanding to show the estimated shot spread pattern. When he reached the firing range and the cutout target, the screen outlined the human shape in white. The gun must have been set up for range practice, because no decent targeting system would mistake a cold, flat figure for a real person. He moved the gun over the torso, watching the sighting dot change from a green "on target" to a red "vital hit" indicator. Red is dead, as instructors were usually fond of saying.

"This is practically sim stuff already," Toreth said. "If you were Service, you'd have an eyepiece attached to your helmet to generate a retinal heads-up display. Or if you're really serious, you can get an implant chip that'll feed the information straight into your optic nerve. Just your kind of thing."

No response. Toreth looked around to find Warrick watching him with an expression Toreth couldn't decipher. "What?" Toreth asked.

"It's strange, but it looks different when you're holding it."

"Yeah?" Toreth lowered his arms and thumbed the sight back down. "Different how?"

"It's ..." And he was practically glazing over on the spot, the very speed of the reaction setting off a hungry heat in Toreth's groin. With an obvious effort, Warrick gathered himself to reply. "It looks like it's alive. No," he corrected himself. "It's that ... it *is* functional now. It's ..."

"Dangerous?"

Warrick nodded, a single, sharp movement, never looking away from the gun. "Dangerous."

"Want to watch me fire it?"

He'd expected a quick affirmative, but Warrick tilted his head a fraction, considering carefully. "I don't know," he said at length. "I really don't. In any case, you can't—the sensors are ..."

Toreth brought the gun up slowly, Warrick's gaze following it until it was too close and his eyelids dropped closed. With his empty hand, Toreth cupped Warrick's face, steadying it, not letting him pull back as he stroked the gun down his cheek. His lips parted slightly, his eyes flickering behind the closed lids, and Toreth grinned. So pliant and willing, so incredibly fuckable—there was nothing left now of the calm, authoritative corporate director who had sent his staff off to lunch.

The sheer fucking *weirdness* of Warrick's sexual kinks never failed to entertain Toreth. Or to turn him on. He moved the gun around, over Warrick's lips, and he jerked his head away slightly. Toreth leaned in and kissed him, the gun cool against the side of his mouth. Warrick was already breathing quick and shallow. He tasted of coffee and a very faint—maybe imaginary—trace of metal.

"You really can fuck with gun oil," Toreth said as he pulled back.

213

After a fraction of a second, Warrick opened his eyes and nodded. "I believed you."

"Uh-huh." Toreth turned the gun over in his hand. "Will it take you long to finish checking the kit?"

"I'm finished now," Warrick said with deadpan seriousness.

Warrick watched in silence as Toreth went over and dropped the bar on the door. For once, their semipublic fucking didn't have to run a real risk of discovery, which would make for a leisurely exploration of this new scenario.

Toreth returned, catching Warrick by the elbow as he passed him, and guided him over to the nearest firing station. He laid the gun on the bench, which was at a perfect height for fucking over. Toreth wondered how often it had been used for illicit purposes. He knew a few people at I&I who'd said that firing guns turned them on. It had never done much for him, but there was no accounting for taste. "Are there any working cameras in here?" Toreth asked.

"No. We had the training center turn off all the electronics, to avoid interference with our sensors."

"Handy. Now, take your shirt off and unfasten your trousers," Toreth said.

The shirt he folded and placed on top of his own jacket in the next station, because he was planning to get plenty of oil around. He pulled Warrick's trousers down to midthigh, exposing him and hampering his movement, and the shiver that went through Warrick would be awareness of both of those.

"Bend over there and get yourself comfortable, because we're going to be here for a while."

Warrick hesitated. "The technicians will—"

"Think you're busy double-checking their work, because you're such a fucking perfectionist. They won't think you're in here getting fucked within an inch of your life."

Warrick turned away and settled down on the bench, bracing his elbows.

"Don't move," Toreth said, "unless I tell you to move. Don't touch yourself."

"Yes."

And that was it—this had to be the record shortest time for persuading Warrick to fuck in public. The cap of the bottle put up more resistance until he finally found the trick to twisting it. He coated his fingers in the cool oil, then leaned on the bench beside Warrick, in the perfect position to watch his face as he felt the first touch of fingers against him.

Warrick's mouth tightened, lips pressing together as his jaw clenched. Toreth teased him, just barely popping the tip of his finger in and out of the ring of muscle. This was an old game, familiar except for the surroundings. Toreth worked his finger deeper with torturing slowness, rewarding stillness with a few more millimeters' penetration, punishing movement with a withdrawal. Under any circumstances it drove Warrick mad, and today it seemed to be particularly effective.

214

Finally he was working one finger all the way in, quick and deep, spicing it with a twist that had Warrick panting and shivering with the effort not to move his hips into the thrusts. Toreth waited for the first sign of relaxation, the first hint that Warrick was regaining control, then drove a second finger in hard beside the first. Warrick clenched around his fingers, the muscles in his back writhing as he struggled to keep motionless. "Bastard," he breathed.

"Now you know why the gym is a good thing," Toreth said. "Because I can keep this up for much, much longer than you can stand me to."

"Bastard." Warrick shook his head, his shoulders tensed.

Swearing was good, for two fingers. Very good, and far too early, and Toreth wondered if Warrick was playing it up to get things over quickly. Half test and half punishment, Toreth slid the second finger out again. Warrick gave a protesting whimper and then, caught by surprise, hissed through his teeth as Toreth drove the remaining finger suddenly deeper.

"God, *please*. Fuck me."

Toreth laughed quietly and returned the second finger. "Not yet."

It was just like work. The first stage was easy. Getting someone to say "I'll tell you what you want to know" was no different from reaching "fuck me." And then after that they would beg for it to stop, or to go on, and that wasn't so difficult to reach either. The real goal lay beyond that. He reached it when whoever he had in his hands knew that begging was hopeless and the only thing that mattered— the only thing that existed in their fucking *world*—was what he wanted. When they ceased to exist and their will was his, that was when he'd won. That was interrogation and that was the game.

He'd started to explain it to Warrick once or twice. He'd always wondered how much Warrick knew, how much he guessed, how much he wouldn't let himself see. Warrick must have known some of it, if only because when Toreth had brought it up in the past Warrick had slammed the conversational shutters down with incredible speed and whatever means necessary, even using the safe word. They'd talked about it exactly once, in the lift at SimTech before the smell of smoke cut the conversation short before they'd had time to do more than start the topic.

You hate interrogations, but you fuck me, he'd asked. *How does that work?*

Warrick's answer had been that he didn't think about it, that the interrogation skills didn't matter, only the physical training and prisoner restraint techniques. Which might all be bollocks, but it obviously helped Warrick sleep at night.

Typical prissy fucking corporate, Toreth thought, pushing deep and twisting until Warrick was whimpering aloud. Not wanting to know about the dirty work that went on to keep their shiny little world safe and profitable. Not so fucking prissy that he wouldn't take the results, though. That he wouldn't do this, bending over the scarred surface of the bench, sweat starting to gleam on his skin. Focusing on the sight in front of him wiped the momentary anger away. Toreth leaned in and bit at Warrick's shoulder, salty-clean against his mouth, pressing in deep with his fingers again.

"Is this what you want?" Toreth asked.

"Yes. God, yes. Don't stop."

No, he wouldn't. Definitely not in the plan. Keeping going until the extra finger Warrick was panting for wouldn't be anything like enough—that was the plan. Going on long enough that when Toreth finally pushed the third finger in, stretching him open with a brutal thrust, Warrick sobbed on a breath and a heartbeat later demanded, "More."

The room was soundproofed well beyond this, but out of habit he brought his hand up over Warrick's mouth—more a warning than a serious attempt to silence. Warrick bucked hard, pushing back onto Toreth's hand. "Good?"

"Smell it on your fingers," Warrick said. "The oil. It's...I can taste the smell."

"Jesus, this really fucking turns you on, doesn't it?" He pressed against Warrick's mouth, forcing his lips open, pushing inside to let Warrick taste him. Filling his mouth as his other hand was filling his arse. Warrick's mouth closed eagerly around his fingers, sucking, his breathing a moan deep in his throat, and the wet heat sent a bolt of lightning jarring down Toreth's spine. Fuck him now, fuck him now—a low chant grew more insistent in his mind, in tempo with the fingerfuck and the pulsing suction heating his blood. Fuck him now, fuck him—

Toreth's elbow bumped something and he looked down to find the forgotten gun. Now *there* was an interesting idea. A very interesting idea, and Toreth tried to hide a smile, even though Warrick wasn't looking at him—was, in fact, totally focused on working his hips hard in counterpoint against Toreth's fingers. When Toreth pulled out his hand, Warrick whimpered once, then stilled, braced against the hard edge of the bench. Thinking he knew what was coming next, and thinking wrong, or at least Toreth hoped so.

The grip of the gun felt cold to Toreth's oil-slippery hand, because despite the SimTech equipment—and the excessive body heat they were both generating right now—the room was still cool. The barrel would be colder still.

He pulled his fingers away from Warrick's mouth, ignoring the determined press of his tongue, then twined them in Warrick's hair, holding him still. "Spread your legs. Wider. Are you ready?"

The nods tugged at his grip. "Please."

"Are you sure? Do you really want it now, already?"

"God, *yes*."

He set the tip of the gun against Warrick's body and began to slide it oh-so-very-fucking-slowly inside. For a moment, there was no resistance from the slick, well-prepared passage, then the invasion of hard, cold metal registered and Warrick tensed reflexively. "What..." And for a few seconds Toreth could see that he really didn't know, that he hadn't guessed, and the delighted triumph kicked through him like downing a glass of vodka. Then realization dawned and Warrick breathed, "*No.*"

Toreth pulled the tip of the gun back, just a fraction, and Warrick followed hungrily. "No?" Toreth tightened his grip on Warrick's hair, and he stopped, trembling slightly, his hips making tiny, helpless movements. "You fucking liar. You want it."

Warrick's breath was hitching as he fought for control. The most he could manage was a tiny, pathetically unconvincing shake of his head.

"Ask for it," Toreth said. He stroked the rounded tip of the barrel down, nudging behind Warrick's balls, caressing him with the slick, solid, *dangerous* weight of the thing. Then he slid it back up, poised against Warrick's hole. "Ask me for it."

The silence lasted for longer than he would have credited before Warrick breathed, "Yes, do it."

"More," Toreth said.

"Fuck me." Warrick jerked suddenly, as if he'd heard the words from someone else, then braced himself. "Fuck me, please."

Toreth released his hair, taking a light grip on his hip instead. Warrick tensed against him in anticipation. "How?" Toreth asked.

For a moment, he really didn't think Warrick *would* ask, as desperately as he obviously wanted it. They'd hit limits before—not many of them—and he wondered if this was one. Then Warrick shivered, his head falling forwards. "With the gun," he whispered. "God. Fuck me with the gun. No..."

"No?"

"*Yes.* Fuck me with—with the gun," he said in a kind of stunned amazement, tasting the words.

He could have gone in hard—he knew Warrick's limits better than he did himself—but he didn't. He kept to the tormentingly slow pace of the earlier game, watching Warrick's face as he worked the gun in and out, fractionally deeper with every return, until he hit the right spot and Warrick's face twisted and he bit his lip. Another few millimeters, with a tilt of the gun, and Warrick moaned aloud.

"Is it okay?"

The gasp was almost laughter. "I can't believe...yes. God, yes. Incredible. But...harder. Please."

Then Toreth looked down, actually saw his hand and what he was doing, and Warrick spread for him, sweating desperation, and the reality hit him like a dose of one of Daedra's more potent fuck drugs, the kind that came with a warning about not using near children and animals. His cock ached, screaming to touch flesh. He pulled the gun back and thrust in, again, twice, again, Warrick's choked reaction sounding distant because Toreth couldn't believe that Warrick was really letting him do this, trusting him this much. Just *taking* it. He wanted very badly to see

Warrick come like this, with the gun inside him, wanting it almost more than he wanted to come himself.

Oil made his fingers slip on the grip, and he curled them tighter around the trigger and the trigger guard. Every thrust now pressed his fingers up against Warrick's shuddering body.

"Let me, please," Warrick was gasping, and it took Toreth a moment to work out what the fuck he was talking about, to remember the instructions he'd given. And it brought a new resolution.

"Move your arms and I'll break them." Fumbling desperately, Toreth managed to unfasten his own trousers one-handed, never letting up the movement of the gun inside Warrick. "This is going to be enough. You're going to come just from this."

"Please." With every thrust, Warrick squirmed back against him as hard as he could without disobeying and releasing his hold. "I can't."

"Yes, you can." Finally, he had his cock free. He touched Warrick's hip, curling his fingers around towards Warrick's cock without making contact with it, then tightened his grip to hold Warrick steady. "It's like this or not at all."

"I can't. Please, touch me, just..."

"It's loaded," he whispered into Warrick's ear, twisting the gun at a new angle—deeper, moving faster.

Warrick choked out a cry, whether in response to the barrel or the words Toreth wasn't sure.

"Did you hear me?"

The response was a contradictory shake of his head. "No, it's n—liar," Warrick panted.

"It's loaded," he repeated, then paused so that Warrick would hear the click. "And that was the safety. My finger's on the trigger. How long do you think it'll be before I slip?"

"No...God, no, I can't—" Then the words were swallowed into sharp panting breaths, closer and faster as Warrick's shoulders tensed, pulling back.

Impossible, utterly impossible, but it was really happening, and the realization snapped his control and his determination to watch Warrick come. He pressed up against Warrick, feeling the cold hard edge of the gun against his hip and the heat of Warrick's oil-slick body against his cock. Four quick thrusts and he was almost there. His hands clenched reflexively and the trigger clicked, seeming deafeningly loud. Warrick jerked forward away from the noise, breath whooping in, then screamed as he came. Toreth felt the strength of it as Warrick's muscles clenched around the gun, and then his own orgasm swept through him, hot and wonderful, while he looked down to watch in dark, delighted disbelief as his come spurted over the gun and his hand, and the curve of Warrick's buttock.

When the spasms stopped, Warrick was leaning on the bench, head on his arms, his fingers gripping the far edge tightly enough to whiten his knuckles. He was still shaking and Toreth wondered if his knees were about to give way. He slid the gun out carefully and laid it back on the bench. It was going to need a hell of a thorough cleaning. Taking hold of Warrick's shoulder, he pulled gently until he came back, away from the support, fingers uncurling reluctantly. Toreth leaned against the wall of the station, sliding slowly down and guiding Warrick down with him until they sat on the floor—Toreth with his back to the panel, Warrick curled against him, his head on Toreth's knees. The only noises in the room came from their breath and the humming SimTech equipment.

Toreth leaned forward to kiss Warrick's shoulder. "It wasn't loaded," Toreth said.

"I know. Hell." He lifted his head slightly, then put it back down. The shivers were slowly subsiding. "I know that. There wasn't any ammunition in the cabinet. But what I didn't know is that it's possible to come just from being so—so—"

"So fucking shit scared?"

"Yes."

"See." He draped one arm over Warrick's shoulders. "I told you. They're not fucking toys."

It took a moment before Warrick started to laugh weakly. "As it were." He looked up at the clock. "If we clean up quickly, we'll have ten minutes to grab a sandwich."

Prodigal

I'm afraid the general cannot speak to you at this time," the young man on the screen said.

"Did you inform her that I had Mr. Nicotera here with me?"

"Yes, sir." The young man looked mildly offended at the suggestion he had failed in his duties. "I'm afraid she asked me to tell you that she will be engaged all day. She apologizes for any inconvenience, but reminds you that the request was made at very short notice."

In other words, Carnac thought bitterly, a very politely phrased "fuck off and don't come back."

When the screen went blank he took a moment to collect himself and then turned to the corporate beside him. "Simply a misunderstanding, I'm sure," Carnac said. "Perhaps we could reconvene the meeting at another time?"

The man's eyes had the flat unreflectiveness of slate. "I don't think that would be in either of our interests, do you?"

"If you would just consider my proposal in a little more detail, I think you'll find —"

"Thank you for your time, Socioanalyst. Peter will escort you out."

This was what he had been reduced to, Carnac thought as the flawlessly polite Peter made sure that he left the premises. Begging favors from lizard-brained corporates and vacillating second-rate career military. So much for the grand machinations of the terrifying spook.

❖ ❖ ❖

The courtyard outside included a shallow pond, artfully curved to complement the line of the building. Ignoring Peter, who still waited just inside the glass doors to observe his departure, Carnac strolled over. A small flotilla of ornamental ducks patrolled the water, inspecting the scrubbed sides for nonexistent weed. Their

220

plumage, natural or engineered, matched the gleaming corporate logo catching the lowering sun above, and a small system of sculpted platforms in the center of the water provided their only, and most unnatural-looking, refuge from endless paddling. Clipped wings, Carnac thought, as he leaned on the rail. Surely that was the only reason the creatures hadn't flown away to somewhere more congenial. Or perhaps pure stupidity.

At least he wasn't corporate, or anyone else's, property, and he was free to fly wherever he wished. Unfortunate, really, that he seemed to lack both inspiration and the ability to let go and take wing. No migration instinct, that was the problem.

"You know," he said to the ducks, "I made a promise. Or not, I suppose, a promise per se. Better to call it a resolution, in the interests of accuracy. I said I was finished with them. The people should get the government they deserved, and choke on it. So why am I here? I ought to know better, you might think. Except, of course, I do know better, and that is the whole point. If you see what I mean."

Talking to himself was, depressingly, the only way to achieve an intelligent and engaging conversation these days. Carnac tried to ration himself, because it really was not a positive sign of mental stability. "But do you suppose it's better or worse than talking to wildfowl?" he wondered aloud.

The ducks ignored him utterly. A piece of litter, blown from who knew where into the pristine corporate enclave, had landed in the barren pond, and the birds were squabbling over it, snatching and rejecting it in turn. Carnac felt in his pockets, finding the expected small packet of ginger biscuits. Colette had taken it into her head that he should eat more, although he wasn't entirely sure that the regular provision of biscuits was adding much to his nutritional regimen. Still, that was Colette all over—well-intentioned, but staggeringly impractical.

He ripped open the plastic wrapper, and an unseemly stampede—could one have a stampede on water?—immediately ensued. The ducks gathered in a shoving, pecking rabble below, sending ripples racing over the smooth surface of the pond. Carnac crushed two biscuits in his hand and scattered the fragments over the water.

"Now that I have your attention—as I was saying. Do you ever consider the reality of objective evil? The existence of things of which one can say only, this is wrong. This must stop." Carnac bit the third biscuit in two, and continued rather less distinctly. "No? Well, at one time, nor did I. And really, for peace of mind, I can't recommend starting. There's no end to it, and no possibility of success in eradicating the problem. The best I can say for it, really, is that the daily prospect of arrest or assassination keeps one alert."

Carnac contemplated the half biscuit in his hand, then sacrificed it for the ducks. "I imagine that most people would advise a career change. Colette suggested I should try my hand at a novel, although perhaps nonfiction might be better. A Socioanalysis tell-all would certainly be as utterly implausible as any of her murder mysteries." He brushed the last crumbs meticulously from his hands. "But in the highly unlikely event that I survived to publish it, then I would quite certainly hate both my reviewers and readers, and as I already hate my clients that would seem to defeat the object of the exercise. It would have to be something intellectually challenging, but ultimately harmless. Poetry, maybe."

Carnac leaned on the rail with both hands.

"How wonderful to be a duck,
With naught to do but flap and fuck.
And represent the corporation,
Engineered to...ah."

The last of the floating biscuit had disappeared into greedy beaks. The ducks were drifting away, pecking optimistically at imaginary crumbs. One of the males, flashing his vivid copper chest feathers, approached a drabber female and received a sharp peck on the head for his troubles. Carnac sighed. "Thank you for providing a most apposite metaphor, anyway."

The light was failing, a late-autumn chill settling quickly over the grassless space. Still Carnac remained leaning on the railing. For all its ugly artificiality, the place provided momentary peace.

As he watched the ducks patrol, Carnac found himself feeling oddly light-hearted. Almost a little drunk. The failure of his meeting with Nicotera and the spineless officer should have left him depressed. And yet, having sunk so low, he found himself experiencing an inexplicable confidence. So what if two more people had provided unnecessary confirmation of the general stupidity of humanity? He would simply find another two, and try again until he hit the exceptional end of the curve.

He had made mistakes. Carnac could admit that, to himself, at least. Some of them he could ascribe to circumstances, but some were the unfortunate offspring of his own faults and limitations. In a fit of pique—and, perhaps more forgivably, disgust—he had cut himself off from the new council he had put in place; entirely as he had predicted, they had failed to survive his departure and slipped out of office and out of history, to be replaced by another set of self-serving idiots of equally dismal character and intelligence. The only pertinent difference was their distrust and dislike of members of the previous regimes, Carnac included. No doubt a few more changes of the guard would dilute memories of his involvement in sedition, but for the moment it was yet another impediment.

Perhaps it would have been better for his long-term goals to stomach their stupidity and stay. Perhaps not. The fact that he didn't have the time, resources, or energy to make a more definitive assessment of that was simply another frustration amongst many.

Before the revolt, failure had been something rare and abhorrent. Since that spectacular disaster, he had failed so often, in so many ways, that the sting was gone. He had held out until now, and could hold out indefinitely, however painful and unpleasant his existence had become. So many forces were arrayed against the change which had to—*had* to—happen within Europe. They would not win, at least not through his surrender. No matter what he had to do, what alliances he was forced to make, he would continue to do what was right until his last breath.

"And what do you say to *that*?" he asked the ducks.

"Excuse me, sir."

The voice didn't belong to Peter, or to Nicotera. When Carnac turned, he found himself eye to shoulder with a most impressive specimen of corporate security. "Feeding the ducks isn't allowed, I'm afraid, sir. This area—"

"No need." Carnac held up his hand. "Really, I was just leaving. Good night, and I hope you have a most enjoyable evening."

Clearly Nicotera selected his security for size rather than brains, because the man stared at him in confusion, before he said, "Uh—and you, sir."

Carnac whistled as he left, not entirely sure whether he was doing it for the benefit of the audience, or for himself.

Carnac stared at the name on the screen. Socioanalyst Camille du Pre. What, Carnac wondered, was the correct emotional response to seeing one's former mentor's name abruptly appear on one's calendar? Apprehension, that would be a good choice. Fear would not be unsuitable. Relief, he decided finally, would have to do. Relief that after months of fictitiously polite negotiations conducted through lawyers, the gloves were coming off. Relief that someone, in however unpleasant the likely circumstances, would confirm that he was still worth consideration.

"If a threat cannot be contained, and to an adequate extent controlled, then it must be eliminated," he murmured.

"Jean?" Colette asked.

"Nothing. A quotation from a training manual—a very basic one."

"I'm sorry, Jean—I didn't know who she was. She simply asked if you had an appointment free, said that she had an urgent need for your services—"

"—and she would pay whatever was necessary to secure them?"

Colette nodded. "So I said that you had time for an initial meeting this afternoon."

"Of course. They must know my finances are delicate—after all, they're the ones who withdrew my license. Once you offered the appointment, she supplied the name freely?"

"Yes. Jean, what are you going to do?"

"Meet her, naturally." He smiled, fooling neither of them. "One can't develop a reputation for letting down one's clients."

"But what if they're planning to—to..."

Carnac turned away from the reception desk screen, looking into his sister's anxious face. "In that case, it makes very little difference whether I go or not. The message has been delivered—one way or another, a meeting will happen."

"But you can't go! It's insane. There must be another way out. What about the contingency plans? Once you're outside the Administration—"

He took hold of her arms, squeezing tighter than he meant to. The sight of his placid, indeed normally almost annoyingly vague, sister panicking was more disconcerting than it should have been. Keeping a clear head was absolutely vital. "Listen to me, Coll. For once, do try to forget that I'm only your brother. Please take what I do for a living seriously, and consider that there is a remote chance I might actually be capable of deciding the best course of action for myself."

After a moment she nodded. He released her arms and smiled a little to acknowledge her acquiescence.

"Then do exactly what I tell you. If I don't return from this meeting, you will close the office—simply lock the door and walk away, leaving all the contents behind. Do not try to contact Socioanalysis. Do not report my disappearance to Justice. Do *nothing* to draw attention to yourself. If they are in a particularly courteous mood, then my corpse will be discovered shortly, the victim of a tragic accident. If not...well, after the prescribed time, then you can have me declared dead. In either case, I don't imagine that there will be any difficulties concerning my will. Do you understand?"

Her brows had drawn together during the speech, almost comically in the gradual gathering of the frown. She drew in a breath, then suddenly she embraced him. "*Jean.* They can't—you're all on your own, and they're a whole department. It's not fair."

"No, it's not. But what can we do about that?" Nothing more, really, than what he had tried to do, which was the reason he was in this mess in the first place.

She still hadn't let him go, and he patted her shoulder, for whatever tiny amount of comfort a physical gesture might deliver. It was oddly and quite unexpectedly satisfying to look back on the last few months they had shared working together. Maddening as she was, she had set her own life to one side and stuck by him without hesitation, and that was gratifying.

He eased back, and tried to smile as reassuringly as possible. "Coll...perhaps there's nothing to worry about. I could be back safe and well in time for dinner. But now, I should go and prepare. I'm sure that whatever du Pre wants, we'll have a great deal to talk about first."

She stopped him as he was entering his office. "Jean—am I in danger?"

He'd rather hoped she wouldn't think of that. "I sincerely hope not." She winced at the word "hope." It wasn't one he used often. "Assuming I have the chance, I will do everything I can to persuade them that you pose no threat. But

224

if you are, shall we say, visited by any persons connected to my former employers, then I advise that you give your full cooperation, whatever they ask from you. I give you my word that nothing you can tell them will hurt me, and they are not, though it pains me to admit it, fundamentally unreasonable people."

Except, of course, in the small matter of supporting an obscene and chronically corrupt regime. But then he had spent the better part of thirty years doing so himself. At the back of his mind, he had always held the illogical conviction that someday he would have to pay for that.

The building the taxi drove him to wasn't an official Socioanalysis office. Instead it was a corporate facility designed to provide highly secure conference rooms for the kind of negotiation where neither party trusted the other sufficiently to enter their premises. It would not, Carnac thought with satisfaction, come cheap. Some small salve to the ego to discover that his disposal would dent a budget or two.

He watched the taxi pull away, then walked in, head high.

In the foyer, sounds dulled by protective glass and explosive-proof décor, he read and authorized a vast quantity of indemnity clauses acknowledging that the terms of the meeting permitted no prior inspection by him of the meeting room; no security personnel belonging to him were to attend; no guarantee of freedom from surveillance had been offered by the other party or parties involved in the meeting, whose identities were not guaranteed to be disclosed; and quite definitely no promises as to his personal safety had been made by anyone.

From the anxious double-checking of his identity and confirmations, and the presence of two lawyers and the chief of operations of the building, Carnac deduced the one-sidedness of the arrangements had caused surprise and concern, and possibly severe doubts as to his sanity. Carnac agreed to everything, with a cheerful smile. Ultimately, at this meeting, intellectual equality was the only factor which mattered and on that score he was far better equipped than any corporation.

The lift took them to the top floor, which in Carnac's experience meant also the most expensive. Up here the physical and technological security measures were hidden even more thoroughly behind corporate luxury. Everything was decorated in cool, neutral colors, the walls hung with expensive, blandly beautiful artwork which slid away from the memory as soon as it was out of sight. Carnac found himself walking briskly down the corridor, buoyed up by anticipation.

He had had no firm expectation that du Pre would in fact be present. However, when the security officer opened the door, she was waiting for him, the only person in the generously sized room. She looked much as she had when he'd first transferred from the familiar tutors of his childhood and early studies to the rather less tender care of those who would train him in the so-called realities of Socioanalytic practice. In all his time with her, no case, no number of sleepless nights, had ever managed to displace a hair in her short, millimeter-perfect dark haircut, or put a wrinkle in her immaculate clothes. Today she was dressed in a dove gray business suit so up-to-date that it perhaps hadn't yet made it onto a catwalk.

She had contrived, no doubt at some expense, to age virtually imperceptibly since he had first met her. The changes he could see were all in her eyes. No amount of money could entirely hide the kinds of experiences they shared. Rising smoothly, she opened her arms. "Jean-Baptiste!"

"Camille," he replied, since they were apparently operating on personal name terms. He pecked her decorously on each cheek.

"It's been too long." She rested her hands briefly on his shoulders, looking up at him with sincerely feigned affection. "You were always one of my favorite trainees, you know. Now, would you like tea? I have chamomile, Earl Grey—I'm sure our hosts can provide anything else you might prefer."

If this was to be the last game, then he refused to be outplayed at this stage. "Chamomile will be perfect—it reminds me of you whenever I drink it."

She gestured him over to the low coffee table, with two armchairs set by it—the more intimate choice, avoiding the walnut expanse of table by the high-grade security glass windows.

No flunkies arrived to make the tea. When she handed him the cup, he inspected it with care, and she coughed discreetly. "Really, if I have to drug you to bring this meeting to a successful conclusion, then I've wasted a terrible amount of the division's money."

True. Nevertheless, he placed the cup on the table untasted. "I would appreciate it if we could come swiftly to the point," he said. "I have clients to see who have genuine cases."

If she knew otherwise, he couldn't tell from her polite smile. "Very well." She set her own cup opposite his and crossed her ankles elegantly. With hands delicately folded in her lap, and the immaculate neatness of the suit, he half expected her to try to sell him an absolutely *superb* property, in a very exclusive development, we've had so much interest, but we offer only to clients of genuine taste and discernment—

"Jean-Baptiste?" she queried.

He realized he was smiling slightly, and wiped the expression away. Hiding from the upcoming no doubt bitter truth in whimsy was beneath him. "I'm sorry, Camille. Do go on."

"Very good. I suppose it would be helpful to set out the terms of negotiation.

I'm here in a technically unofficial capacity, but I'm fully empowered by the head of the division to resolve any questions or difficulties arising—by whatever means necessary."

"Up to and including my death, you mean?" Carnac straightened his sleeve. "I'm flattered that you consider me worth menaces, but forgive me if I am unimpressed, given that I am still breathing after some considerable time."

"Jean-Baptiste, if we had wished you dead at any point..." She let the sentence trail off, a light sauce of manners to disguise the crude flavor of the threat.

"I have measures in place, information kept in reserve..." He returned the courtesy.

"And I'm sure that your precautions are perfectly adequate to deter your political enemies, for now anyway. I'd hope, however, that your opinion of your colleagues hasn't sunk so low that you believe the entirety of Socioanalysis is incapable of countering your safeguards, if we applied our collective minds to the problem."

Carnac conceded the point with a nod. Quite against his will, he recognized the seductive pleasure of the company of someone with whom he felt a genuine intellectual rapport. In all probability they could hold half the conversation in raised eyebrows and minute gestures. They had both been trained to value clarity, though, and kinship did not mean he was in any less danger here. Quite the reverse.

"So what small nuisance value have I suddenly acquired that I've become worthy of notice?" A quiver of nerves he couldn't quite control sharpened his tongue. "Inadvertently stepped on divisional toes, perhaps? Or are you merely tidying up the personnel files? Perhaps I forgot to file an expenses claim before I left."

She ignored the levity. "Socioanalysis isn't as heartless an organization as you have apparently convinced yourself. Every trained socioanalyst is a valued member of the family—even when they regrettably choose to cut themselves off from us."

"It's been a long time since I needed parenting," he said stiffly. "Biologically or professionally."

"Perhaps not so long as all that," she murmured. Before he could reply, she continued briskly. "Do you know how many renegade socioanalysts there are? Not independent, mind. Renegade."

"Actually, yes, I do—four. Counting myself. Two vanished from the Administration, and one is rumored to be here still under a false identity." He gestured languidly, counterpoint to the tension within. "I'm blazing a new path."

She didn't smile. "There is one. Counting yourself. The others have, in one fashion or another, returned to the fold. One, I must confess in the interests of full disclosure, not entirely voluntarily, but I am willing to present an argument that the nature of his criminal activities justified our actions in that case. You've had the chance to find out how lonely life is without your adoptive family, Jean-Baptiste. Now we're hoping you're ready to come home."

His hopes of walking out of the room alive, slim to begin with, reached zero at the conclusion of her speech. Now there was nothing left but to go out in style. "In other words, you want me to resume my former place on a tight leash, propping up the Administration until it collapses under the weight of its own corruption and destroys us all with it," he said precisely. "Forgive me if I am underwhelmed by the offer."

Unexpectedly, du Pre laughed, a perfect tilt of her head making the slim gold chain around her neck catch the light. "Is that really what you think? True, the Administration created our division with that in mind, but current thinking within the higher echelons of socioanalysts is that we have become disinclined to play the role assigned to us. Indeed there is a minority—most of whom until very recently kept their doubts to themselves, as you did—who hold the position that the Administration contains, or rather embodies, deep moral wrongs. There are others who concede that wrongs exist, but maintain that by the very fact it must survive in a wider world, no government can avoid acquiring...a certain moral ambiguity."

Carnac snorted.

"*However,*" she continued. "The majority of us, whatever position we take on the question of morality, agree with your underlying analysis that the Administration in its current form cannot continue indefinitely and that, indeed, without intervention a catastrophic collapse is ultimately inevitable. Perhaps that collapse is decades away, but planning for the long term is what we do."

Against his will, he found himself interested. Hearing one's own argument praised was always a pleasure, if a dangerous one to enjoy now. "And this blinding flash of the obvious occurred when, allegedly?"

"Some time ago. If unthinking support of the status quo was still our goal, then why did we stand aside in the recent troubles? Didn't you ever wonder?"

"You want me to believe that the division wasn't involved at all?" Carnac raised a skeptical eyebrow.

"Did you think we were? I'm sure you would have noticed the perturbations." She shook her head. "No, Jean-Baptiste. The Bureau of Administrative Departments appealed to us for help; we informed them that the situation was entirely unforeseen and we would require time to formulate strategies which we could be confident would deliver the desired outcomes—in the best interest of the Administration, of course. And then we simply watched events unfold."

"You..." Carnac frowned. "I'm not sure I understand."

The admission was surprised out of him, but she didn't comment on the lapse overtly. "Frankly, we approved of the principles behind your actions. The practical implementation was perhaps a little more...robust than some of us liked. But it was clear that you were addressing the problem from a new angle so we decided to allow the experiment to take place. Modeling, however detailed, fails at the chaotic limits and sometimes the empirical approach is the only option." Animation sparked in her face, breaking through the careful mask to lend a crinkle of enthusiasm to the corner of her mouth. "And what an utterly fascinating scenario to observe played out on such an impressive scale. Almost a year later, the analysis is still throwing up surprises."

The sudden gleam in her eyes, more than anything else, convinced him. A hundred clear memories of field training gave it a truth he couldn't deny. Which meant only one thing...

Carnac closed his eyes. He blanked out the other presence in the room—and the no doubt many pairs of eyes watching the meeting—and let the emotions run through him. Sick realization, anger at their high-handed arrogance which had more than matched his own, a far hotter fury at his own stupidity. Disgust that he had imagined he had run so far, and now found the strings were still firmly attached. And, finally, the cold beginnings of acceptance. Anger meant nothing, achieved nothing beyond impairing judgment; the past could not be changed and his purpose was to work with the present for the future. Both of those were saws he had heard many times from du Pre, but they were no less true for that.

He had himself back under control, steady and centered. When he opened his eyes, she made no comment. Socioanalysis worked with only the most civilized forms of humiliation, razor sharpened to open victims without them feeling the incision, and leave them agonized, gutted and bleeding. "I should have known," he said aloud, testing the steadiness of his voice.

"I'm sure you did on some level." The kindness in her voice made him want to punch her, all the more so because it was perfectly genuine. "But to proceed, you had to believe that we had been utterly blindsided. It was the only basis on which you could've made the attempt. We were careful to give no signals, and you had no reason to believe that we sympathized."

"And I'm still not convinced that you do."

"Jean-Baptiste, you worked on your plans for over two years, during which you passed through any number of routine assessments, psychological and professional. You investigated the practical requirements of armed uprisings, and made contacts within the resistance, contacts you actively pruned and shaped. Arrests rose, yet the overall operational efficiency of resistance in the Administration increased—even Int-Sec began to puzzle over it towards the end. To those who knew where to look, you played an overly prominent role in the Athens I&I scandal, including manipulating the assignment of a certain I&I officer—to whom, I'm afraid, we will have to return later," she added drily. "However, with honest hindsight, do you really think that your activities could go entirely unnoticed?"

"I had hoped..." Carnac leaned back in his chair and pinched the bridge of his nose. "Apparently once again my single most generously supplied attribute is self-delusion."

"We have a team looking into it as a factor in successful decision making."

If she had calculated the answer—and of course she had—she could not have chosen a better one to jolt him free of the despair taking root inside. "Successful?" He laughed bitterly. "I think you'll find you're wasting your time."

Her eyebrows lifted slightly. "Far from it! Jean-Baptiste, you sell yourself short. We had merely debated and modeled—you acted. You set out to destroy parts of the Administration architecture while leaving the keystones of organized governance in place, an extremely challenging task, particularly given the resource constraints. Yet, you fulfilled many of your goals at a relatively modest cost in terms of loss of life and property. It was an extraordinary achievement. Our calculations suggest that even the mild social improvements and sense of positive change which your actions brought about are likely to extend the useful life of the Administration by over a decade. Maybe even more."

He gritted his teeth, crushing the ingrained reaction to her praise. "And I'm supposed to be pleased by that?"

She leaned forward in an utterly familiar gesture, one elbow on the arm of the chair, and he braced himself for a hard question. "Why didn't you attempt to unleash a full-scale social revolution? To utterly destroy the Administration?"

"Because the odds were excellent that I would be detected before I could succeed." He paused, then nodded once. "No. Because I couldn't foresee the consequences to my satisfaction. Accurate prediction, as you point out, is impossible with a sufficiently unstable system. All I had were historical precedents, and the evidence was that the immediate costs would be too high and the long-term benefits not proportionate to them. The stronger a political vacuum, the more repellent the specimens it will suck in to fill itself."

"Exactly. You applied your training, for the good of the Administration. And that's what we would like you to continue to do."

"I'm managing quite well as it is." The admission of continued meddling meant nothing now, but it satisfied him.

"I'm sure you're working hard. But—don't you find yourself hopelessly constrained by the lack of resources? By having to expend valuable energy on acquiring influence to barter? By doing your own data gathering, your own risk and security assessments?" She gestured around the plushly appointed meeting room and, as she meant him to, Carnac thought of his own cramped office. "By the simplest little points such as displaying the correct trappings to influence the less discerning?"

"Yes, of course." No point denying it, even though he could see the path it forced him down. A diversion seemed called for. "It would be an interesting political statement, to allow the prodigal to return."

"We feel you would be better suited to a more peripheral association. We would restore your license to practice, as an independent socioanalyst."

"Ah. An expendable asset on the front line."

She shook her head. "Although we could hardly be blamed for that, since you've taken the role upon yourself. However, none of us at Socioanalysis are expendable—we're too valuable. And yet we all are, if the reward is worth paying the price." .

"And as my value is smaller, so I can be sacrificed for a wider range of rewards?" he asked.

"Quite the opposite—you have a great deal of value." She glanced away for a moment, out of the window, her lips pressed together as she considered her words. When she looked back, her gaze was direct. "Let me spell this out clearly, so we both have no doubts. Your break with us, and the old Administration, was public, final, and above all *genuine*. No one will ever be able to prove otherwise. Yet, despite what you might still think, we share the same goals. It places you in a unique position, and I'm sure that the many possibilities inherent in the situation are obvious."

"I will admit I see a great many advantages for the division."

"For both of us." She picked up her cooled tea and sipped it—the prelude, he remembered, to discharging an unpleasant duty. "Forgive me if I say we've been monitoring you closely, and recent successes have not matched past ones. Your activities have become inconsequential. *You* have become inconsequential. I don't say that simply to be hurtful," she added.

"Well, thank goodness for that." He didn't try to refute the other assertion.

"Jean-Baptiste, with the proper resources you could accomplish a great deal. Data, research teams, contacts, and influence: we can supply all of these. All the normal facilities extended to independent socioanalysts, albeit via less direct channels."

Oh, God. No knowledge that it must be forthcoming could prepare him for the offer. Information—to be able to draw on sources of real, accurate information at will, to have it handed over efficiently processed and presented, to be able to place queries and have them correctly answered... The idea had an almost sexual charge, and he wondered briefly if dataphilia was a clinically recognized fetish.

There was simply no way he could stop himself from asking the question. "And in return?"

She inclined her head slightly. "You will work with us towards the eventual reshaping of the Administration into a more stable form. You will share your plans with us and, after a suitable probationary period, we will share ours with you." She hesitated, as though offering him a tacit opportunity to quibble, but he merely nodded for her to go on. Under the circumstances, if no probation had been mentioned he would not have believed her. "In due time you will be admitted into the

231

deliberations of the highest levels of the division, and in return you must simply undertake to share fully and immediately anything of value, whether ideas or information. A two-way flow of data and intellect."

"And that's all?"

"In essence. A practical application of the principle of enlightened self-interest, one might say." She sipped her tea again. "There will be some few other minor conditions."

"Ah. I thought there might be. A little rebrainwashing, perhaps?"

"Hardly." She frowned slightly, as though he'd made an indecent suggestion. "Simply...a refocusing of your priorities. For one, you must give an undertaking to end this ridiculous feud with the para-investigator, Val Toreth. For another, your contact with Keir Warrick must also end."

That those should be the first demands was more of a surprise than on reflection it should have been. Du Pre leaned forwards again, and there was a uncharacteristic delicacy to her voice when she continued. "Para-investigator Toreth supplied emotional weight to your crusade, and Dr. Warrick...well. Sufficient to say that we entirely understand their important representational roles in the psychological coping mechanisms you subconsciously devised in order to break the hold of your deep institutional conditioning. However, by now you must acknowledge that those particular mechanisms have become maladaptive. The outcome of events at I&I can admit no other conclusion. If you require assistance, we will be happy to provide it—entirely on your terms, of course."

It was the first time that Carnac had ever heard the word "conditioning" used openly inside the division—ridiculous, when they must all recognize it. The Socioanalysis family didn't so much have an elephant in the living room as the entire deranged contents of the zoo. "My association with them, both of them, is over. I've had no contact with either for months." Carnac crossed his legs and straightened the seam of his trousers over his knee. "As I'm sure you know."

"We're not omnipotent. Nor can we read minds." She smiled, a little mischievously, which seemed ridiculously out of place. "Not from a distance, anyway."

"Very well: I also have no plans to see or speak to them again. Although if Toreth were to be run over by a rogue taxi tomorrow, I assure you I would shed no tears. I might, in fact, dance a brief jig."

"And Dr. Warrick?"

Carnac sighed, and decided that it would not be an unbearable loss of control to look away. The autumnal blue sky outside was marred only by the faint purple striations of light refracting through the reinforced glass. A modestly sized missile of the shoulder-launched variety could hit it, and the occupants of the room would be startled but unharmed. What a pity that the rest of one's life couldn't be fitted with similar protection. "The best I can say is that I am working diligently on becoming resigned to my situation." Or, as Coll had put it in her typical, aphoristi-

232

cally challenged style, *you need to learn to stop being in love with him, cherie.* "I have, for what it is worth, achieved some not insignificant degree of success—which I freely acknowledge at the moment still rests upon my maintaining a safe distance from him."

It suddenly occurred to him that he was being perfectly honest with du Pre. Alarmed, he looked back, meeting her cool, neutral gaze. "In the meantime," he added lightly, "I'm considering a small research project to refine the parameters of the phrase 'time heals all wounds' to include some more useful scheduling information. Perhaps the division would like to fund it?"

"You never know. Perhaps we might."

It had been a mere joke, but it prompted a more serious question. "Will—would I be obliged to accept other assignments?"

"Not at all, unless you choose to. No doubt there'll be plenty on offer. In any case, our lawyers have advised us of the unimpeachable validity of the cancellation of your training debt."

He laughed sharply. "Oh, please, do tell me that's why we're here: because the lawyers gave up on cracking my clauses. You have absolutely no idea how much joy that would bring me."

"I—" Du Pre relaxed back into the armchair. "There may be a certain measure of truth to the statement, yes."

Again he was conscious of the sense of ease and familiarity. A warmth, almost, inside him. It left him yearning for more—the siren lure of the company of equals. Now that she had baldly pointed it out, he couldn't avoid seeing the clear parallel with, and relationship to, his regard for Warrick; then he found the warm feeling prompted all over again by the knowledge that she would wait for him to explore the connection, and they would both consider such self-examination as time well spent.

"If I return," he said, and held up his forefinger. "*If*—this is simply a nonnegotiable preliminary, not an acceptance speech. If I cooperate, then it would be on the understanding that I&I must be eradicated as soon as is practicable. Absolutely eradicated, not merely rebranded and concealed. If there is no politically acceptable way to arrange the deaths of its employees, then our goal must be for what happens there to become so utterly repugnant to every citizen of the Administration that its dismantling is the only possible outcome."

"We agree that the latter is both an admirable goal and a very useful measure of progress in reforms."

"Is that a yes?"

"You do feel strongly about it, don't you, Jean-Baptiste? If you of all people want a simple yes."

She was teasing, he realized with a shock. Perhaps that was what happened with Socioanalyst du Pre when one had been, in possibility at least, admitted to

233

the inner circles of the division. Suddenly, calling her Camille seemed almost natural. "Nevertheless," he said.

She smiled. "Yes."

His mouth was dry, he realized, and he picked up the tea and took a reckless swallow. "Then I will consider your offer and let you know in due course." He smiled at her over the rim of the cup. "You should know that I never accept a client on the first meeting."

In the living room of his flat Carnac shed his coat, switched off the flat comms, then paused, irresolute. All the way back from the meeting a lingering sense of unreality had kept him waiting for the unexpected twist in the day's story, the sudden shot or a violent swerve of the taxi. Logically his chances of survival had actually increased, but even socioanalysts weren't immune to emotional responses. Far from it, as du Pre had taken pains to point out.

So, he wondered. What next? A book lay on the coffee table and he picked it up—a signed paper display edition of Coll's latest novel—and flicked through it for a minute before he put it back in its place on the shelf. Really, she needed to find a new protagonist. A brief survey had suggested that psychic detectives were positively filling the ranks of popular literature at present, and he had to admit a sneaking pride that it was probably all her fault.

He had been halfway to the office before he had changed his mind and redirected the taxi to his flat. Colette would demand answers and explanations, and he had better things to do immediately than provide them on a level she would understand.

First, he needed to parse them onto a level he himself could understand.

Carnac poured himself a small glass of very expensive white wine (broke he might almost be, but skimping on the luxuries of life was the counsel of despair) and went out onto the balcony. The autumn wind was cool enough that he returned inside to fetch his coat. Warmly bundled up, he contemplated the city below. It wasn't insignificant, he supposed, that he'd remained here in Strasbourg. It had many advantages, but it was inescapably the home of Socioanalysis headquarters. His home. If he had truly wanted to escape them, he might have waddled a little further from the nest. However—to stretch a metaphor harder than Carnac thought entirely tasteful—he had finally found his wings. He could stand alone, and he knew that with a gratifying certainty. Maladaptive coping mechanisms or not, he had learned to survive away from the division and keep fighting no matter how hopeless the odds.

When he was five years old he had realized that he no longer needed his parents. This must be how it felt for those people who only reached that conclusion as adults. He wondered how many at Socioanalysis never experienced the feeling.

Carnac sipped the wine, savoring it. Had he been forced to return to the division out of desperation, he would have resented the necessity no matter what their unexpected political views. That, no doubt, was why they had waited so long to contact him. Now he must consider the options dispassionately, and choose the one which was most beneficial to his own goals.

Despite the sun, the north wind brought a chill to the balcony. When the door to the flat opened, the sudden kick of adrenaline warmed Carnac thoroughly.

"Jean?"

"I'm out here, Coll."

His sister appeared, still clutching her handbag which she abandoned on a chair in order to embrace him tightly. Carnac held his second glass of wine out to one side, and wrapped his free arm around her in return.

"Why didn't you call? I was so worried, cherie, and then I saw the taxi charge come through to the company account, and—are you all right?"

"Yes, I'm perfectly well. Surprisingly so." He kissed her on the cheek. "No damage done, and little prospect of damage in the immediate future."

She stepped back, but her hands lingered on his arms, as though she were afraid that if she let go some force might snatch him away, and she frowned at him doubtfully. "What happened? What did that woman want?"

"Remarkably, exactly what she told you when she made the appointment. Of course, with hindsight that's really no more than one should expect from Socioanalyst du Pre. She's always held the view that lying is a sign of being insufficiently prepared."

"She really wants to offer you an assignment?"

"Rather more than that." Carnac turned away to set the wine on the small wrought-iron table, then took her hands. "In fact, if I accept her offer—which I'm still considering—I may able to employ a new admin soon. Possibly even a researcher or two. I'm sure that you're eager to return to your awful novels."

"But what about vetting staff? What—" Her mouth dropped open. "Oh, Jean, no!"

"I told you, I haven't made my mind up, not quite yet. But the possibility of a 'yes' is certainly there."

"Did she threaten you?" Collette demanded. "You don't have to do what they say. There must be something, some way—"

"Shh." Carnac squeezed her hands. "No threats, I promise. Well, no more than were necessary to add a little color to the occasion and justify the expense of the meeting room. The decision was left quite amicably in my hands."

Collette pulled away. "They can't mean it! Why would they take you back like that, after everything you've done?" When Carnac merely shrugged, she let out a short, exasperated sigh. "Well, then, how can you possibly trust them?"

"For the same reason I can trust you, Coll. Because I know them. Because I understand them." Carnac curled his hand around the cold iron railing. "Because at the end of the day, who else can one trust, if not one's family?"

The Socioanalysis establishment which Carnac approached was peripherally located, occupying a modest, tasteful, and unmarked office building. Most people who knew much about the division at all knew only of the much larger headquarters, right in the center of the city as befitted such an important branch of the Administration. That was just how the division liked it.

He scanned his ID, ninety-nine percent sure that the building would admit him, but curious at the possibility of being wrong.

Inside there was no receptionist, no chairs, no desperately cheerful potted plants, simply another scanner and a pair of lift doors. Carnac stood and waited, examining the familiar white walls hung with shockingly expensive artworks donated by various socioanalysts over the years. It looked more like a gallery where the attendants had been suddenly called away, than an office. He rather thought the walls had had a fresh coat of paint in the time he'd been away. The building's near-invisible administrators liked to keep the décor flawless.

He wondered if someone was occupying his old office upstairs. Probably. And they would stay there, whatever happened. An unofficial association would surely preclude his residence in a divisional building, even one as anonymous as this.

It took five minutes for the lift door to open. Carnac rather hoped he'd interrupted something important, but du Pre looked as unruffled as ever. "Jean-Baptiste." She shook his hand warmly, showing not a trace of doubt. "It's good to see you."

He suppressed the urge to comment that he was quite sure she'd seen him on any amount of surveillance in the past week. "I'll get to the point," he said. "I have one question remaining before I can finally decide whether to resume an association with the division."

Du Pre inclined her head. "Of course. I'll do my best to answer."

No need to query the security of a conversation in that location, but Carnac looked around anyway.

"If you'd prefer, we could go up to my office," du Pre said.

"No. I rather like it here. Near the door."

Du Pre smiled. "If you say no, Jean-Baptiste, then you are free to walk away from here."

timate outcome. "Very well. My question regards assignments."

"As I said, you are free to accept or reject cases from us. I can provide cast-iron contractual guarantees of this."

"And I will be testing the quality of the iron in a very hot furnace, believe me. However, my question is of a more historical nature."

There was a very brief moment of stillness, du Pre's face becoming an expressionless mask before it dropped into lines of polite interest. "Certainly, if it's germane to the issue. If I know about the case or cases in question, then I'll answer now. Otherwise, I may need some time to call on our researchers."

"Oh, I think this one will be quite familiar. It happened some three and a half years ago, when you—or perhaps it would involve less supposition to say 'the division'—assigned a rather dramatically overqualified socioanalyst to perform a loyalty assessment upon a group of people with one of the statistically lowest incidences of ideological disloyalty in the entire Administration. Does that sound familiar?"

Now, forewarned, there was no untoward reaction. "Yes, I do remember a case fitting that description."

"Did you know what would happen?" Carnac left the question deliberately open.

"Not with any certainty." Du Pre pursed her lips a little, nicely conveying her dissatisfaction with imprecision in all instances. "However, we were necessarily working with a rather small, if intensely studied, dataset. But, yes, to answer your underlying question, we deliberately placed certain socioanalysts in situations which we thought would test their suitability for inclusion in the reform project. In your case, the result was rather more dramatic than we had anticipated."

"It's always nice to be an outlier." Carnac considered her answer in more depth for a moment, then nodded. "To pursue the line of inquiry further, you must have known that, provided with the information you gave me a week ago, the possibility would occur to me."

"We discussed it at the strategy meetings before you were approached," she said, no variation in her dry delivery.

"And, of course, I'm sure that your commitment to open and honest revelations about the new Socioanalysis included a plan to actually *tell* me this."

She didn't even flinch at the sarcasm. "It was decided that, since your skills have manifestly not degraded in your time away from us, the probability of you reaching that conclusion closely approached one, and therefore we would wait for you to raise the issue yourself. That was considered the most—" For one of the very rare times in their acquaintance, he thought the hesitation might be genuine. "The most psychologically appropriate course of action."

"Because you think I'm unhinged, or because you hoped I wouldn't ask?"

"Neither of those." She shrugged. "Although I can't absolutely prove it to you, naturally, or dissect the unconscious motives of everyone there. However, I can say that we —in the generic, but particularly myself—wanted very much for you to process the information in such a way as to maximize the odds you would accept our offer. If you wish to question the tactical ethics of the decision, I can contact the others involved and we can hold a case review."

"'Tactical ethics'"—the same mealy-mouthed, prissy abstraction from the real world which had led them to support the Administration for so long. At the same time, the idea of scrutinizing the plans for his own reinduction had an oddly skewed appeal. He wondered what would happen if it were decided he should never have been contacted in the first place.

"So," du Pre said delicately. "May we expect an answer soon?"

"I'd decided to accept before I came here, on the condition that you told the truth." Carnac shook his head. "But, of course, you knew that, didn't you? And so you also knew there was no option to do anything else."

She smiled wryly. "It's so difficult for us to interact truly honestly, isn't it? The price of seeing clearly. Sometimes I think it must be rather pleasant not to know these things about other people."

"I thought that too, once. I decided I was wrong," Carnac nodded around the reception. "But failing blissful ignorance, at least it's preferable to play on a level field, and in a team of equals."

Du Pre held out her hand again, and smiled. "Welcome home."